THE ACCIDENTAL LIFE OF JESSIE JEFFERSON

Adult novels by Paige Toon

Lucy in the Sky
Johnny Be Good
Chasing Daisy
Pictures of Lily
Baby Be Mine
One Perfect Summer
One Perfect Christmas (ebook short)
The Longest Holiday
Johnny's Girl (ebook short)

THE ACCIDENTAL LIFE OF JESSIE JEFFERSON

Paige Toon

SIMON AND SCHUSTER

First published in Great Britain in 2014 by Simon and Schuster UK Ltd
A CBS COMPANY

1 3 5 7 9 10 8 6 4 2

Simon & Schuster UK Ltd
1st Floor,
222 Gray's Inn Road
London WC1X 8HB

Simon & Schuster Australia, Sydney
Simon & Schuster India, New Delhi

A CIP catalogue record for this book
is available from the British Library.

PB ISBN: 978-1-47111-878-4
EBook ISBN: 978-1-47111-879-1

Printed and bound by CPI Group (UK) Ltd, Croydon, CR0 4YY

www.simonandschuster.co.uk
www.simonandschuster.com.au

For Ali Harris: friend, fellow author, and confidante. If you hadn't suggested I write young adult books alongside my yearly chick-lit, my readers would not have this book right now. So thank you!

Chapter 1

'Jessie! *Jessica*! Open the door.'

Not likely. I take another drag of my cigarette and lazily flick the ash out of the open window. I'm not going to waste a perfectly good fag for the sake of my stupid stepdad.

'Jessie, I mean it. If you don't open the door right now, I will break it down.'

Oh, for God's sake. Get a grip, Stu.

'I'm getting dressed. I'll be out in minute!' I call.

'No, you're not. You're on your windowsill smoking and drinking my good cider. It's gone from the fridge.'

He shouldn't have left it in there, then.

'I'm breaking the door down!' he shouts. There's a loud thump.

Blimey, he really has got his knickers in a twist.

'I'm *naked*!' I shout back. 'If you want to get done by child services, go right ahead!'

'Don't you give me that, young lady. What would your mother say?'

'Don't push me, Stu.' His words make my ears burn.

'She'd be so disappointed,' he adds.

I angrily throw the cigarette out the window and storm to the door, wrenching it open. 'To hell with Mum!' I yell. 'She's *dead*, so she can't say anything!'

The look on Stuart's face makes me want to burst into tears, but before he can pull me in for another one of his suffocating hugs, I slam the door shut in his face and lock it again. And then I slump to the floor and bawl my eyes out. I hope he's got the sense enough to leave me be.

'Jessie?' he says quietly, after a minute or so.

No such luck. 'Just leave me alone, Stu,' I blub.

'I want to talk to you.'

'Well, I don't want to talk to *you*.'

'Come on, Jess, I hate seeing you like this. I want to be there for you, help you through this.'

'Please,' I choke out. 'Please, just leave me alone.'

Silence. Has he gone?

'You know I can't do that.'

Nope.

'Unlock the door,' he tries again. 'I've made you a fish-finger sandwich.'

As if that's going to swing it. Although, actually, I could really do with a fish-finger sandwich right now.

'Jessie?' he tries again.

My stomach rumbles. 'I'll be down in a minute,' I relent, and even through the solid wood door I'm sure I can hear his sigh of relief.

'OK,' he says gently.

When I'm sure he's gone, I get up and go to the mirror. My

nose is red, my eyes puffy. My medium-length, light-blonde hair is a bit of a mess, but I like it like that. I grab some make-up from my dressing table and do my best to rectify my blotchy complexion. Damn Stu for making me cry like that. My eyeliner is completely screwed, and my mascara is halfway down my face. I outline my green eyes with black kohl and retouch my mascara, stuffing my pink lipstick into my pocket. Then I pull on my black beanie, grab my camo jacket and climb out of the window.

It's only seven o'clock, so it's not dark yet. It's pretty cold though, considering it's the middle of June. I shove my hands into my jacket pockets and stomp along the footpath in the direction of town. I wonder if anyone is about. I pull out my mobile, but no one has texted me. I click on my inbox just in case I've missed a message and the first one at the top is from Libby – it was sent yesterday. Frowning, I plunge my phone back into my pocket. I can't be bothered to reply. My best friend since she moved to Maidenhead, aged nine-and-a-half, wants to know how I'm doing. If she were *still* my best friend, she wouldn't have to ask that question. Anyone with half a brain can see that I'm not doing very well.

Maybe it's my fault that we've grown apart. But I can't stand to sit by and watch her and her perfect family get on with their lives when mine has been torn apart. She has her mum, her dad and her brothers. I have no one. And I can't help but resent her for it, even though a small part of me knows that's unfair.

OK, so maybe I have Stu, but he's not my real dad. I don't even know who my real dad is. He's as much a mystery to me now as he was when it first occurred to me to ask my mum about him when I was seven.

'It doesn't matter,' she'd told me. 'Stuart is a better father to you than he could ever be.'

That may be so, but she's still a bitch for keeping the truth from me.

I don't mean that. I'm sorry, Mum. I look up at the blustery, cloud-ridden sky and my eyes prick with tears. You're not really a bitch. I have to bite my lip to stop it from wobbling as I take a left towards the park.

There are a group of guys kicking a football around the small pitch. I scan the scene and see smoke trails drifting into the air on the far side of the park, under the trees. I'll bet my beanie Natalie's there. I set off in the direction of the trails, preparing to turn around if I'm wrong. One of the guys playing football scores a goal and his teammates are ecstatic. Honestly, you'd think they're playing at Wembley. I roll my eyes as one of them lifts up his shirt and hooks it over his head like he's Cristiano flippin' Ronaldo.

It's then that I notice Tom Ryder. He's shaking his head with amusement at the guy showing off. He glances my way and I force myself to look past him and not catch his eye. I heard he split up with his girlfriend a few weeks ago, but I doubt he'll be single for long. He's in the year above me, and always seems to have girls after him.

My pulse speeds up as I walk past the game, keeping my eyes trained on the group of four people sitting halfway up the bank. They'd better be my friends because I'll die of embarrassment if I have to turn back now.

'Alright, Jessie?' The sound of Tom's voice makes me jump, I hope not noticeably.

'Hi, Tom,' I reply as casually as I can, barely looking at him.

'Come to watch me play football?' he asks cheekily and I give him a withering look instead of an answer. But that doesn't deter him. He's got so much confidence he could bottle it and sell it on eBay. 'You going to Mike's tomorrow night?' he asks, scratching the top of his head. He has short-ish, brown hair that always looks sort of stylishly messy.

'What's it to you?' I reply. I am, actually. Mike is Natalie's older brother by only a year. Their parents are away this weekend. Party time!

Tom shrugs and grins at me, and my treacherous heart flips.

'Hey!' I hear a shout and turn to see Natalie coming towards me, her hand raised in a half-wave. Relief surges through me and I can't help smiling as she beckons me over. 'I didn't know you were coming out tonight,' she calls.

'Neither did I.' I turn away from Tom, and make my way over to her. I swear I can feel Tom's dark eyes burning a hole into my back as I do so.

As I reach her, she gives me a hug, then pulls me towards the rest of the group. I can't help it: I look back just in time to make eye contact with Tom for a split second before the ball shoots in his direction and distracts him.

God, he's gorgeous. The only trouble is, he knows it.

I say hi to the others, who turn out to be Dougie, Em and Aaron.

Dougie and Em are in sixth-form college. Aaron and Natalie are in the year above me and destined to join them soon. I've only really been hanging out with them for a few months, but I'm already dreading my final year at school, once they've gone.

'What was Tom saying to you?' Natalie demands. Her pale-blue eyes stare at me intently as she pushes her long dyed-black hair from her face. Em turns to me as well. She's less striking than Natalie, with brown hair and a slightly orange complexion.

'Nothing.' I shrug. 'He just asked if I'm going to yours tomorrow night.'

'It's going to be awesome,' she says with a grin. 'Do you want to stay over?'

'Yeah, maybe.' I think about my argument with Stu and the fish-finger sandwich he made me and feel a prickle of guilt. I know he's not going to be happy about me going out tomorrow, too. Natalie passes me her can of cider and I take a big swig and try to put Stu out of my mind. Not that I really need more alcohol – the cider I had earlier has already gone to my head and I'm still hungry. I look over at Tom as he jogs across the pitch.

'Let's go on the zip wire,' Natalie says suddenly, pulling me to my feet. I laugh and follow her.

We're still mucking about ten minutes later when the football game comes to an end. I notice Tom glance in our direction as Natalie drags the pulley back along the line and hands it to me. I climb on and shoot along the cable, squealing with laughter as I jerk up into the air at the other end. I look back over at Tom and he's still standing on the grass, watching me with amusement.

'You want a turn?' I call, buoyed by the cider as I climb off the contraption.

He says something to one of his friends and saunters over. By the time he reaches us, I'm back at the wooden platform and Natalie is raising one eyebrow at me. I smirk at her and pray I'm not blushing.

'Did you win?' I ask Tom, as he climbs up on to the platform and takes the pulley from me.

'Course,' he replies. He's a bit sweaty after the match, but he's still well fit. 'Are you sure this thing's safe?' he asks.

'Who gives a toss? Live dangerously, right?'

He grins at me and my heart flutters. Then he's off.

'Wooooooo!' he yells, as some of his mates catcall and clap.

'You fancy Tom Ryder,' Natalie sing-songs into my ear. I eye the muscles on his arms as he clings to the pulley.

'Who doesn't?' I reply without missing a beat. He's the best-looking guy in school.

Soon all the boys from the football game want to get in on the act and a queue forms, but suddenly I feel a bit sick and dizzy. I gingerly climb down from the platform.

'You were next,' Tom says to me, taking the pulley from one of his mates. 'They can wait.'

'No, no, it's OK.' I wave him away.

'Are you alright?' he asks with a frown.

'I'm fine,' I reply, climbing a little way up the grassy mound next to the zip wire and sitting down. He follows and stands there, looking down at me.

'You don't look very well.'

Actually, I feel sick. Please go away, I think. 'I'll be OK,' I say out loud. Too much alcohol, too little food, *way* too much excitement. I put my head in my hands and try not to throw up.

'Jessie!'

I glance up to see Aaron and Dougie manically waving at me as they stride across the green. They point at the car park behind me, but I can't see over the mound I'm sitting on. Tom looks past me. Before he can say anything, one of the guys waiting for the zip wire shouts, 'What's Mr Taylor doing here?'

I shoot to my feet in an instant and see him slamming shut

7

the door of his little white hatchback. Mr Taylor. Our Maths teacher.

Otherwise known as Stuart, my stepdad.

Shit, shit, shit.

'Better go,' I mutter, getting up and walking away without looking back. I hear laughter and joking in the distance behind me, and I glance up once to see Stu's features set into a hard line.

I'm still fighting the urge to throw up as I get into the car, an urge that overcomes me the moment Stuart drives with restrained fury out of the car park.

'Stop!' I gasp, shoving open the door in time to vomit on the curb.

He doesn't say a word, but he doesn't need to. The air is thick with his disappointment.

Chapter 2

The next morning I wake up with a pounding headache. Light spills underneath the curtains and I slowly sit up and climb out of bed, pulling back the curtains to reveal a beautiful blue sky, yesterday's clouds nowhere to be seen. About time we had some sunshine. I'd probably feel happy if the nausea wasn't taking up so much room in my stomach. A knock on my door makes me jump.

'Get up, Jessie, or you'll be late for school.'

From his tone, it's clear Stuart has not forgiven me.

'I'm up,' I call back.

'Be downstairs for breakfast in ten minutes,' he says firmly.

I don't reply.

'Jessie!' he snaps.

'OK!' I cry back petulantly.

My stomach churns. The last thing I feel like is food, but it's the one thing that will probably make me feel better.

I don't have time to wash my hair today, so I take a quick

shower and fashion it into an untidy braid, then I get dressed in my school uniform, a green-and-white checked dress which is a little higher above the knee than it should be. I still hate wearing it. At least it will be the summer holidays soon so I can dress however I like.

My stomach churns again, but this time the feeling is not hangover-induced. I've been dreading the summer holidays. At least school keeps my mind occupied. I've lined up a few extra shifts at the clothes shop where I work, but that's not really going to cut it. We were going to go to Spain – Mum, Stu and me. Mum had been talking about booking it the week before she died. I'd been complaining because I didn't want to go away on holiday with just her and Stu, and she had said that maybe we could think about inviting Libby, too.

A lump forms in my throat and I quickly swallow. I don't want to cry, not now.

I traipse downstairs to the kitchen. I can see Stuart standing over the toaster, but for a moment I pause in the corridor and imagine that he's Mum. If I squeeze my eyes closed and peek through the blurry crack, it almost could be her, waiting for my toast to pop up.

'Peanut butter or Marmite?' she'd ask. I open my eyes, disintegrating the fantasy, and walk into the room.

'Would you like toast or cereal?' Stuart asks, not looking at me.

He's obviously still really angry. 'Um, toast, please,' I reply cautiously.

It pops up and he puts it on a plate.

'I can butter it,' I say, hoping to placate him. He abruptly hands the plate to me, then turns back to the toaster, putting another two pieces of bread in for himself. I nervously go to stand beside him at the counter. He shoves the butter in my direction.

I'm only five foot six, and petite, so he's taller than me by about six inches. The short-sleeve T-shirts he chooses to wear only seem to highlight his lanky frame. He has dark, messy hair and wears black, horn-rimmed glasses. I pretty much think he looks like a total geek, but apparently some of the girls at school think he's quite hot. Geek chic, I suppose.

'What the hell were you thinking?' he erupts all of a sudden, making me jolt and clutch my hand to my chest.

'Scare the life out of me why don't you!'

'I've had just about enough of this, Jessie.' He stares down at me, waving his butter knife around in his hand. 'How dare you sneak out of your window last night without telling me where you were going!'

'Stu. Put. The. Knife. Down,' I say slowly, trying to keep a straight face. But he looks at me like he hates me, and the urge to giggle vanishes. 'If you've had enough of me, why don't you just kick me out? It's not like I'm *yours*,' I spit. 'At least Mum never lied to me about *that* before going off and getting herself killed!'

The fury slips from his face and is replaced with remorse. 'Hey,' he starts, but I don't give him time to finish, turning on my heel and grabbing my bag from the kitchen floor as I storm out the door.

'Jessie!' he shouts after me, but I'm already gone.

That was a bit stupid, I think to myself as I fling my backpack over my shoulder and walk out of the small close and away from the 1970s townhouse where we live. Now I'm going to have to walk, and school is flippin' miles away.

I have to pass by Libby's on my way, and I make sure I'm on the other side of the street so there's less chance of her spotting me. I keep my gaze trained on the footpath, but instinct takes over and I can't help shooting a look up at her home. Libby's large, detached house is beautiful compared to our shabby little terrace. Her mum likes gardening and it shows, the hedges neatly trimmed, flowers bursting with colour in the beds. Her dad's grey BMW glints in the sunlight on the driveway. I glance through the kitchen window and can see Libby, with her bobbed, ginger hair, sitting with her back to me at the kitchen table, flanked by her similarly ginger-haired brothers. Suddenly her mum appears at the window and her face lights up as she spots me. I quickly look away before she has a chance to wave.

My heart is pounding as my footsteps quicken, the pit of my stomach sick with sadness and regret. Libby's mum always used to make me feel like I was a part of their family. But now Libby and I have nothing in common. I wonder if we ever really did. Just look at her house, look at her dad's car, look at the happy little gathering around her kitchen table. I'm not a part of their family. I'm not a part of anyone's family.

The trouble with having a stepdad who works at my school is that I can only avoid him for so long. I manage it until after first break, but then he corners me in the corridor outside Physics.

'Well, at least you had the courtesy to turn up for school,' he says.

I roll my eyes.

'Don't disappear anywhere at home time. We need to talk.'

'OK, but I'm going out tonight,' I inform him.

'You've had too many nights out recently – you're not going anywhere,' he replies sternly, giving me a hard look as he sets off along the corridor towards his classroom.

We'll see about that.

I turn to go into my Physics lesson and see Tom and one of his football mates, Chris, heading in my direction. I quickly put my head down. I wonder if they saw me barf in the car park last night. How freaking embarrassing.

'Hey, Jessie!' Tom calls. I hesitate outside the classroom door, glancing back to see him grinning at me cheekily. He jerks his head in the direction of Stu's departing back. 'You in trouble?'

I shrug. 'Might be.'

He reaches me and Chris peels off, raising an eyebrow at Tom as he goes. I wonder what that's supposed to mean.

'Is he grounding you?' Tom asks me, bringing my attention back to him.

'Let him try.'

'So you're still coming to the party tonight?'

'Of course.' Does he *want* me to come?

'Cool. See you later,' he says with another grin, then jogs off to catch up with his mate.

I realise I have butterflies in my stomach and I want to be annoyed at myself, but I'm not. Does Tom Ryder, the hottest boy in school, *like* me? I turn around and bash straight into Libby.

'Oof!' she gasps as I knock the breath out of her.

'Watch out,' I snap, pushing past her and into the classroom.

Her hazel eyes crease with hurt and I instantly feel guilty. I hate how she makes me feel like this. I hated how she sometimes made me feel when Mum was alive, too, always siding with her when we argued and never with me. Telling me that I shouldn't pick fights so much, that I should be grateful my mum was so cool. Now Libby just reminds me of how much I took for granted, and I don't want to be reminded. Another reason I've been trying to stay clear of her.

I pull out my chair with a loud screech and slump into it, steeling myself for the misery that is my Physics lesson. Out of the corner of my eye, I see Libby quietly go to take a seat next to Amanda Blackthorn. Amanda smiles brightly up at her and Libby shakily returns her smile. Amanda's closest friend Maria recently moved up north, so her BFF position is up for grabs. I bet Libby takes it. Amanda only lives around the corner from Libby and her life is just as perfect. They're much better suited to each other than Libby and I ever were. I'd say I didn't care, but the truth is, I'd be lying.

After school, I wait beside Stuart's white Fiat in the staff car park. I see him come around the corner with a black look on his face, and he's momentarily surprised to see me standing there. I guess he expected me to split. I will, soon enough. First I'll lull him into a false sense of security . . .

God, when did I become such a bitch?

When my mum failed to turn up for my birthday party, that's when.

Pain hurts my heart and I try to steel it into anger instead. I push off from the car and glare at Stu as he approaches.

'Take your time, why don't you,' I say.

'Get in the car,' he replies, unlocking it.

I begrudgingly do as he says.

'How was your day?' he asks.

'What, so now we're doing small talk?'

14

'Fine,' he says abruptly. 'Forget the small talk. Instead, why don't you tell me when you're going to stop hurting yourself like this?'

I scoff. 'Don't be ridiculous.'

He turns to stare at me. 'You know, no one can hurt you as much as you can hurt yourself.'

'Are you taking the piss? A serial killer could tear my heart out!' I raise my voice. 'Literally, I mean,' I add, because sometimes I feel like my mum's death did that metaphorically. 'I could get raped or murdered or . . . or . . .' *hit by falling glass from a loose fourth-storey window on my way to pick up a birthday cake . . .*

Suddenly I'm gulping back my sobs and I want to get out of the car and run, run, run far away from here, but Stuart's hand is on my arm. I can see pity in his eyes and I want to shake him off, but I don't have the energy so I sit there and cry out the remains of my torn-out heart instead.

'Jessie . . . It's OK. I miss her too,' Stuart says gently. 'I'm here for you,' he adds.

For how long? I think to myself. Why should he look after me, now? He owes me nothing. He was only ever in it for my mum.

That's not true, a little voice inside my head says, but I quash it. Because he's *not* my dad, much as my mum tried to tell me he was as good as one. I have never called him 'Daddy'. He's just Stu.

I roughly drag my arm across my nose and wipe away the tears from my eyes, sniffing loudly. I stare sullenly out the window. 'Are we going home, or what? If anyone sees me sitting here with my *Maths teacher*, I'll never live it down.'

Stu starts up the ignition, but before he pulls away he says,

'You can keep pushing me away, but I'm not letting you go. Just so you know that.'

Hot tears sting my eyes as we drive out of the car park.

Stuart and I settle into an uneasy truce that night. He's smart enough not to make me eat at the kitchen table with him and force polite conversation. Instead we take our bowls of spaghetti bolognese into the living room and sit and eat in front of the telly. He barely raises an eyebrow when I drop a strand of red spaghetti on the carpet. He even lets me watch one of my trashy reality TV shows, which is so not his thing. I want to say that I feel reasonably content, except that at the back of my mind I'm constantly aware that I know I'm going to go to the party at Natalie and Mike's tonight, even if it starts World War III. I wonder if I can persuade Stu to agree on his own terms. Me having a meltdown earlier might have softened his heart a little.

'Thanks for dinner,' I say graciously.

'You're welcome,' he replies, giving me a wary look.

'Stu . . .'

'You're not going out.'

'Stu, please,' I say, muting the TV.

'No, Jessie,' he says firmly.

'Why not?' I try to remain calm. He'll be less likely to agree if I go off on one.

'Because you've been burning the candle at both ends for far too long. You could do with a night in. Natalie and that new crowd you're hanging out with are a bad influence.'

'No, they're not,' I scoff.

'I'm *worried* about you,' he adds.

'You don't need to be worrie—'

16

'Don't I?' he interrupts with a hard look.

'No. You don't.' I look down at my hands, studying my chipped nail polish.

'You're only fifteen, Jessie.' He points out the obvious. 'I'm responsible for you, and you might not like it, but I need to make sure you're safe.'

'I *will* be safe!'

'What, by going out drinking and smoking and doing God knows what else?'

'It's only a party at my friend's house.' I'm trying so hard not to raise my voice. It won't get me anywhere. 'I know I've been difficult lately, but it's hardly surprising . . .' A lump forms in my throat, which is handy because I don't have to act. 'I could do with some cheering up.'

'So we'll watch a movie, eat some ice cream.'

'Oh, for God's sake, Stu! I'm not a child!' I say crossly.

His brow furrows.

'I'll be careful. I won't drink.' Much, I add silently. 'You can even give me a lift there and back.'

'Oh, well, thank you very much,' he says sarcastically. 'Lucky me, spending my evening being your taxi driver.'

'*Please.*' One more try to get him onside and then I'm giving up and going out anyway.

He takes the remote from me, unmutes the TV and glares at the screen.

'Please,' I say again.

He doesn't reply, so I'm taking that as a yes. 'Thank you,' I breathe, getting up and planting a so-rare-it-should-be-in-a-museum kiss on his cheek. I run upstairs to get ready and thankfully, he doesn't stop me.

17

Chapter 3

'Remember, no smoking and no drinking,' Stu says firmly from the driver's seat. We're at Natalie's house, but I've asked him to pull up a little way down the road.

'I promise,' I reply and reach for the door handle.

'Call me. I'll come get you by eleven-thirty, latest. I'm trusting you, Jessie. Please don't let me down.'

Bugger, now he's only gone and put a guilt trip on me.

'OK, OK,' I say with a roll of my eyes as I step out on to the pavement. I turn back to look at him. 'Thanks for the lift.' I force a smile, but can't ignore the doubtful look on his face as I shut the door.

I set off quickly before he can change his mind, the heels of my ankle boots clicking on the pavement as I go. I'm wearing my caramel-coloured shorts that make my legs look really brown and a cream top with lace detail on the long sleeves. My blonde hair is down and blow-dried messy. I'm wearing dark eye make-up and pale pink lipstick. Tom had better appreciate the efforts I've gone to.

The party has already started from the sound of the bass vibrating through the walls as I walk up the footpath to Natalie's house. I hope the neighbours are away. Her parents are pretty laid-back, which is partly why I like her. They don't hang around like a bad smell and try to mother you and make you feel like everything is going to be alright. Unlike Libby's parents. It wouldn't surprise me if they'd actually given permission to have this party, even though the neighbours have been known to complain in the past about the noise levels. Spoilsports.

I ring the doorbell and a minute later Natalie opens the door, a fag in one hand, a can of cider in the other. I'm relieved Stu drove off in the other direction.

'Jessie!' she squeals, dragging me inside and slamming the door shut behind me. She's twisted her hair up into a messy bun with a few strands falling loose around her face. She's wearing a sheer black top and black shorts with wedges.

'Snap!' she says, noticing my shorts. 'You look amazing!' she shouts over the music.

'You too,' I shout back.

'I thought you were grounded!'

'Stu changed his mind. But I would have come anyway. He can't stop me doing what I want.'

'Sorry, I should know you better than that.' She laughs and leads me through to the kitchen. I glance into the living room as I pass, and can see a few bodies lounging on the sofas while a guy wearing headphones hangs over the DJ decks set up in the corner. I wave at Natalie's brother Mike and he lazily waves back. No sign of Tom.

'Are many people here yet?' I ask.

'No, but it's only eight o'clock,' she replies.

I'm instantly on edge. What if he doesn't come?

'What do you want to drink?' she asks.

I could really do with something to chill me out. Cider or vodka usually does the trick, but then an image of Stu's face pops into my mind. I did promise . . .

'Cider?' she tempts me.

'I'll just have a Coke,' I say decisively.

She laughs and passes me a can of cider from the fridge.

'I'm serious,' I tell her with a grin, handing the can back to her. 'My liver needs a night off.'

She gives me a weird look and glugs some Coke into a glass. Then she reaches for a bottle of vodka and jokily tilts it over my drink.

'Maybe later.' I nab my glass before she can spike it.

'Let's go outside,' she says, putting the bottle down on the worktop and steering me towards the French doors to the garden. 'I've been telling everyone they can't smoke inside, yet here I am.' She steps over the threshold and flicks her ash at a shrub.

Dougie and Em are sitting at the table, their faces lit by the candles in multi-coloured glass holders in the centre. We exchange hellos and I sit down next to them.

It still surprises me how relaxed I feel in the company of this lot, considering they're that much older than me. I used to see them around school – Dougie and Em, too, before they went to sixth form college – but didn't speak to any of them. Libby was always a bit scared of them, but they didn't frighten me.

In a weird way, the reason that we started hanging out at all was kind of *because* of Libby. About a year ago, Libby's mum took her out of school for a dentist's appointment and she told me she saw Natalie and Aaron bunking off and smoking. She said Natalie gave her evils. I thought she was probably overreacting until the next day at school, when Natalie slammed into Libby's shoulder in the corridor. Then she'd spun around and pointed two fingers at her eyes and then at Libby, as if to say, 'I'm watching you.' The look on Libby's face – she was terrified. I was so furious on her behalf that I stormed after Natalie.

'What the hell are you playing at? If she was going to tell on you, she already would have!'

Then Mrs Rakeman came out into the corridor and we all broke away from each other.

That weekend, we'd gone to a party for one of our friend's birthdays – the whole year group was invited. His parents were pretty wealthy so they put on a big do at the rugby club, and loads of people from the year above came as well. Libby wasn't that fussed about going – she wanted to stay in and have a girl's night at home instead – but I convinced her to go. Looking back, we had already started to want different things. I just couldn't see it at the time. I thought she'd grow up, too, follow in the same direction as me. But she never did.

Anyway, Natalie and the others were at this party, and Libby was freaking out when she saw them, thinking Natalie was going to start on her. I said I'd have her back and told her not to worry, but later, when we went to the bathroom together, Natalie was coming out of a cubicle. She was still there in front of the mirror doing her make-up when I re-emerged from the toilet myself. I ignored her and applied some lipstick and then I felt her eyes on me in the mirror.

'What?' I snapped, glaring at her.

'I like that colour on you,' she said, to my surprise.

'Have some if you want.' I offered up the lipstick begrudgingly.

'Thanks.' She took it from me, applied some and handed it back as Libby came out of her cubicle looking stupidly pale-faced and worried. But Natalie didn't give her another glance as she walked out.

Later, I saw her at the bar. 'Have you got any fags?' she asked me.

'Nah, I don't smoke.'

'Try it. You might like it,' she said with a cheeky grin.

I just shrugged.

After that, she was friendlier to me at school, smirking at me sometimes if we passed each other in the corridor. Then one day I saw her handing out what looked like little leaflets, and as I passed, she gave one to me. It was an invite to a Halloween party at her house. Word got around that Natalie's parents were out of town and Libby didn't want to go, but I dragged her along.

She was miserable that night. The people there were in the year or two above us, and a lot of them were smoking and drinking. Libby just wanted to go home, but I was having a good time. It was different from the norm. These guys were cool, the music was good, and I was proud of the fact that we – well, I – had been invited.

Libby needed the loo and didn't want to walk through the house looking for it on her own, so I went with her, even though I thought she was being ridiculous. I saw Natalie and asked her where it was.

'Upstairs,' she replied. 'Hey, I like your horns,' she said, pulling me back with a grin. I was wearing sparkly red devil horns and a black dress.

Libby went on up the stairs, glancing nervously over her shoulder at me.

'I'll catch you up,' I called after her, turning back to Natalie. 'I like your tattoo,' I said, nodding at her arm. It was a fake one of a spider. 'Did it hurt?' I kept a straight face.

'It's not real,' she scoffed.

'No shit, Sherlock,' I replied with a grin.

She laughed. 'You got me. I do want to get one, though,' she said flippantly. 'My parents are laid-back, but they're not *that* laid-back . . . Hey, come and meet some people,' she said suddenly.

I felt bad about deserting Libby, but she was being so clingy that night and Natalie seemed alright. She took me outside and introduced me to Em and Dougie, then she lit up a cigarette.

'You want one?'

I shrugged and said sure, but it made me cough and that made them laugh.

'Have a drink,' Natalie said, passing me a glass of what I thought was Coke. Coke and vodka, as it turned out. It made me feel a little bit giddy. Libby came outside soon afterwards and looked shocked to see me sitting at the table, laughing and joking with them all.

'My mum is on her way,' she said tersely.

'Did you call her?' I asked with disbelief, rolling my eyes with disgust when she nodded her assent. 'For God's sake, Libby!'

Things were on edge between us for a while after that, but we eventually seemed to get over it. And then Mum died and everything went to shit.

It still surprises me how quickly my anger dominated my

sadness. At first I retreated into myself. No one could comfort me – I was an orphan and I'd never felt more alone. And then I hit out. I had already missed a lot of school after Mum's death, but I started to skip classes, even though Stu had decided I was ready to go back. One day, I came across Natalie and Aaron in the park and my feet just sort of took me over to them. It was amazingly easy to fall into step with them. They didn't ask questions about Mum. They didn't want to do heart-to-hearts and pat themselves on the back for being there for poor little Jessie. Not like Libby. All she ever wanted to do was ask me how I was, give me hugs and make me cry. I didn't want her sympathy all the time. She kept bringing me down, reminding me of everything that I'd lost and taken for granted.

But Natalie and the others didn't. They were fun, easy, light-hearted. They were shiny and new, and they took me away from myself and my pain for a while. They're *still* taking me away from it.

The doorbell goes, jogging me from my thoughts. Natalie resignedly hands me her fag.

'Hold this for me, Jess.'

She'll be back and forth answering the door all night. Mike is not the getting-up-from-the-sofa type. She heads back inside and I glance down at her cigarette and impulsively take a quick suck. It immediately makes me wish I was drinking. Bugger it, I'll just have a couple. Stu will get over it. Besides, I've broken one promise now, what's the point in keeping the other? I go back into the kitchen and grab the vodka. I'm pouring some into my glass when Natalie returns.

'I *knew* you'd cave!' she exclaims.

24

I look past her to see Tom and Chris in the hallway. It must have been them at the door.

'Hey, Jessie,' Tom says, our eyes locking.

'Hi.' I hand Natalie back her fag and take a sip of my drink. The warmth that flows through my body may well be alcohol-induced, but I have a feeling Tom's presence is majorly contributing.

Two hours later I am having *such* a good time. We're in the living room, the music has been turned right up and loads of us are dancing. I think Tom's gone outside, but I've resisted following him like an eager-eyed puppy dog. We haven't spoken much. There must be fifty or sixty people in the house – some are next door in the TV room where Natalie is setting up *SingStar* on Mike's PlayStation. I've drunk enough to just about allow myself to be dragged in there to 'perform', which is good because that's exactly what Natalie chooses to make me do minutes later.

'Come on, you are *singing*!' she yells, pulling me out of the room and into the next.

'Are you taking me on?' I ask with a grin.

'Hell, no. I'm not that stupid. Who wants to compete with Jessie?' she shouts to the room packed full of people, holding my hand aloft as though I'm some sort of champion. A couple of guys shout drunken, 'yeahs!' so she pulls the boy closest to her to his feet, a dishevelled sixth-former from school who I think is going out with one of Natalie's friends.

'What song?' Natalie asks.

'He can choose,' I say graciously, nodding at my opponent. I can't remember his name, but it doesn't matter because I'm about to kick his arse. Alcohol does wonders for my confidence.

'Something rock or indie,' he tells Natalie as she navigates through the menu.

Perfect.

'"I Believe In A Thing Called Love"!' he shouts, spotting The Darkness. I narrow my eyes at him. Interesting choice . . .

A minute later the whole room is cheering and laughing and half of them are singing along. It's flippin' *hilarious*. I don't quite manage to get the top score because it's a tricky song, but I still get Superstar while he only manages Wannabe. I must have drunk more than I realise to be enjoying myself this much. I never normally sing in public, and whoa, Tom's just walked into the room. Right, I am definitely drunk, because I'm still standing here.

I try not to look at him while my next competitor chooses Hole's 'Celebrity Skin'. The song kicks off and I attempt to give Courtney Love a run for her money. I can tell by Natalie's slightly awed expression that I'm killing it – in a good way. Naturally I win again and risk a glance over my shoulder to see Tom leaning up against the wall with his arms folded. He's wearing black jeans and a light-grey T-shirt, and looks hotter than ever. He grins at me and raises one eyebrow.

A group of girls laughingly shove one of their friends forward to sing next and I push my hair out of my face and get ready to take on my next victim, but then she chooses 'Never Tear Us Apart' by INXS and the ground feels like it's falling away from me. Not that song. Anything but that song.

The last time I heard it was at my mum's funeral. It was one of her favourites . . .

Natalie looks at me, still smiling. She doesn't know what this song means to me. We weren't friends when Mum died; she

26

didn't come to the funeral, she didn't even know what my mum looked like. That's the whole point. Natalie's a new friend, part of my future, not my past. Not like Libby.

She adored my mum, almost always defended her when she pissed me off. Libby used to say my mum was like me. She lived for her music and was young at heart, a free-spirited one-time rock chick. She could have been my friend. But I didn't want a friend. I wanted a mum. Like Libby's. Someone who cooked nice meals and did the gardening and wore age-appropriate clothing and who didn't try to download my music on to her own frigging computer all the time.

I was so mean to Mum about it, and now she's gone and I'll never be able to tell her that I'm sorry. That I loved her. That I miss her.

My throat closes up and there is no way I'll be able to sing this song. So I bolt out of the room well before we get to the lyric about living for a thousand years.

My mum didn't even live to see forty.

I run outside to the garden. There's a bench seat down the back and I need a little time and space to get my head together. I turn to sit down and jolt with surprise when I see that Tom has followed me.

'Are you OK?' he asks with concern, as I slump on to the seat and wipe away the tears trekking down my cheeks.

'I'll be alright,' I mumble as he crouches on the ground directly in front of me. His face is close to mine.

'What's wrong?' His brown eyes look even darker in the low light.

'That song.' I sniff. 'It reminds me of my mum.'

27

I don't know why I just told him that, like it was easy. I never talk about Mum to anyone these days.

He swallows hard and his Adam's apple bobs up and down. He gets to his feet and I fleetingly think that he's going to leave me to it, that this is too much, but he sits down next to me instead.

'It's OK to cry. I know it's not the same, but when my dad left I must've cried every day for six months. Maybe more,' he says.

'I didn't know that your dad left,' I reply shakily, taken aback.

He tilts his chin my way, but doesn't meet my eyes. 'He walked out on us just over a year ago.'

'Where did he go?' I ask.

'America. With some woman he'd been having an affair with for three years.' He sounds bitter.

'God,' I say. 'And you haven't seen him since?'

He looks down at his hands. 'I haven't wanted to. My mum was devastated.'

'But you obviously *do* want to see him,' I say gently, my mind feeling miraculously clear considering the copious amount of vodka I've consumed.

Tom shakes his head. 'I couldn't.'

I have a feeling he *could*, but he feels like he can't, out of loyalty to his mum. If anything, that makes me like him more. 'I'm so sorry.'

'JESS!' Natalie calls from the house. 'Are you down there?'

'Yeah,' I shout back wearily.

She hurries up the garden path and then stops in her tracks when she sees Tom. 'Are you OK?' she asks.

'I'm fine,' I reply. Then, to my dismay, Tom gets up.

'I'll leave you to it,' he says.

I almost blurt after him, 'don't go!' but Natalie takes his place

28

and my heart constricts as I watch him lope back towards the house.

'What's everyone saying?' I ask dejectedly as he goes inside.

'Oh, don't worry about them. They just think you ran off to throw up.'

'Great.' Obviously I'm being sarcastic.

'Did you?'

'No!' I exclaim. 'I just had a bad memory.' I don't want to go into the details.

'About your mum?' she asks uneasily.

'Yeah. But don't talk to me about it or I might cry again,' I warn.

'OK.' She seems relieved. Here's even more proof that she doesn't do heart-to-hearts.

'What did Tom say?' she asks curiously.

'Nothing much.'

'Sorry, I wouldn't have interrupted if I'd known you were out here with him,' she apologises.

'Don't be daft,' I brush her off.

She nudges me. 'You want another drink?'

'No, I think I'd better reign it back in.'

'Worried about Mr Taylor?' she teases.

'A bit,' I admit honestly.

'Fag, then?' she offers. 'I don't have any left, but I can nick one from someone if you want.'

I smile. 'No, it's OK.'

'You are a flippin' awesome singer,' she says suddenly, with a grin, offering her hand for a high five. 'We should form a band.'

'Oh, yeah?' I smirk, half-heartedly returning the gesture. 'And what are you going to play?'

29

'I don't know. I'll just bash about on a drum kit in the background.'

'Sounds like we've got a Number One single, right there,' I say drily.

'I wonder if Tom plays guitar,' she muses, before nudging me again. 'He's so into you.'

'Let's go back inside,' I reply with a smile.

Back in the kitchen I hunt out some snacks. 'I can't go home drunk,' I tell Natalie, who starts pulling crisps and biscuits out of the cupboards. 'Actually, what's the time?' Stu said he'd come for me at eleven thirty, latest. I look around for a clock because my phone is in my bag in Natalie's bedroom. The microwave says 12:33.

'Shit!' I exclaim. 'Is that clock right?'

'Nah,' she brushes me off. 'It's always wrong.'

'What about that one?' I point at the oven's digital display, which reads 10:45.

'No, that needs resetting, too.'

'Bloody hell,' I mutter jokily, stalking out of the room into the corridor. I'll go and get my mobile. I should probably text Stu, anyway. I turn to jog up the stairs, but stop suddenly when I see two people huddled together on the fourth step. They look up and my stomach falls. It's Tom and Isla: his ex.

'Sorry,' I say, as Tom leans towards Isla to make room for me to pass. I thought they split up, but here they are, looking pretty cosy.

I feel nauseous as I go into Natalie's room and hunt out my mobile. There are three missed calls from Stu. Dammit! It's 11.25pm. I've been drinking, I've been smoking, but if I text him

30

now at least he won't hate me for failing him on the time front, too. I type out a message. **Soz. Ready now.**

He texts me straight back to say that he's on his way. I stuff my phone back into my bag and sling it over my shoulder before steeling myself to go back downstairs. Tom and Isla are still sitting on the step, talking quietly.

'Excuse me,' I say as I start to walk down, my heart beating louder in my chest. Once more, Tom moves across for me.

'You off?' he asks, spying my bag.

'Yep, gotta go.'

I don't look at Isla, but I can sense the tension between them. I bet she's trying to win him back, and why wouldn't he be persuaded? She's popular, smart and beautiful. I must look like a mess next to her. If I was Tom, I wouldn't be interested in the crazy girl who cries at parties, either. Biting my lip to stop it from wobbling, I go to say goodbye to Natalie. I find her in the garden, smoking with some of the others.

'I'm off,' I tell her quietly, leaning in to give her a hug.

'No way? Really?' She pulls away with shock.

'Yeah, Stu's on his way.'

'Can't you stay for a bit longer?'

'No, he'll go mental if I keep him waiting.'

'OK.' She looks disappointed. 'Call me tomorrow.'

'I will.' I head back in to the house and to the front door, purposefully not looking back at the stairs as I go out the door.

'You've been smoking,' Stuart says the moment I climb into the car. 'And drinking. You stink,' he adds angrily.

'I'm here, aren't I?' I reply.

'Jesus Christ, Jessie!' he snaps. 'When is this going to stop?'

31

'Please, Stu,' I say wearily. 'I've had a rough night.'

'I don't give a damn!' he raises his voice. 'You *promised* me. You've let me down. You *keep* letting me down! How can I ever trust you when you behave like this?'

'*Please*,' I say quietly, my eyes filling with tears. I don't have the energy. Seeing Tom with Isla hurt me much more than I thought it would. It seemed like there was something between us in the garden, but I guess I was wrong.

'You are something else, do you know that?' He pulls away from the curb, and I don't even bother to brush my tears away on the drive home. He probably thinks I'm crying to get attention, but this time he's wrong. I wish I hadn't gone out tonight. I don't need any more pain in my life.

Chapter 4

'A few of us are heading into Henley this evening,' Natalie says to me the next day, when I answer a call from her on my lunch break.

I'm at work and it's doing my head in to be inside on such a beautiful day. I can see the blue sky above the atrium in the middle of the mall, but the fluorescents down below are sucking the natural light right out of the air, something which never fails to depress me.

'I don't know,' I reply uncertainly. Stuart was still in a foul mood this morning, even after a properly sincere apology.

'Come on, we can go straight from work. There's a load of us going.'

'Who?' I can't help but ask.

'Everyone. Aaron, Dougie, Em, Mike and a bunch of his mates.' She hesitates. 'I don't know about Tom.'

I take a deep breath and try not to let her hear me sigh.

'Did you see him last night with Isla?' I ask the question that has been plaguing me.

'I saw them chatting, yeah,' she replies awkwardly, and humiliation rushes through me. It must be so obvious how much I like him. I wish it wasn't. 'I don't think anything happened, though,' she adds, trying to placate me.

'Whatever,' I say, and she doesn't answer, which only makes me squirm more.

'Oh, please come,' she tries again. 'Even if Tom's not there, it'll still be a laugh.'

Bugger it.

'OK, why not?'

I meet the others at the station after work and wait until I'm on the train before texting Stu. I usually walk home from work because we don't live far from Maidenhead town centre, so he'll be expecting me back around this time. He calls me as soon as he gets the text, but I press divert.

'He's going to do his nut in,' I tell Natalie, who's sitting next to me. The others are chatting noisily and playing about in the seats around us. She rolls her eyes. Her parents are so easy-going that she doesn't get why Stu is overprotective. I try not to let on how worried I am. 'Oh, well, it's done now.'

My phone pings to let me know a message has come in. Uneasily, I take a look. **Get your arse back here right now.**

'What does it say?' Natalie asks, so I show her. 'Oops,' she comments.

'He *will* kill me, you know,' I muse, relatively calmly, as I study the old piece of chewing gum that has been squashed into the back of the seat in front of me.

Ping! **I mean it.**

I bite my lip. Natalie grabs my phone to read Stu's message.

34

'What are you going to say?' she asks.

I shrug as I stare out of the window at a field full of yellow rapeseed flowers. 'I'm already on the train, what can I do?'

'You'd better tell him that,' she suggests.

So I do.

Ping! **Then catch the next one straight home!**

I sigh and type out a reply. **You know I'm not going to do that.**

I wait at least half a minute for his reply. **This is the last straw!**

Unease overcomes me. I wonder if I've finally pushed him over the edge. What's he going to do? Kick me out?

I text him back, **I'm sorry. Really.**

And he replies, **Too little, too late.**

'Shit,' I say out loud, warily showing Natalie our latest exchange. 'Oh, well.' I try to sound light-hearted. 'It's done now. I'd better enjoy my last few hours of freedom before he locks me up for good.'

Some of my bad feelings are miraculously washed away when we arrive at the riverside to see Tom, surrounded by a few of his friends. No girls, I note with relief. I avoid his eyes in a couldn't-care-less manner as we wander across the park to the river. It's a gorgeous evening and the aroma of freshly cut grass, river water and cow parsley fills the air.

'It smells like summer,' I say to Natalie.

'It smells like hayfever,' she replies, followed by a loud sniff to prove her point. We're giggling as we reach the group.

'Hey,' Tom says, leaning back on his elbows and smiling up at me. 'Have you come straight from work?' he asks, thwarting my intentions to ignore him.

'Yeah.' I find myself sitting down closer to him than I was intending to. He's wearing blue jeans today and a faded orange T-shirt with surfer-style graphics on the front. His brown hair has been styled back off his face and his long legs are stretched out in front of him, crossed at the ankles.

'You still working at that clothes shop?' he asks. How did he know that? Oh, that's right. He came in once with Isla. Great.

'Yep,' I reply shortly, taking the cigarette Em has just offered me. 'Cheers,' I tell her, borrowing her matches and obstinately lighting up. I know that I shouldn't, that it'll be one more way to let Stu down, but I'm feeling angsty and it'll help take the edge off.

Tom turns back to his mates. My heart is in my mouth. Why do I have to fancy him so much?

Someone has brought portable speakers and Natalie plugs in her iPod. 'Giving Into It' by Johnny Jefferson comes on.

'This is a bit old school, isn't it, Nat?' Chris says.

'I like it,' she replies defensively.

'You know Johnny Jefferson used to live around here,' says Em, blowing smoke out of her heavily lined lips. 'But he's moved back to LA now.'

'Really?' Natalie asks with a frown. 'I thought he lived up the hill near George Harrison's old house.'

'He did,' Em tells her. 'He and his family left only recently.'

'What are you, some crazy Johnny Jefferson stalker?' Dougie teases her. 'Bit old, isn't he?'

'I still *would*,' she says flippantly. 'Anyway, he's only thirty-six,' she adds and we all laugh because she knows his exact age. She goes a bit red. 'OK, so yes, I do know pretty much everything there is to know about him,' she confesses.

'Are you the reason he fled the country?' Tom asks cheekily.

'I *should* have been his reason for staying,' she replies melo-dramatically, flicking her long hair off her face.

We all laugh and Tom catches my eye and raises his eyebrows at me. Maybe he does like me . . . I just wish I knew where things stood with him and Isla.

Later, much later, we stumble on to the train as a group and make our way back to Maidenhead. I've had such a good laugh tonight, but I know I'm going to pay for it the minute I get home, and the thought is sobering.

Tom appears over the seat in front of me, looping his tanned arms around the back of his seat. 'Are you in for it with your stepdad?' he asks, his brown eyes crinkling at the corners. I can't see his mouth behind the seat, but I think he's smiling.

'Probably,' I reply, trying not to break eye contact as the train starts to slow down on its approach to the station.

'Are you going to catch a cab?' Natalie diverts my attention.

'Nah, I'll walk,' I say, brushing her off.

'I'll walk with you,' Tom says.

My stomach is jittery as we say our goodbyes to the others and walk beside the ring road away from the station.

'I really want to see *Two Things*,' he says, glancing across at the Odeon cinema complex on the opposite side of the road.

'Me too!' I exclaim. 'I love Joseph Strike.' He's well hot – one of my favourite actors.

'Well, I kind of want to see it for all the explosions and stuff, not Joseph Strike, but maybe we should go,' he says casually, and the swarm of butterflies that have been unfurling in my stomach start to go berserk.

'Sure,' I reply as nonchalantly as I can. Does he mean we'll go on a date or just as friends with a bunch of others? It is *killing* me to not ask about Isla. But it would be so embarrassing if he tells me they're back together. He'll think I thought he was asking me out when he clearly wasn't.

Neither of us says anything for a while. I walk with my arms crossed over my chest to keep myself warm because I'm only wearing a lightweight yellow summer dress. I didn't bring the denim jacket I usually wear with this outfit because I wasn't expecting to be going out tonight.

'Where do you live?' I ask him to break the silence.

He jerks his head over his left shoulder. 'Near the Pond House pub.'

'That's ages away!' I exclaim. 'You could have shared a cab with Natalie and Mike.'

He shrugs. 'I don't mind walking.'

'Me neither. Anything to delay the inevitable,' I say nervously. 'He is so going to flip out at me.'

'I can't imagine Mr Taylor flipping out at anyone.'

I screw up my nose. 'OK, so he doesn't really *flip out* as such. He just puts these enormous guilt trips on me. It makes life even more unbearable.'

A good twenty seconds pass before he gently says, 'I'm sorry about your mum.'

'Thanks,' I reply quietly.

'What about your dad? I mean, your real dad,' he asks after a moment.

'What about him?' I reply.

38

'You don't have to tell me, but do you ever see him?'

'I don't even know *who* he is, let alone *where* he is. My mum would never say.'

He sucks the air in through his teeth. 'That's tough. I'm mad at my dad, but at least I know where he is if I really need him. Do you think Mr Taylor knows who your real dad is?'

I frown. 'I doubt it. Why would he?' Then again, Mum knew Stu when they were teenagers. They went out for a bit and broke up. She was eighteen when she fell pregnant with me, but she and Stu didn't get back together again for years afterwards. 'Maybe I'll ask him.'

He glances at me. 'Do you really want to know?'

'Definitely,' I say resolutely. 'Not knowing has been the hardest thing I've ever had to deal with. Well, you know, until Mum . . .'

My voice trails off. Obviously this pales in comparison to Mum dying.

We turn left at the roundabout and start to walk up the hill. I think that's the end of that particular conversation, but then Tom says, 'Maybe your mum didn't tell you who he was for a reason. What if he's in jail or . . . worse?'

I think about that. My mum clearly didn't want me to know anything about my dad – there has to be a reason for that. But even if he *is* a low-life, I need to understand where I came from.

'What could be worse than jail?' I bat back.

'I don't know.' He looks uncomfortable.

'I suppose he could be dead,' I muse aloud, and then I'm swamped by a dark feeling. I halt on the bridge and place my hands on the wall, staring down at the railway lines below. Tom pauses beside me.

'Sorry,' he says softly. 'I don't know why I just said that.'

'You're right, though.' I turn to look up into his eyes, which are full of compassion. 'What if he *is* dead? I always thought he was out there somewhere, but what if he's not?'

'Mr Taylor's OK, isn't he?' Tom says uneasily, hooking his thumbs into his jeans pockets. 'I mean, I know he's not your real dad, but haven't you lived with him for years?'

'Since I was about eight.' I hesitate. 'Sometimes I think he must hate me.' I say it so quietly, that I'm not sure Tom has heard me.

'Of course he doesn't,' he says. 'Why would you think that?'

A train passes loudly underneath us and I watch it go before speaking again. 'I've known him all my life, but even when I was little I sensed that there was something off about the way he sometimes looked at me.'

'What do you mean?' Tom asks uneasily.

'I don't know. It was like he resented me.'

'Oh. Maybe he was sad that your mum had you with another guy instead of him.'

'Stu can't have children,' I reveal, glancing sideways at him.

'Well, that definitely makes sense, then. You probably remind him of what he couldn't have.'

'I bet he wishes I never existed,' I whisper, looking away again.

I feel Tom's hand on my back and I tense up, feeling incredibly vulnerable. I don't usually let my guard down like this. After a moment, he lets his hand drop and stands beside me, gazing down at the railway tracks. I can still feel the warmth of his body beside mine, but I wish he'd left his hand where it was.

I sigh. We both speak at the same time, but I only hear my words: 'I guess I'd better get home.' He nods brusquely and starts to walk on, and I could kick myself because I want to hear what he was going to say.

I'll add it to the list of other things I'll probably never know.

'I live just up here,' I say as we take a right off the main road. I stop at the entrance to my close. 'You don't have to walk me to my door.' I'm half thinking that I might go in the back way: on to the shed and into my bedroom window, a route I take when I want to avoid Stu.

'OK,' he says, looking past me. He probably wasn't going to walk me to my door, anyway. 'Which one's yours?' he asks.

I glance backwards and feel embarrassed as I point at the little house that I call home, with its dark-brown wooden cladding and untidy front garden. The grass hasn't been cut for months. Almost six months, to be precise. A memory comes back to me of mum frantically dragging the tiny lawnmower out of the garden shed on the afternoon of my birthday party.

'Don't bother,' I'd berated her.

'It looks a mess!' she exclaimed, her long dark hair tied up into an untidy ponytail and mud smeared across her jeans and her left cheek. 'I don't want all of your friends' parents dropping their kids off and thinking we live in a dump.'

'Why not, when it's true?' I said sarcastically, then went and listened to my music in my bedroom, turning the sound right up to drown out the noise of her manically mowing the lawn. She was in even more of a rush to go and get my cake after that.

Why didn't I offer to help? Why was I always such a spoilt brat? And why didn't *Stu* ever mow the frigging lawn? But he was visiting his parents that day in Bristol, so I can't even blame him. No, I can only blame myself.

'See you later.' I turn away from Tom before he can see that I'm upset again. He must think I'm enough of an emotional wreck as it is.

Chapter 5

All the lights in the house look like they're off as I approach, so I decide to risk going in the front door. The house is silent when I walk in. It's almost midnight and Stu must have gone to bed already. At least I didn't have to risk getting a splinter from climbing over the back fence again. I feel a small flurry of relief, but it's swiftly replaced with trepidation. We're still going to have a row – it'll just be a delayed one, that's all.

I tiptoe up to my room and collapse into bed. Natalie has texted me for an update about Tom, so we spend ten minutes pinging messages back and forth while I fill her in on all of the details. Afterwards I try to fall asleep thinking about the hottest boy in school, who may or may not fancy me, rather than my disappointed stepdad.

The next morning, I take my time getting up. I can hear Stu pottering away downstairs and I'm slightly surprised that he hasn't come to bash my door down – he never normally lets me sleep in. Eventually I decide I'm going to have to go face the music. I tentatively open the door and step out on to the faded-green carpet on the landing. I can hear the radio in the kitchen as I slowly make my way downstairs. It's ten-thirty so Stu's probably having his mid-morning cup of coffee by now. I poke my head around the kitchen door and see him at our small, round, wooden kitchen table reading the Sunday newspapers, his hair still damp from the shower. A mug of coffee is steaming beside him. So predictable.

I jut my chin out defiantly and walk into the room, steadying myself for the onslaught.

'Hi,' I say.

He doesn't answer.

'*Hello?*' I say more loudly.

He takes a sip of his drink. The silence feels ominous.

'What, so now you're ignoring me?' I know I shouldn't push him, I know I should go and sit down and give him a proper apology, but I can't seem to keep myself from making things worse.

He sighs. 'I don't have anything to say to you.'

'Well, I'm *sorry*, alright? I wanted to go out.' I sound defensive, not in the slightest bit genuine.

He turns a page over.

'Fine.' I go to the cupboard and pull out a mug to make myself a coffee – I could use one after last night. I slam it down on the counter and bang the cupboard door as I do so, just to make a point.

My phone beeps. It's a text from Natalie asking me if I want to go up to Winter Hill with them. I expect Stuart to snap when I ask him if I can go, but instead he says it's fine.

'Don't you mind?' I ask him.

'You're going to go, anyway, so why bother asking for my opinion?' he calmly replies.

I glare at him and walk out the door.

Dougie picks me up in his banged-up Ford Fiesta. Aaron is in the front seat and Em and Natalie are in the back.

'You're still alive!' Natalie jokes.

'Just,' I reply, still smarting from Stu's reaction. I have a distinctly uneasy feeling in the pit of my stomach. I'd almost prefer him to be angry with me than give me the silent treatment.

When I get home later, I pause for a minute in the front garden, staring down at the overgrown grass and tall dandelions with their fluffy white heads. Mum always used to make me wish upon them. One day, just to spite her, I wished out loud that she would tell me who my real dad was. I said it to hurt her, and from the pained look on her face, I know that it did. Now she's gone, I'd do anything to take back every hurtful thing I ever said.

I shove my key in the lock and walk in to a silent house.

'Are you here?' I call aloud to Stuart. No answer.

I find him in the living room, staring at the wall.

'What are you doing?' I demand. He doesn't answer. 'For fuck's sake, Stu, will you talk to me?' I screech.

'Watch your language!' he shouts and I feel a strange surge of relief that I've finally got a reaction out of him.

'You're so useless!' I let rip. 'Do you know what a state this house looks? Why didn't you help out more when Mum was alive? Why didn't you ever mow the lawn? If Mum hadn't had to race around here like a maniac on the day of my party, she might not have been killed!'

45

His eyes are wide open, and when he speaks it's with stunned horror. 'Why are you always such a little—' He stops himself and takes a deep breath.

'Go on! Say it!' I yell, tears filling my eyes. My next question comes out of nowhere. 'Do you know who my real dad is?'

His mouth abruptly shuts.

'Do you?' I ask again.

He looks away from me and the blood drains away from my face. 'Do you?' I ask once more, this time with shock. I step around the coffee table and kneel in front of him. 'Stuart?' I ask, my pulse still racing. 'Stu, please? Do you know?'

He won't meet my eyes.

'I thought that when Mum died I'd never find out the truth ... If you know, you have to tell me.' Tears track silently down my cheeks as I stare at him, my last hope for my world's biggest secret.

Slowly, his eyes meet mine and I know that the answer is yes, he knows.

'Please tell me,' I beg, as the tears continue to stream relentlessly down my neck, soaking the rim of my T-shirt.

He rubs his hands over his face in a frustrated, lost gesture, upsetting his horn-rimmed glasses. He takes them off and pushes his right hand through his hair, studying the glasses in his left. I wait in breathless silence. He shakes his head.

'I don't know, Jessie.'

'Stu, please,' I say again. 'I need to know. It's why I've been so ... *angry* ... I can't move on, I can't say goodbye to her. Not really. I'm so hurt and upset that she kept this from me. *Please ...*' There is a lump the size of a ping-pong ball inside my throat now. 'I just want someone to be honest with me. I don't care if he's in jail. I'll get over it if he's dead. What could be worse than that?'

He shakes his head. 'He's not in jail.'

My breath catches and I freeze, staring at his face.

'And he's not dead,' he adds.

'Then who is he?'

He sighs. 'He has a family. He doesn't know you exist.'

'So that's it? I can't know who my dad is because he doesn't know who I am? Because I might upset his happy little family? Well, tough! What about me?'

'It's more complicated than that,' he tells me.

'How can it be more complicated than that?' I don't understand. I so wish I did.

'He's . . . well known.'

'What?' My brow furrows. Now I'm even more confused. Is he a celebrity? A politician? 'Have I heard of him?'

He nods slowly. 'His name is Johnny Jefferson.'

My world tilts off its axis. Not because I think my dad is Johnny Jefferson, but because Stuart has just told me that my dad is Johnny Jefferson. How could he be so cruel as to openly taunt me?

'How could you?' I ask, my head spinning. Why would Stu mock me like this? To teach me a lesson for acting out?

'I'm not lying to you,' he says solemnly and I want to slap his face. 'I'm not! I'm telling you the truth.'

'I hate you,' I reply bitterly.

'Jessie,' he says firmly. 'Your dad is Johnny Jefferson.'

I stare at him. What is he talking about?

Stu sighs. 'Your mum was a groupie of Johnny's first band, Fence, before they became famous.'

47

'A groupie?' I shake my head in confusion. Aren't groupies really slutty?

'Yes. She followed the band everywhere, was obsessed with Johnny.'

My face flushes. 'Are you being serious? If you're lying to me I will walk out of this door and you will never see me again,' I swear vehemently. Maybe that's what he wants.

'I'm not lying to you,' he replies. 'I swear on your mother's grave that I'm telling you the truth.'

I feel dizzy as now my world completely breaks away from its axis and starts to roll downhill, gathering speed as it goes. I fall backwards and my back hits the wall. I slide down to the floor and stare up at him in shock, looking down at me from his armchair.

'Are you serious?'

'Yes.'

'Holy shit.'

He closes his eyes briefly in resignation at my language, while I ready myself to hear the bedtime story to end all bedtime stories.

'You know that Candy – your mum – was my first love? That we went out when we were sixteen but then broke up,' he starts.

I nod impatiently, because I've heard this story before. They were in the same year at school, and Stu had a crush on her for ages. A few years ago he told me he thought she was the coolest girl he'd ever known – I imagine she was a wild child, while he was a bit of a geek. Anyway, she decided to give him a chance, but after a year they broke up. Mum got pregnant soon after that, and Stu was there for her through the whole thing. But they were just friends until I was about six, when they got back together, although he didn't move in with us for another two years. Those details I know.

'When Candy was seventeen, she went to London to see a new band. Fence. I wasn't much into rock music – not like her – so she went with a friend.' He pauses for a moment. 'She was on such a high when she got back from that concert. She bought her tickets to their next one straight away. It became an obsession. She would travel around the country going to every gig she possibly could, spent all her money on them. She became more and more distant, and then one day she called it off with me.'

'Just like that?' I ask.

'Yep. I was devastated,' he admits. 'I wanted to at least continue to be friends, but she was so into Fence, into Johnny, that she didn't want anything to do with me. I was too much of a nerd for her to be associated with. I'd always known she was out of my league,' he muses.

I feel a wave of pity for him. It sounds like Mum was pretty harsh.

'Anyway, one day, a year or so later, she did come knocking. She was in such a state, really upset.' He looks dazed as he remembers. 'Only a couple of months before that she had seemed so full of confidence, even more than usual. She came to tell me that she was pregnant, that the baby was Johnny's. I asked if she was sure, and she said without a doubt, there hadn't been anyone else. She didn't know what to do, whether to tell him, whether to keep the baby.'

She thought about having me terminated?

'She didn't think about it for long.' Stuart continues hastily, flashing me a sympathetic smile. 'Her parents went absolutely ballistic went they found out – that's partly why she came to me.'

'Did they know the baby was Johnny's?'

'No. Your mum never told them.'

'Why not?'

'Stories about Johnny's women started hitting the headlines.'

'Oh.'

'She was devastated,' he says sadly. 'She hadn't realised that she was one of many. She thought she was special. She was, but only to me.'

'Oh my God.' I try to let all of this sink in. 'But why didn't she ever tell me the truth?'

'She didn't want to lose you.'

'What do you mean? She wouldn't have lost me!'

'She thought that you'd want to get in touch with Johnny. Maybe choose his life over hers.'

'But that's crazy. I wouldn't have left her!'

'Try to see it from her side. Look around you.' He pauses, so I do. I take in the tiny living room with its threadbare carpet and the faded floral hand-me-down sofas – it hurts to acknowledge the left-hand corner which was always her favourite place to sit, with her knees up and her feet tucked underneath her. I stare at the scratched wooden coffee table that she picked up from a charity shop and occasionally bothered to polish, and the curtains that are hanging off-kilter from their hooks, ever since I accidentally grabbed hold of one to steady myself days before she died. We've never lived in a palace. We've never had a fortune. Not, it seems, like my biological father.

'But he might have helped us,' I say, shaking my head. 'We might not have had to live like this.'

'She didn't want to ask for his help,' he says in a tone that implies I should know this. And he's right. Mum was stubborn. She never asked anyone for help, not even her parents, my grandparents, who have never played a big part in my life. Mum never forgave them for that, and now my granddad is dead and gran is in a home with senile dementia. 'She did think about telling you, but when you were older,' Stu reveals.

Em's comment from a couple of days ago flashes in my mind.

'He lived nearby for a while, didn't he?' My real dad, a twenty-minute drive away and I never knew.

Stu nods and stares sadly at his hands. 'She was a mess when he moved back.'

'Was she?'

He nods, and I can see his eyes shining.

'I think she still had feelings for him.'

He coughs suddenly, almost with embarrassment. I'm not sure he meant to reveal that. 'Anyway, I always thought you deserved to know the truth.'

'Did you?' I ask in a small voice.

He looks up at me and slowly nods.

'Thank you,' I say.

He swallows. 'So what do you want to do now?'

'What do you mean?' I ask.

'Do you . . . do you want me to contact him for you?'

I feel faint. Ten minutes ago I didn't think I'd ever know who my real dad was. Now Stu's offering to help me get in touch with him. 'You would do that?'

'Yes.'

A tiny little voice inside asks, *does he want to get rid of me?* But I don't want to know the answer to that question. Not right now. Right now I want to meet my real dad. Whatever the consequences.

Chapter 6

'We have the same hands.'

I look down at our fingers splayed out, our palms pressed together as we lie side-by-side on my single bed. She's right: we do have the same hands. She links her fingers through mine and squeezes, then turns and presses a kiss to my temple.

'I like this song,' she says, as 'Jump Into The Fog' by the Wombats comes on.

'It's cool,' I agree, gently extricating my hand and letting it lie across my stomach. I love her to bits, but I'm not really comfortable lying here holding my mum's hand at my age.

'You have good taste,' she tells me and I smirk. Fancy my mum telling me I have good taste. Of course I bloody do. But I'm content so I don't make a sarky comment. I lean my head against hers and can see her dark hair out of the corner of my right eye, up close and out of focus. Her hair is long and wavy, and looks even more so next to my straight blonde locks. She has caramel-coloured eyes; mine are green. We're different in some ways, but similar in so many others.

I've got her slight build and she'd like to think that we have the same taste in clothes as well as in music. But while I can just about handle her downloading my songs, I draw the line when it comes to her raiding my wardrobe. She kicks one slim leg up in the air and I stare at her toenails, painted cherry red.

'Is that my nail polish?' I ask accusatorily. She giggles and puts her foot down. I smack her knee and lift my own leg up and she mirrors me. It's exactly the same shade.

'Mum!' I squawk as she puts her leg down but continues to laugh. Suddenly she freezes and falls silent.

'What?' I ask.

'Nothing.' She brushes me off. 'Not so keen on this song.'

'What? Why not?' I ask with surprise. It's 'Locked' by Johnny Jefferson. It should be right up her street. I sing along: 'I'm locked inside us and I can't find the key, it was under the plant pot that you nicked from me . . .'

Abruptly she gets up and presses skip on my iPod.

'What did you do that for?' I glare at her.

'Sorry.' She flashes me a small smile.

'That's really annoying!' I berate her, getting down from the bed and stubbornly pressing the back button.

'Fine,' she says curtly. 'I'd better crack on with dinner anyway.' She walks out of the room and I stand there, listening to the strains of Johnny Jefferson's deep, soulful voice as I wonder what the hell that was all about . . .

Now I understand why she reacted that way. My heart aches because I can't ask her about him, and I have so many questions. So many questions that will never be answered. I miss her so much. I roll on to my side, knowing that I could wish on

54

every dandelion in the world, but she'll never lie next to me again.

Stuart asks me to keep the news to myself for the time being, until he's managed to contact Johnny's people. I don't mind, actually. You would have thought that, having found out that my long lost dad is a global megastar, I'd be wanting to shout about it from the rooftops. But I feel strangely private about Stu's revelation, like I want to protect this secret, nurture it, hold on to it while I can. Besides, who would I really tell? Libby would understand, but we're no longer close. I feel sudden regret at the loss of my best friend, but I try to harden up – what's done is done. As for Natalie, she'd be excited, sure, but I doubt that she would take it very seriously.

My head is still spinning. I don't know how this is going to turn out. Maybe Johnny will want nothing to do with me. I know I'm going to be a big chink in the armour of his happy little family. He's married with two kids now, and it doesn't take a genius to work out that I'm probably not going to be very welcome.

Well, tough. I didn't ask him to shag my mum and get her pregnant. His actions have consequences and he's going to have to face up to them.

I feel a flurry of nerves. That's bravado talking. Deep down I feel like a scared little girl.

I'm in a daze the next day at school. I decide to spend lunchtime in the library, so I don't have to talk to anyone. I walk in and am surprised to find Libby quietly reading a book in the corner. I almost turn and walk out again, but she looks up and sees me.

'Hi!' She sounds surprised.

'Hi,' I reply, reluctantly dumping my bag on a nearby table.

'Are you OK?' she asks with a frown.

I nod brusquely. 'Why wouldn't I be?'

'I don't usually see you in here,' she replies, awkwardly tucking her hair behind her ears. It always looks neat and tidy, unlike mine. I couldn't even be bothered to brush it this morning.

I shrug. 'I just needed a bit of peace and quiet.'

Sympathy crosses her face, but she looks down almost before it can register. I haven't rewarded her recent empathy with anything but meanness, so I can hardly blame her. Out of the blue, I miss her, really miss her, and I desperately want to confide in her. Libby understands how much it's killed me not knowing who my real dad is. I can trust her.

I pull up a chair and sit down, confused by my feelings.

The door whooshes open and Amanda walks in. 'There you are!' she exclaims.

I glance at Libby and see her face light up. 'I thought you were ill today,' she says with a smile.

'I had a doctor's appointment,' Amanda reveals with a roll of her eyes. 'Sorry, I tried to text you but idiot Kevin unplugged my charger so my battery was dead.'

I don't know who Kevin is – her brother, her boyfriend – but I don't ask. Now I'm the outsider and I don't want to be here.

'Come on, shall we go and sit on the grass?' Amanda urges.

'Shall we go and sit outside on the grass?' I ask.

'I forgot to put sunscreen on this morning,' Libby replies with downturned lips.

'We can sit in the shade,' I say. 'Well, you can. I'll sit next to you in the sun. I really want to get a tan this summer.'

'I wish I could tan like you,' Libby grumbles. 'I'll just end up with even more stupid freckles.'

'Your freckles aren't stupid,' I say with a grin. 'They're highly intelligent. Doesn't that one speak French?' I prod her arm.

She giggles. 'No, you're thinking of this one.' She prods a freckle on her other arm, then indicates the one I pointed at. 'This one knows how to do algebra.'

We crack up laughing and I drag her outside.

I blink back tears at the memory, feeling an unexpected pang of loss.

'Come on, Libs, it's gorgeous outside,' Amanda says.

'Sure,' Libby replies. She stuffs her book into her bag. Amanda's eyes flit towards me, but she doesn't acknowledge me. We barely know each other, and if Libby has told her anything about me, I doubt it was favourable, considering my recent behaviour.

Libby stands up and hesitantly looks down at me. 'Do you . . . Do you want to come with us?' she asks uncomfortably.

'No, no, it's OK,' I brush her off. 'I'm not feeling that well. Like I said, I wanted some quiet.' I feel like I need to give her some excuse. Any desire to reveal the truth has flown right out of the window.

'OK,' she says, stepping away from me and meeting Amanda's eyes. I'm sure they'll be bitching about me the moment they go out the door. No. Libby is not a bitch. She was a good friend. A best friend. And now she's Amanda's.

I clear my throat and try to gee myself up. Then I see the three computers up against the far wall and an idea comes to me. I relocate myself in front of one of them.

Google: Johnny Jefferson.

Over a hundred and forty million hits come up. The first is his official website, the second his official fan club, but I click on the third link: Wikipedia.

I could write a five-thousand-word essay using all of the information I find, but the things that stick out the most include the following:

His birth certificate says his name is Jonathan Michael Sneeden.
Sneeden, not Jefferson.
His father, Brian Jefferson, left his mother, Ursula Sneeden, before Johnny was born.
Something we have in common.
He was raised in Newcastle by his mother.
So his mother gave him her name? Mine did, too: Pickerill.
His mother died of cancer when he was thirteen.
And mine died at the age of fifteen . . .
After her death, he went to live with his father in London, an aged musician, serial womaniser and recovering alcoholic.
Sounds familiar. Johnny has been described like this, too.
He dropped out of school to concentrate on his music, took on his father's surname and formed Fence in his late teens. They signed a record deal and were global superstars by the time Johnny was twenty.
I would have been born around this time.
At the age of twenty-three, the band split.
How old would I have been then? Three?
Johnny had a well-publicised breakdown, spiralling out of control with drink and drugs.
Like father like daughter?
Two years later, he came back as a solo artist and was more successful

than ever. He met his wife-to-be, Meg Stiles, when she went to work for
him as his personal assistant.

He was 30 when they met, which means I was about ten. I was
consumed with the identity of my real dad around this time.
Libby would remember.

They now have two children together: Barney, three, and a baby boy
called Phoenix.

I have half brothers. I've never had any siblings. Stuart couldn't.
Am I the only one like me out there? Or are there others that I
don't know about, that the world doesn't know about?

My head is still prickling with this thought a while later, when
I open up YouTube and watch some music videos. It freaks me
out to see that I actually look like Johnny: the same piercing
green eyes, the same colour hair. A shiver goes up and down my
spine. What will *everyone* say when they find out the truth?

I manage to avoid talking to people pretty much all day, but later
when I'm walking to the staff car park, I spy Natalie with a group
of Year Elevens.

'Hey!' she says.

'Hi,' I reply.

'Just finished my final exam.'

'Bollocks!' I exclaim. 'Of course you did! Sorry, I meant to
text you and wish you good luck.' I've been so preoccupied. She
was going home after Winter Hill yesterday to revise. Not that
she thought you could do much revision for Maths. 'By now, you
either know it or you don't,' were her words.

Out of the corner of my eye, I see Tom and Chris coming out
of the hall. I try to focus on my friend.

'How did it go?' I ask her.

'It was alright, actually,' she says casually. 'I'm relieved I've finally finished. You coming to Dougie's tonight? His end of exams party is going to be great.'

'Um, I don't think so . . .' Tom and Chris reach our group and start joking around with their mates. They're all on a high after finishing their exams.

'Seriously?' Natalie asks. I look back at her to see her face has dropped.

'I can't,' I reply regretfully.

She smiles kindly. 'Next year will fly by, Jess,' she says, mistaking my mood. She thinks I'm upset because they're all leaving and I'm staying. And a couple of days ago, that would have been my biggest problem – I've been dreading it for weeks – but not now. Now I have bigger things on my mind.

'Come on, come with us. Help me celebrate.'

'No, really, I've got to get home.'

Tom looks over at me. 'You going to Dougie's tonight, Jessie?'

My butterflies lift their dozy heads as he looks at me hopefully, but even they are too consumed with other things to bother taking flight in my stomach.

'No, I can't,' I tell him, noticing Stuart come out of the door near the staff room. I lift my hand up to wave at him and he nods his acknowledgement.

'Are you grounded?' Tom asks.

'Nope, just gotta go,' I tell him, backing away. 'See you later,' I say to Natalie. She looks put out, but hopefully she'll understand soon enough. Tom looks disappointed, too.

I jog over to Stuart. He raises one eyebrow at me over the hood of his car.

'What?' I ask.

'I'm just waiting for you to ask if you can go out with your friends,' he says.

'No.' I open the car door and climb inside.

'Huh,' he says as he appears next to me and starts up the ignition.

'Any news?' I ask eagerly.

'No.' He shakes his head and looks uncomfortable. 'This could take some time.' He glances across at me. 'Don't get your hopes up.'

'But you did contact his people, didn't you?'

'Yes.' He nods. 'I left a message with his lawyer. I'll try him again tomorrow if he hasn't returned my call by then.'

It's three whole days before we hear anything and by then I've chewed all of my fingernails down to the quick and would consider starting on my toenails if only I were that flexible. Stuart comes to find me at lunchtime. I'm in the library again, researching Johnny on the internet. I'm here whenever I get the chance. It's like an obsession.

I can tell instantly that he's heard something. His eyes are lit up and his body is practically vibrating with excitement.

'What is it?' I ask, pushing my chair back and turning to face him.

He glances around the library to check it's deserted. 'His solicitor called me.'

I gasp. He pulls up the chair next to me and sits down.

'He said that you'll need to do a paternity test.'

'Oh.' I feel ill. 'But anyone can see that I look like him,' I say. 'Did you email them any photos?'

'I haven't done, yet.' He presses the tips of his fingers together. 'But don't worry. I'm not surprised they want you to do a test. It's probably just so they can be sure we're serious.'

'What does it involve?' I ask with trepidation.

'A DNA sample, so a piece of your hair would do it. You don't have to go anywhere for it. They're sending the test to us.'

'What?' I'm confused. 'We don't even have to meet anyone?'

'No.' He averts his gaze. 'Maybe when the test comes back positive.'

They think we're wasting their time. 'They don't believe us,' I say dully.

Stu puts his hand on my arm. 'They will,' he replies solemnly. 'But we're going to have to jump through a few of their hoops first, OK?' I meet his eyes and he regards me steadily. 'The important thing is we've made contact,' he reassures me, squeezing my arm. I'm glad he's being positive.

'Alright.' I nod, feeling slightly better. At that moment, I'm really grateful to have Stu in my life.

The paternity test comes by UPS the next day. We carefully follow the instructions and send it back the very same day. It's Friday and I don't want to waste any time by letting this run into the weekend.

I plan to lay low for the next few days, so I've told Natalie I have a stomach bug. I just want to be with Stu right now. I feel closer to him than I ever have. I'm aware of the irony of that, considering my search for his replacement.

It occurs to me that night, the night after I've sent the test back, that Johnny may well know about me by now. I wonder if he's told his wife. I doubt it. I suppose he'll want to make sure I'm telling the truth before he does anything. But if Stu knew Mum as well as he thinks he did, then Johnny'll have to tell her soon.

If Stu knew Mum as well as he thinks he did . . . That sentence carries a lot of weight. What if Mum lied? What if there *was* someone else, other than Johnny? What if Johnny Jefferson is not my dad, after all? Then I really will never know who my real dad is. Anxiety rushes through me, swiftly followed by an almost crushing disappointment as I imagine the paternity test coming back negative. I haven't properly got my head around the idea that Johnny *is* my dad, but suddenly I desperately, desperately want him to be.

The following Thursday, Stuart is waiting for me in the corridor outside my English Lit lesson.

'The result is back,' he says quietly, taking me to one side as my classmates pour out of the classroom behind me. 'It's positive.'

My heart somersaults and I feel dizzy. Libby catches my eye as she follows Amanda out and I see her do a double take. God knows what I look like. I feel like I've seen a ghost.

'Come on, let's go home,' Stu says, and I allow myself to be led by him, too dazed to point out that I'm going to miss my Art lesson.

I've resisted telling anyone else about what's been going on, partly so I won't have humiliation to contend with if Johnny turns out not to be my dad, and partly because I've wanted to keep this secret close to my heart. But now I feel like I'm going to burst.

'What happens now?' I ask when we're in the car.

'He's asked us to go into his office tomorrow.'

'Who?' I feel panicked. Am I going to meet Johnny so soon?

'Wendel Rosgrove, Johnny's solicitor. His office is in London.'

'But I'm going to miss school . . .'

Stu gives me a look. He knows I've skipped school quite a bit recently, and *now* I care about missing classes? My face breaks into a grin.

'Cool,' I say. 'But what about you? Can you get the day off?'

He grins back at me. 'I'll call in sick.'

I crack up laughing and hold my hand up for a high five. He hesitates, leaving me hanging, so I let my hand drop and shrug.

'I shouldn't really,' he says, more in line with the spoilsport stepdad I've come to know and, well, love, I guess. Ew. 'But this is important,' he adds.

I bite my lip and stare out of the window. He's not wrong.

Chapter 7

I must go to the toilet ten times the next morning, and I'm still crossing my legs on the drive to London. I'm so nervous, so excited, so full of emotions that I never imagined I'd experience again, at least, not deeply. When Mum died, anything other than grief felt muted. My heartache dominated everything else, and I didn't think I'd ever feel pure and unadulterated happiness again. I still don't know if I will, but my present intense anticipation is a welcome distraction from my usual pain and anger, that's for sure.

Wendel Rosgrove works just north of Oxford Street in a seven-storey shiny block of glass. That's what it looks like. We've parked in a nearby car park, hanging the expense, and as we walk towards it, past a neatly groomed square surrounded by tall townhouses, I look around for a public loo to relieve myself in.

'You don't really need to go, you know. It's all psychological,' Stu tells me, reading my mind.

'Whatever, I'm busting,' I reply.

'I'm sure there will be a toilet in reception,' he says.

I hope he's right, because we're here. My reflection looms out of the shiny glass door and I see that I appear as small, scared and lost as I feel. I tried to look my very best today. I brushed my hair and fixed it up into a big, loose bun on the very top of my head. I'm wearing my nice yellow sundress again and my only pair of clean ballet slippers, and I resisted applying too much make-up.

But now I wish I'd caked it on. Now I wish I'd left my hair long and messy. I wish I'd worn a beanie hat and my camo jacket. I wish I didn't look like I cared as much as I do.

Stuart pushes open the door and my reflection disappears with it. He stands aside to let me pass into the vacuous reception space. Two women sit behind the large desk ahead of us. One is on the phone. The other glances up and smiles.

'Can I help you?' she asks.

Luckily Stuart takes control because I've lost my voice. 'We're here to see Wendel Rosgrove.'

'Names?'

'Stuart Taylor and Jessica Pickerill.'

She scans a notepad in front of her, then nods. 'Go straight up to the fourth floor.'

'Do you have a toilet?' I interject.

'Of course. First door to your right.' She points to the corridor behind her. I half hop and skip my way towards it, but when I'm safely inside a cubicle, the urge to go vanishes. If this is what I'm like when I'm meeting his solicitor, what am I going to be like when I come face-to-face with Johnny Jefferson?

Another, smaller, reception desk waits for us on the fourth floor, but before we can take a seat as directed, a grey-haired man wearing a pinstripe suit opens the door and pokes his head out.

'Mr Taylor?' he asks, staring straight at Stu, but his blue-grey eyes flit towards me.

'Pleased to meet you,' Stu says confidently, going towards him with his hand outstretched. The man shifts to push the door back with his other hand, relieving his right hand to shake Stu's.

'Wendel Rosgrove,' he says.

'And this is Jessie,' Stu says, turning around and indicating me.

Wendel nods at me. 'Come straight through.' He pushes the door open and I meekly follow Stu through the door.

We follow Wendel down a long corridor, with doors to our left and right. He opens the door at the very end and I'm almost blinded by the light as a view of London at its sunniest comes into focus. We're inside the block of glass, and this is a floor-to-ceiling view of the city. Straight ahead, between a break in the buildings, I can see Oxford Street, bumper-to-bumper with black taxis and double-storey red buses. Mum used to take me shopping there . . .

'Why don't you get a Saturday job in TopShop?' she says as we rifle through the racks. 'There's one in Maidenhead town centre.'

'Yeah, I know,' I reply, vaguely aware of the irony of us coming to London when we have the same shop at home. But this branch is the biggest in the country. 'I think you have to be sixteen,' I reply.

'Oh, that's a shame,' she says. 'You could work in another clothes shop, though? You'd be good in fashion.'

'Yeah, maybe,' I say thoughtfully. I'd love to get a job and have a bit of my own money, but I'm only fifteen – well, I will be next week. We're here on a pre-birthday shopping trip so I can get something to wear at my party.

67

'What about this?' She holds up a dress in front of me. 'Yellow really suits you.'

'Do you think?' I screw up my nose.

'Definitely. I wish I had your skin tone.'

She's always been quite pale. 'I guess I must take after my dad, then,' I say with irritation and she stiffens. Another moment spoiled by the secret that rests between us.

The pain that engulfs me at the memory is breathtaking. I thought this was enough to take my mind off Mum, but I was wrong. Everything about this search for my dad is linked back to her – how could it not be?

'Take a seat.' Wendel brings me back to the present as he goes behind his chunky, dark-wooden desk. Stu and I pull up black leather office chairs in front of him and sit down. The chairs look expensive. Everything in here looks expensive. I glance around at the wooden bookshelves against the wall, neatly stacked with pristine books, and the brown leather sofa to my right, accompanied by a highly polished black glass coffee table.

'Tea? Coffee?' Wendel asks us.

'No, thank you,' Stu replies, and it seems to me that he's lost some of his earlier confidence. Or maybe he never had it in the first place. I quickly shake my head and look away.

'Soft drink?' he asks, and I glance back to see him staring directly at me.

'No, thank you,' I reply quietly.

'Right.' He presses a button on his intercom and speaks into it. 'Coffee for me. Nothing else.' Then he turns and regards us from across the desk. 'Thank you for coming to see me,' he says in a clipped tone without a smile, making me think he's anything but pleased we're here. 'Shall we get down to business?'

Business?

'Can I be completely honest with you?' he asks, and I nod, sensing Stu's impatience beside me. Both of us are clearly wishing he'd get to the point, whatever that is.

There's a sharp knock at the door and a woman enters with a tray. Wendel leans back in his chair as she places it on the desk in front of him. He continues to talk, ignoring her as she pours his coffee and adds a dash of cream.

'We haven't had a situation like this before.' I'm a 'situation'? 'That may surprise you, considering my client's reputation.' So I *am* the only one like me.

The woman turns and goes out of the door without so much as a thank you from Wendel. The man's manners are even worse than my own.

'I have to tell you that I've imagined this day coming on numerous occasions.'

I feel like I'm sitting in the headmaster's office. I'm surprised when Stu speaks.

'In that case, you will have had plenty of time to think about where we go from here,' he says, and I detect a hint of sarcasm to his tone.

Wendel clears his throat. 'It's not that straightforward.'

'Have you told Johnny about me?' I find myself asking. His eyes meet mine.

'He knows,' he replies, his tone neutral.

My heart jumps.

'Does his family know?'

'I'm not at liberty to discuss that,' he replies, making me

shrink back into myself. 'What I would like to know from you, is what you expect to come from this?' He stops short of asking me if I can be paid off. But I know that's what he's thinking, so I answer his unspoken question.

'It's *not* about money,' I tell him firmly. 'I want to meet my real dad. I've always wanted to meet him, or at the very least know who he is. But my mum died nearly six months ago, without telling me who he was. I thought I'd never know the truth, but now I do I'm not going to miss out on this opportunity. So you tell Johnny Jefferson that he'd better come clean to his family about me. Because I'm not going away. I won't be bought. I'm here. And he owes me the courtesy of meeting me face to face.'

Without realising it, I've stood up, my body wracked with tension and my nose tingling as I stare him down from across the table. Whoa. I sit back down with a bump. Then I realise that Wendel is regarding me with something that I would almost call respect, if that didn't sound so cringey. Maybe he's not used to being spoken to like that. Well, like I care who he is?

'OK,' he nods, a hint of a smile on his lips. 'I'll speak to my client.'

Why doesn't he just call him Johnny, like everyone else does?

'But in the meantime, it would be wise for you to keep this quiet. Don't go talking to any journalists—'

'As if I would,' I interrupt.

'If she'd wanted to tell anyone, she already would have,' Stu backs me up.

His faith in me is a *little* unfounded, as I discover the next day when Natalie stalks into work and insists that I go for lunch with her.

'Where have you been?' she demands to know as we sit in the coffee shop in the mall. It's raining today and neither of us brought umbrellas so we don't want to venture far. 'Have you *really* had a stomach bug?'

'Um . . .'

From the look on her face, she knows I'm lying.

'It's true that I haven't been feeling very well,' I tell her.

'What's been wrong with you?' she asks with a frown, sipping her milkshake through a straw. 'Tom was asking about you last night, you know.'

'Really?' I instantly perk up. I've barely thought about him in almost two weeks – I've been so consumed with everything that's going on. 'What did he say? Where did you go?'

'*Now* you're feeling better,' she teases, tucking into her sandwich. 'A bunch of us went round Aaron's,' she reveals between mouthfuls. 'His parents have turned their garage into a games room so we hung out and played pool.'

'What did Tom say?' I urge her to get to the point.

'He just asked where you were.' She flicks her black hair back.

'Did he say anything else?'

'No. But he did look a bit disappointed.'

I can't help grinning as I pick up my own sandwich. But before I can lift it up to my mouth, I have a thought. 'Was Isla there?'

'No, she wasn't, actually. I'm pretty sure they're not together.'

My smile pops back into place. 'Who else was there?' I ask as I take a bite. She fills me in on all the gossip.

'You should have come,' she says eventually, still sounding a little put out. She's not used to me saying no.

I look down. 'I couldn't.'

'Why not? What's going on with you?'

I'm not sure how much more of this secrecy I can bear. I'm dying to spill the beans. I make an impulsive decision. I'm sure Natalie won't tell anyone.

'OK . . .' I lean in towards her. 'I've just found out who my real dad is.'

She frowns. 'Oh. Wow.' She sounds slightly deflated, like she was hoping for something better, and I realise that she has no idea how much I've wanted to know about him all these years. Why would she, when we don't really talk about serious things? For some reason I picture Libby sitting opposite me and can't help feeling a twinge of regret that she wasn't the first person I told. Never mind, the next bit of my news is going to blow her away.

'It's Johnny Jefferson.'

I fight the urge to laugh out loud at the look on her face. Obviously she thinks I'm taking the piss.

'Good one,' she says with a wry look, turning back to her lunch.

'I'm not joking.' I shake my head slowly.

'Ha ha, very funny,' she says sarcastically. 'Have you really found out who your real dad is or were you joking about that, too?'

'Natalie.' I reach across the table and grasp her hand. 'I'm honestly, honestly being serious. My mum was a Fence groupie when she was a teenager.'

She rolls her eyes and extracts her hand.

Bloody hell, she's not going to believe me . . . 'I'm serious!' I exclaim. 'Stu told me. I asked my mum time and time again who he was and she'd never tell me. Then she died.' The smile falls from my face. Natalie still looks sceptical. She doesn't say anything, too worried to look like a fool in case I'm teasing her. But I would never use my mum's death to wind anyone up.

'Why wouldn't your mum have just told you the truth?' she asks with narrowed eyes, holding back from showing any emotion. 'I mean, if your dad is *Johnny Jefferson*,' she says in a comedy voice, 'surely that's big news.'

'She didn't want to lose me, Stu said. She thought I'd want to go and live with him, choose him over her. I mean, he's a mega famous rock star.' I shrug.

She smirks and noisily slurps at the dregs of her drink. 'You should be an actress,' she says when she's finished.

'I am not joking!' I say in a loud whisper. 'Johnny Jefferson is my biological father. I've had to do a paternity test. I went to see his solicitor yesterday in London and he told me to keep quiet about it, so it's actually pretty handy if you don't believe me because I wasn't supposed to tell anyone.'

Something changes in her expression and I think she's starting to come around. Then she cracks up laughing. She literally *hoots* with laughter, bordering on hysterical. 'Are you serious?' she asks again. She's wearing false eyelashes today. They make her blue eyes look even bigger.

'Yes!' I sit back in my chair and grin at her. She lurches forwards and grabs my hand.

'Johnny Jefferson is your dad? *Your* dad?'

'Yes! Shh!'

'Holy shit!' she cries. I lean over and bat her across the head.

'Keep it down, you nutcase. I don't want anyone to hear us.' But the coffee shop is bustling with people and they're all nattering away, so I don't think anyone is paying attention to two

73

hysterical teenagers. I look back at Natalie. She's still staring at me. I'm not sure if it's in disbelief or if she's just reeling from the truth. I hope it's the latter because I'm sick of trying to convince her.

'What a load of bollocks,' she says suddenly with a wry grin, throwing the remnants of her lunch down and pushing her chair back. 'I've got to get back to work.' She stands up. 'Glad you're feeling better, though.' She pats my arm and walks out of the coffee shop, shaking her head with bemusement.

I stare after her with surprise. She still thinks I'm making it up. It makes me think about Libby again, and how things might have been different if she and I were still friends.

The rain has cleared by the evening, so I walk the long way home, my feet taking me on a detour past Libby's house. I slow on the pavement on the opposite side of the street, and cast a look at her house. Her dad's car is on the driveway, but there's no sign of life inside. I feel downhearted, but then, just like the last time I walked past, her mum appears in the kitchen window and she spots me instantly. But unlike last time, I don't put my head down and turn away, so I see her wave enthusiastically. I timidly smile back and she holds up her palm, indicating for me to wait. She hurries out of sight and then the front door opens.

'Jessie!' she cries, beaming, her curly red hair framing her round face. 'How are you?'

'I'm OK, thanks, Marilyn,' I reply uncertainly. My life has changed so much since Mum's death, it's like I don't know her any more. She used to be like a second mum to me.

'Come over and see me.' She beckons to me and I feel obliged to go. 'I haven't seen you for such a long time!' she exclaims as I

74

reach her, putting her arm around me and pulling me in for a squeeze. I awkwardly squeeze her back. She's familiar, yet unfamiliar. 'Have you got time for a cuppa with me?' she implores, and I hesitate before nodding. She leads me through to the kitchen. The house looks the same as it always did, but it feels like an age has passed since I was last here, not just a few months.

'Where's Libby?' I ask.

'She's out at a friend's,' Marilyn replies.

I'd put money on that friend being Amanda Blackthorn.

'She should be back soon. I know she'd love to see you.'

Why do I feel so small and out of place? So much has happened since I last felt comfortable within these walls. Marilyn sets about filling the kettle and putting it on. I pull up a chair at the kitchen table and tentatively sit down. She returns after a while with two mugs full of steaming, milky tea and a plate of biscuits. 'I hope these don't spoil your appetite this close to dinner. I don't want Stuart to be cross with me,' she says, taking a seat next to me. 'But it just feels like so long since I've seen you! How are you?' Her hazel-coloured eyes penetrate mine, and suddenly I wish I hadn't come. Sympathy sets me off every time, and I'm so tired of crying.

'I'm fine,' I reply, blowing on my drink.

'Are you looking forward to the summer?' she asks.

'What summer?' I reply drily, indicating the weather outdoors.

She laughs and rolls her eyes. 'Too true. We're off to Portugal when school breaks up so hopefully the weather will be better there.' She freezes. Does she remember that mum wanted to go to Spain? No subject is safe with me. Perhaps she also wishes I hadn't come in. 'Have you seen any good films recently?' she asks weakly, obviously struggling to think of something to say.

'I haven't been to the cinema for ages,' I reply with a smile, feeling sorry for her. This is why it's easier hanging out with people like Natalie – no awkward questions, no link to the past.

We hear a key in the front lock and she instantly brightens up, leaping to her feet and popping her head around the corner into the hall.

'Libby!' she exclaims. 'You're back! Jessie's here.'

'*Jessie?*' I hear Libby ask with wary disbelief. A moment later she appears. 'Hi!' she says with surprise. She's wearing blue jeans and a light-blue top I recognise from TopShop. She looks like she's lost a little weight. Her mum would call it puppy fat, much to her mortification.

'Hi,' I reply edgily. 'I walked the long way home from town. Your mum spotted me through the window.' I feel like I need to explain my presence.

'I was over at Amanda's,' she says, tucking her hair behind her ears in that familiar gesture.

'Your mum said you were at a friend's. I thought it might've been Amanda,' I reply, trying not to look like it bothers me.

'Do you want to have a cuppa with us, Libs?' Marilyn asks, the hope in her voice obvious.

'Er, alright then,' she says, pulling up a chair.

I have no idea what we're going to talk about.

'Are you going out tonight?' she asks me.

'I don't know,' I reply. 'I might catch up with Natalie.' Libby's face falls a little at the mention of Natalie. 'What about you?' I ask quickly.

'Amanda and I are going to see a film.'

'Are you?' Marilyn chips in. 'Jessie was just saying she hasn't been to the cinema for ages. What are you going to see?'

'*Two Things*,' Libby replies, and I feel a bit gutted as I remember that Tom talked about going to see that with me. I hope I haven't missed my chance with him. 'Come, if you like,' she says casually to me, and out of the blue I really, really want to. I just wish Amanda wasn't going, too.

'Thanks. Maybe.' I follow Marilyn with my eyes as she wanders out of the room. I look back at Libby to see her studying her fingernails and I remember the last time I gave her a manicure. We were having a girls' night in, the week before my fated birthday party. 'Want me to paint them for you?' I'm taken aback to hear the question come out of my mouth. Libby looks startled, too.

'Um, OK,' she says.

My face breaks into a grin, and she instantly mirrors me.

'Shall we go upstairs?' she suggests.

I kick off my shoes at the bottom of the stairs, and you'd think they were made out of lead, because I feel significantly lighter with every step up the stairs I take. We reach Libby's tiny bedroom at the top of the landing, overlooking the road. Her brothers share the larger room at the back of the house. Libby's room looks and smells the same: I'm pleased to see that in her world, at least, nothing much seems to have changed.

'You still love Joseph Strike,' I note, shutting the door and coming face to face with a poster of the actor in all his toned and tanned, bare-chested glory.

'Always,' she replies, bouncing on the bed as she sits down. Her room is tiny, just enough room for a bed under the window, small wardrobe to my left, plastered with pictures of One Direction and McFly, and overcrowded desk to my right. She reaches over and pulls a make-up bag off the desk. I sit down on

77

the bed next to her and cross my legs. She digs around and brings out nail varnish remover and some cotton wool and we set about removing our polish.

'You've been biting your nails again,' she notices with a frown.

'Yeah,' I reply, and then I know that I'm going to tell her why.

'What?' she asks with widened eyes, seeing the look on my face.

'I've found out who my real dad is.'

'*What?*' She grabs both of my hands in hers, her reaction the opposite to Natalie's, the blood draining from her face because she knows what a big deal this is. 'How? *Who?*'

'Stu told me,' I breathe.

'But I thought . . . I didn't . . .' she stutters.

'No, I didn't know he knew either. I never thought to ask him. But he does, and you won't believe it . . .'

'Why? What? Who is it?' She's dying to know. I've never heard so many who, what, whens, hows and whys before in my life.

'You won't believe me,' I say again.

'Yes, I will. You know I will.' She grips my hands a little tighter.

'You can't tell anyone,' I warn.

'I won't!' she exclaims.

My face falls, because she's probably going to think that I'm taking the mick once I tell her, and I really don't want that. Not with Libby.

I take a deep breath. 'It's Johnny Jefferson.'

She doesn't seem to know what to say. I think she's still trying to put two and two together. Then she looks away from me, hurt registering across her face. She does think I'm taking the mick and she's not finding it funny. I can understand why – me making a joke of this would be the biggest insult considering the hours we've spent wondering about my real dad. She probably thinks Natalie put me up to it and we're all laughing behind her back.

'I know you don't believe me,' I say quietly, studying her face. 'But I swear to you, I'm telling the truth.'

I wait a long moment for her to look up, but she doesn't. I sigh. Maybe I should have kept this whole thing to myself for a while longer, at least until it's officially announced. Is that what they'll do? Announce to the world that I'm Johnny Jefferson's daughter? My life will change dramatically. Excitement pulses through me at the thought. I won't leave my friends behind though, I vow silently to myself. I've treated Libby terribly, but I'll win her back from Amanda. And Natalie has really been there for me, so I'll make sure she's well looked after . . .

'Can you go, please.'

Libby's words cut through my thoughts and wound me like a knife.

I stare at her, but she still won't return my gaze. I've never seen an expression like this on her face. She looks . . . almost . . . angry.

'Libby, I'm not winding you up.'

'Just piss off, would you? I don't know what's happened to you, Jessie, but I don't need you coming here and making fun of me,' she snaps. She snatches up the nail varnish remover from the bed and stuffs it back into her make-up bag, slamming the bag on to her desk.

I feel sick as I watch her. 'Libby . . .'

Violently she reaches across and shoves me off the bed. 'Go!'

79

She raises her voice as I stumble to my feet. I hate the idea of her mum overhearing her shouting.

'Libby, wait!' I beg, shocked. 'You *know* me. You know I wouldn't lie to you about my dad.' Tears fill my eyes and I frantically brush them away as I try to convince her. 'It's too important. You might think I've changed – I *have* changed – but I haven't changed *that* much.' I stare at her in desperation and panic, until eventually her eyes lift to meet mine. She still looks angry – furious, even – and the Jessie that Natalie knows would just walk out of the room and tell her to bugger off, but suddenly that doesn't feel like *me* any more.

'I know I've been pushing you away. I know I've been mean to you. But what happened to Mum ... God, Libby.' I hastily wipe my eyes, but still my tears keep coming. 'I would *not* lie to you about this,' I say fervently. 'You know in your heart that I wouldn't.'

Her eyes narrow as she regards me, but I see that her anger is waning, and a small spark of hope ignites within me. 'You're trying to tell me that your dad is Johnny Jefferson?' Her voice remains sceptical.

I gingerly sit back down on the bed. 'I've had a paternity test. There's no doubt about it.'

'How?' she asks with disbelief, bordering on astonishment.

'My mum was one of his first groupies.' My face heats up. I haven't dwelt much on how I was conceived, but now, in front of Libby, I feel embarrassed about this revelation. 'I think they had a thing, going,' I add lamely. 'But I don't know many of the details. Stu has tried to fill me in.'

'Stu told you?' Her brow furrows.

'He's known all along.'

And then I see it: the belief dawning on her face, followed by an eyes–wide-open look of absolute incredulity.

'Johnny Jefferson is your *dad*?'

I can't help it – I start to giggle. 'Yes.'

'Holy . . . Oh my *God*!' she squeals.

'Please don't tell Amanda.' I expect her to scoff and say, 'of course not.' But to my dismay, she doesn't.

'She wouldn't tell anyone,' she says instead, a touch defensively.

'Yes, but you still won't tell her, will you?' I ask hastily.

'No.' She looks put out. 'She's really nice, though, you know. I'm sure you could trust her.'

'I trust *you*, Libby,' I say, my eyes shining. 'I know Amanda is your friend now, but if I ever meant anything to you, you won't betray me.'

Now she scoffs. 'Betray *you*? You should take a good look in a mirror before you accuse *me* of doing that.'

Her tone is bitter and my mouth abruptly shuts.

She sighs and looks deflated. 'Look, I won't tell Amanda.' Then she checks her watch. 'I'm sorry, but I've got to get ready before I eat dinner, otherwise I'm going to be late for the movie.'

'Sure,' I mumble, standing up.

'You're still welcome to join us . . .' she says warily.

'No. But thanks. I'd better get home to Stu.'

I leave as quietly as I can so her mum can't ask me what's wrong.

I can't help feeling deflated. I've imagined the scene where I tell Libby I know who my real dad is so many times, and it was never supposed to go like this.

Chapter 8

Libby and Natalie's reactions eat away at me that night and all of the next day. We can't get hold of Wendel because it's Sunday, but first thing Monday morning I'm on the phone to him while Stu stands nervously by.

'Have you spoken to Johnny?' I ask.

'Yes,' he replies. I struggle to keep my composure.

'I need to know when this will all become official.'

'What do you mean by official, exactly?' he asks carefully.

'Out in the open. It's killing me not to be able to tell anyone,' I say, biting my lip as I spin him a white lie. I've already told two people, with varying results.

He hesitates. 'Oh. I see.'

I wait for him to continue.

'This could be a problem.'

'What do you mean?' I ask with annoyance.

'My client is a very private person.'

'What?' I ask incredulously. That's not how it comes across in the papers.

'*These* days,' Wendel adds. 'Now that he has a family of his own. It's my job to minimise the damage and I've been trying to work out how this can all be contained.'

He's completely sucked the wind out of my sails. *Damage. Contained.* He's making me sound like some kind of natural disaster.

'You would like to meet him?' Wendel asks.

'Yes,' I answer shakily.

'How would you feel about going to Los Angeles?'

His question makes my heart beat just a little bit faster.

'That would be good.' I make a concerted effort to sound more in control. Stu shifts on his feet beside me. He can't hear the other side of the conversation. 'When were you thinking?' I ask.

'My client and his family are going away at the end of the month and would like you to come before then,' Wendel replies. 'How are you placed for next week?'

I swear I can hear my heart beating inside my head.

'I don't break up from school until next Wednesday,' I tell him, aware of Stu's inquisitive look. 'But I might be able to take a couple of days off?' I glance at Stu. He holds his hands out, palms upwards, in a 'tell me what the hell is going on' gesture. 'Can you hold on a moment?' I ask Wendel.

'Fine,' comes his curt reply.

I cover the receiver with my hand. 'He's asking if I can go to LA to meet Johnny and his family next week,' I tell Stuart, unable to keep the plea from my tone of voice.

He looks surprised. 'Oh. Wow.' He pulls up a chair at the kitchen table and sits down, dragging his hand across his mouth. His eyes fall on the receiver. 'Can I?'

Reluctantly I hand over the phone – and the control.

'Wendel? This is Stuart.'

Now I'm the one listening to a one-way conversation, and it's frustrating.

'Mmmhmm … Yes. I quite agree … No, yes, the sooner the better … I imagine early next week, possibly even this coming weekend … I see … OK. Well, that would be excellent … Yes, I appreciate that – things are tight right now … No, thank you … Shall we look into some flights? … Oh, OK, yes, that's great … We'll wait to hear from you, then … Excellent, thanks very much … Sorry? … Oh, yes. No, I'll reiterate that to her … OK, then. Bye bye.'

He ends the call and I'm not sure if I should be infuriated or grateful to him for tying up the loose ends. I stare at him expectantly. He still appears shocked when he meets my eyes.

'Wendel's going to have someone look into your flights. He said they'd cover it.' He clears his throat, embarrassed, and my heart goes out to him. Stu has helped to support me for years, something I've occasionally felt guilty about. 'Johnny and his family are going away at the end of July so you'll have a week with them. Is that OK?'

'It's perfect,' I say, my face breaking into a grin.

'Wendel asked again that you keep this quiet,' Stu says in a warning voice. 'You can't tell anyone, yet.'

I sort of neglected to tell him that I might have already mentioned it.

'Who knows what Johnny will be like?' he adds. 'You don't want your whole life to be uprooted if you later decide to do things differently.'

I don't know what he means by that, but I'm too distracted to ask. I'm going to LA! I jump up and down on the spot and let out a little squeak.

Stu smiles, but he's holding something back. 'Would you like me to come with you?' he asks hesitantly. 'I mean, I know they didn't offer, but I could buy my own ticket.'

My heart swells with warmth for him and I do consider it, but I need to do this myself. 'No, it's OK,' I say. 'It's probably better that I do this on my own.'

That week at school, Amanda continues to hang around Libby like a bad smell. Natalie has finished her last exam so she's no longer at school. Libby makes a bit of an effort to include me and I don't shun her like I have done in the past, even though Amanda clearly doesn't want me around. I want to tell Libby about Wendel booking my flights, but I can't with Amanda there. Libby's careful not to leave her new friend out, and I can't help retreating back into myself. Things are not as they were, and I'm not quite ready to adapt.

I fly on Sunday at midday, arriving in Los Angeles at 3.30pm on the same day. The flight is about eleven and a half hours long, so God knows how I'll entertain myself on the plane. The longest flight I've ever been on was to Italy and that was only about two and a half hours.

Because this is still top secret, I've agreed to stay with Johnny and his family under the guise of being a nanny to his children. I didn't like it when that was suggested to me, but Wendel assured me it's just to keep up a front to the press. He warned me it's for my own personal safety, too. I know he thinks I'm naïve, that I have no idea what I'm getting myself into. Maybe he's right. But there's no turning back now.

On Saturday evening I'm walking home from work when I hear someone call my name from across the street. It's Tom.

'Hi,' I say, my stomach flipping as he crosses the street to join me. He's wearing his footie gear and carrying a football under his arm.

'I'm just heading up to Grenfell Park. You going that way?' he asks with an easy nonchalance.

'I can take a detour,' I tell him, mentally switching the map route inside my head to take me through the park instead of around it.

'Cool.' We fall into step with one another. 'You out tonight?' he asks. 'You've not been around lately,' he adds.

'No, I can't tonight,' I reply hesitantly, thinking of the last of my packing. 'I'm off on holiday tomorrow,' I explain.

'Really?' He glances at me with interest. 'Where are you going?'

'Er . . . LA.'

'LA? Wow, get you. Mr Taylor's splashing out.'

'I'm not going with Stu,' I reply. 'I'm . . . I'm staying with a friend of my mum's.' I breathe a sigh of relief at how easily this explanation falls into place. It's not even a lie. Well, not really.

'How long are you going for?'

'Just a week.'

'Maybe we can catch *Two Things* when you get back.'

'Yeah,' I say with a shy smile, pleased that he remembers. 'I still haven't seen it.'

'Me neither.'

Pause. 'Do you want to text me?' he asks.

'Sure.' My insides swell as I dig out my mobile. 'What's your number?'

He reels it off to me and I feel jittery as I pause on the pavement and punch the number into my phone. I drop my phone back into my bag and we keep walking.

'What are you doing this summer?' I ask him, as he bounces the ball on the pavement in front of us like a basketball.

'Just hanging out. The lads and I are going to Ibiza in August for a couple of weeks.'

Bet he pulls loads of girls. Urgh. 'So are you and Isla ...' Argh, I'm asking the question and I didn't even know it!

'What?' he asks, making me spell it out.

'You looked pretty cosy at Natalie and Mike's party,' I say, feeling myself blush.

He shrugs and bounces the ball again. 'Nah. Once it's over, I don't go back.'

The relief is immense. We chat as we walk. It's easier to talk to him now I'm not worrying about him and Isla.

After a while, I indicate the pathway off to my right. 'I'm going to head home that way.'

He nods. 'OK. Good luck packing.'

'Thanks.'

He backs away, then spins on his heel and jogs through the park. I keep walking so he's out of view before I see him reach his friends.

I have a funny feeling that Tom Ryder and I have unfinished business. I hope that in our case, absence makes the heart grow fonder.

Chapter 9

I put my book down on my lap and stare out of the oval-shaped window at the pale blue sky. We've been flying above the clouds for miles – don't ask me how many. Hundreds. Thousands. But now when I look down I can see the deeper blue of the ocean, far, far below. We'll be flying over America soon. Nerves ripple through me. I can't believe I'm doing this.

I felt oddly emotional saying goodbye to Stu. He walked me to the immigration line and then waited while I made my way through the queue. I had a lump in my throat the whole time, which didn't leave, even as I walked through the doors to an absolutely mahoosive queue on the other side.

I think of our conversation at the coffee shop in the airport, just before I went through to the other side, where he couldn't follow.

'Why did you go back to Mum?' I asked him. 'When she had me? I wasn't yours. She broke up with you and then slept with someone else. Why did you take her back? How could you ever forgive her?' The questions had woken me up in the night, but I hadn't been able to find the right time to ask them that morning. Now they needed to be spoken, and I was running out of time.

'I loved her,' he replied simply. 'I never stopped loving her. People will go to any lengths for the ones they love, whatever the consequences, whatever the sacrifice.' His face softened as he read my mind. 'But you weren't a sacrifice, Jessie. I loved you. I still do, however much you keep pushing me away. That won't change. Even though you're off to bigger and brighter things, you'll always have a home here with me.'

'I'll be back soon,' I promised, gulping back tears.

He nodded. 'I know you will.' He smiled. 'Believe it or not, I'm going to miss you while you're gone.'

It's weird. In a strange way, the last few weeks have made Stu feel more like my dad than ever before. Knowing the identity of my real father has made me appreciate Stu. I feel an intense surge of love for him. *Thank you for telling me the truth*, I say to him inside my head. My eyes shoot open and I stare once more out of the aeroplane window at the blue sky. *But I wish it had been you telling me, Mum*, I add.

There's a dirty grey cloud hanging over LA, and I hear a mother telling her teenage son in the seat in front of me that it's smog. There are no other clouds in the sky, not that I can see from this side of the plane, anyway. In fact, it looks sweltering down there.

I'm Johnny Jefferson's daughter. I pinch myself. I actually do. And it bloody hurts. No, I am definitely not dreaming – my pincer-like grip has left a red mark on my arm. I'm going to stay with Johnny Jefferson! I'm about to meet my dad!

The plane hovers closer to the smog and it makes me think of one of my favourite Wombats' songs, 'Jump into the Fog'. It's the song Mum said she liked when we were lying on my bed together, just before Johnny's song came on. If they hadn't told us to switch off our electrical equipment, I would have put it on my iPod. We pass through the dirty cloud and my heart flutters. I've just jumped into the ... well, smog.

By the time I clear immigration and haul my hefty suitcase off the conveyor belt, it's after midnight back in the UK and I'm starting to feel a little dazed. I try to text Stu to let him know I've arrived safely, but discover that my mobile phone battery is flat – I forgot to charge it up before I flew. I couldn't sleep on the plane. It was all too exhilarating and I was too jittery about meeting Johnny. I got to fly Business Class, and there were so many good films to choose from I didn't want to waste a minute of it by sleeping. Wendel told me Johnny's personal driver, a man called Davey, would be waiting to collect me. I've seen paparazzi shots of Johnny trying to get through the airport with all of his fans going absolutely berserk, so he wasn't about to come and get me himself.

With my heart in my throat, I push the luggage trolley through customs and towards the exit. I'm wearing a T-shirt, denim jacket, black jeans and black ankle boots, which I know I'm going to regret once I get outside, but it was overcast when I left and I needed something comfy on the plane. I suppose I could change? Too late now. I burst through the exit and am confronted with a sea of faces, four people deep. I scan the plac-ards hoping to see Jessica Pickerill, Jessie, Miss Pickerill, any of the above, but I'm feeling woozy with all of the adrenalin and everything starts to look blurry. Suddenly a man with ebony skin wearing a navy blue chauffeur uniform steps out in front of me.

'Miss Pickerill?' he asks, with a raised eyebrow that disappears under the brim of his cap.

'Yes,' I reply with relief.

'I recognised you instantly!' he exclaims, revealing an enormous array of shiny white teeth. He relieves me of my trolley. 'I'm Davey. Right this way, miss!' He moves at great speed, expertly dodging other travellers. He glances at me over his shoulder. 'You look like your father,' he says with a knowing nod, and I feel overwhelmed as I hurry to keep up. He zips out of the airport doors on to the pavement outside and the heat damn near sucks my breath away. I feel a little faint.

'You OK?' Davey asks with a frown.

'I wish I hadn't worn my jeans,' I reply.

'You can change in the car,' he says. 'I'll put the screen up.'

Easier said than done, I think to myself. And then I see the car. It's more like a bus.

'Wow,' I breathe, as we approach the shiny, long, black Mercedes. Davey opens the back door with a flourish and I climb inside. There's carpet on the floor and one long, black leather seat to my left which starts near the door and curves all the way along one side to the back of the car. Opposite the seat, under the window, is a pristine white bar, stereo system and what I'm guessing is a small fridge.

'Shall I put your suitcase here, Miss Pickerill?' Davey asks, indicating the long bench seat. I must look a bit dumbfounded, because he elaborates. 'So you can find something cooler to wear?'

'Oh, y . . . yes, please,' I stutter.

91

'I'll get the air-conditioning started up straight away,' he promises with a smile, shutting the door. He climbs into the front and a black screen glides upwards, separating us. 'So you have some privacy,' he says, as he disappears out of view. His voice sounds over an intercom. 'But I can hear you if you press the red button by the basin,' he tells me. 'Please, help yourself to refreshments, and ask me anything you wish. We'll be at Johnny's in approximately half an hour.'

'Thank you,' I call as he falls silent, but I'm not sure if he heard me. I sit for a moment and try to take in my surroundings. I feel very, very strange. There are seatbelts all the way along the seat, but I leave mine off for a moment. I still feel a bit woozy. Maybe I should have a drink. I lean across and open the fridge. One bottle of champagne, various cans of soft drink, fresh apple juice and, er, *milk*? How bizarre. I could use a drink to calm down, but wouldn't dare open the champagne so I pour myself an apple juice and turn to look out of the window, trying to gather my thoughts.

Everything looks different: the shops, the small bungalows set back behind dry, ratty-looking grass, the wide sidewalks ... I feel like I'm in another world, and I am. I don't even really recognise America from all of the TV series I've been addicted to over the years. Where's the gloss? Where's the shine? Something catches my eye and I see tinsel hanging out in front of one of the tatty houses that we pass. That's not exactly the sort of shine I was talking about. There are more Christmas decorations hanging out in front of a lot of the houses, glinting off the sun. Clearly these people aren't worried about bad luck – Mum used to take our decorations down on the sixth of January, no matter what. Mind you, look where that got her. Before I can think any more about that, it dawns on me: Tinseltown. We're in Tinseltown. Maybe these people leave their tinsel up on purpose.

I down my juice and put the empty glass into a cup holder, then unzip my bag and stare at the contents, my back still damp with sweat from the short journey from the airport to the car. I spot a flash of silver from within my suitcase and grin, pulling the item out. The tinsel has inspired me.

I take off my boots and damp socks, my feet feeling blissfully cool as I ease myself out of my jeans. I throw my denim jacket into my bag and drag my T-shirt over my head, quickly pulling my silver swing dress on, just in case Davey's screen accidentally comes down. Then I stuff the dirty clothes into the inside pocket of my suitcase and let the lid fall shut, not bothering to zip it up again because I'll probably sort my hair and make-up out in a bit, too.

But not yet. I'm still feeling a bit queasy so I pour myself another juice, dig out a packet of crisps from a cupboard, and scoot up the bench seat to the back. I slip my sunglasses back on, put my feet up on the curved part of the seat and try to relax. A smile forms on my face as I stare out of the window again at the wide road lined with ridiculously tall, matchstick-thin palm trees. The sky burns blue above the smog cloud and the big cars reflect the sun, right into my eyes. This is real. This is really real.

'Get out of the car,' Mum barks, an edge of panic to her voice.

'What?' I squawk. 'I'm not getting out in this.'

I glare out of the window at the dark night and the pounding rain lit by the headlamps of passing cars on the other side of the central reservation.

93

Her old Peugeot has broken down – again – and this time we're on the motorway. Mum has managed to get us to the hard shoulder, and on the hard shoulder is where I plan on staying.

'Get out, right now!' she yells as a lorry rattles past us, making the little red car shudder and shake.

'Why?' I raise my voice indignantly.

'It's dangerous!' she screams. 'Do you know how many people die on the hard shoulder every year?'

'Is this one of the things you learnt in your speed awareness course?' I ask her with a sneer. I wish she'd just taken the three points on her licence for speeding so she'd stop going on about it.

'Just get out of the car,' she snaps. 'Walk up the hill to the top.'

'What, and sit in the rain?' I ask with disbelief.

She yanks her door open and climbs out into the downpour as another lorry passes, making the car vibrate violently. OK, it is a little scary here, I'll admit. Suddenly my door is open and she's leaning across the seat and unbuckling my seatbelt. She practically drags me out of there, her wet hair dripping all over me.

'Bloody hell, OK! I'm coming!' I shout, wrestling her hands off me. She shoves me up the hill. I'm drenched instantly and really quite pissed off, thank you very much. Where is she? I look over my shoulder with irritation to see that she's still down by the car, hurriedly getting her bag out of the front passenger seat. At the very least she could have let me get mine. I start to storm back down the hill as she slams the door shut and moves towards me, and then out of nowhere, a car veers off the motorway and clips the back of the Peugeot. I scream with horror as flashes of metal grinding against metal light up the dark night and the Peugeot spins around almost 180 degrees. The other car screeches to a stop further up the motorway as cars and lorries fly past dangerously, and then I'm in Mum's arms and she's *holding me so tight, and I'm so thankful she's safe that I don't even mind the noise of her hysterical cries in my ear.*

I blink back tears as I turn away from the window, regarding the limo's slick interior. We never had money to spend on new cars, ones which didn't break down all the time. The man in the other car on the motorway was unhurt, thankfully, but our little car was written off and we had to share Stu's Fiat after that. The only silver lining was the insurance money, which came through two months later. Mum was so happy that week, planning our summer holiday. Little did we know that there was a ticking bomb hanging over all of our heads, counting down the last few days of her life, a life she could have lost two months earlier, thanks to me.

I try to swallow the lump in my throat as I think about how she probably saved *my* life by forcing me to get out of the car. If only I could have saved *hers*. If only I'd helped out more on the morning of my party. If only I'd told her I didn't even need a cake that year. If only I'd said I didn't want a bloody party. If only she hadn't been walking along the pavement at the exact same moment that a loose window came crashing down upon her, spearing her precious, perfect body with shards of glass . . . If only, if only, if only . . .

Tears stream down my cheeks and my chest shudders as I fight back sobs. I could have been going to Spain next week with her and Stu, rather than sitting here in a limo on my own, in a strange country, about to meet Johnny frigging Jefferson. My crying abruptly stops and I brush away my tears as the surreal feeling intensifies. I'd better pull myself together and sort out my hair and make-up before I completely lose it.

The air-conditioning has cooled the car down – and me down with it. I run my fingers through my hair, hoping it will look tousled and not scratty. Brushing it will only make it look worse. I know that from experience. My make-up hasn't fared too badly so I pop my sunnies on top of my head and apply some powder and lipstick, then pretty much leave it as it is. I don't want to appear too done up. I look down at my silver swing dress and almost snort. OK, so it's a little over the top. It's the sort of thing I'd normally only wear to a party, but I bought it last week at work and wanted to bring it. Who knows what I'll be doing here, where I'll be going out, if anywhere. And quite frankly, I'm a bit past caring what I look like at the moment. I'm certainly not going to bother getting changed again.

My arms and legs are a little chilly now in the air-con and my feet are frozen, so I shrug on my denim jacket and drag out some fresh socks, pulling them on. I'll sort out footwear later, but for now I just want to relax. Ha. As if. I wonder how far away we are.

I lean over and press the intercom button. 'Hi, Davey?'

'Hello, Miss Pickerill,' he replies warmly. 'I thought you might have fallen asleep.'

'No, but I'm dressed now if you want to put the screen back down?'

'As you wish.' The screen glides down and he glances at me in his wing mirror, a twinkle in his brown eyes. 'All set?'

'Pretty much,' I reply with a nervous smile. 'Have we got far to go?'

'Ten minutes. We're just coming into Bel Air now,' he says, and I look out of the window in time to see us pass through a large, wrought iron gate. Now *this* is more like it. Mansions line the pristine streets, landscaped gardens burst with colour, and sprinklers whirr round and round, drenching neatly mown lawns with fat drops of sparkling water. I grin and put my sunglasses back on as the road starts to wind upwards and the ever more enormous mansions begin to retreat behind high walls and impressive security gates.

I'm finding it hard to breathe again and it has nothing to do with the atmosphere.

'Almost there,' Davey calls back to me.

God! Really? I could do with a cigarette right now. I quickly zip up my suitcase and sit with a racing pulse. I won't need my jacket on, will I? Suddenly I'm not sure about the dress. What was I thinking? It's too flashy, too much, too . . . *late*!

'Here's home,' Davey says as we start to pass through tall gates with security cameras pointing down from tall posts on either side. Davey puts his window down and waves at a man in a small office as we pass. If he could see me through the darkened limo glass, he'd think that I look like a rabbit caught in the headlights. Oh no, what about my shoes?

We start to drive down a long driveway. Leafy green trees, rich from the summer sun, partly obscure the house. I look around with panic and realise that I have no choice but to pull my chunky ankle boots back on – never mind, it's 'a look' and I can carry it off. I try to imbue myself with some of the confidence that I normally feel.

The house comes into view: a long, two-storey, white, rectangular building punctuated with large windows. Davey pulls up outside the big wooden front door and gets out of the car. I feel like I can't move. I'm glued to my seat. This is, without a doubt, the most scared I've been in all my life.

Davey opens the door. 'Miss Pickerill?'

I don't know why I haven't already told him to call me Jessie, but now I can barely breathe, let alone speak, so I move to the door and hold on to it for support as I step one chunky boot out. Here I go.

Chapter 10

My feet crunch on the gravel as I climb out of the car and straighten up to see that the front door has now opened and a woman is standing there. She appears to be about thirty and is slim and pretty with straight, blonde hair which just brushes her shoulders.

'Hi!' she calls, coming out of the door. 'I'm Meg, Johnny's wife.'

Now, I recognise her from the papers. I open my mouth to return her greeting, but sensing that my voice is going to come out croaky and quiet, I ramp the volume up a notch and end up sounding louder and more confident than I usually do. 'Hello!'

She comes towards me with an extended hand. She's wearing white shorts and a navy blue top. 'And you must be Jessica,' she says.

'Jessie,' I reply, shaking her hand.

'How was your trip?' She smiles and I think she's trying to sound friendly, but she looks a little stressed.

'It was fun,' I reply, as Davey pulls my suitcase out of the car behind me.

'Shall I take this up to the White Room?' he asks her.

'Yes, thanks, Davey,' she replies with genuine warmth.

I'm curious to see the White Room, whatever it is.

Meg turns back to me and nods towards the door, ushering me inside. 'I'm afraid Johnny's not here,' she says with downturned lips. 'He promised he'd be back in time, but he's running late.' She rolls her eyes good-naturedly, but I detect a definite edge to her voice. 'But come inside and meet the boys.'

I follow her through the hall, then stop short as we step into a huge, cavernous space with floor-to-ceiling glass looking out over the city of LA far below. I thought Wendel's office was amazing, but this is something else.

'Wow,' I say aloud. There's a huge swimming pool right outside on an enormous terrace, but my attention is diverted by a baby's laughter. I look past a charcoal-grey L-shaped sofa to see a little boy with blond hair, standing directly over an even smaller child, who is lying on his back on a shaggy lime-green rug. The older boy has one foot on either side of the smaller boy's waist and is wiggling his hips from side to side while the smaller boy looks up at him and giggles.

'Barney!' Meg cries. 'I've told you not to stand over Phoenix like that!'

Barney pushes his bottom lip out, but steps off the other child, wobbling slightly as he does. Meg rounds the sofas to get to him and kneels down on the floor. 'You mustn't do that,' she says sternly. 'Remember how you fell on him and hurt him?'

Barney looks sad and I feel sorry for him. He was only trying to make his little brother laugh.

Meg glances up at me and smiles apologetically. 'Sorry about that.'

I shrug and wander towards the sofas.

'This is Barney.' She purses her lips at the little boy, and I think that maybe she's trying to keep a straight face. 'And this is Phoenix,' she says with a smile, tickling the smaller boy and making him giggle.

'Hello!' I say as chirpily as I can.

Barney looks over at me with mild interest and then falls to his knees and starts zooming a car across the rug.

'Barney, say hello to Jessie,' Meg prompts.

'Hello,' he says casually, returning to his zooming. Meg casts her eyes heavenwards as the smaller boy sits himself up.

'How old are they?' I ask. It's so weird to think that these two little kids are related to me.

'Barney is four, and Phoenix has just turned one,' Meg replies with a smile.

There's a noise of a car or something – a motorbike? – outside on the drive. Meg's head shoots towards the door.

'I think Johnny's back,' she breathes with relief, but I feel anything but. A powerful thrum of nerves surges through my body and I turn back to face the door with my heart in my throat. I suddenly realise I still have my sunnies on – the sunlight in here is so bright that I didn't notice. I pop them on top of my head as Meg walks briskly past me.

From my position in the living room I can see her open the door and stand in the doorway with her back to me. In the background a figure approaches, wearing a shiny, black motorcycle helmet. He takes his helmet off and his just-below-chin-length, dirty blond hair instantly gives him away: Johnny Jefferson. He reaches Meg, but she doesn't budge from the doorway for a moment. I hear him say, 'Sorry,' and, without a word, she steps aside. He appears contrite as he glances past her, and then he sees me.

His face looks shocked. Meg turns around and meets my eyes and even she looks taken aback, although I don't know why. Johnny composes himself as he pushes his hair off his face and stalks towards me, dropping his motorcycle helmet and gloves on a table in the hall as he passes, but leaving his black leather jacket on.

'Hey,' he says in a deep voice I recognise, coming to a halt in front of me. His green eyes are even more piercing in real life and I feel utterly out of my depth. 'I'm sorry I'm late.' He offers his hand for me to shake and I take it. It's warm and sweaty from wearing gloves.

'It's OK,' I reply timidly.

He's taller than I thought he'd be, well over six foot.

'Jessica, right?'

'People call me Jessie,' I tell him.

'It's good to finally meet you,' Johnny says with a decisive nod. I'm not sure I believe him. This is so weird, so awkward. It's not like I expected any long lost hugs, but … I don't know what I expected, actually.

'Has Meg offered you a drink or anything?' he asks.

'She's only just arrived,' Meg chips in, a little defensively. 'I was introducing her to the boys.'

Johnny jabs his thumb towards a curved glass wall. 'Let me get you a juice or something.'

I'm not particularly thirsty, but I follow him anyway, while Meg hangs back. Behind the curved glass wall is an enormous kitchen, almost as big as the whole downstairs area of our house. There's a big, shiny white table with eight designer-looking chairs of various colours: yellow, red, green, blue. Johnny pulls one out and indicates for me to sit. I'm happy to because my legs feel like jelly. There are two large, silver fridges, and he goes to one of them and opens it, revealing a door full of cans.

'What can I get you?' he asks.

'Just a lemonade or something would be good.'

He sets about getting us both a drink, then shouts through to the living room to ask if Meg wants one, too. She declines. I think she's angry with him for being late.

'So,' he says, placing two tall glasses of sparkling lemonade, on ice, on the table. He pulls up a yellow chair and sits down opposite me. 'Sorry I wasn't here when you arrived,' he says again with a small shrug. He seems a bit tense. He's not the only one.

'Don't worry about it,' I reiterate.

I pick up my glass and he does the same, both of us taking a drink and returning our glasses to the table at the same time.

'How was your flight?' he asks after a moment of awkward silence.

'It was good. I've only ever flown easyJet before, so it was pretty different.'

'Did your stepdad come to see you off at the airport?'

'Stu? Yeah, he did.'

He smiles a small smile at me and I suddenly remember who I'm sitting opposite. This is so weird!

'Daddy!' Barney's breathless voice breaks the silence, as he pitter-patters into the kitchen. Meg appears behind him, Phoenix on her hip. Barney starts to ask Johnny to come and see the car track he's built, but I notice Meg falter in her steps. Maybe it's the

103

sight of us sitting opposite each other at the table, but she seems a bit freaked out as she stays glued to the spot.

'I'll be there in a sec, buddy,' Johnny says to his son, distracted. I glance at him to see him raise one inquisitive eyebrow at his wife.

She ignores him, addressing me. 'Do you want to come and see your room, Jessie?'

'Sure, yeah.' I get to my feet.

She and Johnny follow me out after a slight pause, and I feel distinctly uneasy about whatever unspoken exchange has just gone between them. I don't think Meg wants me here at all, and right now, even I'm beginning to wonder if it was a mistake. I'm so far from home. I know it's ridiculous, because I've only just got here, but I feel a sudden longing to see Stuart.

'This way.' Meg directs me towards a wide concrete staircase.

'Look, Daddy,' I hear Barney say as Johnny tails off behind us to go and see his sons.

'How was Davey?' Meg asks, bringing my attention back to her.

'Fine. He's nice.'

'He's been Johnny's driver for years. On and off,' she adds. 'I used to think he talked in exclamation marks, but he's chilled out in his older age.' She smiles fondly as we turn right at the top of the stairs. 'I still remember him collecting me the first time I flew into LA to work for Johnny. That's how Johnny and I met.'

A waist-high wall on our right safeguards us from falling into the open-plan living room below, and there are doors to our left. I glance inside one open door to see what looks like a child's bedroom.

'That's Phoenix's room,' Meg tells me, pausing for a moment

104

so I can look inside. It's decorated with an underwater theme, a sea of calming blues and greens. The cot is shaped like a fish.

The next room is Barney's and it's even more colourful. His bed is fashioned to look like a fire engine, with a bright red duvet. There are blue bookshelves crammed with books and a small table and chairs in the centre of the room. It looks more like a playroom than a bedroom. I bet he has no idea how lucky he is.

We reach the last door on the landing and Meg opens it up, standing back to let me pass.

Now I see what they mean by the White Room. Apart from my battered purple suitcase at the foot of the bed and the huge, black flatscreen TV, mounted on the wall to my right as we come in the door, everything in the room is white: plush white carpet, the biggest bed I've ever seen, covered with a soft white duvet, four plump pillows and multiple white cushions. Shiny, highly-polished built-in white wardrobes line the walls on the right hand side, and ahead of me are large windows stretching from one side of the room all the way to the wardrobes, revealing the leafy green trees at the front of the house. To my left are two doors.

'Kitchenette and en suite,' Meg reveals with a smile, noting my awed expression.

I suddenly realise I still have my boots on.

'Sorry,' I mutter, quickly bending down to take them off before I ruin the carpet.

'Don't worry about it!' Meg exclaims. 'You don't need to take them off.'

I still feel like I should.

'Honestly, the carpets get cleaned every few weeks anyway,' she tells me, but by then I'm in my socks. I place the boots on the landing outside the door and go in a daze to look inside the first door on my left. Dazzling white stone lines all of the surfaces. There are two basins to my left, a large open shower to my right, and at the back of the bathroom is a huge stone spa bath. Fluffy white towels hang on chrome towel rails.

I open my mouth to speak, but find I'm lost for words. Meg steps past me and opens up the cupboards underneath the sink, revealing rows and rows of jewel-coloured bottles of lotions and potions. I recognise some really expensive brands.

'These are all for you. I wasn't sure what you'd like,' she says with a smile.

I shake my head, speechless. I can't wait to try out all of these products. Meg giggles. I meet her eyes.

'Sorry,' she says, trying to keep a straight face. 'It's just that this was my room when I first came to LA, and I know exactly how you feel.'

I don't think she does, but I don't say it. I have never seen such luxury in all my life.

'Shall I leave you to settle in?' she asks. 'Do you want to unpack or leave it until later? One of the maids could do it for you in the morning . . .'

They have maids? 'No, no,' I brush her off. 'I'm happy to do it myself.'

'That's what I thought you'd say,' she says and I glance at her. 'I was exactly the same,' she adds.

I give her a small smile. Maybe we have more in common than I thought. I hope so. I really don't want her to hate me being here.

'I still remember texting a picture of this room to my best friend,' she says with a far-off look.

106

My face falls as I think of Libby and Natalie. I feel very isolated from them at the moment.

'We thought we'd eat early because you'll be tired after your flight,' Meg says. 'Do you want to have a shower and settle in for a bit? Or would you like a tour of the rest of the house?'

What I really want is to go back downstairs and see Johnny, but I don't feel comfortable saying so. 'A tour would be great,' I reply.

After the boys' bedrooms, there are two more spare rooms, one of which has predominantly gold furnishings, the other green. The penultimate door we come to on our right, as we walk back along the landing, is Johnny's music studio, and it's just like the ones you see in films, with desks full of controls, knobs and dials. Behind a glass screen is another room with a full drum kit in the corner and several guitars mounted on the wall. A round, flattish microphone hangs suspended from the ceiling in the centre.

'And last but not least is our room,' Megs says, leading me out of the studio and to the final door on the landing. She opens it up to reveal a space that is probably as big as my home, spanning from the front to the back of the house with floor to ceiling windows looking down on the swimming pool and the city beyond. It's decorated in colours of green, grey and yellow, with a plush smokey-coloured carpet and a bedspread with a yellow and green symmetrical graphic. The white stone bathroom, to my right, looks out on to the trees at the front of the house. I notice there are no blinds in the bathroom, but Meg answers my unspoken question and flicks a switch. The clear window glass immediately turns opaque.

'Cool!' This place is amazing!

'Want to see downstairs?' Meg asks.

'You mean there's more downstairs that I haven't seen?' I ask with confusion.

'Oh yeah,' she replies flippantly, leading me out of the room. I jog down the stairs after her. Johnny is sitting cross-legged on the carpet, carefully studying a small car.

'Can you fix it?' Barney asks him.

'Hold on a sec, buddy,' Johnny replies in a quiet voice, concentrating on the task. He glances up when we reach the bottom of the stairs, and when he smiles at me my heart flutters in a strange way. But then he looks away again, back at Barney and the car in his hands, and I feel strangely bereft. I wonder what it would have been like if he'd been there for *me* at that age, fixing *my* broken toys.

Meg presses on with the tour before I have time to dwell on that thought. She takes me back underneath the stairs and I see another row of doors, which are directly below the bedrooms. I didn't notice them on my way to the kitchen.

'Study,' she says, revealing a large room with two big desks. 'Johnny's PA comes in most days.'

'Is that what you used to do?' I hope she doesn't mind me asking.

'Yeah,' she replies with a jokey roll of her eyes. 'But unlike Annie, I lived here and pretty much worked twenty-four seven.' She laughs. 'In fact I still live here, and pretty much work twenty-four seven.'

She goes out of the room and opens the next door. Five rows of six comfy-looking red velvet seats steep slightly upwards away from a large screen at the front. 'Cinema,' she says.

'Whoa.'

'Just let me know if there's anything you want to watch and I'll show you how to work it. We even have a popcorn machine,' she adds with a conspiratorial wink.

The next room is the gym, a large space packed full of shiny equipment with a view out to the front of the garden. Flatscreen TVs line the right-hand wall and Meg tells me that a sauna and a shower room are in rooms off to the left.

'It's such an incredible house,' I reply, utterly bowled over as we walk back to the living room. 'I've never been anywhere like this before in my life.'

She smiles. 'What would you like to do now?' She glances at Johnny and then back at me. 'I'll put dinner on in a bit. I hope you like pizza?'

'Yeah, of course.'

'Great.' She shifts on her feet. 'Well, would you like to go and freshen up?'

'Erm, OK. Sure.'

She smiles, and it seems almost like it's with relief. As I climb the stairs it occurs to me that maybe they don't know what to do with me.

At the top of the landing, I glance down in time to see Johnny take Meg's face in his hands and kiss her forehead. She looks up at me and, as we lock eyes, she looks momentarily guilty. She steps away from Johnny and I hear her tell him she'll go and turn the oven on. By then I've reached my room.

I go inside and shut the door behind me, then exhale loudly. I didn't realise I'd been holding my breath.

My head is spinning. I can't believe it. I can't believe any of it. I'm in Johnny Jefferson's house – and Johnny Jefferson is my dad. This is so strange, so surreal.

The feeling stays with me as I go to turn on the shower and open up the cupboard under the basin, pulling out some luxury shower cream. I hope I'll get a chance to talk to Johnny properly, tonight. I want to know what he's like, what he's really like. I want to know my dad, not his rock star persona. I just hope that he also wants to get to know *me*.

All too soon I'll be back at home, back in my tiny bedroom, back in my little house with its shabby front garden, back to the reality of living and breathing every hour of life without my mum. But not yet. Not yet. And right now I need to make the most of every single minute.

Chapter 11

Meg is in the kitchen with Phoenix when I re-emerge twenty-five minutes later, freshly showered and dressed in my caramel-coloured shorts and a floaty black top. My feet are bare, my toenails painted gold from yesterday's pedicure. I spent most of my last day in the UK preening myself for this trip.

'Can I do anything?' I ask.

'No, just take a seat,' she replies, securing Phoenix into his highchair.

'Shall I set the table?' I suggest.

She looks like she's about to say no again, but then she seems to decide otherwise. 'Sure.' She points to a drawer. 'Cutlery is in there. Thanks,' she adds, casting a small smile in my direction.

Phoenix babbles away loudly in his highchair as I get on with the task.

'Are you hungry?' I say to him, passing him a spoon to play with. He can't speak, so he doesn't answer, but he immediately starts to use the instrument to noisily bash the table. A drummer in the making. 'Are you going to be a musician, like your dad?' I ask aloud.

'Not if I can help it,' Johnny interrupts drily, and I start as he appears in the kitchen.

I give him a quizzical look.

'Drink, drugs and rock 'n' roll,' he says and grins at Meg, but she doesn't look too impressed so he spanks her on her bottom. I stand there awkwardly.

'Take a seat, Jessie.' Meg pulls out a chair for me at the end of the table, so I sit down while Johnny organises some drinks and shouts for Barney to come and join us. I watch them all buzzing around: Meg opening the oven and flinching at the rush of hot air as she takes out the pizzas; Barney running in with Buzz Lightyear, yelling; Johnny firmly extricating the toy and batting away his son's complaints as he makes him sit at the table opposite Phoenix; Phoenix rapping his spoon and babbling . . . I get the feeling I'm witnessing a very ordinary dinner time. Except this is no ordinary dinner time. There's a great big elephant in the room and she's sitting at the top of the table. I feel like an outsider, and that's exactly what I am.

'How are you feeling?' Johnny asks me, as he sits down between Barney and me.

'A bit weird,' I admit, and like I'm massively imposing, but I keep this bit to myself. 'It's like my body has been filled up with sand.' I don't know if I'm tired or hungry or something else.

'You're probably jet-lagged,' Meg chips in, as she places the pizzas in the centre of the table and takes the seat opposite Johnny. 'It's, what, the middle of the night, your time?'

'Is it?' I ask with surprise.

'Your body clock will be all messed up,' she points out as she starts to serve up.

'Oh.'

'You haven't travelled to a different time zone before?' Johnny asks.

'No,' I reply, shaking my head. 'Well, aside from going to Europe, but that doesn't really count as it's only an hour. We couldn't afford to go further afield.' Johnny and Meg glance at each other and I wish I'd kept my mouth shut about our financial situation.

'Do you guys travel a lot?' I try to fill the silence.

'Not much at the moment, but I'm going on tour next year,' Johnny reveals, tucking into his pizza.

'That'll be cool,' I say. Surreal moment alert! My dad is a global megastar!

'It's too hot!' Barney interrupts, squealing.

'Give it here,' Johnny says, taking his plate.

'So you live in Maidenhead?' Meg asks, while Johnny blows on his son's pizza.

'Yeah. Not far from Henley, where you used to live, right?'

'That's right.'

'Weird coincidence, hey?' Johnny chips in, sliding Barney's plate back and returning to the conversation.

'Yeah.' It hurts to remember Stu telling me how Mum felt when he moved so close by . . . 'Do you remember my mum?' The question spills out of my mouth as though it has a will of its own. Meg stiffens and Johnny looks taken aback. 'Her name was Candy,' I blurt. 'But maybe you knew her by her full name, Candace?'

113

Phoenix chooses that moment to throw a piece of pizza on the floor, making Meg jump to her feet and curse under her breath as she clears it up.

'We'll talk about this,' Johnny promises me with a significant look. He doesn't add, 'soon', but it's implied.

I nod, as disappointment rushes through me. He clearly doesn't remember Mum and he's just trying to avoid telling me. He needn't worry, because I'm not sure I want to hear it.

After a dinner strained with small talk about school, hobbies and anything else that avoids trickier subjects, I'm almost falling asleep at the table. I feel a bit bad about leaving Johnny and Meg to clear up, but I really am exhausted, so when Meg suggests I call it a night, I don't argue.

I head upstairs to get ready for bed and then remember that I still haven't texted Stu to let him know I've arrived safely. I hunt out my mobile phone charger before realising that I don't have an American power adaptor. I'm sure Johnny and Meg will have a spare.

I head back out of my room, my bare feet making next to no noise on the concrete landing and stairs. Meg and Johnny are talking, with hushed, but irate-sounding voices in the kitchen. Adrenalin pumps through my body as I creep closer. I know I shouldn't listen in, but I can't walk away.

'Look, I'm sorry, alright? But what am I supposed to do?' Johnny is saying over the sound of children's chatter in the background.

'I don't know, Johnny. I ...' Meg's voice tails off. 'I didn't know what to expect, to be honest, but I have a bad feeling about this. About her.'

114

'What's your problem with her?' Johnny demands to know. 'She's only just arrived.'

'Yeah, looking like a right little rock-star wannabe, in her silver dress, boots and sunglasses indoors.'

I feel sick, so sick. I didn't mean to come across like that.

'That's a bit harsh,' Johnny defends me.

'Is it?' Meg asks heatedly.

'She's just lost her mum and discovered that I'm her father, for Christ's sake!'

'Keep your voice down,' she warns, after a moment, but her voice sounds shaky. 'This has all happened so quickly. One minute we know about her, the next she's here! I haven't had enough time to get my head around that fact.'

'You were the one who suggested she come,' he points out irately.

'Only because we're going away the week after next! I wanted to get it out of the way, not have it hanging over us!'

What am I, an *exam*? And why was it Meg suggesting I come and stay? Doesn't Johnny want me here?

'I can't believe how much she looks like you. She has your eyes,' she continues and I have to strain to hear her next words because the kids are starting to play up. 'Although I only saw them when she finally took off her glasses,' she adds sarkily.

'Boys, be quiet,' Johnny hushes his sons. He sighs. 'Look, I know this is hard for you. I know that you didn't want to come back to LA and I get that this whole thing is doing your head in, but we'll be OK. I love you.'

The sound of a kiss, and then I hear her sniff.

'OK?' he asks again, gently.

She sniffs again and maybe she's nodding, maybe she's about

to reply, but I don't wait to find out. I hurry back up the stairs, my heart pounding.

Now I know what she really thinks of me. And to be honest, I just want to click my heels three times and go home.

Chapter 12

'MUM!' I scream. 'Where are you?' I look around in a blind panic, but she's nowhere to be seen. I'm in my house, but it's not really my house and the corridors are long and winding. I hear the television playing loudly so I stumble around the corner into a large and vacuous living room, nearly crying with relief when I see her sitting in her favourite place on our sofa. But she doesn't look at me. Her face is strained, pale, bloodless. It's like she can't see me.

'There you are!' I fight back tears as I run to hug her, but my arms close around nothing. And then I remember. She's dead. And she's never coming back.

I bolt awake out of my dream, but my pain is real, and I'm overcome with silent, whole-body-wracking sobs until, eventually, the lump in my throat subsides and I come back to full consciousness. It's only then that I remember where I am, and it occurs to me that I might still be dreaming. I stretch my arms wide and feel the soft cotton of the enormous bed beneath my fingers. No, I'm not dreaming. I really am in Johnny Jefferson's house.

I take a deep breath, feeling utterly drained. I have no idea what time it is. The electric blackout blinds that I finally managed to work last night are blocking out all of the light from the windows, so it could be midnight or midday, for all I know.

I snuck straight back upstairs yesterday evening after overhearing Johnny and Meg's conversation, but I was too wired to sleep for a long time afterwards, despite my exhaustion.

Meg thinks I'm a wannabe. I feel so humiliated. I only kept my sunnies on inside because it was so bright that I forgot I had them on. And as for the boots and silver dress ... Well, I could carry that look off at night, but even *I* wouldn't normally try to rock an outfit like that in the daytime. I wonder what Johnny thinks of me.

Eventually I drag myself out of bed and try to work the blackout blinds again. The sound of them going up is deafening and I'm worried I'll wake Barney next door and annoy Meg even more. But soon they come to a halt and the light revealed behind them is pale and grey – early morning.

I want to call Stu before the time difference renders it difficult. I wonder if the office downstairs has an American phone adaptor? I switch on the halogens to flood the room and look at the jumble of clothes in my suitcase. What shall I wear? Something that doesn't make me look like a rock-star wannabe, I think resentfully. I settle on a simple blue dress and venture out of my bedroom.

I can hear cutlery clinking against crockery in the kitchen. Someone is up. I pad downstairs in my bare feet and cautiously

118

round the corner into the kitchen. It's Meg and the boys, eating breakfast. They're surprisingly quiet as they tuck into their cereal.

'Morning,' I say groggily and she jumps out of her skin.

'You scared the life out of me!' she exclaims.

'Sorry.'

She recovers quickly. 'How did you sleep?' she asks with a smile, which I find almost impossible to return. Not now that I know how she really feels about me being here.

'Not bad.'

'Do you want some breakfast? There's toast, cereal ... or if you wait a while, Eddie, our chef, will be here and he can do you scrambled eggs or a fry-up or something like that?'

'I'll just have a bowl of cereal,' I decide, not wanting to appear too 'rock-star wannabe' by having a cook cater to my every whim. I am so pissed off about that comment.

She pushes her chair out from the table.

'Don't worry, I can help myself,' I tell her.

'It's OK,' she insists. Martyr. She gets up and fetches me a bowl and spoon, then runs through the vast array of cereals on offer. I choose Cheerios because at least they're familiar.

'I was wondering if you had a US adaptor for my mobile phone charger?' I ask when we're seated back at the table.

'Of course. Sorry, weren't there some in your room?'

'I don't know. I didn't really think to look ...'

'Try the bedside drawer.'

We carry on eating in silence for a bit. I glance over at her bowl to see that it's full of brightly-coloured, flat, Rice-Krispie-looking things. Curiosity gets the better of me. 'What are they?'

119

'Pebbles,' she says with a bashful smile, offering up a box of Flintstones-themed cereal. 'I always go for the kiddie stuff. I've got a sweet tooth.'

I notice the boys are eating plain Rice Krispies.

'I'm a mean mummy,' she jokes, having spotted me looking. 'They have to eat the low sugar variety.'

I don't comment. She *is* mean!

'Do you want to try some?' she coaxes hopefully.

'No, thanks,' I reply flatly. I don't want anything from her after last night's comment.

Her face falls. 'OK.'

Now I feel like a bit of a bitch. I suppose I don't need to give her any more reasons to dislike me. 'Oh, go on, then,' I find myself saying.

She seems happy as she fetches me a fresh bowl and pours some in. I take a mouthful. Oh my God, it's really sweet.

'What do you think?' Her eyes are wide with anticipation.

'I feel like I'm going to be climbing the walls in a minute.'

Meg laughs and I can't help but giggle, too.

'Morning.' Johnny's deep voice punctuates the sound of our laughter. I turn to see him standing in the doorway. His hair is dishevelled and he's wearing a white T-shirt and khaki-coloured shorts. He looks tired, but he's grinning.

'Jesus, Nutmeg, you're not getting Jessie started on Pebbles, are you?' Nutmeg? Is that her nickname? Bizarre. He goes over to her and kisses the top of her head, then, to my surprise, places his hand on my shoulder.

'Any thoughts about what you'd like to do today?' he asks me, the warmth of his touch seeping through the flimsy fabric of my dress. Meg glances our way and he removes his hand.

'I don't know. Won't we just hang here?' I feel oddly disappointed that he's taken his hand away.

'We could do, if that's what you'd like. But we thought you might like to go to Santa Monica beach?'

'I'm still not sure that's such a good idea,' Meg interrupts him nervously.

'It'll be fine,' he brushes her off. 'We'll bring the guys.'

The guys, I later discover, are Samuel and Lewis, two burly bodyguards who also handle the security for Johnny. They follow us in a slick black Mercedes, while Davey leads the way in the limo. I sit in the middle at the back, between Phoenix and Barney in their two car seats while Johnny and Meg take the bench seat up the side.

'You alright there?' Meg asks with a smile. 'Not too squashed?'

'I'm fine.'

'Did you get through to your dad?'

'I call him Stu, not dad,' I automatically correct her. She looks embarrassed, so I quickly continue. 'Yeah, I did, thanks. Thanks for letting me use the landline,' I say to Johnny.

'Anytime,' he replies.

I couldn't get through to Stuart on my mobile, because I forgot that it won't allow me to make international calls. It's only a cheap phone. Johnny told me to use one of the phones in the office.

I think Meg was embarrassed that she hadn't suggested that herself, so she tried to make up for it by coming with me and showing me how to work it. Just as well, because I didn't know what the international dialling code was.

'Call home as much as you like,' she'd stressed before she left

121

the room. Maybe she's feeling guilty, but I can't say I'm not relieved that she's being extra nice to me today.

Stu seemed pleased that I called, but I felt strangely sad to hear his voice and I even felt like crying once we hung up. I didn't tell him that I didn't feel welcome because I didn't want him to worry. This was my choice after all, so I need to see it through. The distance between us feels more than just physical at the moment. I feel like I'm very much in this by myself.

'Hopefully it won't be too busy at the beach,' Meg says, pulling me from my thought. 'We're not normally up and out of the house at this time, are we?' She nudges Johnny. 'Johnny would sleep in every morning if he could,' she tells me good-naturedly.

'Yeah, blood— I mean, *bloomin'* kids,' he corrects himself, stopping short of swearing. He flashes Meg a cheeky look. Beside me, Phoenix starts to whinge.

'What's up with you?' I ask in my best appeal-to-a-little-person voice.

He just continues to wriggle with annoyance.

'He hates being strapped in,' Meg tells me. 'We'll be there soon,' she addresses her youngest son. On the other side of me, Barney begins to moan.

'I'm bored!' he complains. We've only been in the car fifteen minutes.

'Do you want Daddy to sing you a song?' Meg asks.

'Meg!' Johnny grumbles.

'Yeah!' Barney chips in.

'Alright,' he says wearily. 'What do you want me to sing?' He flashes me a resigned look. 'Sorry about this.'

As if I mind getting a private Johnny Jefferson concert!

'"Baa Baa Black Sheep"!' Barney bleats.

'Something else,' he says firmly.

'"Old MacDonald Had A Farm"!' Barney tries again.

'I used to refuse point-blank to sing nursery rhymes,' he tells me wryly. 'But I've given up, now.'

Meg smiles at me, and Johnny gives her a comically withering look.

'I'll do Thomas,' Johnny decides, and Meg claps her hands excitedly. The boys imitate her. 'At least Ringo Starr deems it worthy.'

It turns out that even when he's singing the theme tune from a children's TV show, Johnny's voice is incredible.

'*Thomas!*' he shouts, clapping once and holding his palms out towards Meg in a sort of 'ta-dah' way, leaving a pause for her to fill in the gap.

'*He's the cheeky one,*' she tries to sing, and Johnny winces theatrically because her singing voice is truly awful. I laugh as they continue in this way, going through James and Henry and all of Thomas's other friends. Even Barney seems to know some of the words, and as they get to "square" Toby, I can't resist joining in.

Then all three of us continue to sing at the top of our voices, Meg completely out of tune and me just about remembering the words as the kids bounce up and down in their seats with delight. For the first time since I landed, I feel a little bit at ease.

'Again! Again!' Barney shouts as we finish, while Phoenix claps with delight.

'One more time?' Johnny asks me with a grin.

'Go on, then.'

This time I sing along with him from the start and I don't know why, but he and Meg share a look of surprise. I try not to let it put me off as we get to the fun bit about Thomas being the cheeky one, and all that, but I realise I'm singing alone.

'Your voice is awesome!' Johnny exclaims with amazement, as my singing trails off. He glances at Meg. 'Isn't it?'

'Yes, it is.' She shakes her head, staring at me in a slightly awestruck manner as my face heats up.

'Sing it again!' Barney interjects, but now I'm far too embarrassed.

'In a bit, buddy,' Johnny tells him absent-mindedly.

'Awww!' he moans.

'Seriously,' Johnny says, looking at me directly. 'You've got great tone. Have you taken lessons?'

'Of course not,' I wave him away with a frown, but inside I'm bursting with pride. Johnny Jefferson thinks I'm a good singer!

'Why not?' he asks.

'I don't know.' I shrug. 'I'd feel too self-conscious to sing in public.' SingStar while wasted doesn't count.

I glance at Barney beside me. He grins up at me and he's so cute that my heart unexpectedly swells. I remember that he's my half brother and my bubble of happiness inflates. I turn to look at Phoenix on the other side, but he's back to wriggling and moaning. 'Almost there,' I tell him and he looks up at me. I must have a funny expression on my face because he flashes me a toothy grin, too, and I impulsively stick my hand down his side and tickle his ribs. He starts to laugh like a little nutter and then Barney shouts, 'Tickle me! Tickle me!' and soon they're both in hysterics.

Davey drops us right at the beachfront and as we all pile out of the car, it dawns on me in the most surreal way that I am a part of this family. My happy bubble doesn't burst as we wander along the boardwalk. Soft, white sand separates us from the cool, calm seawater on our left, and tall, skinny palm trees line our path. There's a long pier packed with fairground rides off in the distance.

A couple of women wearing shorts and Rollerblades skate past, seconds later spinning around to look at us with shocked expressions on their faces. They nudge each other and giggle, continuing to skate, but not without looking over their shoulders about five times. I look back at Johnny, but he seems oblivious. Then I notice Samuel and Lewis further behind him. I didn't realise they had followed us, but of course they would have done. It's only about eight-thirty in the morning so there aren't many people around. I think I must've woken up at six-ish.

Barney trots in front of us and Meg, who was carrying Phoenix in her arms, puts him down beside her and takes one of his hands.

'He's almost walking, but he's still a bit unsteady,' she tells me proudly, as Phoenix toddles along the path and then holds his other hand up to me.

'He wants you to swing him,' Meg tells me.

'Oh, OK.' We count to three and then lift him high, while he laughs his little head off. We do this until my arm starts to ache. I hear Johnny say something behind us to his bodyguards, then he jogs forward and scoops up Phoenix from between Meg and me. 'Come on, buddy.'

'Can we go on the rides?' Barney calls to him.

'That's the plan,' Johnny says, as Lewis picks up his pace and goes on ahead of us.

We step off the boardwalk on to the sand and head in the

direction of the fairground. I see what I think is a playground on the sand, but when we approach I realise it's exercise equipment for grown-ups. A ridiculously muscly man is swinging across the monkey bars and when he gets to the end and jumps down, he looks over at us. He freezes and he looks hilarious, like a statue of a strongman. Obviously he's spotted Johnny. Johnny salutes him, but it takes him a few moments to pull himself together and return the gesture. We keep walking and I still can't get my head around the fact that I'm related to a huge celebrity.

The fairground looks closed, and I wonder how long we'll have to wait for it to open before Barney explodes with anticipation, but to my surprise, a smiling man emerges from behind the security fence. He shakes Johnny's hand and then I spot Lewis behind him, scoping out the joint. He must've called before we left home because I'm amazed to discover that we have exclusive use of the rides for the next hour.

We go on everything. Sometimes I take Barney, sometimes I ride with Johnny. I haven't laughed so much in a year. It is the most fun I've had since, well, since singing the *Thomas* theme tune in the car, I think with amusement. We go on the Ferris wheel last. I'm riding with Johnny and Barney, while Meg is with Phoenix in the carriage behind us. I look down to see that the beach is gradually getting busier, and then I see the crowd of people growing on the pier outside the fairground.

'Time to make a move,' Johnny says, and when we come off the ride, Samuel and Lewis are waiting at the bottom with looks of determination on their faces.

'Got it,' Johnny says, without them needing to utter a word. He knows the drill.

There must be about twenty people waiting – not as many as

I'm sure Johnny is used to, but it's still early and there's certainly enough of a crowd to freak me out. Then I spot a photographer off to the side with a long lens, snapping away.

'He's taking photos,' I whisper to Meg with alarm.

'It's fine,' she says calmly. 'The paps always sniff out stuff like this.'

'But what about me? What if they find out about me?'

'It's OK. We're just sticking to the story that you're the boys' nanny, remember? Don't worry,' she tries to reassure me.

But I keep my head down, just in case.

By the time we're back in the car, I'm reeling. That was the strangest experience. The crowd remained deathly silent as we were ushered through them, and then half of them just started to totally freak out. Their screams were ringing in my ears. I thought Lewis and Samuel were big before, but out of the blue they seemed to transform into a brick wall surrounding us as we were rushed off the beach into Davey's waiting limo. The craziest of the fans bashed on the windows, but Davey waited calmly until Meg and Johnny had buckled the kids in, and then he put his foot down.

Johnny's mobile starts to buzz so he takes the call while Meg leans across to get some breadsticks out of the cupboard, passing one each to the boys. Now I realise why there's milk in the fridge – it's for the kids.

'Do you want anything, Jessie?' she offers.

'No, thanks.' I shake my head brusquely.

'You alright?' she checks with a frown, finally noticing that I'm a bit freaked out. She and Johnny appear totally calm.

'Yeah,' I reply breathily.

127

She looks wary. 'Sorry, did that stuff frighten you?'

'Um, well, a little bit, I guess. But it was kind of cool, too,' I say, because as crazy as it was to see all those people staring at us, mostly it was exhilarating.

'Sorry, I should have warned you. I'm used to it now,' she says apologetically as Johnny continues to chat on his phone beside her. The boys munch away on their snacks, totally unaffected by what we've just been through. 'They're used to it, too,' Meg says, reading my mind. 'I was worried about how they'd cope at first.' She looks pensive. 'I don't know if you know about my history with Johnny?'

'Not much,' I admit.

'I'll tell you about it sometime,' she promises as Johnny ends his call.

'Christian,' he tells her before she asks.

Her face lights up. 'Is he OK?'

'Yeah, he's good. Coming over soon for work. Wanted to know if we're around.'

'Did you tell him we're on holiday next week?'

'Yeah, he'll come afterwards.'

'Great. I was thinking it was about time he came to visit.'

I'll be back at home by the time they jet off on holiday. Last night I was ready to leave, but after this morning, a week doesn't feel long enough. The air inside my happy bubble evaporates until I feel nothing.

Chapter 13

We return home to the smell of something sweet and delicious baking in the oven.

'Come and meet Eddie,' Meg says with a smile, seeing my expression.

Barney runs straight past us to the kitchen, shouting 'Cookies!'

We arrive in time to see Eddie sweep Barney up into his arms. He's in his mid- to late-twenties at a guess, is taller than me at about five foot ten or eleven, and has short blond hair and blue eyes.

'Hey!' I can hear his American accent, even in that one word.

'Eddie, this is Jessie,' Meg introduces us with a smile.

He shifts Barney to his other arm and leans across to shake my hand.

'Great to meet you,' he says.

Barney wriggles out of his grasp and runs over to the oven.

'Careful!' Meg and Johnny warn simultaneously, so he freezes in his tracks.

'They'll be ready in two minutes,' Eddie promises.

'Chocolate chip?' Meg asks hopefully.

'Yeah,' he replies with a cheeky grin. 'Would you like tea and coffee on the terrace?'

'That'd be great,' she says warmly, turning to me. 'Annie's probably in the study. Let's go and say hi.'

We leave Johnny and the boys in the kitchen and head to the study where we're greeted by a petite . . . well, she looks a bit like a pixie if I'm being totally honest.

She leaps to her feet and bounds over to shake my hand.

'Hi! Jessie! How are you?' She's tiny – I'm not tall myself, but I tower over her – and she has short, spiky, jet-black hair, twinkly green eyes and a huge smile.

'I'm good, thanks,' I reply.

'She may be small, but she packs a punch,' Johnny says from behind me as he joins us.

Annie good-humouredly rolls her eyes at him, then turns back to me. 'I've just been looking at pictures of you on the internet,' she says to my surprise. She's American, too, like Eddie.

'What? Where?' I ask with alarm.

'In Santa Monica,' she says. 'Don't worry, you can barely see your face. You did a great job keeping your head down. Anyone would think you've had practice at this. Quite a few of the boys, though,' she tells Meg.

Meg frowns and Johnny places a hand on her arm in a reassuring gesture, I think. I guess she doesn't like the boys being exposed to the press.

'Do you want to check them out?' Annie asks.

I don't know about Johnny and Meg, but I certainly do.

Annie relocates herself to her desk and clicks on the mouse. A page full of pictures comes up. There are loads of Johnny and Barney on the dodgem cars – in some of them you can see me zipping behind them on a pink-coloured car, but luckily the focus is on the superstar and his son. Phew. Then we're on the carousel. This time Meg and Phoenix are the subject of many of the shots, too, with her holding Phoenix on a brightly coloured horse. Again, I'm in some of the pictures, but only in the background.

And then there are a bunch of us on the Ferris wheel. There's no mistaking me in these pics, but most of the time I'm looking off to the side and I'm wearing sunglasses anyway. Finally there are a whole bunch of us leaving the amusement park, Barney on Johnny's shoulders, all long limbs and looking completely unfazed by the attention as we head off the pier and across the sand, and Phoenix in Meg's arms, the five of us surrounded by the wall that is Samuel and Lewis. My head is mostly down, so there are very few of my face, but I still feel sick with worry that I've given the game away.

Meg talks quietly and worriedly to Annie, while Johnny stands with his hand protectively on her back. I step away and hesitate a moment, before leaving them to it.

Barney is in his usual spot on the living room rug playing with his toys, while Phoenix is casually making his way around the coffee table, holding on to it for support. Still feeling nervous, I go over to him and offer him my hands, and then help him toddle around the large, open space. Eddie emerges from the kitchen with a tray, glancing towards the open office door with a furrowed brow.

'Is everything alright?' he asks me.

'I don't know,' I reply uneasily.

'I'll take this outside,' he decides aloud, putting the tray down on the coffee table before sliding open the door, picking up the tray again and going out.

Moments later, Meg and Johnny come out of the office. She still has her head down. Johnny glances at me but doesn't smile, which makes me feel worse.

'Come on, let's have a coffee,' he says to her. 'Chocolate cookie, buddy?' he asks Barney on his way past.

I've never seen a child leap to their feet so quickly.

'I'll take him,' Meg says to me with a tight smile, relieving Phoenix's tiny hands from mine and leaving me feeling peculiarly wanting. She lifts him up and clutches him to her as she steps outside, and I feel more like an outsider than ever as I follow her.

They seat themselves at a bench table overlooking the city, but my footsteps falter. I bet they wish I wasn't here, that I didn't even exist. Before I can think about what I'm doing, I turn and bolt.

I'm in my bedroom, sitting on the edge of my bed, chewing my fingernails when Johnny comes to find me. He knocks on the door and calls my name before opening it.

'Hey,' he says, tentatively entering. 'You alright?' He looks distinctly uncomfortable as he stands there.

'I can go home if you want,' I tell him tautly.

His face falls and he looks shocked. 'Why would I want you to go home?'

'I mean, if you don't want me here.' My words rush out.

'Why do you think we don't want you here?' he interrupts.

My eyes unexpectedly fill with tears and I realise how much I want to stay. But I don't want to be constantly making them cross, either.

There's a lump in my throat when I answer. 'All that stuff on the beach. The pics of me. Meg looked so stressed . . .'

'She's not stressed about *you*,' Johnny interrupts again. To my surprise he comes over to me and sits on the bed, putting one hand on my shoulder. 'She's stressed about Barney and Phoenix. She hates the paparazzi getting photos of the boys.'

My heart lifts. This is not about me at all? 'Really?' I ask. 'She's not annoyed with me?'

'Of course she's not,' Johnny brushes me off. 'You're hardly in any of the pictures anyway, and even if you were, she wouldn't blame you. No one would. She's more pissed off at me than anyone,' he adds with raised eyebrows, leaning forward and resting his elbows on his knees.

'Why?' I ask tearfully. The lump in my throat has not shrunk. If anything, it's grown.

He stares down at his hands, crossed in front of him. He has tattoos on his wrists, trailing up his bare arms. 'Meg hates taking them out in public,' he explains. 'She didn't want to move back to LA in the first place.' He flashes me a wry look. 'I persuaded her. But we can't live like that, hiding out from the paps all the time. I'm not going to be a recluse. We've just got to get on with it. The boys don't care,' he adds flippantly.

'They didn't seem bothered at all,' I agree, noticing for the first time how calloused the tips of his fingers are. From playing his guitar?

'Exactly.' It sounds like this is a conversation he's had a lot with Meg, and I'm guessing he gets a bit frustrated, but he clearly adores her. I wish he'd felt that way about my mum. The thought makes me feel sad. If only she hadn't been just one of many.

'What about the pictures that I'm in?' I ask. 'What if they're printed?'

'It's unlikely,' he says, lazily getting to his feet and stretching his arms over his head. 'Not with all the others to choose from, and for now, the boys are the main attraction, not you. Anyway, Annie's on the case.'

She may be small, but she packs a punch ... That's what he said.

'Come on.' He nods towards the door. 'Eddie's biscuits taste much better hot.'

I reluctantly get to my feet. I feel silly for overreacting, for thinking that everything is about me, but I know better than to let my pride get in the way of freshly baked chocolate chip cookies.

Chapter 14

I knot my white sarong around my chest to cover up most of my bright blue bikini. I wore this same sarong lower down around my waist when I took it on holiday to France a year ago, but I feel oddly exposed now.

It's Tuesday, late afternoon, and after yesterday's run-in with the paparazzi, I've been quite content to stay at the house today. Disappointingly, Johnny had to leave us for a meeting with his record label earlier, but he's back now, and Meg has suggested that we all go for a swim together. I still feel like I've hardly spoken to him, but I'm trying to go with the flow.

Meg is applying sunscreen to Barney when I walk through the clear glass poolside gate. He's wriggling and complaining as she rubs it into his cheeks.

'Stay still,' she berates.

'Do you think I'll be alright?' I ask her, feeling the warmth of the sun on my arms. I've tied my hair up into a bun, so I don't get it wet, and my shades are back where they belong: sitting on top of my nose.

'You'll be fine,' Johnny interrupts from behind me. I look around to see he's wearing navy blue swimming trunks and nothing else. His arms and part of his torso are decorated with tattoos. I've seen pictures of him in magazines looking not dissimilar to this, and now he's here in front of me. Alive. Real. My biological father.

'Can never be too careful,' Meg mutters, as Barney continues to protest. She's seemed a bit strained today with Johnny not being around. I don't think she was happy he had to go off for a meeting. We ended up watching a movie in the cinema to pass the time, and I fell asleep for a couple of hours afterwards. My body clock is still messed up.

Johnny goes into what I'm assuming is the pool hut – a medium-sized white painted-concrete cabin to the right of the pool – and comes out with an armful of rolled-up green towels. He goes and drops them over the glass fence that surrounds the pool on to a sunlounger, before returning to the hut. A moment later he re-emerges with a large inflatable crocodile under one arm and a large inflatable shark under the other. He looks comical and I go over to the fence and help to take one and then the other. He returns to the hut. What's he doing now?

I throw the inflatables into the pool and turn to see him appear with a giant double lilo, shuffling his way out of the door. He seems nothing like a rock star and I can't help but giggle as he passes it over the pool fence and returns to the hut. I glance at Meg and she smirks as Johnny re-emerges with an armful of toys and a couple of long, foam tubes.

'Are you done now?' I ask sardonically, and he grins at me.

'Pretty much, chick.' He passes the last of the toys over to me and I drop half of them as he wanders around to the pool gate and comes into the fenced area. He steals Barney from Meg and swings him around in a circle, making him laugh.

'I haven't rubbed it into his arms yet,' Meg says, with slight irritation.

'He'll be OK,' Johnny chides, pressing a kiss to his giggling son's nose. 'Shall we jump in together?'

'Yeah!' Barney shouts.

Johnny puts him down and they go to the edge of the pool. 'One, two, three . . .'

Splash!

The water is shockingly cold, but her grip on my hand is warm and firm. I burst back up through the surface of the lake and my laughter collides with hers as she circles my waist with her hands, instantly making me feel safe and secure. I'm five years old and we're in the Lake District on a camping holiday, just the two of us. I wipe the water out of my eyes and grin at my mummy, who smiles back at me.

'Shall I zoom you?' she asks, her brown hair dripping rivulets of water down her forehead and forcing her to blink her shining caramel-coloured eyes rapidly.

'Yeah!' I shout with glee.

I jolt away from the memory and watch as Barney and Johnny's heads pop back out of the water. Johnny flicks his wet hair out of his eyes and takes Barney's hands, pulling him along.

I look over at Meg to see her face soften as she watches them.

'Can Barney swim?' I ask her. He seems so small.

'Yes,' she replies, starting on Phoenix with the sunscreen. 'But only just, and he still needs constant supervision. So never, ever, *ever* prop the pool gate open.'

137

'Of course not,' I scoff. What does she think I am, an idiot?

'You coming in?' Johnny calls, and I realise he's talking to me.

Still smarting from Meg's comment, I go to the edge of the pool.

'Have a go on this.' He pushes the inflatable shark across the pool. I'm not sure, but, well, OK . . . I fumble with the knot on my sarong and feel self-conscious as I throw it on a sunlounger, then I position the shark in front of me and leap to my fate. The shark wobbles, I scream and try to hold on, and then I tip over and get absolutely drenched, hair and all. So much for not getting it wet. Johnny hoots with laughter, Barney is hysterical and my role as comedy genius is born.

'You knew that was going to happen!' I laugh and splash Johnny. The blue water is blissfully cool, not freezing cold like the lake from my memory. He splashes me right back, but I use the crocodile as a shield. I look over at Meg and see that she has a strange expression on her face as she watches us, but then Johnny splashes me and I have no choice but to get him back.

When I look over again, Meg and Phoenix have gone.

We don't stay in the pool for long. Meg's disappearance seems to have put Johnny on edge.

'Do you think she's OK?' I ask worriedly.

'She'll be fine,' he replies, which doesn't exactly satisfy me. She'll be fine when I'm gone, probably.

There's noise coming from the kitchen when we go back into the house. I follow Johnny into the room, where Meg is feeding Phoenix in his highchair.

'What happened to you?' Johnny asks. 'I thought you were coming for a swim?'

Meg glances at me and then back at her baby son. 'I didn't realise it was so close to the kids' dinner time. Can you go and get Barney dressed?' She sounds a bit snappy. 'You're dripping water all over the kitchen.'

I guess that applies to me, too, I think uncomfortably as I tighten the towel around my waist.

'Eddie has left us some Thai food,' she tells me with what feels like forced brightness. 'We can eat whenever you're ready.'

'I'll go and have a shower. I'll be quick,' I promise, backing out of the kitchen. I think I might have upset Meg. Again.

'Come on, buddy,' Johnny says to Barney. He runs straight past me to the stairs.

'Don't slip!' Johnny calls after him. He still has wet feet.

Barney stands stock still for two seconds and then starts to jump up the stairs, one by one, like a three-foot-high rabbit. I chuckle, despite myself.

'Give me a hand getting him dressed?' Johnny says. He nods towards Barney's bedroom, so I follow him in there, still feeling on edge.

'Can you grab him some clothes from that drawer?' he says, while stripping off his wriggling son.

I do as he asks, choosing red shorts and a navy blue T-shirt with a white shark on the front of it. When I turn around, Barney is standing in front of Johnny, grinning up at him as Johnny vigorously rubs the water from his hair.

'You look so much like each other,' I say, and they both glance at me with their equally piercing green eyes. Phoenix looks more like Meg, I muse to myself as I pass Johnny the clothes.

'Meg was a bit freaked out when she saw how much *you* look like me,' he reveals, pulling the T-shirt over Barney's head.

I wasn't expecting him to admit to that. I shakily perch on the edge of the children's table.

'I never did look much like Mum.'

His jaw seems set in a hard line and he doesn't comment. I want to ask him so many questions about her, but there hasn't been a right time, and we're not alone even now with Barney around.

'When will we tell everyone about me?' I find myself asking. 'I know Meg isn't very happy about me being here,' I add, my voice wavering a little.

'Meg's fine,' he says, brushing me off. When I say nothing, he gives me a sympathetic smile and I know he realises I'm not convinced. He glances at Barney and ruffles his hair. 'I don't think we should rush into telling everyone about you. Once that happens, there's no going back. But we'll talk about it some more soon, OK?'

I don't really know what he means, but I know this is not the time or place to press the issue.

Johnny is still only wearing his swimming trunks and my eyes fall to the scrawly black writing of a tattoo across his left pec. It says *Nutmeg*.

'Is that your nickname for Meg?' I ask.

He touches his hand to it and shrugs. 'Yeah.' He looks a bit sheepish when he meets my eyes again. 'I'll talk to her,' he promises. 'I don't want you to feel uncomfortable being here.'

The next day, Meg comes to find me when I'm outside by the pool.

'How do you fancy coming to a party on Friday night?' She sits down on the sunlounger opposite me.

'Whose party?' I ask.

'Michael Tremway's. He's—'

'I know who he is!' I exclaim, excitedly. He's the executive producer of one of my favourite US TV Shows, *Little Miss Mulholland*, about a teenage girl, Macy, who's trying to make it as an actress in Hollywood. The girl who plays Macy is Michael Tremway's sixteen-year-old daughter, Charlotte.

Meg hands over a ticket and I try to refrain from snatching it, but fail.

'It's Michael's fortieth birthday party,' she tells me as I read that information for myself. 'But I'm sure there will be plenty of young people there, too.'

'Does Johnny know him?' I ask breathlessly.

'Johnny knows everyone,' she replies with a wry grin. 'He doesn't go to many parties these days, but he says he'll come with us to this.'

'Really?' The question comes out sounding like a squeak. Then my heart sinks. 'I don't have anything to wear.'

'What about that silver swing dress?' she suggests, before clapping her hand to her forehead. 'What am I thinking?' she says with a laugh. 'Let's go shopping!'

'But, I . . .'

'Johnny will cover it,' she waves away any concerns. 'He probably owes you about a million bucks in child maintenance, anyway.'

It's a throwaway comment, but it makes my head spin.

That afternoon, Meg and I leave the boys with their dad and take a limo ride, courtesy of Davey, to Rodeo Drive.

I feel like I'm Julia Roberts in *Pretty Woman*. My heart has not stopped racing and, as we step out of the car on to the pristine, palm-tree-lined street, I think I'm going to have some sort of fit. The gleaming white Hollywood sign looms large in the distance and I can't quite believe I'm here.

Gucci, Prada, Armani, Valentino ... The afternoon sun reflects off the glittering windows and I blink quickly as I take in the beautiful jewel-encrusted gowns in the displays. Meg suggests that we go for a wander first, try on a few things and then decide on a party dress. I let myself be lead by her, too stunned to do anything else.

It's only later, when I'm standing in a Roberto Cavalli changing room, staring at the reflection of somebody I hardly recognise, that I remember who I am and where I've come from.

'I'm waiting . . .' Mum's voice cuts through the dense, stuffy heat of the changing room.

'Hang on,' I tell her, struggling to zip up the dress. Her face appears in front of the curtain – just her face, hovering like something out of a bizarre puppet show.

'Mum!' I squawk, checking to make sure she hasn't left any cracks in the curtain for people to peek in.

She ignores my protest. 'Do you need a hand with that?'

She comes in anyway, tutting at me as I reach past her to pull the curtain properly shut. I lift up my hair so she can access the zip.

'There.' She spins me around so that she can get a good look at me. 'Mmm.' She eyes me up and down. 'Yes, I like that.'

'No need to sound quite so enthusiastic,' I say sarcastically.

She smirks. She is not, and never has been, a gushing mum. Not like Libby's mum, who'd be more inclined to say, 'Wow, darling, that's stunning!' even when it's anything but.

I turn around and look at myself in the reflection, while she scrutinises me.

'It's alright,' I say with a shrug, playing it down because that's her speciality.

'Get it,' she says definitively.

'I'll see what else there is, first,' I decide, in part to spite her.

'OK,' she says with a shrug. 'But I'm asking the assistant to put it on hold.'

She knew I'd come back for it, and she was right. I wore the dress at my birthday party, the one she never showed up for.

I blink back tears as I stare at the girl in the mirror. I'm wearing a two-piece slim black skirt and fitted sleeveless top. The top bares my slightly-tanned midriff and has black lace trim around the hem, and the long skirt skims the floor with a slit all the way up to the top of my thigh. I'd have to wear heels. And I'd wear my hair up in a tousled bun with dark eye make-up. I can picture it perfectly. I dread to think how much this outfit costs, but Meg has forbidden me to look at the price tag. Curiosity gets the better of me, and I nearly choke when I see the digits.

'Can I have a look?' Meg's voice snaps me out of it.

'In a sec,' I reply.

I know this is the one. This is the dress. I know that my mum would say, 'Mmm, yes,' or something like that, but that would be enough for me. I wish she were here. I miss her so much.

I try to swallow the lump in my throat and then open up the curtain to get Meg's opinion.

'Gorgeous,' she says, shaking her head. I smile tentatively back at her.

Her comments from my first night here are still niggling away at me, but she seems to be making an effort. I guess Johnny must have spoken to her, like he said he would.

'What do you think?' she asks.

'I love it,' I practically whisper.

'Me too. Do you want to try on anything else?' Pause. 'Or have you made up your mind?' she asks with amusement.

'I don't think this outfit can be topped,' I reply.

She laughs and closes the curtain. 'Let's go buy it, then.'

As I change back into my old clothes, I ask her a question through the curtain. 'Why does Johnny call you Nutmeg?'

She laughs lightly. 'God knows. My name's Meg, but when I worked for him he just started calling me Nutmeg. Now he's got it tattooed on his chest.'

'I know. I saw when we went swimming.'

'He'll probably give you a nickname, soon,' she says drily, and I wish I could see her face so I could read her expression.

'I've already got a nickname. Jessie,' I point out, coming back out of the changing room.

'Of course. Short for Jessica.' She smiles.

I stay standing where I am. 'How did you come to work for Johnny, if you don't mind me asking?'

'Not at all. I used to work for an architect as her PA, and then one of her clients ... Oh! It was Wendel Rosgrove! You've met him.'

'Yeah.' I screw up my nose.

'What?' she asks with confusion.

'I found him a bit intimidating,' I reveal. That's putting it nicely. I actually thought he was a bit of a wanker.

Meg gives me a conspiratorial look. 'I agree with you, but luckily I don't have much to do with him. Anyway, he told my boss that Johnny was looking for a new PA and she suggested me for the job.'

'Wow. As easy as that.'

She laughs wryly and leans back against the wall, crossing her arms. 'Nothing's ever easy where Johnny's concerned.'

'Mmm. No, I suppose not.' I gather up my things, ready to take them to the till.

'I'm sorry about your mum,' she says out of the blue and I stare at her with surprise. 'I just wanted to . . . I just wanted to say that.' She gives me an awkward smile.

'Thanks,' I reply quietly.

Meg shifts on her feet and I sense that she's still got something to say. I tilt my head to one side, expectantly. 'I'm also sorry I've been a bit off since you arrived,' she gives me an apologetic look.

'That's OK,' I tell her, even if she's not entirely forgiven.

'I used to worry that this would happen one day,' she confides. 'That Johnny's past would come back to . . .' Her voice cuts off abruptly before she can say 'haunt us'. She squirms. 'I don't mean it to sound like a bad thing.'

'Isn't it?' I stand up straighter, feeling emboldened. 'I mean, aren't I a bad thing in your opinion?' If she wants to say so, she should say it to my face.

'That's what I'm trying to explain.' She smiles meekly. 'I'm not saying this isn't hard for me. That would be a lie, because Johnny and I have already been through a lot and I actually thought we might be over all the hurdles, that we would get our happily ever after.'

'I'm sorry to spoil it for you.'

'Jessie, you're not listening to me,' she says calmly. 'What I'm trying to say is that, even though this came as a shock, I think you might be good for us. Good for Johnny.' She takes a deep breath. 'I'm kind of glad you're here.'

We stare back at each other for a long few seconds, then she smiles. 'Come on, the saleswoman will think we're shoplifting.'

'Nah, I did enough of that in Armani.'

'What?' she gasps.

'Just kidding.' Ha! Got her.

She rolls her eyes and whacks me on my arm. We're stifling giggles as we leave the changing rooms.

The next two days pass by alarmingly quickly, and soon it's Friday night and time for the party. I wear my hair in a fishtail plait in the end. Meg called in someone to do our hair and make-up and I've never felt more spoiled. The party is here in Bel Air in Michael Tremway's enormous mansion, so it's only a short ride in the limo to get there. Meg looks stunning in a golden-yellow Gucci dress with long floaty sleeves and a short hem which shows off her long legs. She's wearing her hair down, a chunky costume jewellery necklace, and we're both wearing black killer-heels. We went shoe shopping this morning, and yes, they are probably going to kill me by the end of the evening.

Johnny is wearing skinny black jeans with a metal-studded belt and a silver-grey shirt unbuttoned at the top. It's a warm evening so he's rolled up his sleeves and his tattoos are visible. For some reason I imagine Stu with tattoos like Johnny's and the thought makes me smile.

Johnny leans across to open up the fridge. He pulls out a bottle of what looks like champagne. It's called Perrier Jouet and has a pretty white flower decoration up the side. Isn't Perrier mineral water?

'Want one?' he asks Meg with a raised eyebrow.

She eyes him cautiously. 'No, it's OK,' she decides.

'Nutmeg, it's *fine*. You and Jessie can drink it.'

Doesn't he drink alcohol? I know from Googling him that he's been in and out of rehab for drug addiction, but these days he's clean – let's face it, Stu wouldn't have let me come anywhere near him if he wasn't. But I didn't realise that he didn't even drink.

'Jessie's only fifteen,' Meg points out.

'So?' I chip in, a little annoyed. I'm gagging for some alcohol, especially if we're going to a party. 'I drink all the time at home.'

She doesn't look convinced. Or maybe I'm misreading her and she doesn't look impressed.

'One glass won't hurt. It's a special occasion,' Johnny says gently before turning to me. 'Jessie? Do you want a glass of champagne?'

'Yes, please!' I've never had champagne before.

Meg also takes a glass, but Johnny grabs a can of Coke out of the fridge and cracks it open.

I take a large gulp of champagne and nearly cough and splutter it back up again. Jeez, it's fizzy! I prefer cider, to be honest. This isn't sweet enough. But it's a drink so I knock it back as quickly as I can. No sooner have I finished it than we arrive. I look out of the car's blackened glass windows to see crowds of people milling around on the pavement outside a high brick wall. Others are climbing out of limos, being papped by waiting photographers. Meg squeezes Johnny's knee and then turns to me.

'I don't know how much longer we'll be able to protect your identity,' she says, calmly. 'We'll do our best, but just try to enjoy tonight. If anyone asks, stick to the nanny story.'

'OK,' I concede. Why are they so reluctant to tell the world about me?

Before I can ask, the door opens and Davey stands back to let Meg climb out. Johnny and I still haven't had a proper heart-to-heart. Which means I haven't had a chance to ask him the questions that I really need answers for. On the couple of occasions I've brought up Mum, he seems uncomfortable. OK, so he might not remember her, and maybe he doesn't want to talk about it in front of Meg, but he hasn't exactly made an attempt to take me off somewhere, just the two of us. I went shopping with Meg on my own, but it's Johnny who I want to develop a relationship with. What's he playing at? Why isn't he making more of an effort? Maybe he feels awkward. Tough! Life *is* awkward. Irritation spikes me out of nowhere.

Johnny steps out of the car to the flashes of paparazzi camera bulbs. I take a deep breath and try to calm down. I'm about to go to a Hollywood party! I should be excited. Tonight I need to channel fun-Jessie and try and forget all the other stuff. I wait for the flashes to follow him away from the limo, and then I move over to the door and, taking some comfort from Davey's encouraging smile, I carefully climb out, hoping my killer stilettos don't buckle underneath me.

Chapter 15

I can't believe Johnny and Meg aren't blinded by the flashes going off in their faces as they head towards the gates. I'm slightly lost in the crowd as I follow them, my head buzzing from that glass of champagne I drank way too quickly.

Meg looks over her shoulder at me once to check I'm still with them, but Johnny keeps his eyes trained forward. I have my ticket in my hand, and I'm assuming that they're staying ahead of me in a deliberate attempt to keep my identity under wraps. I can't help but feel disappointed, but hopefully they know what they're doing.

My heart jumps as they make it through the gates, with nobody even checking their tickets. And why should they? Johnny and Meg are two of the most recognisable faces in show-biz. But what if I can't get in? I'm a bit panicked as I join the small queue ahead of me. Obviously nobody moves aside for me, like they did for my famous father. Eventually I reach the front and hand over my ticket.

'Name?' a large and formidable-looking bouncer asks.

'Jessie Pickerill,' I tell him with a pounding heart.

He scans his list and seconds later, moves aside.

Meg and Johnny are waiting for me. She smiles brightly, but my eyes are drawn to his.

'OK?' he asks, one eyebrow raised.

'Yeah,' I reply, still on edge. And then I look around.

There's so much to take in. The house is in the distance behind a gently sloping lawn, and on the lawn there is a vast array of colourful old-fashioned fairground rides: a carousel, Ferris wheel, flying chair-o-planes, a helter-skelter and teacups. I feel like I'm back on Santa Monica Pier, except these rides are in somebody's *garden*!

The house in the distance is an enormous three-storey mansion made out of cream stone, with pillars all the way along the front. The winding path is lined with pink and white flowers and lit with real-fire torches, although it's not dark, yet. I notice golf-kart-style buggies going to and from the house along the path. In a daze, I follow Johnny and Meg to the karts. There are no photographers inside the gates – at least, not that I know of – so I'm hoping I'll relax soon. I wish I'd had another glass of champagne.

Just as I think that, I see serving girls in red and black 1950s dresses standing beside the karts holding wooden trays full of champagne glasses. Some of the liquid inside them is clear and fizzy, the others are coloured raspberry pink or pale orange. There are a few tall glasses of juice, too.

'Champagne, Bellini and Rossini,' the serving girl nearest to us reveals. I check out her reaction to Johnny. She keeps her cool, but her eyes watch him beneath lowered lashes as he leans across and takes a juice. She looks amazing – she could be an actress or a model with her red lipstick and dark hair tied up in a high ponytail.

'I'll take a Bellini, please.' Meg helps herself, ignoring the girl's obvious fascination with her husband. I wonder how she copes with it. I'd hate it if I were her.

'What's that?' I ask Meg, nodding at the pale orange liquid in her glass.

'Champagne and peach puree. The Rossini is Champagne and berry puree. Will your stepdad kill us if you have one more glass?'

'Let him try,' I scoff, reaching for a berry drink and taking a sip as I climb on to a waiting kart. Mmm, this tastes much better than that stuff in the car. Johnny and Meg sit behind me, facing backwards, him with his arm draped around her shoulder. He seems so into her, but surely she must feel insecure when so many women are obviously interested in him?

Pop music is blaring out of enormous loudspeakers all around the garden, but it doesn't drown out the sound of screams and laughter coming from the fairground rides as we drive past them. I can smell popcorn and candy floss and spy a couple of hot dog stands, with servers dressed in 1950s-style striped red and white costumes and matching hats.

The kart doesn't pull to a stop outside the house, but instead drives along beside it. We round the corner to the back garden and are greeted with the sight of a large oval-shaped swimming pool with two slides going into it on either side, and a fountain in the middle spurting out jets of crystal clear water. There are loads of people splashing about – mostly younger ones, from what I can see – and quite a few girls in bikinis and bare-chested

151

guys in shorts lazing about on sunloungers dotted all around the pool. This makes Mike and Natalie's party look laughable in comparison.

Beyond the swimming pool, the sprawling garden continues, and off in the distance I can see a log cabin set within silvery white tree trunks.

I can't believe one person owns all of this. I've never seen anything like it in my life.

Inside, the house continues to astound me. Two wide winding staircases curve up and away from the ground floor of a double-height, white marble-lined lobby. Impressive flower displays sit on top of what look like antique carved wooden side tables.

A distinguished-looking man wearing a casual white shirt and black trousers greets people as they arrive. It takes me a few seconds to recognise him as Michael Tremway. There's a woman who must be his wife beside him. She looks young, and I remember reading somewhere that he remarried someone who is about twenty-five years his junior. She's young enough to be his daughter. I wonder what Macy thinks of her.

'Johnny,' Michael says, warmly, as we reach him. 'Meg. You look stunning, as always.' He kisses her hand first and then shakes Johnny's. I hang back, but Johnny steps aside and brings me in. 'And this is Jessie, my—'

'Our nanny,' Meg smoothly interrupts.

Was Johnny just about to introduce me as his daughter? I feel a surge of annoyance towards Meg for cutting him off. Who is she trying to protect, me or them? I have a feeling it's the latter.

Michael shakes my hand and smiles, his grey eyes crinkling at the corners. He turns around to his wife.

'You remember Colleen.' She steps forward and kisses Johnny's cheeks, doing the same to Meg. She has a high-pitched, slightly cloying voice.

'It's great to have you back in LA,' I overhear Michael saying to Johnny.

'Yeah, well, can't argue with the weather,' Johnny replies. 'Happy birthday, by the way,' he adds.

There's a commotion behind us. I whip around to see a girl, who must be about my age, in a skimpy red bikini and with long, dark, dripping-wet hair, sitting on her bum in the middle of the lobby. She looks shell-shocked. Michael Tremway stalks through the crowd.

'How many times do I have to tell you not to run on the marble with wet feet!' he exclaims with exasperation as he reaches her.

The girl blushes a deep beetroot as she scrambles to her feet.

'Screw you,' she hisses, deliberately bumping into Colleen as she heads to the stairs, making her gasp and wobble on her high heels.

I stare after the girl, dumbfounded, as I realise that that was Macy from my favourite TV show. Charlotte Tremway, I correct myself in my head.

Michael laughs lightly. 'Teenagers,' he mutters. 'Can't live with them, can't live without them.' Then he turns to say hello to the next people to arrive.

I can't help but feel bad for Charlotte for being dismissed by her dad so easily.

A while later, I decide to go and explore on my own. I feel like Meg's on edge having me around threatening to blow the big

153

secret. I leave her and Johnny sitting inside with a few people from Johnny's record label and go for a walk around the fairground.

My heels sink into the grass as I walk past a hotdog stand towards the old-fashioned dodgems, snatching up a Bellini from a passing waitress on the way. Mmm, yum. This one's even nicer than the berry one. I wish I had a friend here to share this experience with. I miss Natalie. She'd go crazy at a party like this!

Thinking about her reminds me that I'm going home soon. But I've barely got to know my so-called dad at all. I can't imagine ever knowing him, not like I do Stu. Once more I feel a pang of homesickness. Absence definitely makes the heart grow fonder in my case. I wonder if Stu's missing me. Probably not. I bet he's enjoying the peace and quiet.

Katy Perry's 'California Girls' is blaring out of the garden speakers as the dodgem ride up ahead comes to an end. The combination of perky music and alcohol makes me decide to have a go. By a stroke of luck, I manage to swipe a just-vacated car beside the barrier. I hold my almost empty glass between my knees and take in my surroundings while I'm waiting for the ride to start. The ages of the people around me range from about ten to sixty. There are a few teenagers who look pretty cool. They shout across the cars to each other and, as the ride starts off, my eyes are drawn to the back of one boy's head. He has black, messy hair and even from behind I can tell he's probably pretty cute. I nip in between a couple of kids and he rounds the bend up ahead, allowing me to catch a glimpse of his face. Whoa. I was right. He's gorgeous. Absolutely gorgeous. Tanned with dark eyelashes and sculptured cheekbones. I wonder if he's an actor? *I wonder if he has a girlfriend* . . . Maybe he's gay. An old biddy crashes into the side of me and then hoots with laughter. I giggle as I turn my wheel all the way to the right and reverse away from her, crashing backwards into the front of another car. My head jerks forward on impact.

'Hey!' I hear a guy behind me jokily complain as I put my foot down. I look over my shoulder with a grin to see that it's *him*. My eyes widen, while his narrow, and he leans forward with determination as he chases me. I dart in between two more cars and take a hard right to come up behind him. He spies what I'm up to and I laugh at his mock outrage. All of a sudden he spins his car around so we're facing each other, heading for a head-on crash. I squeeze my eyes shut, then, ouch!

'No head-on crashes!' the guy running the dodgems shouts at us.

The boy purses his lips at me and I try to keep a straight face as we find ourselves riding side by side. I grab the opportunity to down the rest of my drink.

'Are you drinking and driving?' he asks with faux horror. He has an American accent. 'Bad girl,' he mutters.

'You don't know the half of it.' I turn my wheel sharply to the left and veer into him.

'Hey!' He laughs, doing the same to me. All of the cars slow to a stop as the ride comes to an end. Damn.

'Everybody off!' the dodgem car operator shouts.

Our cars have stopped beside each other. He shoots me a sideways look and raises one eyebrow. 'I hate to think what you're like on the road.'

'I don't have a licence,' I reply flippantly, trying to look cool and not too ungainly as I go to climb out of my car.

'No?' He looks surprised as he hops out of his own and holds his hand down to me. He has a tattoo of a comic-book style POW! on the outside of his right forearm and a bunch of braided leather straps around his wrists. I take his hand instinctively, the slit on my dress flashing the length of my leg as I step on to the smooth metal. At least with him holding my hand I won't slip in my heels and make a tit out of myself. 'How old are you?' he asks, as a girl of about ten barges past me to get into my car.

'Fifteen,' I reply, glaring at the little brat. He looks surprised, and then I realise I'm gripping his hand hard, so I drop it like a hot cake. His fingertips were rough like Johnny's. 'You play the guitar,' I say without thinking.

'Yeah.' He looks confused. 'Have we met?'

'No, just a lucky guess.' I nod down at his hands.

'Aah,' he says.

Even with the extra inches on my shoes, he's taller than me by half a foot.

We reach the barrier, trying to avoid people rushing to take over the empty cars. A couple of kids who miss out moan loudly. I spy the old biddy who hooted with laughter looking a bit sneaky as she stays in her car. 'Cheeky cow,' I mutter.

'Who?'

'Her.' I nudge and point. 'That old lady, sticking in her car for another ride.'

He grins and tuts. 'Guess she's gotta get her kicks from somewhere.' We step down on to the grass and it's then that I notice his T-shirt: it's grey with a faded black line drawing of a wombat on the front, playing an electric guitar.

'You like The Wombats?' I exclaim.

'Yeah, man, they're cool.' His bluey-grey eyes stare out at me from behind a few wisps of black hair that have fallen down across his forehead. 'I'm going to see them in September.'

'No way! I'm so jealous.'

'Can't you get tickets?' He hooks his thumbs into the belt loops of his skinny black jeans.

'I won't be here, then,' I reply sadly, handing my empty glass to a passing waitress.

'Where will you be?'

'Maidenhead, innit.'

'What?'

I giggle, amused by my insider lingo. 'England.'

'Is that where you're from?'

'You're quick,' I tease. He grins and my insides go all jittery.

'Obviously I knew you had an accent.' Pause. 'You look *really* familiar. Have I seen you around?'

'I doubt it. I've only been here since Sunday.' I fold my arms.

'What's your name?'

'Jessie.'

'I'm—'

'Jack!' a guy interrupts him with a shout. We break eye contact and look over to see four other teenagers from the dodgems waiting approximately ten metres away: two girls and two guys, one of whom is responsible for calling his name. 'Are you coming on the slide?'

My spirits dip.

'There in a bit,' he calls back nonchalantly, his gaze returning to me. 'I'm Jack, by the way.'

'So I heard.' I purse my lips, sensing that we still have his friends' attention. One look over and I'm proved right – they haven't moved. In fact, one of the girls – a tall, skinny blonde in a floaty lilac-coloured dress – seems a bit put out. Is she his girlfriend? Perhaps not, if he's still here chatting to me, but I bet she wants to be. Who wouldn't? For some reason, at that very moment, my brain chooses to show me a mental snapshot of Tom laughing.

'You wanna come with us?' Jack asks me, jerking his head in their direction while simultaneously jerking my focus back to him.

'Sure.' I'm leaving soon, and how many Hollywood parties am I likely to be invited to? I'd be stupid for not making the most of tonight. Jack is super-cute, and it's not like Tom and I are even going out.

I follow him over to the group. The girl I noticed earlier shifts on her feet, but shoots daggers at me.

'Hey guys, this is Jessie.' Jack introduces me, then points to each of his friends. 'Morgan, Miles, Bryony and Lissa.'

They all say hi – some more enthusiastically than others. Morgan is tall and skinny with short dark-blond hair and scuffed blue jeans, Miles is a bit shorter and broader with dark hair dyed orange at the tips – he's dressed all in black – and Bryony is my height with medium-length dark hair. Lissa, the blonde one, barely even meets my eye. The girls are wearing expensive-looking dresses, which makes me feel better about my outfit, especially because the boys are pretty scruffy.

'Take your time,' Lissa says moodily to Jack.

'You don't have to babysit me, darlin'. I would have met y'all over there,' Jack replies in a fake country accent. Lissa huffs. 'So what's your story?' he asks me in his normal voice as we walk on. 'Who are you here with?'

'My . . .' I almost say 'my dad', but I catch myself just in time. 'Just some people who know Michael.' I force myself to say Michael and not Michael Tremway so I don't sound completely clueless.

'Are you an actress?' Lissa asks over her shoulder, in a slightly condescending way.

I throw my head back and laugh. 'Hell, no.' She looks even more put out as Jack smirks.

'What about you?' I ask him. 'Why are you here?'

'Oh, my dad knows Mike.'

Mike, not Michael. Bugger. I didn't sound as clued up as I had intended.

'How long are you in LA?' he asks as we reach the helter-skelter.

'Just until the day after tomorrow,' I reply, as he passes me a mat to use on the giant slide.

'What a shame,' Lissa comments cattily, her disposition visibly improving.

'Chill out, Lissa,' Jack snaps. She stomps up the stairs huffily in front of us. We follow her to find a short queue at the top.

'Excuse me!' I move to one side as someone pushes past me, then I see who it is.

'It's the pushy old lady from the dodgems!' I tug on Jack's arm and we look after her with astonishment.

'Who are you calling an old lady?' she shouts angrily over her shoulder.

Shit, she heard me! I clap my hand over my mouth.

'I'm forty-nine!' she yells at the top of her voice as she shoves her way to the top.

Jack and I glance at each other and crack up laughing. The

sound of her squealing as she rides down the slide only makes us laugh harder.

I'm still giggling when I come down the slide myself, and even the sight of Lissa whispering to Bryony at the bottom doesn't wipe the smile from my face. Jack is behind me anyway, so I turn around to wait for him.

'I wouldn't get too close to him if I were you.' I glance over my shoulder to see Lissa and Bryony have edged forward, but it's Bryony, not Lissa, who spoke.

I raise one eyebrow. 'Is he trouble?' I'm being completely sarcastic, but it's lost on them.

'Yeah,' they both reply in all seriousness.

'OK. I'll keep that in mind tonight.' As if I'm going to fall for him in the next few hours. I roll my eyes and turn back in time to see Jack whizz down the slide. Trouble or not, he's hot.

'Are you sure we don't know each other?' he asks again as he walks over to me.

'Trust me, if I knew you, I'd remember you.' I can't believe I said that without blushing.

He chuckles and shakes his head. 'You really remind me of someone.'

And then it hits me. Does he mean Johnny?

'What?' he asks because I must've looked a bit on edge.

'Nothing,' I brush him off.

'Come on.' He touches his hand lightly to my back and a shiver goes down my spine. 'Catch you later,' he calls back to his pals.

Taylor Swift's 'I Knew You Were Trouble' starts to play out of the speakers and it's everything I can do not to laugh out loud. Maybe Taylor's trying to tell me something.

Jack digs his hand into his pocket as we walk, pulling out a crumpled packet of cigarettes. He nods up ahead. 'Let's go around the back. The music's better.'

'You don't like Swifty? I prefer indie rock myself, but you can't deny a catchy tune when you hear one.'

'My little sis is obsessed. But there's only so much Taylor Swift a guy can take.' He pauses and offers me a cigarette. I'm semi-tempted, but I decline. I don't really need one and I'm sure Meg and Johnny wouldn't approve.

'I bet Harry Styles would agree with you.'

'Who?' he asks through a trail of smoke as we keep walking.

'Harry Styles from One Direction. He went out with her.'

'Oh, them.' He glances at me. 'Now it's all coming out. I thought you liked good music like the Wombats.'

'I do!' I exclaim. 'Anyway, you're the one with a Zayn Malik comic-book tattoo.' I grab his wrist and twist his arm so his tattoo is on show. 'He's got one like this, only his says ZAP!'

Jack stops in his tracks and stares at me directly. 'Zayn?'

I shrug. 'He's in One Direction too.'

'Jesus Christ,' he says with a grin. 'Katy Perry, Taylor Swift, One Direction ... You are so not a rock chick.'

I frown. 'Who says I like Katy Perry?'

'I saw you dancing away to her on the bumper cars.' He raises one eyebrow at me and keeps on walking.

'Did you?' He noticed me before I noticed him? We reach the path lit by torches, hanging back as a kart whizzes past.

'Moments before you nearly took me out,' he adds, crossing the path to the grass on the other side.

'Yeah, well, this is coming from someone who has a One Direction tattoo,' I tease.

'I do *not* have a One Direction tattoo,' he says firmly, stopping again and facing me.

'He who protests too much,' I say in a pretend plummy accent.

'I bet I got mine done first,' he says.

'Bet you didn't.'

'How much?' He raises one eyebrow.

'How much what?'

'How much do you want to bet?'

I laugh. 'Are you serious? You really want to have a bet about this?' I hesitate. 'OK, you're on,' I decide. 'What are the odds?'

'The loser has to jump in the pool naked.'

My mouth falls open. 'No way.'

'OK, in their underwear,' he concedes, walking on.

'Are you taking the piss?' I walk after him. 'There is no way in hell I'm getting into that pool in front of all of those people. I wouldn't get in, even if I was wearing a bikini.'

'Why not?' He takes a casual drag and eyes me up and down, a smile playing about his lips. My stomach ties itself in knots as he takes me in.

'I'm not that much of an exhibitionist,' I reply. 'I saw Macy slip over on the marble earlier in her wet bikini. Fell flat on her arse.'

'Macy?'

'Yeah, you know, Michael Tremway's daughter.' There I go again, saying Michael instead of Mike.

He grins. 'You mean Charlotte?'

'Hey?' Then I realise my mistake and start to laugh. 'I've been calling her Macy inside my head since I arrived. *Little Miss*

162

Mulholland is one of my favourite TV shows.' Was it really uncool to admit that? Oh well, add it to the list.

Jack looks amused as he takes a final suck on his cigarette and flicks it on the ground. I step on it and grind it into the grass with the sole of my shoe. 'You trying to start a fire?'

'You sound like my mom,' he says wryly.

At least he's got one.

That's the first time I've thought about *my* mum all evening. 'I need another drink. At least they don't seem to care about the age limit here?' I pause. 'How old are you, anyway?'

'Eighteen,' he replies. 'And here that's still underage. Good thing it's a private party. You can get away with a *lot* of stuff.'

The way he says 'a lot' seems ominous.

We spy a serving girl near the corner of the house and swipe a couple of glasses. The music is louder than it was when we arrived and there are a few less people in the pool. The sky is now dark blue up above, an orange tinge visible on the horizon behind the far-off trees. I wonder what time it is. I hope Meg and Johnny aren't looking for me.

Jack sits down on a sunlounger and stretches out, crossing his legs. He pats the one beside him.

'Take a seat.'

I'm careful not to flash my knickers as I do. From here we have a perfect view of everyone in the swimming pool and the house behind it. All of the lights are on inside now and the windows are casting a warm glow which reaches us even from this distance.

Cold War Kids' 'Hang Me Up To Dry' comes on the sound system. 'I like this song,' I say.

'My bro's DJ-ing,' he tells me.

'Is he really? That's cool.'

'He won't be playing any One Direction, though,' he says to mock me.

'Aw, I'm so sorry for you,' I mock him right back. 'Come on, then, I'm not jumping into the pool naked or in my underwear, so you may as well just tell me when you got your tat done,' I say, taking a sip of my drink.

'About four years ago.'

'Bullshit!' I splutter. 'That would have made you fourteen!'

'Yep.'

'You're not allowed to get tattoos until you're eighteen! Believe me, I checked. At least, not without parental consent and there's no way in hell I was getting that.' I remember that particular argument with Mum. Libby was on Mum's side, as usual. She couldn't believe I was considering getting a tattoo. It was a month or so before Mum died, but even then we'd already started to grow apart. I try not to dwell on it. I'm having too good a time to spoil it now. 'Is it different over here?'

'I don't know,' he says. 'My older brother's buddy did mine.'

'Didn't your parents go mental?'

He shrugs. 'My parents don't really mind what I do.' My face falls and he notices. 'Not minding is not the same as not caring,' he points out. 'They're just pretty laidback, that's all.'

'Oh.' They sound like Natalie's parents, and that's not so bad.

'What are yours like?' he asks.

'Um …' Conversation killer alert! I seriously don't want to talk about this. 'Is that Macy?' I sit upright as I see a girl coming out of the house.

Jack follows my gaze. 'You mean Charlotte?'

Whoops. Did it again. 'That's the one.'

He smirks. 'You want me to introduce you?'

'You *know* her?'

'I know *Charlotte*,' he says pointedly. 'She's a friend of my sister's.'

'No way! Is she nice?' Out of the blue I feel nervous. 'I mean, is she . . .'

'A bit of a bitch?' he interrupts. 'Oh, yeah, comes with teen star territory,' he says nonchalantly. 'But you seem to be able to handle yourself.'

I raise one eyebrow. 'What's that supposed to mean?'

He grins, but ignores me. 'Here she comes.'

I look back over to see her approaching the pool. A couple of her friends sitting on nearby sunloungers stand up and wave her over. Jack gets another cigarette out of his pocket, but stays where he is. I decline his offer, too edgy to smoke, ironically. She glances over at us and her face lights up.

'Hey, Jack!' She leaves her friends looking after her as she heads over to us. 'Where's Agnes?'

Who's Agnes? Is that his girlfriend?

'Not here tonight,' he replies.

'Oh yeah, I forgot about her and Drew.'

She leans over and gives him a hug, then spies his cigarette. 'Oh, let me have a drag.' She takes it from between his fingers, but he doesn't seem to mind. She perches on the edge of his sun-lounger, facing away from me. Her dress is low-cut at the back and she's so skinny, I can see her ribs as she inhales deeply.

'I needed this,' she mutters, taking another long drag before handing the cigarette back.

'You want one?' Jack asks.

'No. Mike'll go crazy if he sees me.'

Mike? Does she call her dad, Mike?

Jack taps her shoulder and jerks his head in my direction. 'This is Jessie, by the way.'

I've been sitting here, watching this entire exchange and feeling totally left out, but now she swivels around and looks almost surprised to see me. I didn't know I had invisible powers.

'Oh, hi,' she says, then frowns. 'Sorry, *who* are you?'

'Jessie,' I repeat.

'That doesn't answer my question.'

'Jessie likes your show,' Jack says calmly.

'Oh.' That seems to placate her, strangely.

'She's over here from England for a few days.'

'I love England!' she says, warm all of a sudden as she swings her legs over Jack's to face me. 'Which part?'

'Berkshire.'

She wrinkles her nose up.

'It's not that far from London,' I explain.

'I love London,' she says, her blue eyes widening. 'It's so pretty and so ...' She thinks for the right word and comes up with 'quaint.'

I'm not sure about that, but I'm too distracted to comment. I can't believe I'm sitting here talking to Charlotte Tremway.

She pats Jack's thigh and nabs his fag again. 'So how have you been, baby?'

'Yeah, I'm good. You know me.'

'Yes, I do.' She blows smoke over the top of his head and I seem to have invoked my powers of invisibility once more. I don't even want to know what she means by that comment. She certainly seems very comfortable with him.

'Are you all set for the seventh?' she asks.

166

'Pretty much,' he replies as he takes his cigarette back. 'My band's playing a gig on August seventh,' he tells me.

'Cool,' I say.

'*Way* cool,' Charlotte adds, not looking at me. 'I'm still working on getting you guys on my show.' She pats his thigh again.

'Charlotte, do you want a drink?' one of her friends calls from nearby.

'There in a minute,' she replies over her shoulder, in a bored-sounding voice.

Are all of the girls in LA complete bitches? Much as I'm a fan of the show, I really wouldn't mind if its leading actress buggered off right about now.

'So what's up with you?' Jack asks her, and I start to think that maybe it's time I went to find Meg and Johnny.

'Usual crap. C driving me insane. Mike being an A-hole. Did you know he's letting them kill off Bessie in this next series?'

'You know I don't watch it,' Jack replies, while I wrack my brain to think which character is called Bessie in real life. I give up. I can't be bothered to think right now and I find myself tuning out.

'Maps' by Yeah Yeah Yeahs is playing now. I lean my head back on the sunlounger and look up at the stars that are starting to appear overhead. I hum along.

'OK, you're starting to win back some of my respect,' Jack says. I realise his comment is directed at me.

'*You've* still got a long way to go,' I reply without missing a beat.

'How do you two know each other?' Charlotte interrupts with a frown, her eyes drifting to the slit up the side of my skirt and my bare midriff.

'We met tonight,' I tell her, sucking in my tummy as a

precaution. I am so not Hollywood skinny. At that point I see Lissa and Bryony on the terrace. They've spotted us.

'Charlotte!' Lissa calls.

Great, they're friends. Of course they are.

'Where the hell have you been?' Charlotte exclaims as she scrambles off Jack and hurries over to her.

Alone again. At last.

'Heart-Shaped Box' by Nirvana starts to play. Johnny looks a bit like a cleaner-cut Kurt Cobain, I muse. I should probably go and find Johnny and Meg soon. But I really don't want to leave Jack, yet . . .

'Your brother has got good taste in music,' I say, forcing Johnny and Meg out of my mind for a bit longer.

'Come meet him,' Jack says suddenly, standing up.

'OK.' I get up, touched that he wants me to meet his brother.

'You know, you still owe me a forfeit,' he says as we walk alongside the pool. 'I won the bet.'

'Yeah, yeah.' I brush him off. 'I told you I'm not getting naked or going into the pool in my underwear.'

'In that case . . .'

I scream as he sweeps me up in his arms and carries me a few steps to the pool. In a panic I hook my hands around his neck. 'Don't you dare!' I squeal. 'This is a Roberto Cavalli dress!' Not words I ever thought I'd say.

He grins. 'You can buy another one.'

'My dad got it for me!' And I've just realised I haven't even said thank you. What's Johnny going to think if I have to get back into the limo dripping wet? What will Meg think? That's what a rock-star wannabe would do. 'Don't you dare,' I warn again, more seriously.

'You owe me a forfeit,' he repeats, more slowly this time. I'm instantly aware just how very close his lips are to mine. Heat floods my body as I stare back into his eyes.

'JESSIE!' I start with surprise as I look past him to see Johnny standing on the other side of the pool. Jack sees him, too, and suddenly I'm back on my feet. 'We're going,' Johnny shouts, beckoning me over. He doesn't look too happy. My heart sinks for more reasons than one. I don't want to go, yet. And I don't want to piss off my new dad.

'You know Johnny Jefferson?' Jack asks with confusion, and I'm aware we have Charlotte, Lissa and Bryony's attention.

'Yeah,' I reply warily. 'He's ...' I don't want to lie. 'I'm ... I help out with their kids.' Well, it's sort of true.

'You're the nanny?' OK, he came to that conclusion himself. Not my fault. 'Lucky kids,' he adds, glancing over at Johnny.

I laugh weakly.

'If my nanny looked like you, I wouldn't be thinking about moving out.'

'You don't have a nanny,' I scoff, before I can register the fact that he was flirting with me.

'She's fifty-one, the size of a small car and she's looked after me since I was a baby. Are you calling me a liar?'

'You have a nanny?' I ask in disbelief.

'Yep.'

'Well, OK, then!' I say breezily, looking back over at Johnny. He coolly points to the terrace by the house and I nod my acknowledgement. Meg is there, too.

All of a sudden I feel very flat. 'Well, it was nice meeting you,' I manage to say.

'What are you doing tomorrow?'

My sinking heart does an about-turn.

'I don't know,' I reply. 'Probably not much.'

'Do you want to do something?'

I can't keep the smile from my face. 'Sure.'

He grins. 'Give me your number.'

I'm about to reel off my mobile when I remember it doesn't work here. I've been using Johnny and Meg's landline all week. 'I don't know what it is.'

'Are you trying to blow me off?' he asks warily.

'No! No, I swear I'm not. Give me your number and I'll call *you*.'

He looks bemused as he digs his hand into his pocket and pulls out his wallet. He extracts a card from inside.

'You have *business* cards?' I take it from him.

'You could do with some,' he replies with a wink, stuffing his wallet back into his pocket.

'I'll call you,' I tell him with a smirk, walking away, distinctly aware of the nearby girls watching me.

'You better,' he calls after me. 'Otherwise I'll track you down.'

By the time I reach Johnny and Meg, Johnny is tapping his foot impatiently.

'Ready to go?' Meg asks with a smile.

'Yep,' I reply.

I look back at Jack as I climb on to a waiting kart. Lissa, Bryony and Charlotte have swarmed him, but I know he's still looking at me, even as I turn away.

Chapter 16

'Good time?' Johnny asks when we're safely back inside Davey's limo. There's a sharpness to his tone and I'm not sure why.

'Yeah,' I reply.

'So you met Jack Mitchell.'

'Is that his surname? We didn't get that far.'

'You looked like you were getting pretty far to me.' He gives me a pointed look.

'Johnny,' Meg interrupts with a frown. 'Leave her be.'

'You don't need to fight my battles for me.' The words are out before I know it. Meg looks surprised.

'Hey, chill out, chick, no one's battling anyone,' Johnny quickly says, his green eyes narrowing with apprehension.

'Sorry, force of habit,' I reply, my face heating up. Meg looks a bit put out as she turns and stares through the window. I notice Johnny put a protective hand on her knee.

Suddenly I feel annoyed. And over the course of the short journey home, my bitterness grows and eats away at me. How dare he act like he cares about what I get up to? Why am I even here? He's not a father to me. He's no one.

No, sorry, *my* mistake, I think sarcastically. He's *Johnny Jefferson*. The *big celebrity*. *Somebody*.

But it feels like he's nobody to me.

I'm fuming by the time we get back to his house. Slam-doors fuming. Annoyingly, Davey is waiting to close the car door behind me, but the front door is *mine*.

BANG!

'What the hell?' Johnny spins around.

As soon as I do it, I realise that I might have woken Barney and Phoenix, but I pretend not to care. 'Sorry, didn't mean to wake your precious children,' I say sarcastically.

Meg's eyes widen with shock. She gives Johnny a significant look and sets off up the stairs. I know she's checking on the boys and relieving the babysitter, but I'm glad she left us to it. Now Johnny will have to face me himself.

'You've had too much to drink,' Johnny says calmly and it winds me up even more.

'Screw you!'

'You've only just got here and you're sounding like an American.'

I storm towards him. 'Would you rather I said fuck you? Fine. Fuck you!'

'Hey!' he raises his voice and I can see that I'm getting to him.

'Take it outside!' Meg hisses from the landing as a door upstairs opens and I see the concerned-looking babysitter venture out. I glare up at Meg and then Johnny stalks to the door leading out on to the terrace and slides it open. He points out-

172

side, his jaw twitching with irritation as he stares at me. I stomp across the living room and step over the threshold. He slides the door shut.

'What's up with you? I thought you had fun tonight. Why are you acting like a brat?'

'Why should you care?' I bite back.

'You're going to have to help me here,' he says with forced calm. 'I haven't had to deal with many teenage girls in my time.'

'My mum was just a teenager when you shagged her and got her pregnant. Do you ever think about *that*?'

He reels backwards and even in the low-level light I can see that I've stunned him. My heart is beating wildly. Where did that comment even come from? But it's about time we had a conversation about my mum.

He takes a deep breath, and I'm taken aback when he finally says: 'I *do* think about her.'

'What?' But my voice instantly sounds smaller.

'Just . . .' He looks worn out as he walks over to a chair and sits down, hunched-over with his elbows resting on his knees. He nods at the one opposite. 'Sit.'

I do as he says. 'So you really remember her?' I struggle to get the words out past the lump that has so swiftly lodged itself in my throat.

'Yeah, I remember Candy.'

It shocks me to hear him say her name. Stu made it sound like Mum was just another girl to him, but maybe there's more to the story. 'What . . . What happened between you?' I ask.

He sighs. 'She followed the band, you know?' His eyes are piercing in the light spilling through on us from the living room. 'She came to every concert before we made it big, and I'd see her right up at the front. Candy was hard to miss.'

'Why?' My voice comes out sounding like a whisper.

He meets my eyes. 'She was beautiful. Anyone could see that. But there was something else about her. She had a free spirit. I guess ...' He pauses, looking past me to the living room. 'I guess I was drawn to her.' He meets my eyes again.

I look over my shoulder through the floor-to-ceiling windows, but there's no one there. I wonder if Meg's gone to bed. I doubt Johnny would be being quite so open with me if she were around.

'What happened?' I ask, but he looks hesitant. 'I need to know.' I don't want to beg him. I shake my head and hot tears fill my eyes. 'She's not around any more to tell me.' The lump is colossal now, but I don't want to break down and detract from this conversation now that we're actually talking. It's too important and my time here is running out.

'Christ,' he mutters, getting to his feet. I watch him as he goes to the small outside bar area. He digs around in a cupboard under the counter for a bit and comes back with a packet of cigarettes. He pulls one out as he walks, popping it between his lips. He looks unhappy as he stands beside me and lights it, the glow from the flame adding to the light cast from inside. He sits back down.

'Meg is going to kick my ass,' he says in a low voice, his accent taking on an American twang that I've noticed comes through occasionally.

'Why?'

'I gave up.' He takes a long, slow drag and in a weird way he feels more familiar to me. This is the image I had of him in my head before we met. More rock star, less doting husband and father.

174

'Can I have one, while you're at it?'

He glances at me. 'It's a filthy fucking habit,' he says through a puff of smoke as he exhales.

'I know.' I hold my hand out, palm upwards, and he stares at it for a moment. Then he stubs out his cigarette.

'No, none for you, and none for me. Like I said, it's a filthy habit.'

He's trying to be responsible for me all of a sudden? Normally I'd be annoyed, but actually I'm strangely touched. 'Tell me about my mum,' I press.

'I noticed her at the first concert she came to.' I realise I'm holding my breath as he continues. He looks far away as he remembers. 'She was standing right at the front. It was dark, but I could see her. She was so into the music. I liked the way she danced, the way she lost herself . . .' He smiles wryly. 'When we slowed things down she just stood there and stared at me.' He shrugs. 'I couldn't take my eyes off her, either.' Pause. 'I thought about her after that night.' I'm transfixed, watching his face as he speaks. 'And then she turned up at the next concert.'

I picture the scene: the good-looking rock star singing a slow song to the beautiful young girl . . . It gives me shivers. No wonder she fell hard for him.

'Jesus, I could do with a drink,' he says.

'No, don't,' I warn.

He raises one eyebrow. 'Don't worry, girl, I'm not going to crack.'

'I didn't know you didn't drink. I mean, I know . . .' Hmm, this is embarrassing. 'I read about your drug addiction on the internet,' I admit.

'Yeah. I'm damned if I'm going to go there again.' He eyes his cigarette on the floor. 'Those bastards make me want to

175

drink. Drink makes me want to take drugs. I'm better off if I say no to the lot of it.'

'Come on.' He points over to the other side of the deck. He gets up slowly and starts to walk off, so I have no choice but to follow him. We walk around the swimming pool to the grey, polished concrete outdoor table and he slides across the bench seat, patting the space beside him. The city is sprawled out before us. It's a cloudless, starry sky and the moon is almost full. The glow from the moon and the far-off city lights illuminate Johnny's face in a muted glow.

'What happened at the next concert?' I ask.

He stares down at the view. 'It was concert number three.' I wait patiently for him to continue. 'She was there again, standing right at the front. It was in a bar, a smaller venue. Usually we'd head off after the gigs, go to a club or something, but this time I persuaded the guys to hang around. I saw her ordering a drink at the bar and went over.'

I'm holding my breath again. 'I want to know every detail,' I say firmly.

He indulges me. 'I didn't look at her as I ordered a whisky on the rocks, but I could sense her tensing up beside me. I turned to face her and said hi.' He grins and gives me a sidelong glance before looking back at the view. 'She broke eye contact first.' He chuckles again as the memory comes back to him. 'She always broke eye contact first.'

Funny that he should remember something like that.

'When did you have your first kiss?' I meant it when I asked for the details. It's weird because it's about my mum, but for some reason I need to know exactly what happened. Maybe I just need to know that she meant something to him.

'Aah . . .' He shifts awkwardly and pushes his hand through his hair. 'I tried that night.'

'She turned you down?' I ask with disbelief.

He starts to laugh. 'She put her hand, right here.' He gently punches his own chest. 'And told me, "I don't think so . . ."'

'You're shitting me? She didn't even let you kiss her?'

'She told me why later.' He shrugs. 'She said she knew I'd lose interest in her once she put out.' He smirks. 'Her words, not mine.'

'Was she right?'

'I don't know,' he says slowly. 'I don't know.'

'But you obviously kissed eventually.'

'Well, I was pretty pissed off that she turned me down.' He glances at me. 'But she kept coming to the concerts, kept standing right at the front with those big, doleful eyes of hers, and . . . I couldn't resist. We had a few . . .' His voice trails off, then he finds the word he's looking for: ' . . . *followers* at the time.'

'You mean groupies,' I say, disliking the term and what it stands for, but equally, not wanting him to lie to me.

He looks abashed, but doesn't correct me. 'There were a lot of girls. It was just as we were starting to make waves. Record companies were starting to show interest, talking about record deals. We weren't short of . . . *attention*.'

'Groupies,' I chip in again.

'Anyway,' he moves on. 'I know Candy could see it. I knew she was jealous, but still she kept coming, and, well, I started to think it was just the music she liked. Until one night I got a roadie to give her a backstage pass. I didn't know if she'd come back, but I was talking to a couple of blondes when she did and I remember the look on her face. I thought she was going to turn and bolt, but I caught her before she could.'

'What did she look like?' I ask. 'If you can remember . . .'

'Oh, I can remember. She looked freaking hot, that night.' He shoots me an apologetic look. 'Sorry.'

'It's OK, I want to know.'

'Well, she did,' he continues. 'She was wearing a sheer black top and jeans. She had her dark hair down and her eyes seemed bigger than usual. I wanted her bad.' He glances at me again, unsure if he's said too much, been too open. 'Are you sure you want to hear this?'

'Definitely,' I reiterate.

'I told her she was killing me.' Suddenly he looks agitated, rubbing his hand over his mouth and pushing his hair back again. 'I shouldn't have. I wouldn't have. I shouldn't have . . .'

'Shouldn't, wouldn't, what?' I interrupt impatiently. What's going through his mind?

'I screwed up, OK?' he snaps suddenly. 'I shouldn't have taken her back with me.'

'You regret sleeping with her?' I don't know why the thought hurts me so much.

'No. No.' He shakes his head, looking down. 'I don't regret that. She was beautiful. I liked her. A lot,' he says again, and I know he means it in more ways than one. 'It was what came afterwards that was so messed up.'

He scratches his head again and looks behind us to the bar. 'Christ, I want a drink.'

'No. Don't.' Am I pushing him too far?

He turns around. 'I won't.' He shakes his head again. 'I

178

won't,' he says again, more firmly this time. I sense he's talking to himself, more than he's talking to me.

'What happened afterwards?' I press gently.

He doesn't say anything for a long time. I try to be patient, but it damn near kills me. I see him swallow and I think he's hurting, but I can't be sure and it makes me realise that I still don't know him at all. Finally he speaks. 'Meg . . .' He jerks his head back towards the house. 'Before Meg, I was different. I didn't do commitment. If I liked someone, I pushed them away. I did that to . . . your mother.' He sighs. 'We hooked up a few times after that night, but then she started asking questions, started wanting some sort of commitment from me. So I told her it was just a casual thing, that she shouldn't go getting any ideas. She was angry. I knew she would be. I guess I proved her right. The whole reason she knocked me back in the first place.' He sighs. 'She left and I didn't think I'd see her again. It hurt, you know? More than I thought it would. But that same day we were offered a record deal, and by lunchtime we were offered another deal by an even bigger label. By the end of that week, our manager had been approached by four different record labels – all of them major – and they had a full-on bidding war over us. I didn't have time to think about Candy. I had to focus on Fence, on the guys, and making the right decision.'

I notice his leg is jigging up and down underneath the table. He bites his fingernail and stares up at the moon. 'We still had two more gigs to play on that tour before we had to start recording our debut album. The label we signed with wanted us to tour Europe, so there was a lot going on.'

'Did you see Mum again?' I ask.

'She came to the next gig. She turned up unexpectedly,

didn't call me to say she was coming. I was shocked because I thought she'd given up on me for good.'

'What happened? What did you say to her?'

His leg jigs more violently. He shakes his head quickly. A bad feeling settles over me. I remember Stuart telling me about this.

'You hooked up with another girl in front of her.'

He doesn't deny it. Then he nods quickly. 'And at the next gig?' I hardly dare to ask. He said he had two more gigs.

'She didn't come,' he says quietly. 'That was the last time I saw her.'

The lump is back, well and truly. I place my hand to my throat, but I can't get rid of it. I really need to cry. No, I need to sob. I want to bawl my eyes out for Mum and how she must have felt. How heartbroken she must have been.

Johnny swivels on the bench seat to face me. I don't want to look at him, but I do, and when I meet his eyes I'm surprised to see that his have filled with tears. 'Why didn't she tell me about you?' he asks sorrowfully. 'I don't get it. I know I screwed up. I know she must've been angry.'

'Heartbroken,' I correct him.

He looks miserable as he nods, conceding.

'But she still should have told me.' Now I detect an underlying edge to his tone. He glances at me. 'I had a right to know.'

'What would you have done?'

He looks away again. 'I don't know.' Then back at me. 'But you, me, we should have known each other. It's been *fifteen* years, Jessie.'

'Tell me about it,' I snap with a spark of irritation.

'Christ,' he mutters. 'First Barney and now you.'

'Barney?' I'm confused.

'Meg didn't tell me he was mine, either.'

I'm shell-shocked. 'You're joking. What? How long?'

'She was with someone else when we ... You know ...' His voice trails off again. Bloody hell, he really is something. The tabloids didn't need to exaggerate his reputation as a woman-iser at all. Then I realise what he's just said.

'She didn't tell you she was *pregnant?*' I ask with astonish-ment. I didn't think Meg was that ... God, I want to say devious, but I know Mum kept quiet about me, too.

'It wasn't her fault.' Johnny is quick to defend her. 'She didn't know the baby was mine. Christian was my best mate. She and I were together first, but I ... well, I did her over and ... Hell, you don't want to know all this stuff.'

Actually, I do. 'Tell me.' I remember him saying that Christian was coming to visit. Is it the same man? Surely not. I ask the question.

'Yeah,' Johnny tells me. 'It's all water under the bridge now. Meg didn't know about Barney being mine, not until he was older and he started to look like me.'

'He looks *just* like you,' I agree.

'She did the right thing in the end,' he says simply. I have a feeling that he makes it sound a lot simpler than it was. Maybe I should take Meg up on her offer to give me her side of the story sometime. But tonight is about Mum.

'Mum didn't tell you because she didn't want to lose me,' I say quietly. 'She thought I'd leave her. That I'd prefer to have ...' I look around. 'All of *this*, rather than the life *we* had.' I turn to stare at Johnny face-on. 'She was wrong.'

181

He meets my eyes for a long few seconds, then nods. 'I get it.'

'She was my mum.' Tears fill my eyes. 'Nothing would have made me choose you over her.'

He reaches over and places one hand on my shoulder. 'But you could have had us both.'

A tear rolls down my cheek and I brush it away. Another one immediately follows.

'I could have helped you,' he says. 'I could have helped *her*.'

I shake my head. 'She wouldn't have wanted your help. Not after what you did.'

'I would have apologised,' he says. 'Hey, I'm not saying I would have changed. It's taken me years of buggering up big time to do that,' he says cynically. 'But we could have had a relationship. You and I could have had a relationship.'

I sniff loudly and then laugh tearfully.

'At least we can have one now,' he adds, squeezing my shoulder and letting his hand drop.

I nod quickly, staring down at my hands resting on the table.

'It's late,' he says. 'You should get to bed. And I'd better go and face the music.'

'She won't really give you hell for smoking one cigarette, will she?' I ask with a frown, as we get up from the table.

'Do you know how much she's been going on at me to quit?' He raises one eyebrow. 'Nah, she'll be OK. She always is. And that's why I love her so,' he adds in a gently comic voice as we walk around the swimming pool towards the house.

His words make me smile, but the warmth I feel is followed by a prick of jealousy. I hope Meg knows how lucky she is. If

Johnny had felt that way about my mum, how different would my life be?

'So what about you and Jack Mitchell, hey?' The irked look is firmly back in place on his face.

'Do you know him?' I ask.

'I know his dad,' he replies.

Aah, OK. 'Well, Jack wants to see me again.'

'Does he, now?' Johnny does *not* sound amused.

'I'm going to call him in the morning,' I say, feeling a little torn, even as I say it. After waiting forever to meet my dad, am I really going to blow him off to spend part of my last day with some random guy? Erm, yes. Such is the problem with chemistry. Besides, now that we've finally had our heart-to-heart, I'm sure I'll see more of Johnny after this trip.

Perhaps Johnny senses my determination, because he doesn't argue. 'Just watch out for him,' is what he says. 'His dad Billy was worse than me, back in the day.'

'In what way?'

'He partied *hard*.'

'Who says Jack is like his dad?' I ask with mild provocation.

'The apple rarely falls far from the tree.'

'Speak for yourself,' I snap, but he winks at me. I take a deep breath, realising that he's teasing me.

'I'm going to lock up and switch the lights off down here,' he says as we go back inside. 'Go get some rest, it's pretty late.'

'OK.' I yawn widely, tiredness washing over me like a wave. Everything seems quiet upstairs. Meg must've gone to bed. I start to walk up the first couple of steps and then stop, remembering something. 'Johnny?' I call over to him as he locks the sliding door.

'Yep?' He flicks off a light and heads my way.

'I meant to say earlier, thanks for the dress.' The black lace Roberto Cavalli has made me feel special all night long.

'You're welcome,' he says with a warm smile. 'You look beautiful.'

I return his smile and carry on up the stairs, but I hear him murmur, 'Just like your mum.'

Chapter 17

I can hear Meg doing breakfast for the boys in the kitchen when I come out of my room the next morning. I have a headache and feel decidedly ropey from the booze I drank last night.

Eddie doesn't work on weekends, and I can't hear Johnny downstairs. He's probably still in bed after our late one. It's where I should be. Despite my exhaustion, I didn't sleep well. And thanks to my continuing jet lag, I'm still waking up at the crack of dawn. I'm sure I would have been able to doze off again if it weren't for my mind ticking over. So much happened last night. If it wasn't the conversation with Johnny playing over and over in my head, it was the conversation with Jack. Jittery nerves ripple through me when I think of him. I wonder if he was serious about catching up today. I'm still feeling torn. I know that I should probably forget all about him and spend my last day with my family, but I'm drawn to him and that's something I can't control.

I take a deep breath before I reach the kitchen.

'Hi,' I say meekly to Meg, staying where I am in the doorway.

'Hey.' She sounds less friendly than normal. She's feeding Phoenix in his high chair. Barney is humming away to himself as he munches his way through a bowlful of Rice Krispies.

'I'm sorry about last night.' I don't usually find apologies easy, but this one needs to be said. 'I didn't mean to kick off. I think I had a bit too much to drink,' I admit.

'It's OK.' She seems slightly appeased. 'Johnny said you had a bit of a heart-to-heart.'

'Yeah. I feel better after talking to him.'

'Good.' She smiles up at me.

I go over to the table and pull out a chair. She spoons another mouthful of cereal into Phoenix's waiting mouth. He looks like a little bird.

'I don't suppose you have any headache tablets?' I ask.

'In the cupboard next to the fridge.'

I get up and hunt them out, helping myself to a glass of water from the dispenser on the front of the fridge. It makes ice, too. I thought that was pretty cool when I found out.

'Help yourself to toast or cereal,' she says. 'Sadly, no Eddie today.'

I said goodbye to him yesterday. 'Actually, didn't he leave some pancakes in the fridge?' I ask.

'Did he?'

'He told me that he would, seeing as he wouldn't be here to cook my last couple of breakfasts.'

'Aw, that was sweet,' she says.

'Tell me about it.' I get up to look and there, on a plate in the centre of the fridge, is a stack of about ten thick, fluffy, American-style pancakes.

186

'Awesome.' I half laugh as I say this, pulling the plate out and showing it to Meg.

'Whoa,' she says.

'Pancakes!' Barney shouts, his eyes lighting up as he spies them.

'Will you guys have some?' I ask.

'Yeah, whack 'em all in,' Meg replies with a grin.

Johnny appears when we're down to the last few.

'Hey,' he says, leaning down to peck Meg on her lips.

'Urgh.' She grimaces and pulls away, giving him a dirty look.

'I'll come back when I've brushed my teeth,' he says with a wry grin, patting me on my shoulder as he strolls back out of the kitchen.

'I hate it when he smokes,' Meg mutters, pushing her plate aside.

'Yeah, sorry about that,' I say guiltily. 'I think that might've been my fault.'

'He's a big boy,' she replies darkly, but then her face softens. 'I can't complain too much. He's changed a lot for me.'

I remember what Johnny told me last night. About Christian. 'You still haven't told me how you went from being employed by Johnny to being married to him,' I say.

She glances at Barney. 'Hmm, yeah, I did say I'd tell you about that. But now's probably not the right time.' She ruffles Barney's head and gets up to clear the table. Story of my life. When is it ever the right time?

After breakfast I go and get Jack's card from my bedside table. I nearly had a fit this morning wondering where I'd put it because

187

I didn't take a bag last night, but then I remembered I stuffed it in my bra. It was still there this morning, looking slightly worse for wear.

Annie put a phone up in my bedroom after that first morning, so I don't have to go back downstairs to the office. I feel nervous as I pick up the receiver. Is this too early? It's only nine-thirty. Will I look too keen? Probably. Have I got anything to lose when I'm leaving tomorrow anyway? Probably not.

I stare down at Jack's card. It's black with yellow, scratchy-looking writing. Underneath his name it says 'All Hype', which I'm guessing is the name of his band. There's a mobile number, email address and web address.

Hmm. I know what will pass some time so I don't look too keen.

I skip downstairs and round the bend into the office. It's empty because Annie, like Eddie, doesn't work on weekends. I pull up a chair and switch on the spare desk's computer.

A quick internet search brings up several hits for Jack Mitchell, mostly photos of him in the band, snapped by fans. My heart flips as I click on one, revealing a hot and sweaty, but still undeniably sexy, Jack singing into a microphone with a guitar hanging on a strap around his neck. He's gorgeous. His black hair is wet with sweat, and his T-shirt is damp, too, but he radiates sex. I can see his POW! tattoo on the arm holding the mic, the leather wrist straps also visible. I wonder when this pic was taken? Only recently, I'm guessing. I'd love to see him play in person. I remember with a sting that Charlotte said he had a gig at the beginning of August.

Charlotte! I haven't even thought about her since last night. I can't believe I met Macy from *Little Miss Mulholland*! Libby would do her nut in. All of a sudden I feel sad. Sad and tired. How did I let us grow apart so badly? She was a good friend to me. When I get home, I really need to try and make it up to her somehow, but I have a horrible feeling that we'll never be as close as we were.

I sigh and click on another link. And at the sight of Jack looking drop dead gorgeous in yet another on-stage shot, some of my bad thoughts fly out the window.

I make it until ten-thirty before I call him. He sounds sleepy when he answers. My heart is pounding like a jackhammer.

'Hi, Jack? It's Jessie.'

'Jessie . . .'

Shit! He doesn't remember me! Have I got the wrong number? Was that a seven instead of a one on his card?

'Oh, Jessie!' he suddenly exclaims. 'Jessie from last night, right?'

'I said I'd call.' I try to sound casual.

'So you did.'

My nerves intensify. Did he definitely want me to? I press on. 'Have I woken you up? You sound half asleep.'

'I kind of actually still am.'

'You want me to call back later?'

'No, as wake up calls go, this one's pretty good.'

He sounds like he's smiling so I relax a bit. 'I'm glad to hear it.' Pause. 'Did you stay late last night?'

'Couple more hours.'

I wonder what he got up to. Whatever it was, I hope it wasn't with a girl.

'My bro got me on the decks,' he elaborates.

'Did he?' Phew. 'What did you play, One Direction?'

189

He laughs a deep, low laugh that sends a shiver up and down my spine. 'I would have played them for you if you'd stayed.'

'Bullshit,' I reply with a grin.

'Yeah, you're right.'

Warmth spreads through my belly.

'What are you doing later?' he asks.

'No plans for this afternoon.'

'I can't do this afternoon. I've got band practice. I forgot my sister persuaded my bandmates to play at her birthday party tonight.'

'She asked them without asking you first?'

'She knew I'd say no.' He says this fondly.

'Why?'

'You'll understand when you meet my sister.'

What's he saying? 'Er, when am I going to meet your sister?'

'At her party, tonight.' He says it like it's a sure thing.

I laugh. 'I haven't told you if I'm busy, yet.'

'Are you?'

'Well, I . . .' Shouldn't I be having a last dinner with Johnny and Meg? 'I'd better check with Johnny and Meg first. Make sure they don't need me.'

'OK,' he says slowly.

'But it should be fine,' I tell him quickly. I really, really want to see him again. And at least I can spend the day with Johnny, Meg and the boys. Barney and Phoenix will be asleep tonight, anyway.

'Cool.'

'Do you want to tell me your address?' I ask.

'I'll come and pick you up if you like.'

'That would be great. What time?'

'Seven-thirty? It will give me an excuse to get out of here.'

'Is that all I am to you?' I tease. 'An excuse to get you out of helping?'

'Oh, you're much more to me than that.'

What a flirt!

'See you later,' he says.

'Wait, don't you need my address?'

'I know where Johnny Jefferson lives. Everyone does.'

'OK, see you later.'

'Bye.'

I have the biggest smile on my face as I hang up. I flop back on to the bed and beam up at the ceiling. Thoughts of Tom flicker through my mind, making my smile waver. I wonder if he's thought about me much since I left. He's probably on his way to Ibiza where he won't be short of attention. I try to close my mind off to him – and my guilt along with it. I should live in the here and now while I can. It's been a long time since I felt happy and full of anticipation.

I glance out of the windows at the trees and the blue sky beyond. So how am I going to spend my last day with Johnny? Swimming pool. Easy. Better apply lots of suncream though. Sunburn is not an accessory I plan to utilise.

I climb off the bed and go to the tall white wardrobes, opening the one on the left. My bikini is three drawers down – freshly washed and laundered yesterday afternoon by Carly, one of the two lovely maids. The other maid, Sharon, is sweet, too. She tidied up my room and made my bed when I went down for breakfast. It's going to be a bit strange going back to my tiny house at home. I stand on the fluffy shagpile carpet and do a three-sixty degree turn around the room. Yep, it's going to be hard.

Johnny is watching TV when I return downstairs, my white sarong tied around my waist. It's a testament to how much more comfortable I feel around him now.

'Going for a dip in the pool. You fancy it?' I ask him.

'Um …' He looks pretty engrossed in whatever it is he's watching. Racing cars of some sort.

'I'll join you,' Meg says, coming out of the kitchen. 'Come on Johnny, it's Jessie's last day.'

'Yeah, alright,' he says, reaching for the remote and switching off the telly. 'Be out in a sec.'

I walk outside and stand for a short while on the warm stone, looking up at the sky. The day is not too hot, yet. It's perfect. I go and stand on the top step of the pool and stare down at the city. The sky is clear, the smog not too bad for a change. I glance over at the polished concrete bench table where Johnny and I sat last night. It seems so unreal: the party and then coming back here. I still feel very much like I'm in the middle of a dream, and right now I wish I had access to some strong sleeping tablets, because I don't want to wake up.

I step back out of the pool, take my sarong off and throw it on a sunlounger. Then I walk down to the deep end, take a deep breath, and dive.

After a while, Meg brings the boys out and gets them dressed and suncreamed-up beside the pool. Johnny appears and wanders to the pool hut, and I tread water and watch with amusement as he brings out all of the inflatable toys.

'You going to try and master the shark today, Jess?' he asks me.

192

'Only if you do the croc,' I reply.

Barney is dressed and ready so Meg lets him into the pool area. 'Can you take him, Jessie?' she calls.

'Sure.' I swim to the shallow end and stand up. 'You going to jump in?' I ask him.

'Yeah!' he shouts, putting his toes right at the very edge.

'One, two, three, go!' I shout and he leaps in, creating quite a splash. I laugh and grab his slippery little body and he giggles as I whizz him through the water.

I look over at Meg to see her smiling. She stands up with Phoenix and carries him into the pool, zooming him towards me as Barney takes off on his own towards her. I bounce up and down with Phoenix, making him giggle.

Johnny carries the crocodile over and stands on the edge, launching himself on to it and instantly upending himself. Barney laughs his little head off. I do too, and as I swim Phoenix through the water to his dad, I can't help but feel melancholic. It occurred to me at the beginning of this week that I am a part of this family. But only now am I starting to feel it. I'm going to miss this. I'm going to miss *them*. I really don't want to go home.

Chapter 18

'Be careful,' Johnny says. We're sitting in the living room and I'm playing with the spare iPhone he's leant me for tonight. I look up and see that he's serious. He nods at the phone. 'Davey's number is stored in there. He's expecting you to call him for a lift.'

'Jack might give me a lift back,' I reply with a frown.

'If it's Jack's sister's birthday, Jack will be drinking,' Johnny says with a pointed look. 'I'd rather just know you're using Davey,' he adds.

'OK,' I reply noncommittally, looking back down at the super-cool phone.

'Jessie.'

I look up again.

'Promise me you'll call Davey.'

'OK, OK, I'll call Davey!' I exclaim. Jeez.

He raises one eyebrow at me, but he looks amused.

'You look good,' he says. 'Nice T-shirt.'

I smile at him. 'Thanks for getting it for me.'

'Any time.' He rakes his hand through his hair and rests his arm on the back of the sofa. We're sitting beside each other as I wait for Jack. I'm nervous, but the iPhone – and Johnny's worrying – is taking my mind off things.

I read the boys a bedtime story a little while ago – my last one – and now Meg is putting them to bed.

We went for lunch this afternoon at a cute little café on Melrose Avenue, followed by a shopping spree. I felt like a princess, spoilt rotten. I think Johnny was trying to make up for lost time. Either that, or he's feeling guilty because I'm leaving tomorrow. He actually seemed disappointed that I'm choosing to spend my last night with Jack instead of him and Meg. I almost changed my mind, but Meg encouraged me to go out and enjoy one last night in LA with people my own age. More nerves ricochet through me. Jack's late . . .

I'm wearing skinny black jeans and a cream, grey and black fitted T-shirt with sparkling red graphics on the front. I'm going for the rock chick look and I hope I've made the right choice. If I arrive and they're all wearing ballgowns, I'm going to look like a right div. I've got my hair down and dishevelled, my eye make-up dark and glittery and my army-green strappy wedges on. Meg took me for a mini-pedi on our way home while the boys watched cartoons on the in-car DVD players, and my toenail polish is now dark red.

The buzzer goes, jolting me to life.

'There's your ride,' Johnny drawls, lazily getting to his feet.

'You're not seeing me to the door, are you?' I ask worriedly, as I stuff the iPhone into the new bag I bought earlier.

'I was going to, yes,' he replies with a funny look.

195

'Well, you can't. I'm supposed to be your nanny. You're hardly going to check up on me, are you?'

'Bloody hell,' he mutters, shaking his head.

'What? What would you rather I said?'

'I'd rather we just come the hell out with it and tell everyone you're my daughter.'

Hope surges through me. 'Really?'

Perhaps he thinks better of it. 'We'll talk about it soon,' he decides and I feel flat again. 'Be the nanny tonight.'

My eyes narrow as I regard him.

'Jessie, it's for your own good,' he says when he sees my expression. 'Once it's out there, your life will never be the same again.'

Hmm. I'm not at all convinced that's a bad thing.

'Trust me,' he implores. 'Come on, before he presses the buzzer again and wakes the boys up.'

'OK.' I start to walk past him.

'Oi.'

He grabs my arm and I jolt to a stop and stare up at him. To my surprise he wraps his arm around my neck and pulls me towards him, kissing the top of my head. 'Have a good time,' he murmurs, letting me go.

I smile warily and turn to walk into the hall, but my eyes are shining at his unexpected tenderness. I take a deep breath, opening the door before I have a chance to exhale. The sight of Jack standing there, leaning against a shiny black expensive-looking car, makes me want to gulp for more air.

He's even better looking than I remembered: tall, slim and tanned with ripped grey jeans and scuffed Chelsea boots. He's wearing a black T-shirt with a yellow drawing of a family of stick figures on the front, and his black hair is messy and falling down across his forehead again.

'Hey,' he says, grinning.

'Hi.' I reckon the butterflies in my stomach could practically fly me over to him. Maybe I won't risk it; I'll use my feet instead. I pull the door shut behind me and walk over to the car. He opens the door and I climb in, then he shuts it behind me. The interior is dark grey and smells of fresh leather. I can tell from the sign on the steering wheel that it's an Audi, but I don't know which sort. His family must be wealthy, that's what I'm thinking. And I guess they are – especially if they were invited to Michael Tremway's last night. I don't imagine he mingles with normal people. Like me. Am I out of my depth?

Too late to be thinking about that. Jack opens his door and climbs in, glancing across at me.

'Nice T-shirt.'

'Thanks.' I nod at his. 'Yours is cool, too.'

'My sister made it.' He starts up the car and sets off down the driveway. 'It's my one concession to making an effort for her birthday.'

'Is she a fashion designer?' I ask as we wind our way along the drive to the gates at the end.

'No, but she wants to be.'

'How old is she?'

'Sixteen last week.'

'Am I underdressed?' I ask as he slows down on the approach to the gates.

'No, you look hot.' He grins and nods up at Samuel in the security hut beside the gate door. The gates start to open and I wave at Samuel as we pass through.

197

'That's Samuel. He told me a good joke earlier,' I say, trying to keep my cool. Jack just said I look hot!

'Really?'

'You wanna hear it?'

'Sure.' He turns right on to the main road and we continue to wind up the hill.

'OK. A woman gets on to a bus with her baby. The driver says, "Urgh, that's the ugliest baby I've ever seen." Fuming, she goes to the back of the bus and sits down, complaining to the man next to her: "That driver just insulted me!" The man replies, "Go back up there and tell him off. Go on, I'll hold your monkey for you."'

Jack bursts out laughing. 'That's funny.'

'Told you. Want to hear another one?'

'Sure.'

'Went to the zoo. There was only one dog in it. It was a shitzu.'

He sniggers with amusement.

'OK, I've got one. A sandwich walks into a bar. The barman says, "sorry, we don't serve food."'

I giggle. 'Two goldfish in a tank. One of them says, "How do you drive this thing?"'

We carry on like this, and after a while I realise my nerves have gone. We're still winding our way through the hills – the road has levelled out a bit so we've stopped climbing. 'Where's the party?' I ask.

'It's at my house. Just up here.'

I can hear the music pumping before we see the house, but then we round a corner in the hill and there's a long, white wall surrounding a boundary with a red-tiled rooftop visible behind.

'Here we are.'

Quite a few cars are parked on the road, everything from Porsches to shiny new Beetles, and a couple more are pulling up behind us. Someone toots their car horn and Jack looks out of his rear-view mirror. He holds his hand up in a half wave and then reaches into the central compartment and pulls out some sort of remote. He presses a button and the white wall starts to slide open. I stare up at the sandy-coloured Spanish-style villa on the hill. It looks enormous. His family must be *mega* wealthy. What does his dad actually do? Johnny said he knew him – that he used to be wilder than him. Why didn't I think to ask Johnny what he did? Whatever it is, one thing's for sure, Jack and I are from two very different worlds.

OK, maybe technically not any more. Now I know that I'm Johnny Jefferson's daughter I should fit right in, but all this extravagance is not me. I feel daunted.

But wait. Jack thinks I'm a nanny. That's pretty ordinary, right? And he still invited me. So he must not care about all this material stuff.

My head is buzzing with all of these thoughts and I'm so preoccupied that I don't immediately notice the girl in a short pink dress, standing on the driveway in front of what looks like a six-car garage.

'I'm in trouble,' Jack murmurs.

'What? Who is she?' She has an edgy black-haired bob, is wearing thick black eyeliner and hot-pink lipstick and she doesn't look happy.

Please don't let her be his ex-girlfriend, or even worse, his current girlfriend.

'That's Agnes.'

199

'Agnes?' Isn't that the girl that Charlotte mentioned yesterday?

'My sister.'

The relief is short-lived. As soon as he pulls up in front of her, she stalks to his door and yanks it open. 'Where the hell have you been?'

'Chill out, sis,' Jack says calmly. 'I just went to pick up Jessie.'

'Jessie?' She's glaring as she peers into the car, but she jolts with surprise when she sees me.

'Oh! I couldn't see you with the sun reflecting off the car,' she says.

'Agnes, meet Jessie, Jessie meet Agnes,' Jack says slowly.

'Hi,' I say weakly. 'Happy birthday.'

'Humph.' She straightens back up again and Jack flashes me an apologetic look.

'Am I gatecrashing?' I whisper, feeling nervous again as he unclicks his seatbelt.

'No!' he brushes me off and climbs out of the car. Warily, I do the same.

'Miles, Eve and Brandon have already set up,' she tells Jack crossly.

'Sounds like they've got it all under control,' he replies smoothly as I make my way around the front of the car to the two of them on the other side, nearest the house.

'Why didn't you tell me what you were doing?' she asks irately, while I hang back a few feet.

'You were busy getting ready.' He puts his hands on her shoulders. He's taller than her by about four inches. 'Relax.'

The glare on her face wavers and for a split-second she looks like she's going to cry. But then the glare is firmly reinstated.

'Are you wearing that?' she indicates his T-shirt and then stares back up at his face.

'Yeah. It's my favourite.'

'Whatever,' she snaps, but even as she turns away from him she looks slightly mollified. She glances at me and gives me a quick once over. I have a horrible feeling I'm not dressed at all right, but it's too late now. She stalks off towards the house. 'Go and check on the band,' she snaps over her shoulder.

'Yes, Ma'am,' Jack replies. He looks at me and rolls his eyes. 'I warned you.'

Erm, he didn't really warn me *that* much.

'Are you sure I'm OK to be here?' I ask worriedly, as he comes to stand by me.

'It's my house, too. Come on.'

He points his keys at the car and it beeps as he locks it. He doesn't walk across the tiled courtyard towards the intricate-carved, wooden front door. Instead he leads me around the right-hand side of the Spanish-style villa, underneath shady, fat palm trees and beside greenery bursting with pink, orange and red flowers. The view is in front of us as we emerge from the side of the house, and it's of the city, similar to the view from Johnny's.

The garden steps downwards – a flat expanse of green lawn and then a steep slope, followed by two more flat expanses and two more steep slopes. There is a large rectangular swimming pool on the first flat expanse, set within a terrace of peachy-coloured floor tiles and enormous potted palms. Hot pink and yellow flower-shaped candles are floating on the blue water. A bunch of cool kids are milling about the terrace and garden, laughing and chatting and drinking colourful cocktails. I spy a bar laden with drinks near the pool, with two young guys wearing black T-shirts serving. To our right is what looks like a smaller house in the same style of architecture, but then I realise the music is coming from there. I can see a bunch of people through the four wide-open double doors.

'Game room,' Jack tells me. 'I'm just going to make sure the guys are all set up.'

Labrinth's 'Earthquake' is blaring out of huge speakers outside the games room as I follow him over there, the beat pumping through my body.

'Who's DJ-ing tonight?' I shout.

'A few of us,' he shouts back. 'I've gotta do a set, too.'

'What about your brother?'

'Not here tonight.'

What? Not at his sister's birthday? That seems a bit weird. But we reach the double doors and Jack's mates spot him, so I don't get a chance to quiz him further. One guy takes a running jump and practically lands on him. A few others swarm around him, backslapping him and doing complicated handshakes.

Jack laughingly shoves off the guy who did the running jump and is still half hanging around his neck. He's dressed in a grubby-looking white T-shirt and skinny jeans with a metal studded belt. His light-blond hair is styled in a slick quiff and he looks like he could be a member of the band. I spot one of the guys from the fairground last night. He breaks away from Jack and goes over to a drum kit on a raised platform. Yeah. He does look like a drummer.

It's then that I notice the absolutely stunning, skinny, dark-skinned girl standing on the platform adjusting the mic stand. She has slick, shiny black hair combed into a boy cut and she keeps furtively glancing at Jack, but she doesn't go over. I watch Jack and see the blond guy saying something in his ear. They both glance at the girl, but now she appears to be steadfastly ignoring them.

Uh-oh. I have a bad feeling about this.

Then Jack seems to remember me. He looks over and as he does so, the blond guy throws one arm around his neck. Jack good-naturedly smacks him in his stomach and he lets go again, but he follows Jack over.

The music is not as loud in here because the outside speakers are facing the garden.

'Jessie, Jessie, Jessie,' the blond guy says playfully, winking. His eyes are deep blue and he's very good-looking. He leans forward and shakes my hand. He's tall – as tall as Jack – and he has a tattoo of a seagull on his right shoulder.

'This is Brandon,' Jack says with a wry grin, as Brandon straightens back up.

'You're in the band,' I say. I remember Agnes saying Brandon, Miles and . . . Eve. Oh. I look at the girl on the stage again. That must be her. 'Earthquake' comes to an end, followed by an unnatural silence.

'Crap!' Brandon curses, running away from us over to some DJ decks.

'What an idiot,' Jack mutters, smiling, as Brandon hurries to put another record on.

'What does he play?' I ask, glancing at Eve and unfortunately catching her eye. She quickly looks away.

'Bass guitar. He sings a bit.'

'What about you?' I ask.

'Lead.'

'You sing, too?' I remember seeing the picture of him with the microphone touching his lips. Sigh.

'A little. But it's mostly Eve.' He looks over at her and back to me. Does he seem guilty?

'Shall we get a drink?' I ask. I think I'm going to need one to get through this party.

It turns out the cocktails by the pool are piss-weak, but Jack tells me he has a sneaky bottle of whiskey in his bedroom. The house inside is big, albeit smaller than Johnny's. There's a large living room, which is in keeping with the Spanish villa style of the place. The rooms are crowded with a lot of dark-wood furniture, and there are carpets, curtains, cushions and rugs throughout, in contrast to Johnny's minimalist pad. Old-fashioned artwork in ornate frames hangs on the walls. Again, I wonder what Billy Mitchell does. This does not look like a wildman's pad.

'Where are your parents tonight?' I ask as Jack leads me up the wooden staircase.

'My mom and dad are divorced,' he tells me over his shoulder. 'Mom and Tim will be around somewhere.'

'Is Tim your stepdad?'

'Stepdad Number Two,' he says drily, turning left at the top of the stairs. We walk a little way along the corridor – there appear to be about six bedrooms up here – and he opens the second door on the left.

I follow him in. This is more like it. His bedroom doesn't resemble the rest of the house at all. Posters of indie-rock bands line the walls and his clothes are draped over the bed and the back of a chair. Books have toppled over on his bookshelves and the wardrobes are half open, with the contents spilling out on to the floor.

'You don't have a maid, then,' I joke.

'Actually we do.' He purses his lips together as he looks over at me. 'She's been ill since Thursday.'

'Bummer.' I'm being sarcastic.

'Tell me about it.' I think he is too. But then again, I don't know him that well.

He opens one of his drawers and roots around, pulling out a bottle of whiskey. I go over to the window and look out. He has a view over the garden and the city beyond. People are dancing by the pool now. Oh no, is that Lissa?

'Please tell me that's not Lissa,' I say.

A second later he's right by my side, his arm brushing against mine and making my hairs stand on end.

'That's her,' he says.

'Damn.'

He laughs softly. 'She was quizzing me about you when you left last night.'

'What? Why?'

'When she saw you leaving with Johnny Jefferson.'

My heart skips a beat. 'What did you tell her?'

'Nothing.'

He cracks the bottle open and takes a swig, grimacing slightly as he swallows. He offers the bottle to me. I take it hesitantly. 'Don't you have any Coke?'

'Whiskey *and* coke? You are a bad girl,' he says in a slightly dirty voice that sends shivers up and down my spine again.

'I don't mean that sort of coke.' I pull a face. 'Coca-Cola, you idiot.'

He laughs. 'I know. Yeah, I'll get you something soft to go with it.' He rummages around in his top drawer again and pulls out a small hip flask, filling it up to the brim.

'Go on, then, I'll have a quick swig,' I decide, nicking the bottle from him. I knock some back. Urgh, it tastes disgusting! 'How can you drink it straight?' I ask, coughing.

He laughs and puts the cap back on. 'I'm hardcore.' He pockets the hip flask and I catch a glimpse of his tanned, toned navel before he tugs his T-shirt back down. Phwoar! 'Come on.'

I'd prefer to stay here alone with him, but I suppose it *is* his sister's party . . .

We go back out into the corridor to the stairs, just in time to see a woman reach the top.

'Hi, you!' she exclaims brightly. She looks to be about forty or so and is wearing a medium-length, multicoloured print dress.

'Hey, Mom.' Do I detect a slight weariness to his tone?

'Who's this?' she asks, looking past Jack to me.

'Mom, this is Jessie. Jessie, this is my mom.'

I quickly step beside him to say hi. She's slim and tall with a wide smile and dark wavy hair that comes almost to her waist. 'Hello, Jessie,' she says pleasantly, then to Jack, 'Hurry on downstairs. Agnes was looking for you earlier.'

'OK, Mom.' Definitely weary.

We step back while she passes us and heads along the corridor. Jack looks at me and rolls his eyes as we start to walk down. What's the deal with them? I think she seems nice.

We grab a couple of soft drinks on our way past the bar and Jack ducks behind a potted palm to top them up with whiskey. I try to keep a straight face as I wait for him. I look over to see Agnes talking to Lissa by the pool, along with that other girl from last night, Bryony.

Jack reappears and Agnes chooses that moment to notice him. She calls and beckons him over. He takes a large gulp as we walk and I follow his lead. Whoa. I instantly feel light-headed. That was quick.

Lissa is saying something to Agnes as we approach. She's looking me up and down. Bryony turns around to scrutinise me, too, and I groan inwardly. I'm not sure any boy is worth this much girl bitching.

To my surprise, Lissa's face breaks out into a huge smile as we reach them, and her delight seems directed at me. 'You're Johnny Jefferson's nanny?'

Oh, shit.

'You told her.' Jack sounds accusatory as he speaks to his sister.

Agnes looks guilty, while Lissa looks put out. 'Is it a secret?' she asks me.

'Erm, no, not really.'

'So, who's looking after the kids tonight?' she asks.

'Meg and Johnny,' I reply cagily.

'What are they like?' Bryony chips in eagerly.

'Would you quit with the inquisition?' Jack snaps. 'Haven't you ever heard of a confidentiality clause?'

Lissa looks back at me and I shrug. Yeah, I bet Johnny's staff would have had to sign one of those. Come to think of it, I'm surprised they didn't ask *me* to sign one, although I would have been pretty pissed off if they had . . . I'm family, not staff.

Jack takes my hand and drags me away from the gaggle of girls.

I barely register the warmth of his grasp before he lets go. 'I'm going to have to go and check on Brandon soon. He wants me to play my set next, but let's just chill out for a bit.'

We reach the steep slope leading to the second, lower level.

Jack jogs down, holding his drink aloft, and turns to look back up at me.

'I'm not sure my wedges will survive.' I kick up my feet to show him my shoes.

'I'll catch you,' he promises.

'Oh, you know all the lines,' I joke, but inside I'm swooning. I edge down the slope and then let momentum take over and run the rest of the way, trying not to spill any of my drink, but failing. He steadies me at the bottom and my laughter falters as I look up into his blue-grey eyes, my hand wet from sticky liquid that has sloshed over the side. To my embarrassment, I can't help blushing.

I pull away from him and shake my hand dry, then set off across the grass. There's nobody down on this level – they're all up by the pool or over by the games room – but we walk to the next slope anyway, sitting a few feet down and facing the city.

'So Agnes is sixteen. How old's your brother?' I ask, nursing the remains of my whiskey-spiked cola.

'Twenty.'

'What's his name?'

'Drew.'

Drew. Why does that name sound familiar? 'Oh, Charlotte mentioned him at Michael's party.'

'Yeah.'

'Any other brothers or sisters?'

'Nope.' He glances at me and raises one eyebrow. 'This is a lot of small talk for someone who's going home tomorrow.'

'What would you rather do?'

He grins cheekily.

'Sorry, pal, I'm not that easy.'

But right now, I wish I were. I take a sip of my drink and grimace. Even with the Coke, it tastes like shit. He chuckles and looks away. His side profile is so sexy.

'It's just the three of us,' he reveals. 'There are two years between each of us. My parents were meticulous about pregnancy planning.' He takes a large gulp of his own drink, but doesn't pull a face. 'What about you?' he asks.

'I'm an only child. My stepdad can't have children.'

'No dad on the scene?'

Eek! 'Yeah, he's around.' And then I suddenly remember Barney and Phoenix. 'Actually, he has two kids of his own, so I have half-brothers.'

'You forgot you had half-siblings?' he asks with amusement.

Whoops. 'He's only recently remarried.' I quickly change the subject. 'What about your parents? When did they split up?'

'They got divorced about eight years ago.'

'And your mum has remarried twice since then?' I'm unable to keep the surprise from my voice.

'Things were messed up for a long time between my parents,' he says. 'This conversation is getting a bit heavy.'

I fall silent, trying not to feel snubbed. I take a large gulp of my drink. The sooner it's gone and I can get something else, the better.

'Sorry,' he says abruptly, picking up on my mood. 'I don't really like talking about it.' He sighs and falls back on his elbows, sliding his feet further down the slope so that he's stretched out. 'It's just that my dad was a bit of a bastard back in the day. Mom used to put up with a lot of crap. But I don't think he ever expected her to call it quits, to find someone else and file for divorce.'

What, so now he's opening up to me? 'Was that Stepdad Number One?' I ask tentatively.

'Yeah. She and Rob only lasted a year, though. Then Dad came back on the scene, screwed around a bit more before she moved on again with Tim. He looks after her, which is what she needs – someone reliable. And rich.' He doesn't look happy. 'They've been married for four years now.' He delves into his pocket and pulls out a familiarly crumpled cigarette packet. 'Damn,' he mutters, realising he only has one.

'What does your dad actually do?' I finally get around to asking the question as he lights up.

'He's a singer.' He inhales. 'Used to be in a band.'

'Which one?' I watch him blow out the smoke and fight the temptation to ask him for a drag. After hearing what Johnny said last night about smoking, I'm starting to think it would be cooler to quit. The usual predictable lecture takes on a whole different meaning when it comes from one of the world's most legendary bad boys.

'Casino Girl?' He says it like it's a question, but he doesn't need to.

'I know them. My mum used to play their music.'

'They haven't done anything for a while,' he tells me.

'Johnny told me he knew your dad,' I say.

'Yeah, they know each other. Dad hung out with him and his crowd for a while, back around the time Johnny went solo.'

'And your mum put up with him messing around?'

He pauses. 'Mmm. Agnes has been pretty screwed up over it. She won't talk to Dad these days.'

'Oh. That's hard.'

'Yeah.' He falls silent, staring at the view. 'Drew chose to live with Dad, so Agnes doesn't speak to him, either.'

So that's why he's not here tonight. 'That must be really tough on you,' I say.

'It sucks,' he says sombrely. 'I hate being caught in the middle.'

'I can imagine.' So that's why his sister was so keen for him to be at her party. He's effectively her only sibling. She must depend on him a lot. I feel a wave of pity for her.

'I don't know why I'm talking about this,' he admits suddenly. 'I don't normally.'

'Maybe it's because I'm going home tomorrow. You won't have to see me again, so it's easy.'

'Hmm. Maybe.' He looks across at me and my heart flips at the serious expression on his face. He looks at my lips and my heart begins to flutter.

'Jack! There you are!'

We whip our heads around to see Brandon standing above us. 'You missed your DJ set, bro. Ryan swapped with you, so you're on later, now.'

'Oh, right. OK.'

'Agnes wants us to kick off soon. You ready?'

'Yeah.' He gets up, and I do the same, dusting dead grass off my jeans. I wish we could stay here, just the two of us. Brandon flashes me a mischievous smile. 'Sorry to drag him away, but he's in demand tonight.'

Jack's raised eyebrow at Brandon doesn't go unnoticed. I wonder if there was a double meaning to his 'in demand' comment. Is he talking about other girls? The thought makes my heart sink, but I won't be around after tonight, so I guess it's not really anything to do with me.

211

Chapter 19

I lean against the wall, keeping out of the way as I watch Jack and his bandmates hook themselves up to their equipment on the small stage. It's pretty packed in here, now. More people have arrived and even more have come across to the games room from the pool terrace. I'm paying particular attention to Eve and the way she and Jack seem to be avoiding eye contact. They haven't even said two words to each other since we turned up. I'm almost certain there's something between them.

'If you're the nanny, how come you went out with Meg and Johnny last night? Who was looking after the kids?'

Oh, God, it's Lissa again. She leans against the wall beside me. I turn my head to face her, thinking on my feet. She just doesn't want to let this go.

'They got someone else in to help because they thought it might be nice for me to have a last night off,' I tell her calmly.

'But this is your last night,' she points out.

'They're very kind,' I say sweetly.

The space is suddenly filled with the almost deafening strains of an electric guitar and I shoot my head around to see Jack, Brandon and Miles rocking the stage, while Eve nods her head to the music and hangs coolly off the mic stand. The party crowd has gone berserk. Agnes, in her hot pink dress, is standing right at the front, holding her arms aloft and jumping along to the beat. Eve stills and starts to sing staccato lyrics into the mic, pulling away and nodding her head while the music punctuates her words. Jack catches my eye and winks. I grin back up at him.

'You know he's only into you because you're leaving, right?'

Is she still here? I turn to face Lissa, wanting to put an end to her know-it-all attitude. 'So Jack doesn't do commitment? Well, that's good, because neither do I.'

Not strictly accurate … OK, I haven't had a proper serious boyfriend, but that's not because I don't want one. Tom pops into my mind again, but even the memory of him doesn't take the sting out of Lissa's comment. Not that I want her to know that she's got to me. I meet her gaze. My comment seems to have thrown her.

'You're suited for each other then,' she says, huffily flicking her platinum blonde hair back off her face.

Job done. Without another word, I push off from the wall and immerse myself in the dancing crowd – then I let myself go to the music.

They play five songs, all of them potential hits in my opinion. The crowd moans when they finish playing, but the DJ almost instantly pipes the music back up again. Jack lifts his guitar strap over his head and props the electric guitar up against the wall, then jumps down from the stage, his eyes on me. Agnes catches him first, throwing her arms around his neck.

I notice with a jolt that Charlotte Tremway is also here. She has her hand on Brandon's chest and is staring up at him with a flirtatious smile. He sure doesn't seem to mind. She pulls away and turns to Agnes and Jack, grabbing Jack's face in her hands and pressing a kiss right on his lips. My insides prickle with jealousy and my eyes somehow find Eve in the crowd. She's seen them, too, and I turn to watch her push her way through the people dancing and exit through the games room doors.

Before I have a chance to process what I've just seen, I feel someone's hands on my hips. I look over my shoulder to see that it's Jack.

'Hey,' he says.

I swivel round to face him, my emotions all muddled up. He grins down at me, seemingly unaffected by all the attention he's getting. I don't know what to think. I don't like that he's got a terrible reputation, but even that doesn't stop me from being unbelievably attracted to him. He starts to dance with me and he's so close and hot and sexy that I make an impulsive decision. I'm just going to enjoy tonight. Tomorrow all of this will be irrelevant, anyway.

'I've got to go and do my set,' Jack shouts in my ear after a while, his hand on my waist. He nods towards the DJ decks set up on the other side of the room. 'You wanna come and help me?'

'Are you kidding?' I grin up at him.

He smiles at me and takes my hand, making me feel even more jittery as he pulls me through the crowd. A couple of times he's accosted by girls who are way too tactile for my liking, and who clearly pretend I'm not there. Jack is friendly, but not flirtatious and he doesn't let go of my hand. We finally make it to the decks and he lets go to greet his mate, a tall, sandy-haired guy with headphones on. I recognise him from last night. Jack pats his chest and nods at me.

'You remember Jessie?'

'Hey, Jessie. Morgan,' he says. That's right. He takes the headphones off and passes them to Jack. Jack pulls me behind the decks as Morgan ducks away. Jack rifles through the records and quickly pulls one out of its sleeve, being careful not to dirty it with fingerprints. He swaps it over with the one on the right-hand deck, and as the record on the left approaches its end, he expertly speeds his own choice up so the beats melt into one. Then he flicks a switch and his own song – 'I'm Not Going To Teach Your Boyfriend How To Dance With You' by Black Kids – seamlessly takes over.

OK, I really want him to kiss me now.

He nods at the records, indicating for me to take a look, and I dance along to the song as I rifle through them. I have no idea how to work the decks – although looking at him do it, I *really* want to learn – but for now I'll stick to helping with song choices. I stop when I come to the Wombats and my heart flips at the smile Jack gives me.

It's the most fun I've ever had in an hour, and the time passes way too quickly. All too soon, Miles arrives to take over.

Despite the laidback atmosphere, I'm feeling ridiculously strung out. I fancy Jack so much and I know I'm going to be on edge until his lips are on mine, but I know I have to chill out if I don't want to put him off. Jack pulls me into the crowd and I let my inhibitions leave me and drape my arms around his neck as we dance. Out of the corner of my eye I can see Charlotte and Lissa looking over at us, but I don't care. Right now it's just Jack and me.

I stare up into his blue-grey eyes, which look darker in this light, and he stares right back at me as every nerve ending in my body stands on edge. It's like there's an electric current between us. His toned chest presses up against mine and I feel his muscles ripple underneath his T-shirt as he moves. Then his fingers are in my hair, his palm cupping my jaw as he bends down and kisses me. My stomach cartwheels over and over as my lips open, our tongues touching as our kiss deepens. He's such a good kisser. I feel dazed as he pulls away, his face still close to mine.

'Shall we go to my room?' His question comes with meaning and I'm a little shocked. I am *not* that sort of girl – I've never been with a boy in that way and I'm not about to lose my virginity to someone I've only just met – but God, I want to be with him alone, away from all this female attention.

'Sure,' I breathe, as he tugs me away, a sense of urgency in his grasp as we storm out of the games room. Neither of us speaks as we cross the pool terrace. I'm vaguely aware of eyes following us, and I try to tell myself not to care what they think because tomorrow I'm gone and I'll never see them again, but I still feel a little anxious.

It's quieter inside the house. Jack lets go of my hand as we go up the stairs and my trepidation increases as we arrive at his bedroom door. I follow him inside and wait uncertainly by the door as he pulls the curtains shut. His movements slow, become more deliberate as he turns on his side light and pulls an iPhone out of his pocket. A beat fills the room like a heartbeat as the dark and moody strains of Placebo's 'Running Up That Hill' begin to play out of the speakers on the desk.

Jack comes my way unhurriedly, reaching his arm past me to the door. I step aside, sick with excitement and nervous energy as he turns the lock. And then his hands are in mine, intent in his eyes as he leads me to the bed.

'I'm not ... I can't ...' I stutter, all of a sudden unsure of myself and what I've got myself into.

'I just want to kiss you again,' he murmurs, and then his lips are on mine, his hands in my hair and I fall down to the bed with him, wanting nothing more than to kiss him back.

No, I want more than that ... I'm lying if I say otherwise. But I can't. I barely know him. He eases himself on top of me, his body weight crushing mine in the most deliciously pleasant way. His leg slides between mine and I feel a dart of desire as I realise that he wants me, too. I can feel him. Oh, Jesus, we'd better stop now.

A phone starts to ring and he reluctantly breaks away from me.

'It's yours,' he says, looking down at my bag.

What? Who's calling me at this hour? He rolls off me and I climb off the bed and grab my bag, digging around and pulling out the ringing iPhone. Eh? It's Davey.

'I thought you didn't have a phone,' I hear Jack say.

'I borrowed it for tonight,' I quickly reply. 'Hello?' I answer breathlessly. My lips feel swollen.

'Hello Miss Pickerill,' Davey says warmly. 'I'm outside the gates, waiting for you.'

'But I thought I was going to call *you*.' I grab Jack's wrist and check the time on his watch. Blimey. It's one o'clock.

'Mr Jefferson said I should collect you now.'

You have got to be kidding me. Johnny's worse than Stu. At least at home I could stay out and just sneak in.

'Shall I come inside to find you?' Davey asks, and I detect an authority to his tone that I haven't witnessed before.

Disappointment and resignation swirl through me. 'No, I'll come out,' I tell him.

'I'll see you in five minutes.' That sounds like a warning.

'OK.' I end the call and turn to look at Jack. 'My ride's here,' I say regretfully.

'I could've given you a lift home,' he says with a frown, propping himself up on his elbows.

I give him an unimpressed look. 'You've been drinking.'

He sighs heavily with discontent as I stuff my phone back into my bag and hang it over my shoulder.

'You going to see me out?' I prompt.

'Of course. Yeah.' He jumps up and I go to the door. I feel his warm hand on my back and then he's leaning past me to unlock the door. I glance over my shoulder again and then his lips are on mine and we're kissing with a passion I've never experienced before in my life. It makes me feel giddy. As he breaks away and stares down at me, I'm overcome with the urge to cry. I bite my lip and turn away. He doesn't touch me as we walk back downstairs.

'This way,' he says in a low voice, taking me to the front door. He opens the door, pressing a button on a buzzer beside it. I hear the sound of the automatic gates sliding open.

'I can see myself out,' I say, not wanting Davey to spot Jack and make any assumptions, however right they may be.

'OK,' he says, a pained look on his face. 'I don't want you to go,' he mutters, pulling me to him.

218

Our last kiss is so sweet.

Tears fill my eyes as I walk away, trying not to look back.

'Bye, Jessie,' he calls.

I spin on the soles of my feet and walk the last couple of steps backwards.

'Bye, Jack. I'll see you round.'

But I know that I won't.

I try to fix the sight of him standing in the doorway into my mind as I flash him one last smile. I round the corner to the waiting limo, trying to swallow the lump in my throat as I see Davey get out of the car.

'Miss Pickerill,' he says, opening the door for me.

I don't let myself cry until I'm safely inside.

Chapter 20

I sob myself to sleep that night and I'm still miserable when I come to the following morning, my eyes stinging and puffy. For the first time in a very long time, my tears are not for my mum. There's a strange relief in that, even though the pain is still acute.

I lie there for a while and stare up at the ceiling. It's early, but I won't be able to fall asleep again. I don't want to go home. It's too soon. I've only just met my new family. I have a dad! And I have half-brothers who I barely know. I don't want to play a minor part in their lives. I want them to know me. I want them to know I'm their big sister. I feel a fondness when I think of them, a fondness which I'm certain will develop into proper blood-is-thicker-than-water-style love. I want to watch them grow and not feel like a stranger every time I come to visit.

And then there's Jack . . . I've only just met him, but he's got right under my skin and I hate that we're over when we've barely even started.

I'm still close to tears when I venture downstairs for my final breakfast. My flight is at two o'clock. I can't bear to pack my bags yet. My clothes probably aren't all going to fit anyway, not after the shopping sprees I've been taken on. It feels like we went to Melrose Avenue days ago, but so much has been packed into these last couple of days, and last night was a long one.

A shiver goes through me as I remember Jack's lips on mine, his body pressed up against me. My whole body tingles as I think about kissing him, touching him. I bite my lip with nervous exhilaration as I imagine what might have happened if Davey hadn't called. How far would we have gone? And how much willpower would I have needed to tell him to stop?

Meg and the boys are having their usual breakfast, and Johnny is also drinking a cup of coffee at the table when I mope into the kitchen.

'Hey, kid,' he says.

'Hi!' Meg exclaims. 'How was your night?'

'Shorter than I wanted it to be.' I give Johnny a pertinent look, but he shrugs innocently.

I pull out a chair and slump into it.

'You want me to get you something?' Johnny asks casually, the first time he's offered since I got here.

'No, I'm not hungry.'

'You been drinking again?' He raises one eyebrow.

'That's not why I'm not hungry,' I mutter.

I glance over at Phoenix opening his little bird mouth as Meg feeds him. Barney pretends his spoon is a plane as it crashes into his cereal.

'Barney, don't make a mess,' Meg chides, and the urge to cry overwhelms me.

I shove my chair out from the table and rush out of the room. The sliding doors are open wide – the warm morning air wafting into the living room. I hurry outside and give up – I can't fight my tears. I walk across the terrace and let my sobs take over.

'Hey, hey,' Johnny says gently from behind me. 'Jessie, what's wrong?'

I turn around and crash into him, burying my face in his chest as I cry. Hesitantly, his arms come around me, and I realise it's the first time we've actually hugged.

'Shh,' he soothes. 'Shh, it's OK. What's wrong?'

'I don't want to go home,' I find myself blubbing. 'It's too soon. I've only just got here.' And then I can't speak any more because I'm crying too much.

'Shh, shh,' he says again, rocking me slightly. I feel closer to him then in that moment than I ever have. 'You don't have to go home,' he says in a deep voice.

What? I pull away and look up at him, tears continuing to streak their way down my cheeks.

'You don't have to go home if you don't want to,' he says again, rubbing my tears away with his rough thumbs.

'But I . . . But my flight is at two o'clock,' I stutter.

'So we'll cancel it,' he says calmly, his green eyes staring down at me.

'What? You mean it? I can stay?'

He half laughs. 'I'm only just getting to know you, too.' He pushes a strand of hair out of my eyes. 'You remind me of her, you know. Candy.'

I jolt, but I shake my head. 'We look nothing alike.'

'You do. More than you know. You have her smile . . . Her nose . . .' He lightly taps my nose with his index finger. 'The

222

shape of her eyes . . . OK, the eye colour is mine,' he concedes. 'I don't want you to go home, yet, either.'

My head is buzzing with everything he's saying. I so want to believe him. 'But what about your holiday? Aren't you going away tomorrow?'

'You can come with us.'

Hope surges through my heart and I can barely speak. 'Are you serious?' I finally manage to ask.

'I wouldn't joke about this,' he says.

'But what about Meg? Would she be OK with me staying?' My questions tumble into one another.

'I don't have to ask her permission,' he says as my optimism takes a nosedive. It feels like I've just got Meg on side and I don't want her to hate me all over again. 'She'll be fine,' he says, as though trying to reassure me. Maybe he's trying to convince himself, too.

'I'll help out around the house more,' I blurt. 'I'll look after Barney and Phoenix. I'll . . . I'll . . . I can help Eddie cook—'

'Enough!' He laughs. 'You don't have to do any of that. Well, only if you want to. But we really need to talk to your stepdad, OK?'

Shit. I forgot about Stu. How's he going to feel when he hears I don't want to come home yet? I feel a twinge of guilt, but shrug it away. I *have* to stay.

'Shall we go and call him together?' he suggests.

'Hadn't you better run it past Meg first?'

He pulls a face. 'Yeah. I guess that would be a good idea.' He rubs my arms with his hands and steps away from me. 'I'll be back in a sec.'

My heart continues to race as I pace the terrace, too restless to sit down. A few minutes later he reappears at the door and I swear I'm going to burst with happiness when he grins at me. 'Come on,' he beckons me inside. 'We've got a phone call to make.'

Chapter 21

Stu sounds so pleased when he realises it's me on the other end of the line and I feel guilty about what I'm about to say.

'All packed?' he asks.

'I'm thinking about staying,' I exclaim.

Silence. 'Pardon?'

'I'd like to stay for a bit longer,' I say. 'Johnny says it's OK.'

'Oh. Right.' He sounds taken aback. Johnny motions for the phone.

'Johnny wants to speak with you,' I tell him.

'Oh! Right.' Exactly the same words, but now he sounds on edge. I pass the phone over.

'Hey. Good to talk to you.' Here I am, at the other end of a one-way conversation again. 'Yeah, that's right. And I'd like her to stay.' Pause. 'If you're OK with that?'

He'd better be, I think to myself as I sit there biting my nails and staring idly at Johnny's tattoos trailing up his arm.

POW! I'm reminded of Jack and butterflies flit through me.

Stu agrees, on the understanding that I'm home well in time for the next school term, earlier if I change my mind about staying.

Johnny pats my back as I say goodbye to Stu. He goes out of the office, leaving me to it. I promise Stu I'll continue to call him often, and he tells me he'll set up Skype so he can see my face.

Afterwards, I go upstairs to my bedroom and sit on the bed, trying to take everything in. I'm not going home. I am *not* going home. I can't believe it. I'm staying. I'm *staying*! I'm going to be in LA for the summer! Getting to know my new dad! My new family!

And Jack . . .

What about Tom? I feel surreal when I think about him. I'm sure that when I see him again, I'll still have feelings for him, but he's so far away. It occurs to me that maybe he'll have a holiday romance with a girl in Ibiza, and the thought stings. But the pain is muted because of Jack and the possibilities there. What will he say when I tell him I'm staying?

'He's only into you because you're leaving.' Lissa's words come back to haunt me. Jack doesn't do commitment . . .

I should text him. We're flying in Johnny's private jet to the Virgin Islands tomorrow, and from there we'll be sailing by yacht to a secluded island for a two-week holiday in beach huts over-looking the ocean. Johnny has booked the entire resort so we'll have the island to ourselves. I can't actually get my head around that. It sounds too good to be true.

Anyway, the holiday means I won't be seeing Jack for a while, but I need to let him know I'll be back in LA soon. Of course, I could let him stew, but it would serve me right for playing games if he hooked up with another girl in the meantime. No, I'll definitely contact him, but today I just want to let all of this sink in.

226

There's a knock at my door, stirring me from my thoughts.

'Can I come in?' Meg calls.

'Sure,' I call back. I study her as she walks into the room. She doesn't *look* annoyed. But I haven't forgotten her saying she wanted to get me out of the way before their holiday.

'Hi,' she says.

'I hope you're OK with me being here a bit longer,' I say hesitantly. 'I don't want to cause trouble between you and Johnny.'

She smiles wryly and shakes her head. 'Johnny and I have been through much worse than this, I can assure you.' She perches next to me on the bed. 'I understand why you want to stay,' she says gently, her brown eyes full of compassion. 'And you're right, it *is* too soon for you to be going home. You and Johnny have got a lot of catching up to do.'

I exhale with relief. 'It's not just Johnny,' I find myself telling her. 'It's Phoenix and Barney as well. I've never had siblings before. It was always just Mum and me. And Stu.'

'The boys adore you, too,' Meg says.

She sighs and I tense up again, wondering what she's going to say next.

'Look, I'm going to be honest with you,' she continues. 'I was *terrified* when Johnny told me about you. I know he told you about Barney and how I kept quiet about him being his son for over a year after he was born.'

I nod. Johnny must've filled her in on our conversation from Friday night.

She swallows and looks down at her hands. 'Trust me, I know how bad that sounds. You probably think I'm a heartless bitch, but I swear I thought I was doing the right thing.'

I open my mouth to say that I don't think she's heartless, and she's proved herself not to be a bitch, despite initially calling me a wannabe rock star, but she carries on before I can say anything.

'I'm sure you've heard all about Johnny's struggles with drink and drugs?'

'Yes.' Is she finally going to tell me about how she and Johnny got together?

'Right, unless you've been living on Pluto for the last ten years,' she says sardonically. 'Well, he and I had a thing going on, when I worked for him as his PA. I fell for him. I didn't want to – I knew he was bad for me – but I couldn't help myself. He had *serious* issues with commitment.'

Her words make me think of Jack, but I try to concentrate.

'Johnny's oldest friend Christian used to hang out here in LA with us occasionally – he was writing Johnny's biography.' She pauses, maybe thinking better of telling me all this. 'Anyway, I won't go into it all now—'

'Please do,' I beg. 'I'd really like to hear it.'

She hesitates. 'OK. So anyway, when things got really rocky with Johnny, I left LA and went home. Christian, who had always looked out for me, sought me out and we became friends. And eventually more than that,' she says quietly.

I wait for her to go on.

'Johnny went mental when he found out.' She looks at me, her eyes alight as she remembers. 'He told me he loved me, that he wanted me to come back to LA with him, and . . . I refused. I couldn't do that to Christian. But I . . . Well.' She shifts with embarrassment and looks away. 'Things got out of hand. We . . .' She turns her palms outwards, but doesn't say the words. 'I fell pregnant.' She appears smaller somehow as she relates this to me. 'And on the day I went for my first scan, I realised that

Johnny was never going to change for me.' She takes a deep breath. 'This is still surprisingly hard to talk about.'

'I appreciate you telling me,' I say. And I do. She's showing me respect by trusting me with her story. I'm not just anyone. I'm Johnny's daughter and she's treating me like part of his – her – family. Affection swells inside me as I process this fact.

'I knew I should have said something to Christian … To Johnny … But I honestly believed that Johnny would have run a mile if he'd known I was pregnant, and Barney could have been Christian's. I wanted him to be …' Again her voice trails off. 'When he was born with dark hair and blue eyes, I was so relieved I'd made the right decision.' She smiles at my confused frown. 'I know, Barney could not be more blond or green-eyed now, but it took him a fair few months to get there, and by then I found myself in a bit of a pickle.' I know she's putting it mildly. 'I saw Johnny again for the first time when Christian's mother died.' She freezes as she realises she might be reminding me of my mum's death.

'It's fine,' I reassure her.

'Johnny saw a photo of Barney and put two and two together. That year was a mess. Christian and I broke up – as you'd expect – and Johnny was with this evil … Urgh!' She grimaces. 'This complete … urgh! Horrible, horrible girl …'

Wow, she must've been pretty awful to invoke that reaction.

'But he and I sort of became friends again, although he was still seriously messed up … And eventually he sorted himself out, broke it off with the bitch from hell. Sorry.' She flashes me an apologetic look, but I'm grinning. 'And he and I got back together.' She smiles. 'So that's it. You know the not-quite-fairy-tale story of our relationship.'

229

'Sounds like a whirlwind,' I comment.

'Anyway, all I'm trying to say is that I understand why your mum might have felt that keeping the truth about Johnny from you was for the best.'

My insides contract. I didn't know this is where we were headed and I'm not sure I'm ready to talk to Meg about it. Whatever she and Johnny went through, she doesn't know anything about my mum.

'She obviously thought she was doing the right thing—'

'She was wrong,' I interrupt. 'Barney missed out on a year of his dad's life, but at least he won't remember that. Phoenix had him from the start. I'm fifteen . . . I shouldn't have had to make do without a father.'

Bloody hell, I feel like crying again. Meg looks mortified.

'Sorry,' I say. 'I know it's not your fault. You're not my mum. But what I wouldn't give for her to be here, right now, so I could have it out with her . . .' My voice shakes as I say this, trailing off as the tears spill out of my eyes and run down my cheeks. I angrily brush them away.

'I'm sorry,' Meg whispers, rubbing my back. 'I can't imagine how you must be feeling, but I'm here for you if you need me. We all are.'

I nod, the lump in my throat too big to say thank you.

Chapter 22

'Here's your iPhone back,' I say later that evening, handing it to Johnny. He's lounging on the sofa reading *The Sunday Times*. He must've had it brought in especially. 'Thanks for lending it to me, even if Davey did turn up sooner than expected,' I add wryly.

He looks amused. 'Keep it.' He holds it back up to me.

'What? Are you serious?' An iPhone? I think I'm going to pass out with excitement!

'Annie will help you switch over your contacts in the morning, if you like. She's good at stuff like that.'

I stare with unbridled glee at the phone in my hands.

'On the issue of Davey ...'

I look down to see him regarding me with a serious expression as the newspaper rustles in his hands. 'You're *fifteen*. I don't know what you get away with at home, but here you'll stick to a curfew. One o'clock is *late*. Are we clear?'

I nod meekly, and it's only afterwards that I realise I succumbed far more easily to Johnny than I ever have with Stu. What's with that?

We're all in a flurry the next morning with the packing. Meg won't hear of Carly or Sharon packing any of the bags for her, and I'm with her on that. I want to make sure I have my very favourite things with me – most of them are the new clothes I've bought while I've been here. Annie comes to find me in my bedroom, just as I'm zipping up my bag.

'Johnny says he's given you the spare iPhone?' She's wearing shorts and a T-shirt and is dressed more casually than usual, but she still looks like a pixie with her short, dark hair and twinkling green eyes.

'That's right.' I grab it from my bedside table and smile at her. I decided against calling Jack last night because I didn't want to appear too desperate. It nearly killed me to resist.

'Do you want me to change over your contacts while you're away?' she asks.

I frown. 'While I'm away? Is there no chance we can do it now so I can take it with me?'

'There's no cellphone reception on the island,' she says.

'What?' My face falls. But how am I going to text Jack? 'Are you serious?'

'I'm afraid so,' she tells me sympathetically.

'What about email?' His card had his email address.

She shakes her head. 'Sorry. When Johnny and Meg want to get away, they *really* want to get away,' she says.

'But ... What if there's an emergency? What about calling my stepdad?'

'There will be a satellite phone on the island for emergencies,'

232

she reassures me. 'I'm sure you can call your stepdad on that.'

Phew. But what about Jack?

'So shall I change over your contacts from your old cell so you have your new iPhone ready when you get back? You'll have to leave them both with me.' She holds out her hand, but I hesitate. There's no way I can go for two weeks without letting Jack know that I'm still here.

'Can I bring them down to you in a minute?'

'Sure. But don't be long. I'll send Davey up for your bag,' she says, turning to leave.

'OK,' I reply, distracted. I'm wondering where I packed Jack's card. I upzip my bag again and dig around in a panic, upending all of my neatly-folded clothes. My head is swimming and I have no idea where it is. Shit, damn, bollocks! Where the hell is it? Oh God, what an idiot! It's in my purse. Dur!

Davey knocks on my door and I ask him to hang on while I zip my bag back up. He comes in and takes it, while I hunt out the card in my purse. My heart is beating fast and I make four mistakes as I type the number into a new text message. Johnny calls out to me and I shout that I'm coming. I wish I had more time to think about what to write, but I settle on:

> It's Jessie. This is my new number. I'm still here! I didn't go home. I'm off on holiday and out of contact for two weeks but then I'll be back. Hope to see you???

I press send and go out of the room, clutching the phone in my hand. How long before we get to the airport? Argh! I've just remembered Annie wants me to hand over my phones now! I can't! She comes out of the office as I'm walking down the stairs.

'So, you want to give them to me?' She nods at the iPhone I'm still holding.

'Can I take this one with me?' I ask desperately.

'There's no phone recep—'

'I know,' I interrupt. 'But what if someone calls me between here and the airport?'

She regards me with amusement. 'I can swap your contacts over when you get home, if you like?'

'That would be great!' I exclaim, wanting to hug her.

Barney comes awkwardly down the stairs, carrying a Playmobil fire engine.

'Come on, buddy, you can't take that,' Johnny chides. 'Who's going to carry it for you?'

'I will,' I offer, and Barney flashes me such a cute grin that I forget about the text message I've just sent. For all of five seconds. Then it's on my mind again.

It's on my mind the entire way to the airport.

'Waiting for someone to call?' Johnny asks wryly.

I nod, staring down at the phone. Come on, Jack. Text me back. I'm so preoccupied that I barely take in my surroundings as we climb up the few stairs to the small silver aeroplane in the private airfield half an hour out of the city.

'You're going to have to switch that off now,' Meg says gently as I take a seat in a cream-coloured leather armchair.

Ping! My heart jumps as a message comes in and I scramble to read it.

Wow. Cool. Call me when you get back. Jack.

That's it? I don't really know what I expected, but no kisses? Not even an explanation mark?

What am I thinking? He's not that sort of guy. I know that. I send a quick one back. **Will do.**

Then I switch off my phone, knowing that I'm going to spend the next two weeks worrying that I shouldn't have replied to him so quickly.

The beach huts we're staying in are quite small, but by no means basic. I have one all to myself and it has a large raised bathtub behind the bed so I can soak myself in bubbles and look out of the front doors to the still ocean beyond. There are a few staff on hand – although Meg tells me there are probably four times as many behind the scenes – but we wake up each morning to fresh fruit and a massage on the beach, followed by snorkelling. I even learn to scuba dive, which opens up an incredible new underwater world.

Our afternoons are spent walking through lush vegetation, chilling out on the beach with one of the many books on the bookshelves in my hut, or going on boat rides around the neighbouring islands. We have dinner on the beach, watching the sun set over the ocean, and eating fresh fish and things like lobster, which I've never tried before but have discovered I really, really like.

I feel guilty about Stu, at home in our little house, missing out on a summer holiday and no doubt missing my mum, and probably even me.

I speak to him a couple of times – just quickly, to touch base. The satellite is a great big bulky thing that doesn't exactly make conversations easy, but it does the job. He tells me that Natalie has been calling for me and that he told her I'm staying with my biological father. She was shocked, he said, but there has been no mention of Johnny Jefferson between them. I'm sure she still thinks I'm pulling her leg about that. I miss her, regardless, and I'm glad she's been calling for me.

As for Jack, well, I think about him a lot, too. To be honest, the first few days I *obsess*. But then I start to calm down. I'll have just over two more weeks left in LA before I go home for the next school term, so what will be, will be. I've been through too much with my mum to have to endure any sort of heartache over a boy. I won't let that happen.

Towards the end of our holiday, I'm lying on the soft sand staring up at the stars. They're so bright. Brighter than I've ever seen. I'm waiting for a falling star. I've seen three since I've been here, and I know that if I watch and wait for long enough, I'll see another one.

I hear footsteps pad across the sand and look over to see Johnny approaching.

'Hey, girl,' he says, sitting down on the sand next to me. 'You alright?'

'I'm good,' I reply, glancing up at his pale face in the moonlight. He lies back on the sand beside me and we stare up at the stars.

'I'm trying to spot a falling one.'

He says nothing for a long time, and I'm surprised to hear how choked he sounds when he speaks.

'Do you ever think your mum is up there, looking down at you?'

Tears automatically spring into my eyes and the requisite lump forms in my throat.

'I'd like to think so.' My voice is shaky. 'But I don't know.'

'I still miss my mum,' he says, and I hear him swallow, trying to compose himself. 'But it does get easier.'

'She died when you were a bit younger than me, right?'

'I was thirteen,' he reveals. 'She had cancer, so she was sick for a couple of years before that.'

'That's so sad.'

'I had time to get used to it—' He stops himself. 'No,' he says sharply. 'There still wasn't time to get used to it.' He speaks more gently. 'It was still a shock when she died. I can't imagine how you must have felt losing your mum so suddenly.'

I really want to cry now, but the need to talk is stronger so I try to hold back my tears. 'Were you there when she died?' I ask, turning my head to look at him. He continues to stare upwards at the bright night sky, but he nods.

'Yeah, I was there. She was asleep. Or out on drugs,' he reveals. 'The nurses had tried to get me to go back to Christian's house – we were friends, even back then. I was staying with him and his family when she was really ill.'

'Not with your dad?'

'No, he came to collect me after the funeral. I had to go down to London to live with him, but I hardly knew him.' He glances across at me. 'So I guess I know a little bit about what you're going through.'

I nod quickly and turn my head upwards again. 'I wish I'd been there when Mum died,' I manage to say.

'Hey.' He reaches over and takes my hand, but I'm gone. I can't hold back my tears so I sit up on the sand and clutch my hand to my swollen throat and try to speak through my tears as Johnny sits up beside me. 'Stu had to go and identify her body,'

I tell him. 'I didn't see her again. The casket was closed. I wanted to say goodbye, but Stu wouldn't let me. She was too . . .'

I can't speak. I can't say it out loud. She was cut up. Her beautiful face was all cut up from the broken window falling out on her.

'I'm sorry. I'm sorry,' Johnny says as I cry. He wraps his arm around my neck and pulls me into him and I snot into his T-shirt.

'I miss her so much,' I sob. 'I miss her. I wish she was here. I'm so sad she's gone and I'll never get to see her again. I was such a bitch to her!' I cry.

'No, you weren't,' Johnny says firmly.

'I was!' I exclaim. 'I was always saying horrible things, pushing her away.'

'You're a teenager!' he erupts. 'That's what teenagers do! She knew you loved her.'

'But, what if she didn't . . .'

'Of course she did,' he mutters with a voice wracked with emotion as he holds me tight. 'She knew you loved her. Don't you think we all have regrets? I could have been nicer to my mum. I was always going on at her about how she should have stayed with my dad, should have made things work. She even taught me how to cook when she was really sick and all I could do was moan about how I'd rather be playing video games.' He breathes in deeply, his chest expanding and shaking as he exhales. I don't need to look at him to know that he's crying.

'She knew you loved her,' I say, muffled into his chest.

'She did.' He nods quickly. 'And Candy did, too. I know you didn't have time to prepare yourself for her death, but neither did she. And as far as I can tell, that's a good thing. I can't imagine how much it must have hurt my mum to know that she was dying, to know that she was leaving me with a shitty excuse for a father. I didn't know him. He was a stranger to me.'

He looks down at me. 'I don't want to be a stranger to you. I'm sorry I wasn't there for you, that I haven't been here for you. But you probably would have hated me if we'd met years ago. I was screwed-up like my dad. Meg saved me. Meg, Barney and Phoenix saved me. I'm only the man I am now because of them. Thanks to them, I'm ready for this, ready to be here for you. I *want* to be here for you,' he says fervently, then he hesitates and his voice is gentler. 'I want to tell everyone you're mine,' he says.

My heart skips a beat.

'Annie is drawing up a press release,' he tells me quietly.

I swallow.

'We'll wait until we get back to LA before putting it out. OK?' he asks.

'Yes.' My voice comes out as a whisper. *Finally!* I wish I could be a fly on the wall when Natalie, Em and Libby see the news. And Tom! What will he think?

Johnny reaches over and rubs my tears away. His fingers are rough, as always. 'I know it's going to change things for you. I know it's going to be hard.'

He's wrong, that's not what's going through my mind. I *want* the world to know he's my dad. I'm sick of the pretence. I'm proud he's my dad and I want to shout it through a megaphone.

'But it's ridiculous that people are going around thinking you're my nanny,' he continues darkly.

I smile at him. 'I'm ready,' I say. 'Really. I want people to know. I hate pretending.'

He smiles and squeezes my shoulder. 'Good.'

Chapter 23

It's early August by the time I return to LA, relaxed and bonded with my new family. It's been a blissful two weeks, having proper quality time together, and it's exactly what I needed. I feel full of fight and determination and much more like my old self. If Jack isn't interested, bollocks to him. If he was only into me because I was leaving, like Lissa said, then I'll find out soon enough. But I'm not going to let him get to me. I send him a text on the day we get back, keeping it casual.

I'm back in LA if you want to catch up sometime?

That's not to say I don't check my phone incessantly until he replies, nearly driving Annie mad when she finally nabs it to swap my contacts over from my old cheapo phone. He replies just as I'm going to sleep and trying not to get myself all worked up about him again. 'Keep your cool' is my new mantra.

I've got a gig Wednesday night. Come?

I think twice about replying so quickly, but I can't be bothered to play games, so I type out another message.

Sounds good. Where and what time?

To my relief, he texts me back straight away with the venue and the time. He says he'll leave a ticket on the door, but he doesn't offer to come and collect me. I guess he'll be busy setting up. Either that, or maybe Jack Mitchell has gone cold on me. But he still invited me to his gig and I've got nothing better to do for the next two weeks. Anyway, I can give as good as I get.

When I tell Meg and Johnny about my plans, they ask Annie to hold off putting out the press release about me until the end of the week, giving me a couple more days of anonymity so I can go to the gig without being harassed. I'm disappointed to have the news postponed, especially when it feels like I've waited an age for it to come out, but I guess it makes sense.

On Wednesday afternoon, while I'm trying to pass the time before I can sensibly start to get ready, I walk past the music studio and hear voices coming from inside. I tentatively push open the door and see Christian sitting at the control desk and Johnny behind the glass screen, hanging his guitar from a strap around his neck. He leans forward to talk into the microphone suspended from the ceiling in front of him.

'Can you—' he starts, then he looks past Christian to see me. 'Jessie, you want to come in? I'm just about to show Christian something I've been working on.'

241

'Yeah,' I say enthusiastically, smiling brightly at Christian.

He arrived last night – a tall, broad, good-looking man with shaggy dark hair and warm brown eyes. I liked him instantly, although he seemed a bit taken aback by me.

'Jesus Christ, she looks like you,' he exclaimed to Johnny. Meg smacked him on his bum and berated him for swearing.

'I didn't say the F-word,' he says.

'Shh!' she warns, but it's clear he's only teasing her. It's unbelievable, looking at the three of them, to think about what they went through. I can't comprehend that they're still friends considering their past and everything I know about Barney, yet here they are.

Christian pats the chair next to him so I go inside and sit down. I'm filled with a growing sense of excitement as I watch Johnny tune his guitar. He asks Christian to adjust a couple of dials, then bends down and picks up a long lead from somewhere, plugging it into his guitar. He starts to strum a slow, gentle tune: a lullaby. I'm rapt. How I wish I could play the guitar like that. And then he steps up to the mic and starts to sing, his deep, soulful voice filling the room and filling up my senses as I watch, transfixed.

It hits me again. That's my dad, right there. That, *there* ... That *Johnny Jefferson*, right *there* behind *that* glass, is *my* dad. MY dad. How can my life have taken such a turn?

I don't know about Christian, but all of my hairs are standing on end. This song is full of emotion and it's truly beautiful – a love song. The lyrics say something about a girl with a warm smile who became a teacher and her unconditional love for her subject, and then it hits me like a tonne of bricks that this is not a song about an *actual* teacher, it's a song about Johnny's mum.

242

Maybe even *my* mum. Didn't Meg say Christian's mum died not so long ago, too? I look across at Christian and see that his eyes are shining. Mine immediately fog up and I struggle to hold myself together as I watch Johnny through the glass.

When he's singing, his eyes are downcast, and when the instrumental kicks in, he steps back and looks down at his guitar, giving himself up to the music. When he plays out the final few chords, Christian and I furtively wipe away our tears. Christian gives Johnny the thumbs up. I know why. I'm too choked to speak, too.

'You like it?' Johnny asks him, looking a little lost, almost boy-like.

'Yeah.' Christian says gruffly. 'Yeah, I do.'

Johnny smiles sadly and starts to lift his guitar strap over his head, but he pauses, glancing back out at us. He presses his mouth to the mic. 'Something more upbeat?'

Christian gives him the thumbs up again.

'Yes!' I nod eagerly.

And then he kicks off with a jaunty melody, an acoustic version of one of his more recent hit singles. I can't help it – I start to sing along.

Johnny's eyes dart up to meet mine and he grins as he sings, raising one eyebrow. Then he stops singing and playing suddenly and jerks his head backwards. 'Get in here,' he says.

'What?' I shake my head, confused.

'Get in here and sing with me.'

'Go on!' Christian urges, shoving my chair. The wheels underneath my chair roll me about a foot closer to the studio door.

'I . . . I can't do that!' I erupt, putting my feet down to stop the motion.

Johnny's shoulders slump, but he's not giving up. 'Get. In. Here,' he says firmly.

'No!'

'Jessie.' Hmm, that's a very no nonsense tone.

'Forget it.' I shake my head determinedly. 'I don't sing in public, remember?'

'What about *Thomas The Tank Engine*?' Johnny asks with amusement.

'Eh?' Christian chips in. We've lost him.

'Come on,' he beckons me inside again.

'You'll regret it if you don't,' Christian points out.

Something twinges inside me and I realise that he's right. I will regret it if I don't. And I don't want to have any more regrets. Johnny waits patiently, staring at me with those very green eyes of his. Bugger it. I stand up and saunter into the studio, pursing my lips as Christian claps and cheers in a completely OTT manner.

Johnny grins at me and pulls another mic down from above our heads. He says something into the first mic to Christian. 'You'll have to press that ... Blah, blah, blah ...' I don't know what he's talking about, but Christian seems to know what to do, as he twiddles some dials and knobs on the control desk in front of him. Johnny leans past me and says, 'Testing, testing, testing,' into the spare mic and then Christian's voice comes into the room, sounding like he's on speakerphone, and he tells us we're good to go.

Johnny turns to look at me as he starts to play the same song. I grin down at his fingers strumming the guitar, truly wishing I could play too, and then the first verse kicks off and Johnny starts to sing. I know this song like the back of my hand – it's one of his biggest hits – and I nod my head along for a bit, then step forward and start to add little bits of harmony to the occasional lyric. Johnny raises his eyebrows at Christian and I glance at him to see him looking impressed. When the chorus kicks in, I sing along to the whole thing, still doing the occasional harmony, and before I know it, we're singing the rest of the song together.

Johnny strums the last note and throws his arm around my neck, pressing a kiss to my forehead while I blush furiously. Christian claps and cheers, but this time he's being genuine – I can tell that he's blown away – and I'm bursting with pride.

'Isn't she amazing?' Johnny exclaims, looking out of the glass.

'Properly un-bloody-believeable,' Christian replies, shaking his head while I continue to blush. 'Jessie Jefferson is a great stage name,' Christian says and I laugh because I think he's joking. 'Seriously,' he adds.

I glance at Johnny, who shrugs. 'It's got a good ring to it.'

'No,' I say shortly, my smile falling from my face. 'My name is Jessie Pickerill.'

Christian leans back in his chair. 'Johnny's mother's name was Sneeden, but he changed it to Jefferson.'

'Leave it, Christian.' Johnny cuts off his friend. He shakes his head quickly, abruptly, as he lifts his guitar strap over his head. 'It's too soon.'

'It will always be too soon,' I point out firmly, trying not to get upset. 'My mother's name was Pickerill.' I'm not going to choose Johnny over her, like she feared.

'You could be double-barrelled,' Christian presses on, not realising how touchy I'm feeling.

'Christian!' Johnny snaps. 'Let it go.'

Christian looks taken aback and I feel bad for him, but at least Johnny understands.

'Sorry,' Christian says a little defensively.

'It's OK,' I brush him off, keen to change the subject. 'Hey, what's the time?'

He checks his watch. 'Getting on for five o'clock.'

Is it too early? Nah. 'I might go and get ready,' I tell them.

'Ready for what?' Christian asks, as Johnny and I walk out of the studio.

'She's going to see a band tonight. You might've heard of them – All Hype? They're Billy Mitchell's kid's band?'

Christian's brow furrows, thinking. 'They sound kind of familiar.' I remember Johnny telling me Christian used to be a music journo. 'Where are they playing?' he asks me.

'A place called The Rider, near Melrose Avenue.'

He nods. 'That's a good venue.' He turns back to Johnny. 'We should go?'

What? I don't want my dad gatecrashing my date. Is it a date?

Johnny glances at me and scratches the stubble on his jaw.

'Why don't we?' Christian presses.

'And cramp Jessie's style?' Johnny asks with a grin.

Then again, Johnny turning up at Jack's gig would be amazing press for his band . . .

'You could come,' I say with a shrug.

'Great,' Christian enthuses. 'I love checking out new bands.'

'Aren't you jet-lagged?' Johnny asks wryly. 'You usually are,' he adds.

'We don't have to have a late one,' Christian replies. Pause. 'Do we?' He sounds slightly worried now.

'I don't do late ones any more,' Johnny says cynically, then,

'Sure, we can go if you want. I don't know whether Nutmeg'll fancy it.'

'Shall I ask Jack to put aside a couple more tickets?' I ask.

'Nah, don't trouble him. Annie'll sort it.'

'Cool!' He is going to *love* me for this!

Chapter 24

Earlier this afternoon, Annie prompted me to send out a message to everyone in my contacts book, alerting them to my new mobile number. I don't hear from anyone for hours, and I begin to think that none of them care about me, but then I remember the time difference and realise it's the middle of the night in England. My first text comes through to me when I'm in the limo on the way to Jack's gig. I pull my phone out of my purse and see that the message is from Natalie. I smile as I read it.

> **What the hell? You've gone to see your dad? Who the hell is he? I'm assuming he is NOT Johnny Jefferson ;-)**

I giggle out loud and type out a reply, while Johnny and Christian ignore me. Christian is drinking a beer, while Johnny and I sip lemonades. I declined to have a glass of champagne after Christian told me how expensive Perrier Jouet actually is –

over a hundred pounds a bottle! I nearly had a heart attack. Stu would be proud of the fact I'm not drinking. Meg opted not to come with us – she's more of a pop girl, she said to my surprise and Johnny's joke disgust.

> **Good to hear from you! Sorry I've been awol. I'll call you tomorrow for a proper chat?**

I feel a pang of homesickness for her. I miss her. I wish she were here. To my delight, she replies straight away. **You'd better xxxxxxxx**

We leave it at that. But I will tell her the truth tomorrow before the press release goes out, and if she still doesn't believe me, she will soon.

While I have my phone out, I decide to send Jack a quick text, too.

> **Johnny & his friend, a music journo, are coming to your gig tonight with me. Good luck!**

Seconds later another message comes in and it's like my phone has given me an electric shock, the way I whip it back out of my purse. But it's not from Jack. It's from Tom. My heart jumps as I read it.

> **Hey you! In Ibiza. Have proper bad hangover. Been thinking of you a bit. Back next week if you want to do something?**

I feel a bit dazed. I've been trying to put Tom out of my mind since I've met Jack, but now I see him in my head so clearly, crouching in front of me at Natalie's party, after coming to find me when I bolted.

I stare down at the text. Tom's been thinking of me. That makes me feel warm and fuzzy inside. I put my phone back into my bag, confusion muddling my brain.

There's a line of people snaking out the front door of the venue when we arrive. Johnny directs Davey to take us around the back.

'But my ticket will be at the front,' I say worriedly to Johnny. 'Shall I get out and queue?'

'Nah.' He shakes his head and gives me a weird look. 'You'll be alright.'

Hmm. I suppose I *am* with Johnny Jefferson.

There's no one around the back, but then the black metal door bursts open and a blonde girl wearing a headset pokes her head out, spies the limo and grins. The door of the limo opens and I see Davey standing there, and behind him, Samuel and Lewis. Where did they come from? Did they come ahead to the venue? They must have done.

'After you,' Johnny says to me. I climb out on to the pavement and wait, flanked by Johnny's security guards. Christian comes next, gently ushering me towards the door. I still half expect the girl with the headset to demand to see our tickets, but she doesn't. I look back at Johnny.

'Cheers, Bud,' he says to Davey as he climbs out. And then the screams start. I don't know where they come from, who the girls are or how they spotted us around this side of the venue – maybe they saw the limo drive past – but Christian presses me forward, and moments later, Johnny and Samuel are inside with us. I guess Lewis must be waiting outside for our exit later.

My head is spinning. 'Is this what it's always like?' I say to Christian.

He looks at me like I'm bonkers. 'That was nothing,' he tells me.

The girl leads us down a corridor and then I feel Johnny's hand on my back and I instantly feel calmer somehow.

'Do you want to wait backstage?' the girl asks over her shoulder.

'Nah, let's go and get a drink,' Christian says, glancing at Johnny for agreement.

'Cool.' Johnny nods.

The music from the venue outside the corridor is muted, the bass a dull thumping, but we come to a door and when the blonde whooshes it open, the noise is deafening. The venue is crowded, the bar is packed and the stage is dark and empty. Samuel goes first, looking almost comical in his size and posture – but despite his penchant for silly jokes, he is *not* someone to be messed with.

We're about a quarter of the way through the crowd on the dance floor, en route to the bar, when Johnny is noticed. At first it's just shocked looks and excited nudges as the crowd parts in front of us, but like a ripple, the news spreads outwards and then the crowd swarms around us. Nobody screams, though – maybe that would be too uncool – but all eyes are on him. Eventually we reach the bar – Samuel goes first, clearing a space – and then the bartender appears miraculously.

'What are you having?' Johnny bends down and asks me in my ear.

'Erm ... Whiskey and Coke?' I ask hopefully. I may have been good in the limo, but now that I'm inside I feel so jittery about meeting Jack that I kind of want a drink.

251

'Try again,' he says, deadpan.

I pull a face.

'Let her have a beer,' Christian suggests genially. 'A light one?'

Johnny raises one eyebrow at me. 'I'd prefer cider,' I tell him with my best smile.

'They won't do cider here,' Christian chips in. 'Go on, get us a couple of beers, mate.'

Johnny shoots him an unimpressed look, then leans in and asks for two beers and a Coke. My shoulders slump, so I'm surprised when Christian gives me a cheeky thumbs up. Then a bottle of beer is in my hand and I realise Johnny is drinking the Coke. Result! I can't believe I got served in here, actually. Definitely a perk of having Johnny around, I'd say.

'Cheers!' Christian says and we all chink bottles. That's when I look around to see that there are dozens of sets of eyes staring straight at me. I jolt with shock. Whoa, this is so weird. They must be wondering who I am, why I'm here with Johnny Jefferson. I take a sip of my beer. It doesn't taste too bad. Johnny asks Christian about someone called Sara – maybe that's his girlfriend – but I tune out.

I wonder if Jack got my message? I feel a hand on my waist and spin around, coming face to face with the boy himself. Butterflies instantly take flight in my stomach and heat radiates from the place where he's touching me.

'Hi.' He seems guarded as he looks past me to Johnny, but Christian is saying something into Johnny's ear and he's distracted.

'You alright?' I ask cautiously, then his eyes are on me and my heart flips. I'd almost forgotten how good-looking he is.

'Yeah,' he says uncertainly. 'I just got your text.'

'Thought I'd better warn you.'

'Thanks.' He smiles a small smile. 'Catch you afterwards?' He looks past me again.

'Sure.'

He squeezes my waist and then turns around, making his way back through the crowd. My eyes follow him until he's out of sight, then I turn around to see that I've finally got Johnny and Christian's attention.

'Who was that?' Christian asks.

'That,' Johnny replies, giving him a significant look, 'was Jack Mitchell.'

'Aah,' Christian says knowingly.

My face burns as I take another gulp of my drink. Johnny and Christian grin at each other. A man appears on the stage, setting up or doing something. Johnny pats Christian on the chest and nods towards the stage, indicating for us to go closer. We start to make our way through the crowd, but then a man stops Johnny and they backslap and greet each other enthusiastically. Johnny pulls him forward.

'Christian, you know Billy?' Johnny says, and he and Christian do a complicated handshake while my head spins. Jack's dad?

'And this is my daughter, Jessie,' Johnny says. Billy's eyes widen and he looks shell-shocked for a split second before regaining his senses. He leans forwards and shakes my hand the proper way.

'Well, well, well,' he says, looking back at Johnny. 'I didn't know you had a daughter?'

Johnny shrugs. 'Neither did I,' he says. 'So, how's life treating you?'

I can't hear Billy's reply, but I'm hardly paying attention anyway. Johnny has just told Jack's dad that I'm his daughter. For the first time, it really hits me that the truth is about to come out. And my life really *is* going to change.

Billy stays with us to watch the band, and as the crowd around us start chanting and looking up at the stage, the atmosphere is charged.

I lean up into Johnny's ear. 'You just told him I'm your daughter!' I exclaim.

'Everyone's going to know the day after tomorrow anyway,' he replies with a shrug.

'But I haven't even told Jack!'

'Tell him tonight.'

He *so* doesn't realise what a big deal this is to me . . .

The girls in front of us start screaming and their reaction is contagious because more join in as the band take the stage, and then BAM! Jack and Brandon start pounding on their guitars in unison while Miles bashes the hell out of the drum kit behind them. Eve bounds on to the stage, wrenches the microphone out of the stand, and starts to sing the hell out of the venue. It's amazing – *they're* amazing – even more so than at Agnes's party. This venue, this crowd, it's unbelievable. I jump along and throw my hands up in the air, while Johnny, Christian and Billy coolly nod their heads along to the beat beside me. This just makes me giggle. Johnny raises one eyebrow at me, but I ignore him and carry on dancing.

Jack looks so sexy up there, I fancy him even more and I didn't think that was possible.

He's singing into the mic, doing background harmonies, and then the lyrics cut out for an instrumental break and Eve turns around to face him, bouncing on the stage in front of him, while he plays the life out of his electric guitar. He grins at her and a horrible feeling overcomes me.

This is different to last time. Last time they could barely look at each other. Now there is definitely chemistry. Major chemistry. What the hell has happened in the two weeks I've been away? So much for not letting a guy get to me. If he isn't interested in me any more, I know without a shadow of a doubt that I'll be devastated.

No. No. I am stronger than that.

I force myself to carry on dancing, to not appear bothered as Eve spins around and continues to sing. But I watch them closely over the next couple of songs, and I'm sure that something is up. When they slow things right down, she looks over her shoulder and sings a sad, soulful song to him – and he stares right back at her for a good few seconds – before she faces the crowd again. It makes me feel sick.

I stare up at him, the urge to dance well and truly out of the window. Luckily no one else is dancing now, anyway, as this is a chilled-out track. He looks down at the crowd, his eyes moving left and right, stopping near me. I think he's seen his dad, because he nods his acknowledgement. Has he seen me? No, probably Johnny. And then his eyes are on mine, and I swear time contracts as he and I stare at each other.

Eve starts to sing to him again, but this time he doesn't smile at her. He almost looks ... irritated. As for me, well, I don't want to be here any more, but I refuse to look like an idiot and leave.

Someone grabs my arm and I turn around to see Agnes.

'Hey!' she exclaims. 'I thought you went back to the UK?'

'Change of plan!' I shout back, surprised that she'd want to talk to me. She looks strangely pleased to see me, actually. Her edgy black-haired bob is mussed up and she looks cool in a dark-red top and what I'm guessing is her trademark thick black eyeliner.

'He was bummed!' she shouts.

'What?'

'Jack!' she tells me. 'He was bummed when you left!'

I glance up at the stage, confusion making my head feel fuzzy again. Eve has her arm around Jack's neck while he plays his guitar.

'Trust me,' Agnes shouts in my ear as she sees my face fall. Then she freezes, looking past me. She must've seen Johnny. I glance over my shoulder, but it's not Johnny she's seen, it's her dad. He looks torn-up as he stares at her. I turn back in time to see Agnes pushing her way through the crowd.

My heart sinks and I impulsively glance up at Jack. It's clear from the troubled look on his face that he saw this exchange. He's shaken, but he doesn't stop playing. His gaze returns to mine, but I only meet his stare for a few seconds before I force myself to look away.

Jack told me Agnes wasn't speaking to his dad, and there's my proof. Their family is just as dysfunctional as mine from the looks of that.

The gig is awesome, and despite my concerns about Jack and Eve, I'm pleased for him.

'They were good,' Christian comments afterwards when the band has finally exited the stage after their raucously demanded encore. He seems genuinely impressed. Billy nods, seeming pleased. The club's music has started up again, but it's not as loud as the band were.

'Yeah,' Johnny agrees.

'Come get a drink?' Billy suggests, patting Johnny on the back.

'I'm only on the soft stuff these days,' Johnny replies.

'Ah man, what's happened to you?' Billy exclaims. Johnny just shrugs and Billy tuts with mock disgust. 'This is what happens when you settle down.'

'You should try it,' Johnny replies pointedly.

'Nah.' Billy brushes him off with a cheeky grin which looks just like Jack's. 'Not for me.' He leads the way back to the bar, but Jack intercepts him.

'Hey, boy!' Billy shouts, engulfing him in a hug. Jack awkwardly detaches himself, smiling with embarrassment at Johnny, Christian and me, while Billy heartily shakes him. 'Johnny, you know my boy, Jack?'

'Hey, Jack,' Johnny says in a cool, calm and collected way as they shake hands. Jack looks a bit fazed, but is trying not to be. Johnny introduces Christian and they shake hands, too.

'You guys were great,' Christian says with genuine enthusiasm.

'Thanks.' Jack seems touched.

'And you know Jessie, of course,' Johnny says drily.

'Yeah.' Jack's blue-grey eyes meet mine for what seems like an age as those treacherous butterflies sweep through me once more.

'Have you seen Agnes?' Jack asks his dad apprehensively.

Billy shifts awkwardly and shrugs. 'Nah. She took off. She'll come back.'

'Jesus Christ, Dad. I told you not to screw it up.'

'I'm sorry, alright?'

Johnny and Christian exchange a look, and Johnny jerks his

head in the direction of the bar, his intention being to leave them to it.

'Hang on,' Billy interrupts them, putting his hand on Johnny's arm. He turns back to Jack. 'Come on, drink first. We'll go and find your sister afterwards.'

Jack hesitates, but then he glances at me and seems to change his mind. He nods.

'Same again?' Johnny asks me when we near the bar.

'Yes, thanks.'

I jump with surprise as Jack takes my hand and pulls me a couple of steps away from the others. I look up into his eyes and I'm thrown by the expression on his face.

'Are you OK?' I ask hesitantly.

He doesn't answer immediately. 'I don't know,' is what he replies with, which only baffles me more. 'It's good to see you again.'

He might've said it's good, but he doesn't exactly look pleased.

And then it's like slow motion, the slim, dark-skinned hands sliding around his waist from behind and I find myself eye-to-eye with Eve as she rests her chin on Jack's shoulder.

'I've been waiting for you,' she says to him, but her eyes are unwaveringly on me.

He unclasps her hands from around his waist. 'I'll be there in a minute,' he says steadily.

'Don't keep me waiting much longer, baby,' she says, kissing his cheek and giving me a meaningful look as she sashays off.

Despite what my earlier intuition was telling me, I'm still shocked. Jack stares at me helplessly, and then out of the blue,

Johnny appears by my side, his arm draped around my neck and his lips on my temple as he gives me a perfunctory kiss.

'Time to go,' he says firmly. He must have seen the exchange and wants to take me away before I get even more hurt. I glance up at him to see that my assumption is correct: Johnny is staring Jack down, anger flashing in his eyes.

'Give me a moment,' I plead. I'm not ready to walk away, yet. He nods down at me, then gives Jack one more pointed look, before turning back to Christian.

Jack shakes his head at me, and I sense he's conflicted.

'How long have you and Eve been an item?' I ask outright.

'We're not. I mean, we sort of are. On and off,' he tries to explain, but I don't think I want to know.

'Well, good luck with that,' I say bitterly, turning away.

'Jessie!' He grabs my hand and wrenches me back, pulling me to him so that my fist is pressed hard against his chest. Then his eyes narrow. 'You haven't been honest with me either, have you?'

I don't say anything, so he pulls me closer. 'You're not the nanny, right?' he says in my ear. He pulls back only to give me a look, and from my expression, he'll know he's guessed right. And then he leans in and says, 'And I bet you're older than fifteen, too.'

I pull away, confused. What is he saying? He glances towards Johnny with a dirty look on his face, and then I get it. He thinks I'm with Johnny. *With* Johnny.

'Urgh!' I shove him in his chest. 'You moron!' I shove him again, to his surprise. 'He's MY DAD!'

The look on his face is one of pure shock. I don't care. How dare he think that about me!

'You stupid dickhead!' I shout, just to ram it home. I glare at Johnny to see him looking bizarrely impressed, and then I turn and storm out of there, feeling safe in the knowledge that my newly protective dad is close behind.

Chapter 25

My head is reeling that night, and the next morning I don't want to eat anything. I'm so cross with myself for falling for Jack – and so quickly! But more than anything I feel crushed. I really, really liked him. And I was stupid enough to think that he liked me, too.

'The press release is going out tomorrow morning,' Annie tells me around lunchtime. 'Just in time for the weekend papers. So if you want to tell your friends and family before it breaks, you'd better do it today.'

I can't believe it is finally happening! But I don't have any family to tell, only friends. I've never been particularly close to Stu's parents, and Mum's parents were equally useless, as grandparents go. The only family I have is Stu and he already knows.

I wonder if Johnny has told his dad. I go outside to find him. He's sitting on a sunlounger, scribbling on a notepad. He's wearing dark sunnies and swimming trunks, and his tanned torso is decorated with tattóos that I still don't know the meaning of. It's kind of cool that my dad is considered hot by so many women. Although the thought of someone my age fancying him, like Natalie or Em ... Yuck.

'Annie says the press release is ready to go out. Have you told your dad?' I ask him.

'I called him this morning, actually,' he reveals.

'Really? What did he say?'

He stares up at me, but I can't see his eyes behind his dark glasses. 'He wasn't that surprised.'

Oh. 'Does he ... Will he ...'

'You'll meet him soon,' he promises. 'He wants to come over in September, so you'll just miss each other, but maybe next time.'

'Next time?' I ask hopefully. We still haven't discussed exactly when that might be or what's going to happen when I finally go home.

He puts his pad down. 'You know Stuart really wants you to finish your GCSEs. And he's right. So get through this year in the UK and then we'll see, OK? In the meantime, you can come back for holidays if you want.'

'That would be great!' Happiness sweeps some of my anguish about Jack away.

He smiles up at me, then takes off his glasses and his green eyes are concerned. 'You feeling alright today? After last night, I mean.'

I shrug, feeling downcast again. 'I'll be fine.'

'Don't let him get to you,' he says seriously, glancing at his notepad.

'You writing a song?' I ask.

'Yeah. Do you write?'

His question catches me off guard. The truth is, I do. I always have. But I've never told anyone about it apart from Mum. 'A little,' I find myself admitting. 'Only poetry and stuff, not songs.'

'Songs are poetry put to music,' he replies with a smile. 'If you ever want me to look at anything you've written, just give me a shout.'

'Thanks,' I say, knowing full well that I never will.

I turn to go back inside. 'Jess,' he calls me back. 'We need to talk about a few more things before you go home. Stuart said he was sure you'd want to stay at the same school?'

I frown. 'Yes?' Of course I don't want to change schools. What's he going on about?

'OK, well, I've got someone looking into security, which I understand might be a bit weird for you at first, but it's necessary.'

'What are you going on about?' I ask the previously unspoken question.

He looks confused. 'Obviously you're going to need a bodyguard.'

I laugh out loud. He's joking, right? A bodyguard following me to school? Hanging around me all day when I'm at work or going shopping or chilling out with my friends? That's ridiculous! What would everyone say? I stare at his face. Shit. He doesn't look like he's joking. 'I don't want a bodyguard,' I say, as panic rises up inside me.

'But Jessie,' he argues. 'You don't have a choice. As soon as this news comes out, the paparazzi will be after you. You might even be a kidnap threat. I want you to move to a more secure house, too. I mentioned it to Stuart, although I know he has reservations about me helping financially.'

'What? You've talked to Stuart about moving?'

'Yeah, and I get that he doesn't want me waving my wallet around, but that's tough. I need you safe.'

'No way,' I say fervently, backing away from him. 'No bloody way. I am not moving.'

Johnny looks shocked as he gets to his feet. 'You can't stay where you are,' he says cautiously, taking a step towards me. 'It's not safe. Wendel has checked it out and you won't be secure—'

'I am *not* moving!' I blurt out, my bottom lip wobbling. 'That was my mum's house! I grew up there! She's still there, in every room, and I'm *not leaving her*!' I'm practically yelling now. Johnny's face drains of blood as I run into the house and up to my bedroom, slamming the door behind me.

What the hell? I can't move! I *won't*! The little spare room in our house is still full of all of her things: her clothes, her make-up, her jewellery. Neither Stu nor I have had the guts to go through any of it – we just put it all in the room and shut the door. But I go in there sometimes. Sometimes, when I need to be near her. And it smells of her. The room, her *clothes*, even the house still smells of her! I'm not leaving her behind. No way. No frigging way. I burst into tears and bury my face in my pillow.

Ten minutes later there's a knock at my door. It's Johnny.

'Hey, chick,' he says wearily. 'Can I come in?'

I don't respond, but I know he's there. The bed dips at the end as he sits down. He sighs heavily and I risk a glance at him. He's facing away from me, hunched over in a defeated sort of pose.

'I need to talk to you,' he says in a voice thick with emotion. I sniff my response and he looks over his shoulder to see that I've emerged from underneath my tear-sodden pillow. He looks concerned. He looks exhausted.

264

'Are you ready for this?' he asks.

'Ready for what?'

'Ready to be my daughter?'

My heart jumps. Does he want me to forget about him? Has he had enough of me? Doesn't he want me to be a part of his life any more? Am I too much trouble? All of these thoughts rush through my head at once.

'What are you saying?' I ask waveringly. 'Don't you want me to be here any more?'

His face falls. 'Of course I do!' he exclaims. 'This ...' He motions to the two of us. 'You and me, we're good, right? Nothing is going to change that. I'm talking about them,' he points out the window, 'out there. Are you ready for everyone else to know that you're my daughter?'

I bite my lip, tears springing into my eyes again. 'I don't know,' I admit. I thought I was, but I don't think I've actually considered the reality of how much my life – and even Stu's – will change.

'Because we don't have to do this. We don't have to put out that press release. That's the reason we've been holding off. We wanted to give you time to get used to the idea of not being who you are any more. But I don't know if you're ready.'

So he has been keeping the truth about me quiet for my benefit, not his. What else did he just say? *Not being who you are any more*. It sounds strange, but I think I understand what he means. I was just little Jessie Pickerill before. A nobody. But soon the world will think of me as Jessie *Jefferson*, and I'll be considered a whole different person.

'But I've already told some people. I've told Jack.' It hurts to say his name out loud. 'And what about my friends back home?'

I wanted them to read about me in the papers. Wanted to prove them wrong in the biggest and brightest way possible. It sounds petty, but it's true.

'You can still confide in them,' Johnny says. 'If you trust them,' he adds. 'And despite him acting like a little prick last night, I'm sure Jack Mitchell can be trusted with a secret or two. He's certainly had to deal with a bit, with his dad,' Johnny says drily, but my heart flutters at his words. I don't want to think about why. I don't want to still care about him, not after seeing him with Eve. I try to put him out of my mind and focus on the immediate conversation.

'What I would *like* to do,' he says, 'what I've just been talking to Meg and Annie about . . .' I sit more upright and give him my full attention. ' . . .is put out a press release telling everyone that I have a daughter, but that she'd like to remain anonymous because she's still at school. That way you can stay at your school, in your house. We'll have to put it out quick – I'm thinking now, today – because pictures of you and me at the bar last night could spring up at any point and then there's no clawing back the story. There are already rumours online,' he says with disgust. Urgh, God! Do other people think the same as Jack? That I'm his bit on the side? That's revolting!

'No one has posted any pictures on the internet yet. Luckily we have Wendel on the case, and because of your age, because of your request for anonymity, if we send out the release now, we should be able to stop anything going to print if there are photos from last night out there. The press owe me a few favours, anyway.' I try to take all of this in. 'You can still come clean to your friends,' he continues. '*If* you trust them,' he adds again, flashing me a significant look. 'But everyone else will be

266

ignorant, including – hopefully – anyone who might be a threat to your security. No one would expect my daughter to be living where you are, so it's a pretty good smokescreen. Even if someone recognises your face from a blurry internet shot, it's unlikely they'll put two and two together. Sorry,' he says, seeing the defiant look on my face from what he said about my home. 'But it's true,' he says gently. 'I still don't like it, but I understand. I know you're not ready to leave yet. When you are, we'll talk again.'

I nod, and immediately afterwards want to cry again, this time with relief more than anything else.

I can't believe Tom texted me last night. I still haven't texted him back, but I will. I wonder if he is one of the 'friends' that I'll be telling the truth to? First things first: I ring Natalie.

'Hi!' she exclaims when she answers.

'Hi!'

'I thought you were going to call me earlier?' she says. I'd forgotten I said I would when I texted her from the limo. 'I was going to go and get ready for bed in a minute,' she adds.

'Sorry. It's been a bit hectic here.' It went through my mind to call her last night when I got back from the gig, but my head was all over the place, and after the way she reacted when I told her about Johnny, I still wasn't sure I wanted to confide in her.

'Where are you?' she asks.

'Still in LA.'

'When are you coming back?'

'A week on Sunday,' I reply.

'So are you going to tell me what's going on? You're with your real dad?' She sounds a little detached. I suppose she feels like

I've shunned her by barely seeing her before I went away, and then disappearing for weeks. I can't blame her.

'Yeah,' I say slowly.

'Wow. That's mental.'

I hesitate. 'You know what I said about Johnny Jefferson?'

'Yeah,' she replies carefully.

'Well, it's true.'

I hear her snort. She doesn't sound very amused. 'Have a look online,' I say calmly. 'We're putting out a press release today so the news that Johnny has a daughter will be up there soon. But we're not telling anyone that it's me. We're going to try and keep my identity a secret.'

Silence.

'Natalie? I mean it. You can't tell anyone who I am. I want to remain anonymous.'

More silence, then, 'This is getting a bit beyond a joke, Jess.'

I take a deep breath, and I can't help but sound angry when I speak. 'How would I know that there's going to be a press release put out about Johnny Jefferson's fifteen-year-old daughter who wants to remain anonymous because she's still at school? Hey? Why else would I be in LA for God's sake?'

She doesn't answer.

'Call me back when it hits the news,' I say, and then I hang up.

Bloody hell. Next I ring Libby.

'Hey!' she exclaims as warmth rushes through me. It's good to hear her voice. 'I got your message about your new number. I've been meaning to text you.'

Then why didn't she? Probably because she still hasn't forgiven me for treating her the way I did.

'I would have called you sooner, but it's been a bit full-on here and—' My voice cuts off as I hear a girl speaking in the background.

'Hang on a sec,' Libby says, and the line is muffled while she covers the receiver. She comes back on the line. 'Sorry, I'm staying over at Amanda's,' she says casually.

'Oh, right.' This revelation should hardly be surprising, let alone hurt me, but hurt it does. Has Libby spent every day of her summer holidays getting closer to Amanda, having sleepovers and living in each other's pockets, like she used to do with me? I wonder if she misses me, even a little bit? I press on, because this needs to be said. 'I just wanted to tell you that that secret I told you about, you know, the one you're not allowed to repeat to anybody?'

She hesitates before answering. 'Yes . . .'

'Well, it's about to hit the press.'

'Oh!'

'Johnny is going to tell everyone he has a daughter, but he's not going to release my name, Libby. So you still have to keep quiet about it. Don't tell Amanda,' I add, wincing at the thought of her doing just that, the moment she hangs up.

'I've already told you I won't,' she snaps.

But even as we end the call, I'm not sure I believe her.

I bring up the text from Tom. I think for a long while before replying.

> I'm still in LA. Lots to talk to you about when I get home. Definitely still on for that movie x

I press send and flop back on to the bed. Thinking about Tom reminds me how much I do like him. He *is* gorgeous with his

269

brown hair and brown eyes. Boy-next-door hot and his texts show he likes me back. But then there's Jack. Rock-God-in-the-making, Jack. I roll over and hug a pillow to my chest. My phone beeps again and I snatch it up.

You free this afternoon? Want to grab a coffee?
Agnes x

I bolt upright. Agnes? How did she get my number? What's she doing texting me? There's only one way to find out. My head is buzzing as I reply with a yes.

Chapter 26

'I'd rather you didn't go,' Johnny says when I ask if Davey can take me to the Mondrian Hotel. Apparently there's a bar there with a swimming pool where Agnes claims she likes to hang out. She says she'll grab a table with a view.

'Why not?' I feel crushed. I'm desperate to find out why she wants to see me. What if it's about Jack?

He puts his mug down on the kitchen table. He, Meg and the boys are having an afternoon snack of tea and chocolate chip cookies. I still don't have an appetite.

'Annie is putting the press release out any minute. You might be followed.'

'I won't be if I leave now,' I say quickly.

He stares at me. Meg puts her hand on his knee. 'Let her go,' she says. 'The limo is darkened anyway, so Davey will get her back without being papped.'

Johnny sighs. 'OK,' he mutters. 'But be careful.'

'Thanks!' I run upstairs to get ready.

*

Agnes is already at the Skybar, as I discover it's called. I half expect to see Lissa or Charlotte with her, but she's sitting alone on a cushioned bench, in front of a wall of glass overlooking the city, her face in an e-reader with a cup of coffee on the table in front of her. The bar is open-air, with a swimming pool taking up a large chunk of the floor space. Giant, white, square-shaped 'beds' are dotted around the space, providing very laidback seating.

'Hi,' I say when I reach her table.

'Hi!' she exclaims, jumping to her feet and kissing me on my cheeks. She's wearing flats and I'm in heels, so we're about the same height. 'I'm glad you came.'

I tentatively take a seat beside her, leaning my back against one of the cushions pressed up against the glass, and trying not to look down. It's almost enough to give you vertigo. Agnes is wearing a short dress with a geographical pattern on it. I'm in a navy blue maxi dress. We've both got our sunnies on.

'I was surprised by your text. How did you get my number?' I ask.

'I stole it from Jack's phone.' Her reply is causal, but I tense up when I hear his name.

'I'm sorry about Eve,' she surprises me by saying.

'What about her?' I try to sound unbothered.

'She really needs to get a life. No girl should fall for my brother,' she adds, and I wish I could see her eyes behind her dark glasses.

I raise one eyebrow at her.

'He told me about Johnny being your dad.'

I freeze. Now it all becomes clear. She's suddenly interested in me because of Johnny.

'Well, I'd appreciate it if you kept that to yourself.' There's a sharpness to my tone, and I'm sure she can hear it.

'Oh, Jeez.' She waves me away. 'I don't care about crap like that. You think I haven't heard enough gossip? Been subjected to enough of it, myself?'

I instantly feel humbled. I guess when you come from this kind of background, finding out a rock star has a secret child is no big deal.

She beckons a waitress over. 'You want a coffee?' she asks me.

'I might just have a lemonade,' I tell the waitress. It's late in the day, but it's still hot and humid. 'I'm confused,' I say to Agnes when the waitress has gone off again. 'Why did you invite me here?'

She shrugs. 'You seem interesting. Different. There's not much of that around here.'

'Oh.' I feel strangely honoured. 'What about Jack?'

'What about him?'

'Well, you know, if he's back with Eve ... Do you really think he'll want me hanging out with you?'

'If I let that sort of thing bother me, I wouldn't have any friends at all,' she says drily.

Does she mean ...?

'Jack gets around a lot,' she clarifies, seeing the look on my face.

Great. Yes, she does mean that. The waitress returns with my drink. I take my sunnies off and clean them on my dress.

'I wasn't lying yesterday, though. He really was bummed when you left.'

I glance at her. 'What do you mean by that, exactly?'

273

'Moping around, looking like a sad, sorry little puppy dog. He's not usually like that over a girl.'

Hope sparks inside me, and I wish it wouldn't. I don't want to care about him. Not now. Not after last night.

'That's what I thought,' she says calmly.

'I didn't say anything.'

'You didn't have to.' She leans forward and takes a sip of her coffee. 'I can tell by your expression that you're still into him.'

What does this girl want with me?

'Hey, you wanna come with me to Lottie's house later?' She surprises me with a complete change of subject.

'Lottie?' I put my sunglasses back on.

'Charlotte. I call her Lottie. Known her since we were kids,' she says.

'Charlotte Tremway? Is she having a party or something?'

'No, she's just hanging out with some friends.'

'Sorry, I just don't know why you'd be inviting me to Charlotte Tremway's house.' Obviously I've been there. I went there for Michael's birthday, but that was with Johnny. 'I don't know her. I barely know you.'

'Yeah, but you will. And this is a good place to start.'

Bizarrely, I find myself agreeing. I don't know why. Agnes even talks me into going back to hers first, as she seems to think she has something perfect for me in her closet to wear. Again, I have no idea why I agree to this. Going back to Jack's house? Surely not smart. But then I figure, what the hell. I've got nothing to lose. And if Agnes really thinks I'm interesting? Well, the feeling is mutual. There's certainly something about her, and in the absence of my friends back home, I could do with some girl company.

Her car is valet-parked at the hotel, so we wait outside the foyer until a gleaming white Ford GTI pulls up. I still can't get used to the wheel being on the opposite side of the car, so when she climbs into what is the passenger's side in the UK, I'm momentarily confused. Then I realise my mistake and get in the car beside her.

'I thought you were expecting me to drive for a minute,' I say.

'My friends and I all drive each other's cars. I wouldn't have minded,' she replies nonchalantly.

'I don't have a licence,' I say. 'I'm only fifteen and a half.' Wait a minute. 'Haven't you just turned sixteen?'

'Yeah, and?'

'Do you have your licence?' I'm suddenly a little bit worried.

'*Yeah*!' She laughs. 'You can get your licence at sixteen here.'

'Oh, right.' Actually, I think I do know that from watching American TV shows. 'Are you sure Charlotte isn't going to mind me gatecrashing?' I seem to be doing a lot of that lately.

'Hell, no. The more the merrier.'

I have to ask, even though the question makes me feel ill. 'So has Jack slept with Charlotte, too, then?'

'No,' she scoffs. 'They've messed around, but he's not that stupid. She'd have him by his balls.'

That doesn't make me feel much better.

'What about Lissa?' I know I'm not going to like this.

'Same,' she replies.

OK. No sex, just ... *messing*. Yuck.

'Bryony?' I ask wearily.

275

'No, not Bryony.'

Phew.

'Yet,' she adds.

Bloody hell . . .

'As for Eve,' she says. 'Yeah, I'm sure they've gone all the way.'

No! I didn't want to ask that question and I certainly didn't want the answer. I feel like I could throw up now.

'But she's not right for him,' she adds flippantly.

It doesn't take long for us to get back to her house, and during that time I've had to text Johnny back and forth and convince him that yes, it *is* a good idea to go to Charlotte's place with Agnes. He finally gives in, but I don't doubt that Davey will be collecting me, probably sooner than I would like him to.

Agnes takes me upstairs to her bedroom, and I can't help but feel on edge wondering if Jack will appear at any moment. But soon we're inside Agnes's bedroom and I start to relax. Posters of bands and sexy young actors plaster the walls, and her wardrobe doors are open to reveal rows of neatly hung clothes and tidy racks of shoes. Her double bed is unmade, its hot pink sheets crumpled in a mess on the floor. Fairy lights are twirled around the white iron bedhead and candles and incense sticks are lined up on the windowsill. The room smells of incense and perfume. It's strangely comforting. I have so few belongings in my room at Johnny's. Being here makes me miss my room at home – and my friends.

I sit on the bed while Agnes goes to her wardrobe. I see on the wall that she has the same picture of Joseph Strike that Libby had behind her door: the film publicity shot of him from *Sky Rocket*, looking all toned, fit and gorgeous with his top off.

'Have you seen *Two Things*?' I ask, making conversation while Agnes rifles through her clothes.

'Yeah, it's awesome. Have you?' She glances over at me.

'Not yet. I'm supposed to be seeing it with a guy I know when I get home.' It's surprisingly satisfying being able to say this to Jack's sister.

'Oh, *really*? Anyone special?'

Excellent. She's taken the bait.

'Maybe.' It's not a lie. It's just too hard to be thinking about Tom with everything that's going on over here.

'Hmm.' She turns back to the wardrobe and finds what she's looking for. 'Here it is!' she chirps, throwing me an emerald-green-coloured garment.

'Try it on,' Agnes urges.

I turn my back on her and pull my maxi dress over my head, replacing it with the green ... Erm, what is it? It barely covers my bum, but it does. Just.

'Is this a dress or a top?' I ask uncertainly.

'A dress.' She says it like I should know. 'Try it with this.' She passes me a skinny purple belt, so I put that on, too.

'Shoes?' I ask, glancing down at her feet. They're at least a size larger.

'Your heels look great,' she says. 'So does your hair.'

I've got it down today.

'But your make-up could do with some tweaking.' She motions for me to sit at her desk, and there's something about her which is strangely persuasive, so I do. Five minutes later, I'm wearing shimmery gold eyeshadow across my lids with black mascara and black eyeliner – not quite as thick as she wears hers. I'm not sure I could carry that off. Peachy blusher and

277

lipgloss finish off the look. Finally, she passes me a chunky gold necklace and a handful of mismatched, mostly gold bracelets. I slip on the bracelets, and she spins me around to do up my necklace.

'Perfect,' she says approvingly.

I regard my reflection in the mirror. I do look pretty hot, even if I do say so myself. My legs are tanned and look longer than they ever have, and my eyes – whoa – they look really green, complimented by the dress.

'You're good at this,' I tell her.

She grins. 'Keep telling me that.'

'You're good at this,' I say again and she laughs.

'I really want to go to art school,' she reveals.

'Jack told me you want to be a fashion designer,' I remember.

'Did he?' She looks pleased.

'Is he going tonight?' I ask hesitantly, stuffing my maxi dress into my bag.

She averts her gaze. 'He might be. But don't worry about it. We'll have fun no matter what, OK? Just stick with me.'

'So tell me about Johnny?' she says on the drive to Charlotte's house.

'What about him?' I ask warily.

'Have you always known he was your dad?'

'No. No, I found out only recently.'

Who knows why I feel I can trust her not to spill my story to the gossip mags, but for some reason I do.

'I can't believe Jack thought he was my ... That I was his ... Ew!'

'My brother is an idiot.' I'm glad to see she agrees with me.

'Johnny looks just like you. Jack was too busy battling the green-eyed monster to notice.'

I screw up my nose. 'He wasn't jealous.'

She glances across at me. 'Aren't you listening to me?' She tuts. 'If you like him as much as I think you do, play it cool. He won't be able to resist. But,' she adds, before I can deny it, 'he's trouble. Especially when it comes to girls. Don't say you haven't been warned.'

I recognise Charlotte's house as we approach. Actually, I recognise the wall surrounding it – I can't see the house.

She pulls up in front of some high wooden gates and waves up at a camera perched on the gateposts. Moments later, the gates open and she drives through them. I didn't even notice the driveway when I came here last, but I can see the back of the house up ahead, behind the ostentatious swimming pool with its big slides and OTT fountain, and then I see the log cabin between the silvery tree trunks on my right. Dozens of coloured lanterns hang from green branches and there's a small group of girls and guys sitting around on deck chairs and seats fashioned out of logs outside the cabin. Agnes stops the car.

'We're not up at the house tonight?' I check.

'Nah. Lottie hates her stepmom. Her dad has just given her the cabin so she won't legally divorce him as her guardian and move out. If anyone needs her own space, it's Charlotte,' she says wryly, unclicking her seatbelt.

'Why doesn't she live with her mum?' I ask.

'Her mom's in New York.' She glances at me and gives me a sad little shrug. 'They're not close.'

I can't imagine having a mum and being estranged from

her. Especially not now I know how easily they can be lost forever.

There's music playing out of a stereo as we walk towards the group. It's not too loud, and the atmosphere is chilled-out and laidback. I hope I'm not overdressed. I see Charlotte wearing a gold mini dress with a low-cut cowl neck and I relax about my appearance. But only slightly. Lissa and Bryony are here, and I can't say I'm happy to see them. I quickly check, but I can't spy Eve. I wonder if she moves in the same circles as this crowd. I doubt it. Eve seems too cool for them. How I hate admitting that.

'Hey, everyone,' Agnes says, as we become the centre of attention. 'You remember Jessie.'

'Hel-*lo*!' Lissa says, freaking me out slightly with her intonation. 'Here's Little Miss Jefferson herself!'

What? Uh-oh.

I turn, gobsmacked, to Agnes.

'I swear, I didn't say a thing.'

'She didn't have to,' Charlotte interjects, with a smirk, as she gets to her feet. 'With your blonde hair and green eyes and job as "the nanny",' she says mischievously, 'who else could it be?'

'Has the press release gone out?' I try to comprehend what's going on.

'Dur. Where have you been all afternoon?' Lissa says.

'It's all over the news,' Bryony chips in. 'The social networking sites are going crazy.'

I look around the group to see a few people holding smartphones. Lissa smiles nastily at my discomfort.

Has my cover been blown? What about my anonymity? What

280

about my home? I don't want bodyguards! No, no, no! 'Does everyone know it's me, or just you guys?' I ask with growing panic.

'What are you so worried about?' Lissa asks with a sneer. 'Isn't being Johnny Jefferson's daughter better than being just *another* one of the *millions* of girls he's screwed?'

'Urgh, shut up, that's disgusting!' I snap.

'Like your mum, I'm guessing,' she adds evilly, and my mouth clamps shut. I'm too shocked to speak.

'Back off, Lissa,' Agnes warns crossly, grabbing the nearest smartphone.

'Hey!' complains the guy she snatched it from.

'Lissa, either cut the crap or go home.' To my surprise, it's Charlotte who has said this. They stare each other out for a few seconds, but then Lissa gets up.

'Whatever. I'm going to refresh my drink.' She sets off towards the log cabin, snapping over her shoulder at Bryony to follow her. She hesitates only a moment before doing so.

Charlotte rolls her eyes at me. 'Don't worry about her. She's always a bitch, but we love her anyway.'

I realise I'm shaking. How could anyone love *that*?

'Hey, don't freak out,' Charlotte says, looking concerned as she notices the state I'm in. 'Your identity's still safe. Nobody else knows that it's you.'

'She's right,' Agnes breathes, handing the phone over to me. 'Your name hasn't been mentioned. It's only speculation at the moment.' I take the phone, feeling like my feet are about to give way.

'Why don't you sit down,' Charlotte says, firmly manoeuvring me on to a log seat. Maybe she's only being nice to me because

281

of who my dad is, but right now I don't care if it's not genuine. I just want someone to look out for me.

I stare down at the phone. The words are blurry, but I force myself to focus and read the comments.

GuessGirl says:

> I saw her last night! She was with Johnny at the All Hype gig.

Mousey replies:

> I saw her too! I didn't know who she was at first. Thought she was just another blonde bimbo hanging off his arm.

TreeHugger joins the conversation:

> I know. I thought that too. But don't you think she looked like him?

Mario moans:

> I wish I'd taken a picture!

My heart races when Beagle says:

> I got one, but it was so dark in there, you can hardly see her.

Beagle attaches the photo and I suck in a sharp breath as I narrow my eyes and peer at it. There I am, standing next to Johnny. But the resolution is grainy and you can barely make out my face, only that I'm small and blonde. I look up at the group, who are all staring at me fixatedly.

This is so weird. Here I am, surrounded by a bunch of people I hardly know – or even *like*. I should be with Natalie or Libby or Em, or even Dougie or Aaron. Or Tom, I think with a pang. They should be comforting me and helping me through this. I stare back down at the phone in a surreal daze.

'I'll get you a drink,' Charlotte says. 'What do you want?'

'I'll just have a Coke or something,' I murmur, and then it hits me that I wish Jack were here, more than anyone else, and the thought makes me ache inside.

I take a deep breath and try to inject some normality back into my voice as I pass the guy his phone back. 'I'm Jessie, by the way.'

'I know,' he replies calmly, and I look around to see that they're all still staring at me.

'Feel free to tell me who you are,' I say flippantly.

'I'm Peter,' he replies with a grin, cueing off a round of introductions, not that I'll remember all of their names. There are three guys and six girls here, not including Agnes and me.

Agnes sits down next to me, and Charlotte returns with our drinks. Someone turns the music up.

'How long are you in LA?' Peter asks me while Agnes and Charlotte catch up. He's got very short, dark hair and brown eyes and a shadow of stubble on his jaw. He looks like he should be tall, but he's sitting down so it's hard to tell.

'Not for much longer,' I reply distractedly. 'I've got to go back

283

to school at the beginning of September.' I'm not in the mood for small talk, but I try my best to be sociable.

'Bummer,' he says.

'How do you know Charlotte?'

'We work together.'

Oh my God. I've just realised who he is. He's Zachary from *Little Miss Mulholland*! He plays Macy's long-lost brother.

'Are you . . .' My voice trails off. 'I recognise you. Sorry,' I say, my face heating up.

He laughs. 'Don't apologise.'

'How's it all going? On the show, I mean? Back in the UK you've only just started.'

'Yeah, it's going great. I love it. I've got this killer storyline coming up.'

'Can you tell me about it?'

He grins over at Charlotte, who has started to pay attention.

'I'll keep your secret as long as you keep mine,' I joke.

'That sounds fair,' Charlotte interjects with a smile. 'This guy is going to be huge.'

As Peter fills me in on the show's gossip, I start to feel better. Lissa and Bryony venture back outside, but I manage to ignore them, and it's not too hard with Peter, Agnes and Charlotte distracting me. I'm still taken aback by how nice Charlotte is being, considering she practically ignored me the last time I came here, but even if she does have an ulterior motive, it won't kill me to be friendly.

I hear the sound of a car coming along the drive and look over my shoulder, along with everyone else.

'Your bro's here,' Lissa says to Agnes in a singsong voice, her eyes darting towards mine. My stomach cartwheels and I quickly

284

avert my gaze, trying to think of something to say to Peter so I'm not looking at Jack when he arrives. But I can't think of anything. I hear car door after car door slam – how many of them are there? Is Eve here? Now my stomach churns, but I force myself to focus on Peter. I rack my preoccupied brain.

'Have you always wanted to be an actor?' I ask.

'No, I only got into it recently, actually. I was scouted on Santa Monica beach.'

'No way? That's so cool. Did you have your abs out?' I ask cheekily, trying to sound light-hearted.

He laughs, then shrugs. 'Might've done.'

'Just as well you can act, then, hey.'

'It's pretty lucky.'

The paparazzi shots of me with Johnny at the fairground come to mind. Will he secure an injunction against getting them printed?

'What's up?' Peter spies my expression, so I tell him, aware of Agnes, Charlotte and a couple of others getting up to greet Jack and whoever else has just arrived. I steal a glance at him to see he's with Miles and Brandon.

'I wouldn't worry. As long as they don't print your name and address back home, no one will suspect it's you.'

I turn back to Peter. 'I hope so. Thanks.' I smile gratefully at him, and then his attention is diverted as Jack reaches down to shake his hand. He sees me and freezes.

'Jessie,' he says with shock.

'Howdy,' I reply, staring up at him directly.

Damn him, he's still sexy as hell.

285

Chapter 27

I stay where I am as he bends down and kisses my cheek, his right hand clasping my head, and then Agnes tugs him backwards.

'Hey!' he exclaims crossly.

'Leave her alone,' she warns teasingly, smacking him on his arm before going over to speak to Miles.

Charlotte hooks her arm around Jack's neck and peers up at him. 'What do you want to drink?'

'What'cha got?'

'Soda?' she suggests.

'Whiskey?' he counteracts with a grin.

'I can get you a beer – that's the best I can do.' She lets go of him and turns to Brandon, who raises one eyebrow at her. I have a feeling there's something going on between those two. 'Beer?' she asks him. And then Jack crouches down beside me and all of my attention is on him. He's wearing another cool printed T-shirt and his hair is falling across his forehead.

'What are you doing here?' he asks, and I wish I could tell what he's thinking.

'Agnes brought me.'

'Agnes?' We both glance over to see her laughing at something Miles has said.

I try to keep my cool. 'She nicked my number from your phone,' I reply casually. 'She said she wanted to get to know me for some strange reason.'

'Have you guys met before?' Peter interjects, and Jack starts. I'd forgotten he was there, too.

'Once or twice,' I say drily, not taking my eyes from Jack's face.

'Of course,' Peter says, holding up his phone as he remembers the social networking sites. 'You were at the All Hype gig with Johnny last night.'

'That's right.' I lean back and force myself to include him in our conversation. 'Did you go?'

'I missed it, unfortunately. I was filming.'

I want to say, 'you didn't miss much', just to wind Jack up, but that would be cruel, as well as a lie, so I say, 'Shame,' instead. 'They were good. Johnny and his mate Christian thought so, too.'

Jack's eyes light up. 'Really?'

'Really.'

Charlotte hands a bottle of beer down to Jack and goes over to chat to Brandon.

'Where's Eve tonight?' I ask.

'I don't know. Haven't seen her today.' He looks awkward as he takes a swig of his beer, and when he stands up my heart sinks. He's going to go and talk to someone else and I *really* want to go home, now. But he pulls over a log seat instead and I hate how much my mood instantly improves.

'So the news is out?' He nods at Peter's phone and Peter hands it over again.

'Yep,' I reply curtly as he scrolls through the comments. 'They don't know who I am, yet, though.' He returns Peter's phone and Peter gets to his feet and stuffs it into his back pocket.

'Gotta take a leak,' he says, wandering off towards the cabin.

Jack pushes his hair back and leans forward, resting his forearms on his thighs. He glances at me, a flicker of doubt passing across his face. 'Sorry,' he mutters, his lips downturned. 'I was being a dick.'

'About what?' I ask sweetly, and he has the grace to look embarrassed.

'Anyone with half a brain can see that you look just like Johnny. I don't know what I was thinking.'

Is that all he has to apologise for? I take a sip of my drink and look away.

'I'm sorry about Eve, too,' he says quietly.

'Is she your girlfriend?' I have to ask.

'No.' He frowns. 'But it's complicated. We've had this . . . *thing* going on.'

Ouch. It hurts even more to hear these words come out of his mouth.

'She's the lead singer of the band,' he continues, looking a bit helpless. 'When we fight, it makes things difficult. For all of us.' He looks over at Brandon and Miles, then back at me.

'Yet it's so easy to be with me and her at the same time?' I say sarcastically.

'I'm sorry,' he says again. 'I screwed up.' I look away from him. 'But I'm glad you're here,' he adds.

'I won't be for much longer,' I reply facetiously.

Agnes skips over and pulls me to my feet. 'Come dance with me, Jessie,' she says, sticking her tongue out at Jack as she leads me away. I want to stay with him, but I know it's for the best if I don't. So I try to have a good time, even if I can't help but know exactly where he is at any given moment over the course of the next hour.

Johnny texts me after a while, wanting to know where I am and if he should send Davey to collect me.

'I'll take you home,' Agnes says when I mention it to her. 'I need an early night, anyway.' She turns to say her goodbyes and I do the same.

'Come hang out with me again soon, OK?' Charlotte says, hooking her arm around my neck. She has really bad beer breath. 'I still need to hear all about Johnny,' she slurs into my ear. 'What's he *like*? He is so freaking *hot*.'

I grimace. Now I know the real reason for her being nice to me – she has a crush on my dad. Ew!

Jack detaches her. 'See you later, Lottie. Might be time you quit drinking.'

'You can talk,' she snaps after him, as he leads me away. My heart is racing as he turns to Agnes.

'Can I hitch a ride with you?'

'Really?' Agnes asks with astonishment as we follow her to her car. 'Not like you to leave a party early.'

Jack shrugs and Agnes gives me a significant look over the car roof as he climbs into the backseat behind her. I get in and shut the door, looking out of the window to see Lissa talking to someone on her phone at the back of the log cabin.

Agnes beeps her horn as we drive off, and Lissa's head shoots up to see us leaving. She looks panicked, I don't know why.

'What's up with Lissa?' I say out loud.

'She's always a bitch. Don't worry about her,' Agnes says, brushing me off.

'No, I mean, she looked shocked to see us leaving.'

'She was probably shocked to see *Jack* leaving,' Agnes points out, raising her eyebrows at her brother in her rear-view mirror.

'And who could blame her,' Jack bats back. I look over my shoulder at him and he stares straight back at me, a smile playing around his lips. The car feels a lot smaller than it did on the way here.

Agnes turns the volume up on the stereo and we drive for a while without speaking.

'Which way is it?' she asks out of the blue.

Er, I don't actually know.

'Left,' Jack directs her. Phew. At least he knows where we're going. I haven't really paid attention since Davey's been taking me most places. After a while, I start to recognise where we are.

'Jack . . .' Agnes says uncertainly.

'What?'

'Are we being followed?'

He and I both look behind us at the same time. There's a black vehicle tailgating us. 'Take a right here,' he says warily, but as she indicates, he suddenly shouts, 'No! Keep driving!'

And then I realise what he's seen. Paparazzi. Dozens of them. Waiting in the bend of the road leading to Johnny's gates. Agnes swerves and goes around them, but in doing so, she gets their attention.

'Jeez!' Jack curses as he peers out of the rear window. I follow the line of his sight to see a hoard of men with long-lens cameras manically climbing into their cars and screeching away from the curbs in pursuit of us.

'Cover your face!' Agnes shouts at me.

'What with?' I exclaim, looking around.

Jack unclicks my seatbelt and squeezes my waist. 'Climb back here,' he says with urgency. I don't hesitate, half clambering, half being pulled between the two front seats to the back. I bury my head in his chest, his arms wrapped around me as he holds me tight.

'Where will we go?' I ask, my voice muffled against the warmth of his T-shirt.

'Back to ours,' he says loudly enough so Agnes can hear.

It's a frightening journey. I don't look up, but I can hear Jack's commentary as paparazzi pull alongside us, and even though I'm pressed against his chest, I can still see the camera flashes going off as they try to catch a glimpse of me inside the car.

'It's OK, sis, you're doing good,' Jack says in a low voice at one point, and his caring concern for Agnes, the way he's holding me to him, protecting me, makes my stomach swirl with jittery nerves. Despite how hairy the ride is, I don't want it to end.

It does, though, and when we're safely inside the gates of his mum and stepdad's property, his grip on me loosens. I slowly pull away and look at him. My vision is blurry from squeezing my eyes shut, but his proximity makes my heart flip.

'OK?' he asks, his blue-grey eyes coming into focus and increasing the flight speed of the winged creatures in my stomach. He's staring at me intently.

I nod quickly. 'Yeah.' My voice is barely more than a whisper. His right hand is still on my stomach, his left around my waist, and his touch is making me feel breathless.

Unfortunately he lets me go to lean forward and rub Agnes's shoulder. She glances at him in the rear-view mirror and exhales loudly. Then she looks back at me.

'You'd better call Johnny.'

I nod. 'I know. What were they doing?' I'm so confused. 'Johnny said they wouldn't harass me. That he'd get an injunction.'

'He might get an injunction against publication, but no one can stop them from harassing you,' Agnes says darkly.

'But they weren't even up at the gate,' I say, momentarily side-tracked as Jack sits back in his seat and the whole left-hand side of his body presses into mine. 'They were waiting down the road.' I try to focus. 'Did somebody tell them I was coming? Lissa was on the phone . . .'

'Lissa wouldn't—' Agnes starts.

'Wouldn't she?' Jack interrupts sharply.

They exchange a look. 'I know she's jealous of Jessie, but she wouldn't rat her out to the press. That's the lowest of the low.'

Agnes gets out of the car and yanks Jack's door open. 'Don't jump to conclusions,' she says. 'The paps are slippery little suckers.'

She steps aside and I feel deflated as Jack climbs out, leaving my right-hand side cool from the absence of his body. I edge out of the car after him.

We go to the games room. I call Johnny while Agnes goes up to the house to tell her mum we're home. Jack sits over in the corner, absent-mindedly plucking his guitar strings as he waits for me to finish.

'I'll send Davey to collect you,' Johnny snaps when I've filled him in. I can tell he's angry that I went out without Davey tonight, against his better judgement.

'There's no rush.'

'Half an hour, max,' he warns, ending the call.

I turn around, and look at Jack. I sigh heavily.

'You alright?' he asks.

'Not really. This is all too weird.'

I wander over to him. He's leaning against the wall with his guitar in his hands, his legs stretched out and crossed in front of him.

He starts to play a jaunty little tune and then he begins to sing, and I laugh out loud when I realise what the song is and who it's by: One Direction. He doesn't know all of the words, but he makes some of them up and it's so funny. He sings the penultimate line of the chorus, 'Tonight let's get some . . .'

I join in for the last line of 'Live While We're Young'.

He gives his guitar one last strum and grins up at me as my heart flips over and over. I want to hate him, but I can't. He props his guitar up against the wall and stands up, coming towards me with a raised eyebrow.

I shake my head with amusement as he reaches me, grinning down at me. 'You're a shithead,' I tell him as he puts his hands on my waist.

Agnes chooses that moment to come back into the games room.

'Jeez, Jack,' she chastises. 'Hasn't she been through enough?'

He sighs loudly, and pretends to be frustrated, but he winks at me.

Agnes passes me a large glass of something red and fizzing on ice. I hope it's alcoholic.

'Cranberry and lemonade,' she says.

No such luck.

We go and sit on the grass slope and look down at the multi-coloured city lights. Jack is sitting between us. He strikes a match and I glance across at his face, lit by the flame's orange glow.

'Urgh, do you have to smoke?' Agnes complains, shifting away from him. 'You're starting to stink like Drew,' she says of their older brother.

'Did you speak to him last night?' Jack asks with interest.

Last night? Oh, at the All Hype gig. I wonder who he was.

'Briefly. He asked me to go to lunch with him sometime.'

'That'd be good.'

She doesn't say anything and I feel bad for her, being estranged from her dad and her brother, just like Charlotte is estranged from her mum. It's no way to live.

'My mum died in January,' I say slowly. Jack inhales sharply on his cigarette and out of the corner of my eye I see Agnes leaning forward to look across at me. 'She would never tell me who my real dad was. And when she died, I hated her for that ... and for leaving me.' I whisper the last bit. I look across at Agnes. 'If there's any chance at all that you can make amends with your brother and your dad, do it,' I urge. 'Because they could be gone tomorrow.' I stare back at the view. 'My stepdad was the one who told me about Johnny. I've treated him badly ever since Mum died – and before, probably – but he's a good guy.'

My phone starts to ring and I sigh, pulling it out.

'Miss Pickerill?'

'You know, I keep meaning to tell you to call me Jessie,' I say wryly to Davey.

'As you wish,' he replies warmly. 'I'm outside the gates. Can Mr or Miss Mitchell buzz me in?'

'I'll be with you in a bit.' I end the call.

'I'll walk you out.' Jack gets up.

'Keep your hands to yourself,' Agnes mutters, also standing.

I smirk and glance up at him as he rolls his eyes.

'I'll call you,' she says to me. 'We'll catch up again.'

'I'd like that,' I reply with a smile, and then Jack and I walk around the side of the house towards the courtyard-cum-driveway. I can see up ahead that there's a control panel on the side of the gate.

'Stay where you are,' he tells me. 'The paps are probably still out there.' I hang back as he goes ahead to press the button. Davey drives in and Jack closes the gates again, keeping the prying eyes out.

Jack jogs back over to me while Davey gets out of the car and opens the back door. I start towards him.

'Wait,' Jack says to me, holding his hand up and making me halt in my steps. 'She'll be there in a minute,' he calls over his shoulder to Davey. Taking my arm, he leads me back around the side of the house where it's more private.

'What is it?' I ask, confused.

His brow is furrowed. 'Can we start again?'

'In what way?' I ask.

'Let's hang out. Go see a movie or something.'

'What about Eve? What about your band? Isn't that going to make things *difficult*?'

He sighs and stares at me directly. 'You're only here for, what? Another week or so?'

'And then I'll be gone again. That's pretty convenient, hey?' I raise one eyebrow at him.

He shrugs. 'You'll be back.'

I sigh with regret. 'I've gotta go.' I nervously smooth the front of my dress down and then remember it's not *my* dress. 'Shit! I'm still wearing your sister's dress!' I hastily glance towards the courtyard where Davey's waiting.

'Give it to me next time I see you,' he says. 'I'll pass it on.'

'Or I could give it to *her* next time I see *her*,' I reply with meaning.

He looks momentarily downcast. I undo the necklace and take off the bracelets. 'You can give her these, though.'

'Why don't I give her the dress now, too?' he asks cheekily, eyeing me up and down before laughing at the look on my face. 'Come on, Jessie,' he pleads, his shoulders slumping. 'Let me take you out on a real date.' He doesn't give up, does he?

'Fine,' I snap with a melodramatic sigh. 'But only if you promise to sing One Direction to me again.'

He perks up and my heart flips. '*Baby say yeah, yeah, yeaeah . . .*' he sings softly.

'No, you can't kiss me,' I interject, knowing where he's going with the lyrics to 'Kiss You'.

'Are you sure?' he asks, trailing the fingertips of his right hand down my bare arm and sending a shiver up and down my spine.

I step away from him. 'Yeah. I'm sure.'

When I'm safely back inside the limo with Davey, I exhale loudly. I can't believe my willpower was that strong. *You're a tough little cookie, Jessie Pickerill*, I think to myself with a smile.

Jessie Jefferson, I silently find myself correcting.

Chapter 28

'Oh my God.'

'Stop saying that!' I laugh. I'm on the phone to Natalie and she finally – *finally* – believes me.

'I can't believe it.'

'Stop saying that, too,' I reply with a smile. This has been the most repetitive conversation of my life.

'I can't believe it.'

'Natalie. Snap out of it!'

'When are you coming home again?' At last she has something new to say.

'A week on Sunday.'

'I saw Tom yesterday, looking very fit, tanned and utterly gorgeous. He asked after you.'

Despite my rollercoaster ride with Jack, this makes me feel happy. 'He texted me from Ibiza,' I reveal.

'No! Did he really?'

'Yeah.' I sigh. Then I tell her about Jack.

'Whoa,' she says, and I don't quite know if it's whoa good, or whoa bad. 'Do you have any pics of him?'

'Look up All Hype online. He's the guitar player with the black hair.'

'OK, I will.'

I hear Johnny shout for me from downstairs. And there's something about the tone of his voice that makes me think it's urgent.

'I've gotta go,' I say quickly. 'I'll call you again soon.'

'OK,' she says.

'Bye.' I hang up quickly, then run to the door. 'I'm here!' I shout over the landing wall to Johnny in the living room below.

'Can you come down?' he asks, his voice strained and his expression tense.

'What's wrong?' I ask quickly, hurrying along the landing and down the stairs. Meg is sitting on the sofa, cuddling Phoenix to her and rubbing his back. She looks upset.

'My dad's had a heart attack,' Johnny tells me.

'Oh no,' I breathe.

'He's in hospital,' he says. 'They think he'll pull through.'

'OK,' I reply. Phew.

'I've got to go to him,' Johnny says, glancing at Meg. She stares back at him with compassion, then she looks at me.

'We've all got to go,' she says gently. 'The boys and me.'

Obviously, I don't know him, so that's fair enough. But hang on . . . What are they saying?

'Have I got to leave too?' Finally it sinks in.

'I'm sorry,' Meg says.

'I don't know how long I'll have to be in the UK, but it could be some time,' Johnny says softly, as all of this computes. 'More likely to be weeks rather than months, but that still takes you into your school term.'

But what about Jack? What about Agnes? I've just got to *leave*?

'Obviously we can see each other while we're in the UK,' he says. 'But I'm afraid we've all got to leave LA today. There's always the next holidays,' he continues to speak, but inside I'm a mess. 'Maybe you could come back for Christmas?'

I look up at him in a daze and see him glance at Meg. She nods in agreement.

'I'm sorry,' he says, touching my arm. 'But you've got to go and pack. Carly can help you. We're leaving in a couple of hours.'

'I don't need any help,' I reply automatically, and then I go back upstairs to my room, my mind reeling. I can't believe this is it. This is me going home. I feel sick as I pull my suitcase out of the wardrobe and start to pack away my things.

I'm done quickly – packing everything I've bought and brought with me. When I'm ready, I grab my phone and slump down on to the carpet, my back against the wall.

I dial Jack's number.

'I knew you wouldn't be able to resist my charms,' he says when he answers, and I know he's smiling.

'I'm going home,' I tell him sadly.

'When?'

'Now. Today.'

'Why?' He sounds taken aback. 'Is this because of Lissa?'

'Lissa? No. Why do you say that?'

'We think she *was* the one who told the press you were on your way to Johnny's. Agnes has been leaving shitty messages on her phone all morning.'

My heart sinks even further. I knew I couldn't trust Lissa, but her betrayal is still difficult to bear. She must really despise me.

'No, it's not about Lissa,' I reply. 'Johnny's father has had a heart attack. He's got to go and see him, and obviously I can't stay here alone.'

'No way. Can't you . . . Isn't there . . . You could come and stay with us?'

I laugh out loud, despite myself. 'I don't think that would go down too well with Johnny. He doesn't think very highly of you,' I point out.

'Mmm.' Is he squirming? 'We didn't even get to say a proper goodbye.'

'What, like the last time?' I ask without amusement. 'You cheered yourself up pretty quickly after that. I'm sure you're capable of doing it again.'

'Ouch,' he says gruffly, falling silent for a bit before finally asking: 'When will you be back?'

'Christmas. Maybe even when I have my school half term in a couple of months.' Johnny did say holidays.

Pause. 'That's not so bad.'

'Are you better at emails than you are at texts?' I still remember the bluntness of his text when I told him I stayed.

'Kinda,' he replies. 'But yeah, let's stay in touch this time. You can't escape me by running off to another country.'

I bite my lip. 'Oh no, what about Agnes's dress? I'll ask Johnny's PA to send it,' I decide.

'I'll tell her. She'll want to email you too, you know.'

'I'd like that,' I reply with a smile. And I would. I really would.

Jack and I have unfinished business, I think to myself as we hang up, and I'm immediately hit with a sense of déjà vu as I remember that that's exactly what I thought about Tom when I left England to come here.

I exhale loudly and look around the room one last time, before kneeling on my suitcase and struggling to zip it closed. I manage. Just.

Barney is jumping up and down outside his bedroom door when I emerge, tugging my weighty bag behind me.

'We're going on a plane! We're going on a plane!' he shouts, and I wish I had his enthusiasm.

'I know, cheeky monkey. Are you excited?'

'Yeah!' he shouts, running back into his room. I smile as I pass, glancing in to his bedroom to see that, for once, Meg has enlisted Carly's help with packing his things. We really must be in a hurry.

'You ready?' Meg calls to me, as I pass Phoenix's room.

'I think so.' I leave my suitcase on the landing and go inside. Phoenix is babbling away to himself in his cot. He's usually asleep at this time, but there's too much going on today.

'Davey's going to take the luggage separately,' Meg tells me as she packs nappies and baby wipes into a bag. I wander over to the cot and peer down at Phoenix, who smiles up at me. 'We're going by helicopter,' she says, as I tickle his chin and make him giggle.

'Helicopter?' I look over at her.

She smiles at me. 'It lands on the roof. It'll avoid us being tailed by paps the whole way on the road.' She doesn't look impressed. 'By the time Davey gets to the airfield with our bags, we'll already be on the plane.'

'Are they still outside the gates?' I ask worriedly. A bunch of cars followed us all the way home last night, and there were even more paparazzi waiting at the gates, but they couldn't see me inside the darkened glass of the limo's windows.

'I'm afraid so. It was like this when the press found out about Barney. But it'll blow over. Hopefully when you come back at Christmas, everything will have calmed down.'

'Hopefully,' I murmur. She didn't mention half term, but maybe I can swing it somehow. Christmas seems so far away.

'Even if you had stayed, it would have been hard for you to go anywhere,' she points out.

That gives me a little comfort. But not much.

Libby rings me when we're in the living room, listening out for the helicopter.

After waiting longer than I thought I'd have to for her call, I'm now too preoccupied to talk.

'Hi,' I answer, tapping my foot on the floor. I'm sitting on the sofa next to Johnny, who's also tapping his foot on the floor. We both have magazines in our hands, but neither of us appear to be reading.

'Hi,' she says.

'I can't really talk right now,' I tell her bluntly.

'I'm sorry I didn't call you sooner,' she blurts out.

I close my eyes briefly. It's a relief to hear her say that. I get up and go out of the living room door to the terrace.

'It's just that I still feel like I don't know you any more,' she says quickly.

I nod, even though she can't see me. 'I get it,' I reply. 'If we'd been close, like we used to be—'

'I would have called you every day,' she finishes my sentence for me.

302

There's a helicopter in the distance. I wonder if it's ours?

'I'm coming home,' I tell her. 'We're leaving today. Johnny's dad has had a heart attack.'

'Oh, I'm sorry.'

'I think he's going to be OK, but it means I have to leave sooner than I was supposed to. Can we catch up when I get back? There's so much I want to tell you.'

The helicopter is coming closer.

'That would be great.'

Johnny comes out on to the terrace with Phoenix in his arms, closely followed by Barney. 'Look, helicopter!' he says.

'Copter!' Barney replies, jumping up and down.

'Here, put these on,' he says to me, passing me my hat and sunglasses. 'Just in case.'

'Was that Johnny?' I hear Libby say in my ear. She sounds shell-shocked.

'Yeah.' I pull the hat on and pop on my sunnies.

'Oh my God, Johnny Jefferson is your dad,' she says, as though it's only just hit her. I know how she feels.

I smirk. 'I'll see you soon,' I say.

And then the noise of the helicopter landing on the roof drowns out our goodbyes.

As we take off, headsets on and the pilot's voice in our ears telling us about the flight time, I look back down at Johnny's ultra modern house, gleaming white in the baking hot afternoon sun. There are still a few paparazzi waiting outside the gates, despite Davey's diversion, and their cameras are pointed up at us.

Meg's voice comes through the headset. 'That'll make a good shot for the tabloids,' she says wryly. 'Our sneaky escape.'

The pilot swerves off to our right and I inhale sharply. This is actually quite scary – a bit like a fast fairground ride. That thought makes me think of Jack and me on the dodgems and I can't help but smile. At that very moment, as I look out of the window at the mansions nestled in Beverly Hills below, I see his house. Maybe it's my imagination, but I swear I can see some-one – him? – sitting on the slope of the grass looking out at the view. I wonder if he sees me too.

I'll email him when I get home. I hope he keeps in touch. Like I said, we have unfinished business.

Stuart comes to collect me from the private airfield where we land. Johnny, Meg and the boys are going by chauffeur to Johnny's dad's place in Essex. Johnny would have had a chauf-feur collect me, too, but Stuart wanted to come. And I'm so happy to see him.

An immigration official came on to the plane to check our passports, so all we have to do is walk down the steps and into the building. I see Stu through the glass as I head towards him – he's wearing his typical uniform of white T-shirt and denim jeans and he suddenly feels so familiar. I don't run to him, but when I go through the door and into his arms, the force of our bodies slamming into each other takes my breath away. I've never hugged him like this before in my life.

I pull away and smile up at him, and he down at me, and I notice his glasses have come loose so I reach up and straighten them. He looks past me and stiffens, and I know that Johnny has entered the building. I step away from Stu and turn around, and then they're shaking hands – my new dad and my stepdad, the man who has raised me all of these years and who I've never properly appreciated. I wrap my arm around Stu's waist again and give him a hug, and I notice something pass over Johnny's expression as he regards us. He steps backwards, flanked by Meg and his boys.

When all is said and done, it's still 'them' and 'me', I think pensively, as Meg comes forward to be introduced. But maybe that will change. One day.

We walk outside to the waiting limo and Stu's little white Fiat, the cars a strange reflection of the two very different worlds laid out before me. Both Stu and Johnny look awkward and I think that they can see it, too.

Meg comes forward to give me a hug, while Stu and Johnny make small talk. 'See you soon, Jessie,' she says, quietly. 'You've got my number. We'll catch up while we're here, OK? Maybe you can come and meet Brian when he's perked up a bit?'

My grandad . . .

I nod quickly. 'That would be good.'

She steps back while I crouch down to speak to Phoenix. 'Come here, you.' He flashes me a toothy grin and toddles towards me. He's grown more steady on his feet even in these last few weeks, but I hope I never forget holding his hand while we walked along the boardwalk at Santa Monica, on my first morning there. 'Bye bye, baby.' I fight back tears as I take him in my arms and squeeze his chubby little body, then I watch him toddle off to hang on to his mummy's leg. I turn to Barney. 'See you later, B,' I say.

'Where are you going?' he asks, his forehead furrowing with confusion.

'I've got to go in that car.' I point at the Fiat. 'But I'll see you soon, OK?'

'I wanna come with you!' he says.

'No, you've got to go in the shiny new one,' I reply with underlying humour.

'Aw!' he moans, his shoulders slumping dramatically.

I laugh and open the back door of the limo. The driver jumps out of the front seat and apologises because he didn't get there first.

'It's fine,' I wave him away. 'Look!' I say to Barney, and we both peer inside. 'Go and see what's in the fridge!' He eagerly clambers inside, but I tug him back. 'Kiss first.'

He pecks me on my lips and turns away and I fight back tears as I straighten up. Meg smiles sympathetically and touches my arm with tenderness as she and Phoenix climb into the limo. Stu nods at Johnny and then at me, before going to climb into the Fiat. He's giving us some space.

'I've got this,' Johnny says to the limo driver, who returns to the driver's seat, leaving us alone.

I stare up at the dad who I am yet to call dad. I know I'll see him again soon, but this feels like the end of something. Hopefully it's the start of something else.

'Come here,' Johnny says gruffly, pulling me into his arms as tears start to spill from my eyes. 'I'm sorry we had to cut your trip short,' he apologises again.

'It's fine,' I manage to choke out as he lets me go. I don't want him to leave yet. It feels too soon.

'We've still got a lot of catching up to do,' he says, running his thumb along my cheek and wiping away some of my tears. 'And I really want to buy your stepdad a new car,' he mutters with a smile.

'He won't let you,' I tell him. 'He couldn't bear anyone to think that he told me about you so he could benefit.' It's true. I know him well.

Johnny rolls his eyes good-naturedly and says, 'Try to convince him.'

I nod, but I know nothing will do that.

'See you later, chick.'

I freeze as he presses his lips to my forehead, trying to etch this moment in time into my memory.

He turns away abruptly and climbs into the limo, and I suspect he's feeling emotional, too.

The limo driver appears again to shut the door before returning to the front, and then I stand and watch my funny little family drive away from me.

'Bye, Dad,' I whisper.

Then I look over at Stu, waiting patiently for me in the Fiat. I go and climb into the passenger seat, next to him. The car smells comfortingly familiar, even if it is a pile of shit.

'Alright?' he asks cautiously.

'Yeah,' I grin. 'Yeah, I'm alright. Let's go home. I'm dying for a fag and a drink.'

'I really hope you're joking,' he says warily. 'I thought you might have grown up since you've been away.'

I collapse into giggles as we drive away from the airfield.

But in truth, I *have* grown up. I've changed. And I might be going back to the same town, the same little house, the same school and the same friends, but one thing's for sure, life will never be the same again.

I'm excited to see what it has in store for me next.

Acknowledgements

I don't think I will ever start an acknowledgements page without thanking my readers first and foremost. I can't tell you how much your messages and online reviews make me smile, so please say hi if you haven't already @PaigeToonAuthor and on Facebook.com/PaigeToonAuthor. Also, stay tuned to www.paigetoon.com because I have some exciting plans for 2014 . . .

Big thanks to the brilliant children's team at Simon & Schuster, but specifically to my editor, Jane Griffiths, and also Kat McKenna, Elisa Offord, Catherine Ward, Nick Stearn, Laura Hough, Sam Webster, Dominic Brendon, Becky Peacock and Maurice Lyon. Thank you also to my editor Suzanne Baboneau and Emma Capron on the adult team.

Thanks to Isla Bell for reading an early manuscript for me and feeding back, and also to Susan Rains for her help with my Americanisms. And thank you also to my new YA agent Veronique Baxter from David Higham – I'm excited to be working with you from here on in!

Thank you to my friend and fellow author Ali Harris for giving me the idea to branch into young adult books in the first place – I'd be lost without our weekly catch-ups over tea and biscuits!

And, yes, I know this is a little bit weird, but thanks to Meg – the character who kicked off the Johnny madness in the first place. I hope you don't mind Jessie taking your story forward! (Please note: faithful readers of *Johnny Be Good*, *Baby Be Mine* and ebook short *Johnny's Girl*, don't worry – you will hear from Meg again. Just stay tuned to www.paigetoon.com for forthcoming details ...)

Thank you to the lovely ladies in my local coffee shop for keeping me topped up with tea at my favourite table in the corner: Wendy, Becky, Milly, Jo, Sarah, Clare and Wendy's daughter Paige (yes, it is very confusing to hear your mum talking about you!).

Thanks always to my parents, Jen and Vern Schuppan for their unwavering belief in me, and my lovely in-laws, Ian and Helga Toon for all of your help and support. And also of course, my amazing husband Greg Toon and my cheeky little children Indy and Idha. We really do make a great team and I love you all very, very much.

Paige Toon

Don't miss the new Jessie Jefferson novel, coming Spring 2015!

Life as the undercover daughter of a rock god isn't going to be easy. How will Jessie adjust to her old boring life again after spending her summer living it up with her famous dad in LA? With tough decisions ahead (and not just choosing between two hot boys), can she cope juggling her two very different lives?

Summer may be over, but Jessie's story is just beginning…

WIN!
enter our
#rockstarselfie
competition

find out more at sugarscape.com

sugarScape

Win! The ultimate rock star prize with Sugarscape and Paige Toon!

We've teamed up with Sugarscape to offer one lucky Paige Toon fan the chance to be the star of social media! You could win the ultimate rock star kit: a leather jacket from ASOS, a Fuji Instax 8 instant polaroid camera and a signed copy of *The Accidental Life of Jessie Jefferson*!

To enter, simply take your own 'rock star selfie' – don your coolest sunnies, red lippy and glitter eyeliner, or just a guitar and your skinnies ... whatever it means to you to look like a true rock star. Then, upload it to Twitter, Facebook, Pinterest or Instagram using the hashtag **#rockstarselfie** and tag Simon and Schuster Children's Books.

For full details of how to enter (and to view the terms and conditions), visit www.sugarscape.com. The competition closes on 27th February 2014 and is open only to residents of the UK and Ireland.

Paige Toon

Want to know how Johnny
and Meg got together?
Read on for an extract of
JOHNNY BE GOOD
to find out...

Prologue

'Sing! Sing! Sing!'

No. I can't.

'*Sing! Sing! Sing!*'

No! Stop it! And for God's sake, cut that bloody music!

'SING! SING! SING!'

Argh! My palms are so slippery I almost dropped the mic. I'm in bad shape. I can't sing. I can NOT sing. But they won't stop. I know they won't stop until I deliver. And I shouldn't disappoint my audience. Okay, I'm going to sing! Here comes the chorus . . .

> *I'm locked inside us*
> *And I can't find the key*
> *It was under the plant pot*
> *That you nicked from me*

That's not my song, by the way. And when I say I can't sing, I mean I *really* can't sing. When you're as drunk as I am, you could be forgiven for thinking that *if only* Simon Cowell were in the room, he would say, 'Girl, you've got the X Factor.' But I'm under no illusions. I know I'm, in his words, 'distinctly average'.

As for the audience . . . Well, I'm not singing to a 90,000-strong crowd at Wembley, but you've probably guessed that by now. I'm in the living room of my flatshare in London Bridge. And the music comes courtesy of my PlayStation SingStar.

The person who's just grabbed the mic from me is Bess. She's my flatmate and my best friend. She can't sing either. Jeez, she's hurting my ears! Next to her is Sara, a friend of mine from work. And then there are Jo, Jen and Alison, pals from university.

As for me? Well, I'm Meg Stiles. And this is my leaving party. And that song we're making a mockery of? That's written by one of the biggest rock stars on the planet. And I'm moving in with him tomorrow.

Seriously! I am not even joking.

Well, maybe I'm misleading you a little bit. You see, I haven't actually met him yet.

No, I'm not a stalker. I'm his new PA. His Personal Assistant. And I am off to La-La Land. Los Angeles. The City of Angels – whatever you want to call it – and I can't bloody believe it!

Chapter 1

Ouch. My head hurts. What sort of stupid person has a leaving party the night before starting a new job?

I'm not usually this disorganised. In fact, I'm probably the most organised person you're ever likely to meet. Having a leaving party the night before I had to board this plane to LA is very out of character. But then I didn't have much choice. I've only just got the job.

Seven days ago I was a PA at an architects' firm. My boss, Marie Sevenou (early fifties, French, very well-respected in the industry), called me into her office on Monday morning and asked me to shut the door and take a seat. This had never happened in the nine months I'd been working there and my initial reaction was to wonder if I'd done anything wrong. But I was pretty sure I hadn't so, above all, I was curious.

'Meg,' she said, her heavy French accent laced with despair, 'it pains me to tell you this.'

Shit, was she dying?

'I do not want to lose you.'

Shit, was *I* dying? Sorry, that was just me being ridiculous.

She continued, 'All of yesterday I toyed with my conscience. Should I tell her? Could I keep it from her? She is the best PA I have ever had. It would *devastate* me to let her go.'

I do love my boss, right, but she ain't half melodramatic.

'Marie,' I said, 'what are you talking about?'

She stared at me, her face bereft. 'But I said to myself, Marie, think of what you were like thirty years ago. You would have done anything for an opportunity like this. How could you keep it from her?'

What on earth was she going on about?

'On Saturday night I went to a dinner party at a very good friend of mine's. You remember Wendel Redgrove? High-powered solicitor – I designed his house in Hampstead a couple of years ago? Well, anyway, he was telling me how his biggest client had lost his personal assistant recently and was having a terrible time trying to find a new one. Of course I empathised. I told him about you and how I thought I might die if I ever lost you. Honestly, Meg, I don't know how I ever managed before . . .'

But she regained her composure, directing her cool blue eyes straight into my dark-brown ones as she said the words that would change my life forever.

'Meg, Johnny Jefferson needs a new personal assistant.'

Johnny Jefferson. Wild boy of rock. Piercing green eyes, dirty blond hair and a body Brad Pitt would have killed for fifteen years ago.

It was the chance of a lifetime, to go and work in Los Angeles for him and live in his mansion. To become his confidante, his number one, the person he relies on more than anyone else in the world. And my boss, in a moment of madness, had suggested me for the job.

That very afternoon I met up with Wendel Redgrove and Johnny Jefferson's manager, Bill Blakeley, a cockney geezer in his late forties who had managed Johnny's career since he split up with his band, Fence, seven years ago. Wendel drew up a contract, along with a strict confidentiality clause, and Bill asked me to start the following week.

Marie actually cried when I told her it was all done and dusted;

they'd offered me the job and I had accepted. Wendel had already persuaded Marie to waive my one-month-notice period, but that left me only six days, which was daunting, to say the least. When I raised my concerns, Bill Blakeley put it bluntly: 'Sorry, love, but if you need time to sort your life out then you're not the right chick for the job. Just pack what you need. We'll cover your rent here for the first three months and after that, if it all works out, you can have some time off to come back and do whatever the hell it is that you need to do. But you've got to start immediately, because frankly, I'm sick to fucking death of buying Johnny's underpants since his last girl left.'

And so here I am, on this plane to LA, with a shocking hangover. I glance out of the window down at the city. Smog hangs over it like a thick black cloud as we fly towards the airport. The distinctive white structure of the Theme Building looks like a flying saucer or a white, four-legged spider. Marie told me to look out for it, and seeing it makes me feel even more spaced-out.

I clear Customs and head out towards the exit where I've been told there will be a driver waiting to collect me. Scanning the crowd, I find a placard with my name on it.

'Ms Stiles! Well! How do you do!' the driver says when I introduce myself. He shakes my hand vigorously as his face breaks out into a pearly white grin. 'Welcome to America! I'm Davey! Pleased to meet you! Here, let me take that bag for you, ma'am! Come on! We're this way!'

I'm not sure I can handle this many exclamation marks on a hangover, but you've got to admire his enthusiasm. Smiling, I follow him out of the terminal. The humidity immediately engulfs me and I start to feel a little faint so it's a relief to reach the car – a long black limo. Climbing into the back, I slump down into the cool, cream leather seats. The air-conditioning kicks in as we exit the car park and my faintness and nausea begin to subside. I put the window down.

Davey is rabbiting on about his lifelong ambition to meet the

Queen. I breathe in the outside air, less humid now that we're on the move, and start to feel better. It smells of barbeques here. The tallest palm trees I've ever seen line the wide, wide roads and I'm amazed as I stick my head further out of the window and gaze up at them. I can't believe they haven't snapped in half – their proportions are skinnier than toothpicks. It's the middle of July, but some people still have sad little Christmas decorations hanging out in front of their tired-looking homes. They twinkle in the afternoon sun – no wonder they call this place Tinseltown. I look around but can't see the Hollywood sign.

Yet.

Oh God, how can this be happening to me?

None of my friends can believe it, because I've never been that fussed about Johnny Jefferson. Of course I think he's good-looking – who wouldn't? – but I don't *really* fancy him. And when it comes to rock music, well, I think Avril's pretty hardcore. Give me Take That any day of the week.

Everyone else I know would give their little toe to be in my position. In fact, make that their whole foot. Hell, throw in a hand, while you're at it.

Whereas *I* would struggle to give up more than my big toenail. I certainly wouldn't relinquish a whole digit.

That's not to say I'm not thrilled about this job. The fact that all my friends fancy Johnny like mad just makes it even more exciting.

Davey drives through the gates into Bel Air, the haven of the rich and famous.

'That's where Elvis used to live,' he points out, as we start to climb the hill via ever-more-impressive mansions. I try to catch a glimpse of the groomed gardens behind the high walls and hedges.

The ache in my head seems to have been replaced by butterflies in my stomach. I wipe the perspiration from my brow and tell myself it's just the side effects of too much alcohol.

We continue climbing upwards, then suddenly Davey is pulling up outside imposing wooden gates. Cameras point ominously down at us from steel pillars on either side of the car. I feel like I'm being watched and have a sudden urge to put my window back up. Davey announces our arrival into a speakerphone and a few seconds later the gates glide open. My hands feel clammy.

The driveway isn't long, but it feels like it goes on forever. Trees obscure the house at first, but then we turn a corner and it appears in front of us.

It's a modern architectural design: two storeys, white concrete, rectangular, structured lines.

Davey pulls up and gets out to open my door. I stand there, trying to control my nerves, as he lifts my suitcase out of the boot. The enormous and heavy wooden front door swings open and a short, plump, pleasantly smiling Hispanic-looking woman is standing beside it.

'Now then! Who have we got here?' She beams and I like her immediately. 'I'm Rosa,' she says, 'and you must be Meg.'

'Hello . . .'

'Come on in!'

Davey wishes me goodbye and good luck and I follow Rosa inside, to a large, bright hallway. We go through another door at the end and I stop in my tracks. Floor-to-ceiling glass looks out onto the most perfect view of the city, hazy in the afternoon sunshine. A swimming pool out on the terrace sparkles cool and blue.

'Pretty spectacular, ain't it?' Rosa smiles as she surveys my face.

'Amazing,' I agree.

I wonder where The Rock Star is.

'Johnny's away on an impromptu writing trip,' Rosa tells me.

Oh.

'He won't be back until tomorrow,' she continues, 'so you've got a little time to get yourself unpacked and settled in. Or even better, out there by the pool . . .' She nudges me conspiratorially.

I lift the handle on my suitcase and try to ignore my disappointment as Rosa leads me into the large, double-height open-plan room. The hi-tech stereo system and enormous flatscreen

TV in the corner tell me it's the living room. Furniture is minimal, modern and super, super cool.

I'm impressed. In fact, I'm feeling less and less blasé about this job by the minute, and that's not helping my steadily swirling nerves.

'The kitchen is over there,' Rosa says, pointing it out behind a curved, frosted-glass wall. 'That's where I spend most of my time. I'm the cook,' she explains before I get the chance to ask. 'I try to feed that boy up. If I were a bartender I'd have a lot more joy. He likes his booze, that one.' She chuckles good-naturedly as we arrive at the foot of the polished-concrete staircase.

'Are you okay with that, honey?' She glances back over her shoulder at my suitcase.

'Yes, fine!'

'We should really have a butler here, but Johnny don't like a lot of staff,' she continues, as she climbs the stairs ahead of me. 'It's not that he's stingy, mind, he just likes us to be a tight-knit family.' She turns right. 'Your room is over here. Johnny's got the big one at the other end, and behind them doors there you've got your guest rooms and Johnny's music studio.' She points them out as we go past. 'Your offices are downstairs, in between the kitchen and the cinema.'

Sorry, did she just say cinema?

'I'll show you round later,' she adds, slightly out of breath now.

'Do you live here, too?' I ask.

'Oh no, honey, I got a family to go home to. Apart from the security staff, you're the only one who'll be here overnight. And Johnny, of course. Okay,' she says, clapping her hands together as we reach the door at the end. 'This is you.' She turns the stainless-steel knob and pushes the heavy metal door open, standing back to let me pass.'

My room is so bright and white that I want to put my shades on. Windows look out over the leafy trees at the back of the house and a giant super-king-size bed is in the centre, covered by a pure white bedspread. White-lacquer floor-to-ceiling wardrobes line one wall, and there are two doors on the other wall.

'Here you've got your kitchenette, where you can whip yourself up some food if mine ain't good enough for you.' From her jovial tone I'm guessing that's not likely to be the case. 'And here you've got your en-suite.'

Some en-suite. It's enormous, with dazzling white stone lining every surface. A huge stone spa is at the back, and a large open shower is to my right, opposite double basins on my left. White fluffy towels hang on heated chrome towel rails.

'Pretty nice, huh?' Rosa chuckles. She walks to the door. 'I'll leave you to settle in. Why don't you come on down to the kitchen when you're good and ready and I'll get you something to eat?'

As the door closes behind her, I start jumping on the spot like a mad woman, face stretched into a silent scream.

This place is mental! I've seen rock star mansions on *MTV Cribs*, but this is something else.

I kick off my shoes and throw myself onto the enormous bed, laughing as I look up at the ceiling.

If only Bess could see this place . . . It's such a far cry from our dingy flatshare back home. It's getting on for midnight now in England and she will have hit the sack long ago, sleeping off her hangover before work tomorrow. I decide to send her a text to wake up to in the morning. I climb off the bed, smiling at the feeling of the thick white shagpile carpet between my toes, and grab my phone from my bag.

Actually, I think I'll send her a picture. I slide open the camera lens instead, snapping the massive room with the (now slightly crumpled) bed in the middle. I punch out a message:

CHECK OUT MY BEDROOM! HAVEN T MET HIM YET BUT
HOUSE IS AMAZING! WISH YOU WERE HERE X

She is going to die when she sees the outside view. I'll have to send her that tomorrow.

I decide to unpack later and instead go and see Rosa downstairs. I find her in the kitchen, frying chicken, peppers and onions in a pan.

'Hey there! I was just preparing you a quesadilla. You must be starving.'

'Can I help?' I ask.

'No, no, no!' She shoos me away, minutes later delivering the finished product, cheese oozing out of the edges of the triangular-cut tortillas. She's right: I am starving.

'I would offer to make you a margarita, but I think you just need feeding up, judging by the state of those skinny arms.' She laughs and pulls up a chair.

My arms *are* skinny compared to hers. In fact, every part of me is skinny compared to Rosa. She's like a big Mexican momma away from home.

'Where do you live, then?' I ask, and discover that home is an hour's drive away, where she has three teenage sons, one ten-year-old daughter, and a husband who works like mad but loves her like crazy from the way she smiles when she speaks of him. It's a long way for her to travel, but she adores working for Johnny. Her only regret is that she's not often there to see him tuck into the meals she leaves for him. And it breaks her heart when she comes in the next morning and finds the food still in the refrigerator.

'You have got to make that boy eat!' she insists to me now. 'Johnny don't eat enough.'

Hearing her speak about 'Johnny' is strange. I keep thinking of him as 'Johnny Jefferson', but soon he'll just be Johnny to me as well.

I do already feel like I know him, though. It's impossible to live in the UK without knowing about Johnny Jefferson, and after a lunch break of Googling him when I worked at Marie's, I now know even more.

His mother died when he was thirteen so he moved from Newcastle to live with his father in London. He dropped out of school to concentrate on his music and formed a band in his late teens. They signed a record contract and were global superstars by the time Johnny was twenty. But he spiralled out of control at the age of twenty-three when the band broke up, before coming back almost two years later as a solo artist. Now thirty, he's one of the most successful rock stars in the world. Of course there are still rumours of his dodgy lifestyle. Drink, drugs, sex – you name it, Johnny's probably done it. I don't mind the odd drink, and I'm not a prude, even if I have had only three serious boyfriends, but I'm really not into the drug scene, and I've never been attracted to bad boys.

Rosa heads off at six-thirty and urges me to get outside by the pool. Ten minutes later I'm on the terrace, clad in the black bikini that I bought for my recent holiday in Italy with Bess. The sun is still baking hot so I stand on the steps in the shallow end and tilt my head back up to catch the rays. The glittering blue water is cool, but not cold, and I don't flinch as I immerse myself fully. I swim a few laps and decide then and there to swim fifty every morning. I did so much walking in London that keeping fit was effortless, but everybody drives cars here so I might need to work at it.

After a while I climb out and spread my towel on the hot paving stones beside the pool, forgoing the sunloungers so I can trail my fingers in the water. My hangover is long gone, and I lie there feeling blissfully happy, listening to the sound of the water filtering through the swimming pool and the cicadas chirping in the undergrowth. High overhead a distant aeroplane leaves a long white streak in the cloudless sky and out of the corner of my eye I can see little black birds swoop down to drink from the pool. I begin to feel dozy.

'Is this what I pay you for?'

I jolt awake to find a dark figure hovering above me, cutting out my sun. I'm so shocked I almost fall in the pool.

'Whoa, shit!'

I rummage around to try to pull my towel out from under my bum so I can cover myself up, but it drops in the water.

'Bollocks!'

I hastily scramble to my feet, realising all I've done in the last few seconds is curse at my new boss.

'Sorry,' I blurt. His eyes graze over my body and I feel like he's undressing me. Which isn't that difficult, because I've barely got anything on as it is. I cross my arms in front of my chest, desperately wanting to retrieve my soaking towel from the pool. Unfortunately, though, that would involve bending over, which is not something I feel comfortable doing right now. I look up.

He's actually quite tall – about six foot two, I estimate, compared to my five-foot-seven-inch frame – and is wearing skinny black jeans and a black T-shirt with a silver metal-studded belt. His dirty blond hair falls messily around his chin and his green eyes, with the light of the swimming pool reflected in them, look almost luminous.

Christ, he *is* gorgeous. Even more so in real life than in pictures.

'Sorry,' I say again, and his mouth curls up slightly as he reaches down behind me to drag my sopping-wet towel out of the pool. I instinctively want to step away from him, but the only way is backwards and into the water, and I think I've made enough of a tit of myself as it is. He straightens himself back up and wrings the towel out, muscles on his bare arms flexing with the movement. I notice his famous tattoos and can't help but feel on edge.

I remember my sarong is hanging on one of the sunloungers behind him, but he makes no attempt to move for me as I awkwardly sidestep him before hurrying over to grab it. I quickly tie the still-way-too-small green piece of material around my waist.

'Meg, right?' he says.

'Yes, hi,' I reply, watching him while shading my eyes from the sun as he rolls the wet towel up into a ball and aims it at a basket six metres away. It goes straight in. 'And you, er, obviously, are Johnny Jefferson.'

He turns back to me. 'Johnny will do.' I note that he has a few freckles across his nose that I've never noticed in photographs.

'I was just, um, taking a break,' I stutter.

'So I figured,' he replies.

'I didn't think you'd be back until tomorrow.'

'I figured that also.' He raises an eyebrow and delves into his jeans pocket, pulling out a crumpled cigarette packet. Sitting down on one of the sunloungers, he lights up and casually pats the space next to him, but with the way my heart is beating, I figure I'd be safer on the sunlounger opposite instead.

'So, Meg . . .' he says, taking a long drag and looking across at me.

'Yes?'

'Do you smoke?' he asks, not offering me a cigarette.

'No.'

'Good.'

Hypocrite. I think it, but I don't have the guts to say it.

'How old are you?' he asks.

'Twenty-four,' I reply.

'You look older.'

'Do I?'

He flicks his ash into a two-foot-high stainless-steel ashtray and narrows his eyes at me. 'There's a lot of pressure with this job, you know.'

Oh, okay, not really a compliment, more a concern.

'I can handle it.' I try to inject some confidence into my voice.

'Bill and Wendel seem to think so.' He sounds quite American, which is surprising considering he spent the first twenty-five years of his life in England. 'Got a boyfriend?' he asks.

Hey, hang on a second . . . 'What's that got to do with anything?'

'Don't get touchy,' he says, looking amused. 'I just want to know what the chances are of you getting homesick and buggering off back to Old Blighty.' *Now* he sounds English . . .

His stare is making me feel uncomfortable so I hold his gaze for only a couple of seconds. He remains silent and I sure as hell don't know what to say to him.

'You haven't answered my question.'

Question? What question? Oh, boyfriend question . . . I'm finding it difficult to focus.

'No, I don't have a boyfriend.'

'Why not?' he bats back immediately, before taking another long drag on his cigarette.

'Er, well, I did have one but we broke up six months ago. Why?'

He grins, stubbing out his fag. 'Just curious.' He gets to his feet. 'Want a drink?'

I stand up quickly. 'I'll get it.'

He gives me a wry look over his shoulder as he wanders over to the other side of the terrace where there's an outdoor bar area. 'Chill out, chick, I'm perfectly capable of getting myself a drink. What are you having?'

I opt for a Diet Coke.

He returns with two large whiskies on the rocks and hands one over. I look down at it and back up at him. His expression is blank. Did he hear me?

'Um . . .' I say, but the next thing I know he's dragging his T-shirt over his head. Oh my God, I don't know where to look. I take a large gulp of whisky as he stretches out on a sunlounger.

Right then and there, the ridiculousness of the situation hits me. This is nuts. Johnny Jefferson – *the* Johnny Jefferson! – is here in front of me, so close that I could actually reach out and touch him. I could tweak his nipple, for crying out loud! Imagine if I sent Bess a picture of *this* view. A small snort escapes me at the thought.

'You alright?' He glances over at me.

'Yes,' I answer. But, embarrassingly, I start to giggle.

'What's so funny?'

'Nothing,' I quickly reply, but inside my head my mind is going into overdrive . . .

Nothing? A week ago I was working in an architects' studio in

London and now I'm in LA, in a rock star mansion, sitting on a sunlounger next to a half-naked rock star! If that's not surreal, I don't know what is.

He knocks back his whisky in one and I hold out my hand for the glass.

'Another?'

He hesitates for a moment before offering it up. 'Why not.'

About time I start doing my job. I get up and hurry to the bar area, finishing the rest of my drink. I survey the bottles in the cupboard under the bar, searching for the whisky. I spot a can of Diet Coke and consider switching but think better of it. What I need right now is some Dutch courage. And a few shots of tequila wouldn't go amiss . . . Ooh, there *is* a bottle of tequila in here, actually. I glance over at Johnny Jefferson, sprawled out on a sunlounger and facing away from me, oblivious to my beverage dilemma.

No, Meg, no. No tequila for you.

Oh, bugger it, I'll just have one.

I take a quick swig from the bottle and almost spit the booze back out as it sears the back of my throat. I desperately, *desperately* want to cough. Instead I swallow furiously and choke back the tears.

I need water. Water!

Or perhaps another swig of tequila would help?

Oddly, it does.

'You know what you're doing over there?' Johnny calls out.

Whoops, I've been ages.

'Yes, just coming!'

I approach the sunloungers, trying not to get distracted by the sight in front of me.

'Cheers.' Johnny chinks my glass and takes a gulp as I sit down.

His chest is toned and smooth and he has a dark tan. There's a tattoo of some writing right across his trouser line. I can't read what it says, but *phwoar* . . .

Oi! Focus, Meg, focus!

'So Rosa said you were away on a writing trip?'

'Yeah. Trying to get everything together for next week.'

'What's happening next week?' I ask.

He looks a little surprised. 'The Whisky?' he replies.

'More whisky?' I ask. Jesus, he really *does* have a drink problem.

'No, *the* Whisky,' he says.

'I don't understand.' I look at him blankly.

'Girl,' he says, 'don't tell me you don't know about my comeback gig at the Whisky – you know, the *venue?*'

'No, sorry, I don't.' My face heats up. 'Should I have heard about it?'

He laughs in disbelief.

'Sorry,' I say, 'but I don't really know much about you.'

And then I begin to ramble like a lunatic . . .

'I mean, I'm not really a fan.'

Shut up, Meg.

'I don't mind some of your songs but, well, you know, I kind of prefer Kylie, to be honest.'

Why the bloody hell did I admit *that*?

'But at least you haven't ended up with a mad stalker,' I continue. 'I could know anything and everything there is to know about you. I could know your favourite colour, the brand of shampoo you use . . .'

Christ Almighty, ZIP IT! Nope. It just gets worse . . .

'At least I'm not a star-fucker.'

ARGH!

'I should hope not, Meg,' he says, stubbing out his second cigarette in five minutes. 'That would be going above and beyond the call of duty.'

'Another drink?' I offer weakly, the reality of everything I've just said starting to sink in. I'm going to lose my job. I'm going to lose my job before it's even started.

'Nah, I've got to shoot off.' He stands up. 'I'm going to hook up with some pals in town. Ring the Viper Room and reserve us a table for eight.'

'Sure. Er, where . . .'

'In the Rolodex in the office. You'll find all the numbers you'll need in there.'

'Is that eight people or eight p.m.?'

'Eight people. Get them to hold the table. I don't know what time we'll be there.'

So I'm still employed, then? I get up hastily and take his empty glass from him, unable to meet his eyes. I turn away and notice in the reflection of the glass window that he's watching his new PA's departing derrière as she makes her way inside to the office.

Half an hour later Johnny Jefferson comes downstairs and finds me tapping my fingers on one of the two big desks in the office. I'm still feeling nervy, despite the tequila, and I'm not quite sure what to do next.

'Table all booked?' he asks, hooking his thumb casually into his jeans pocket. They're the same ones he was wearing earlier, but he's changed into a fitted cream shirt with silver pinstripe.

'Yes, and champagne chilling on ice. I didn't know if you wanted the car so I called Davey just in case. He's waiting on the driveway.'

'Cool.' He nods. 'Thought I'd have to take the bike.'

At least I got that right.

He stays standing in the doorway for a moment, staring at me, his hair still damp from the shower.

'Right then, I'm off.' He pats the palm of his hand on the door with an air of finality.

I try to resist asking, but can't. 'When will you be back?'

'Tomorrow,' he answers. 'Probably.'

And then he's gone. And suddenly the house feels very empty indeed.